Rejected

The Delivery Co. series

Lane Northcutt

Published by Lane Northcutt, 2022.

For information contact:

Lane Northcutt

lanenorthcutt@yahoo.com

ISBN: 978-1-7355827-3-3 (paperback),

978-1-7355827-2-6 (eBook)

Cover design by DePaul Vera © 2022 Lane Northcutt

Copyediting by Natalia Leigh at Enchanted Ink Publishing

First Edition, 2021

10 9 8 7 6 5 4 3 2 1

For my ideal reader, my wife, Shannon.

Chapter One
Ahna

"Now!" yelled Scorcher.

Ahna put all her weight into her legs as she pulled upward on the metal bumper. Her hand almost slipped on the snow, but she managed to keep hold of it. With the help of Scorcher and Sticks, they pushed the car to the side of the road. No matter how many she'd helped move along the way, it was always difficult. Having only one hand didn't make that any easier either.

Abandoned cars were becoming a normal occurrence. Their bodies were typically rusted and missing multiple pieces. That was helpful when it came time to move them out of the way. Other times, they were able to find some that had somehow managed to remain untouched by the war or roaming bandits. That meant they still had additional parts for them to use for armor or to repair their wagons. In fact, the wagons had practically become half car, almost literally.

They had found a few trucks along the way and used their frames to support the wagons, which made for a sturdier ride. They had also covered the sides of every wagon in car parts, so they looked like a rolling junkyard. Looks didn't matter as long as they had protection. Of course, the added protection meant more weight for the horses, which ended up meaning slower travel days. Felan pushed the horses more than she should've at times, but Ahna didn't say anything to her about it. Besides, she was the only one who knew where they were going, so Ahna figured it was best to let her do what she wanted.

Sticks pulled himself back into one of the wagons once they'd finished moving the car out of the way. Felan snapped the reins, and the wagon lurched forward. Once the wagons finished moving past her, Ahna brought up the rear, Scorcher appearing from behind the last wagon to join her.

"Not tired?" asked Ahna.

"Nope," said Scorcher.

She could see him fighting off a yawn. She chuckled.

"Sure about that?"

Scorcher nodded. "Figured you could use some company."

"I'm capable of walking back here by myself, you know."

"Never said you weren't. Besides, bothering you is more fun than sleeping." He smirked.

Ahna smiled back, feeling a welcoming warmth beneath her armor.

You should bother me more often.

Snow silenced their steps as they followed the caravan, the creaking wheels of the wagons accompanied only by the occasional cry of the wind. Trees danced as they continued down the decimated highway, sunlight warming their faces as it began its decent. Beneath the fur and leather, Ahna could finally feel her body coming back to life. It wouldn't be long until they were able to set up camp and finally rest after an exhausting day.

The wagon came to a halt in front of them, its wheels sliding slightly on the icy road.

What now?

Ahna and Scorcher exchanged a quick look before heading up to the front of the caravan. A familiar sound flooded Ahna's ears, reminding her of the graveyard of Tent City. Rushing water. She had her mouth half open to ask Felan why they'd stopped before she saw the answer for herself.

A bridge.

Unlike many bridges they had crossed along the way, this one was made from rope and wooden planks. It was suspended over a large gap in the road, a gap that stretched to either side as far as she could see.

"What's going on?" asked Scorcher. His bow was already in his hands, his head on a swivel, alert.

"See for yourself," she said, gesturing in front of her.

Ahna and Scorcher walked toward the bridge. On both ends, it was secured to large rocks that were almost as big as the wagons. She wasn't worried about the ends of the bridge, though. It was the middle that would cause problems. At least every other plank was missing or damaged. There was a large gap near the middle of the bridge where no planks existed at all.

Maybe we can go around.

"What're you thinking?" asked Scorcher.

"Not much of a choice here, is there?" asked Ahna.

Scorcher shook his head. "Doesn't look like it, no. I don't see another way over or around this gap—not within view, anyway."

He had a good point. It didn't matter if there was another way around if it wasn't nearby. They couldn't afford to backtrack or get lost looking for another way around, but they also couldn't risk the bridge collapsing. Either way, it wasn't going to be an easy decision.

"You're right," said Ahna. "But how do we get across the bridge? It's missing half the planks."

Scorcher stared at the bridge for a moment, his eyes narrowing. She liked his thinking face, the way his eyes focused and his jaw clenched. His eyes widened, and he let out a laugh, then hurried toward the trees nearby.

"What are you doing?" Ahna called out. "Scorch!"

When she caught up to him, he was already cutting into a log on the ground. She watched as he cut pieces of the bark, taking notice of his muscles peeking through his shirt.

Later, Ahna!

"You gonna watch me or help?" asked Scorcher, raising his eyebrows.

"Help what? Make new planks for the bridge? That's gonna take forever."

"Close," said Scorcher, chuckling. "We're making two long planks."

Ahna's eyebrows met as she tilted her head slightly. "Huh?"

"If we can cut this log in half and make it flat on both sides, we might be able to put it on the bridge and make it across."

That's actually pretty smart.

"How'd you know how to do this?" asked Ahna.

Scorcher scoffed. "Sticks isn't the only one who's good with his hands."

Oh, I know.

"Sorry. It's a great idea," said Ahna. "How can I help?"

"You have your knife on you?"

"Yep." Ahna patted the knife on her waistband.

"Good. Go to the other end of this log and start cutting. Once we get it cut in half, then we can smooth out the other sides."

Ahna started to pull her knife from the sheath, then stopped. "Why don't we use the axe?"

Scorcher stopped, looking up at her. It took a second for him to realize what she'd said fully. Then he laughed.

"The axe, right. You wanna go grab that while I keep cutting? I'm almost halfway through this side."

Ahna nodded, then walked back to the caravan. Felan was leaning against the side of the wagon talking to Wick. They stopped when Ahna came close.

"Done playing around in the forest?" asked Felan.

"If you call fixing our problem playing, then no," replied Ahna. "Where's the axe?"

Felan pointed behind her.

Ahna walked the length of the caravan, inspecting each wagon until she reached the last one. Inside, she spotted the crates of tools and other supplies. The handle of the axe was sticking up from a barrel near the back, so she climbed in to retrieve it. Before climbing out of the wagon, she tossed the axe outside, freeing up her hand.

"Ow!"

Oh no.

Ahna jumped out of the rear of the wagon to see Sticks on the ground, holding his head. She hurried over to him, offering her hand. He pushed it aside.

"I can do it myself."

He pushed himself up from the ground, struggling a bit more than usual.

"Trying to kill me, or do you enjoy throwing axes at people now?" asked Sticks.

"I'm sorry, Sticks. I had no idea you were standing there. You okay?"

"It'll take more than an axe to the face to kill me," he said, laughing. Ahna laughed too before pulling a small cloth from her pocket.

"Hold still."

She placed the cloth against the cut on his forehead. He winced but didn't pull back. Ahna patted the cloth against it gingerly, wiping away most of the blood.

"How bad's the cut?" asked Sticks.

"Barely noticeable," said Ahna.

"Good. I can't have you ruining my face. It's my best feature."

Ahna laughed. "I couldn't make it any worse if I tried."

They both laughed. It was nice to finally have a moment like this with Sticks given all the times they'd argued in the past. She figured it wouldn't last, but it was a nice change of pace.

"What's going on?"

Scorch.

Ahna turned to see Scorcher standing behind her. His arms were crossed as he stared at them, waiting for a response.

"Scorch," said Ahna, "you finished with the log already?"

"I hit a knot in the wood. Instead of waiting, I thought I'd help you find the axe. Guess you don't need my help."

"Calm down, Scorcher," said Sticks. "She found the axe all by herself."

"Oh."

"Then she threw it at my face."

Scorcher chuckled but remained tense. The way they stared at each other made Ahna's heart race.

"Yeah, sorry about that, Sticks," said Ahna, rushing to pick up the axe. Once she had it in her hand, she joined Scorcher. "Let's finish the job, huh?"

She smiled at him, but he only nodded before grabbing the axe from her hand.

"Let's go."

Ahna was relieved the wagons weren't that far from the log. Scorcher had become quiet and hadn't looked at her once since the conversation with Sticks. That bothered her. She wasn't expecting all his attention to be on her, but to be completely ignored was a different story. They'd hardly fought in the four months they'd been traveling, and she didn't want to start. She asked about the only thing she knew he'd not be upset to discuss.

"I hear they have really nice beaches out West."

Scorcher continued cutting into the log, wood chips flying like debris from a grenade. She could've watched him cut wood all day. If they hadn't been in a hurry to get somewhere, she would've tried to find a reason to need more of it, though he might not have listened to her if she did. It didn't seem like he had even heard what she'd said. She'd never seen him angry—not with her, anyway. It was strange. With every swing of the axe, Ahna felt as though she were watching their relationship whittle away. Finally, he stopped and stood to face her, the log now in two behind him.

He thrust the axe in her direction.

"Your turn."

Sweat around the handle of the axe almost caused her to drop it before she even started to chop. He had split the log in two, but now she had the more difficult job of trying to trim the other side to be flat. It might not have been that difficult if not for the fact that she couldn't hold the log while cutting into it.

You have to know I can't do that.

Ahna knelt down to the log and raised the axe behind her head, taking aim.

"Hold on," said Scorcher. He knelt down beside her and wrapped his hands around the coarse bark, holding the split log in place. "All right, go ahead."

Ahna couldn't help but smile before continuing. He cared about her. Even when he was upset, he cared.

I'm pretty lucky.

She swung the axe repeatedly, chipping away the remainder of the bark and creating a flat surface. It had taken a little while, but they finally had long flat planks. They just had to stay in place for them to ride across, and everything would be all right.

This was a good idea. I don't know what we'd have done otherwise . . .

Ahna stood and wiped the sweat from her brow. She handed the axe back to Scorcher, who placed it in his waistband. After counting to three, they lifted the planks together, Scorcher taking the brunt of the load. She was able to carry her end, though. She'd been practicing plenty on doing everything she could to keep up with everyone else. She almost didn't think twice about her missing hand . . . besides the occasional nightmare and phantom pain associated with it. She'd gotten used to it, but that didn't help make it any better.

Ahna and Scorcher reached the bridge with the planks and dropped them to the ground, getting a slight break.

"Beaches, huh?"

Ahna felt the side of her mouth rise slightly. She nodded.

"Yeah. Wick said they run up the whole side of California and are better sand than we've seen before."

Scorcher's eyes widened as he smiled slightly. He chuckled.

"Cool." His mouth hung open. "You think they have different fish than we did back home?"

Ahna shrugged. "I don't know what kind of fish we had there, so . . . no clue."

Scorcher laughed, then nodded. "Right."

He clapped his hands, and sawdust formed a cloud around him. Then he started picking up one of the planks.

"Scorch?" asked Ahna.

He stopped, then looked up at her. "Yeah?"

Ahna swallowed before continuing. Her mouth was dry, as though she had inhaled a handful of sawdust. She cleared her throat, then continued.

"We're good . . . aren't we?" she asked.

Scorcher dropped the plank and walked over to Ahna, pulling her into him. His arms wrapped around her, calming her. He kissed her hair.

"Of course we are. Just because I get upset with you a little doesn't mean I hate you. You know that, right?"

He pulled her away from him, his hands on her shoulders as his emerald eyes stared into hers. Ahna smiled, nodding.

"Yeah."

Scorcher smiled back.

"Good," he replied, letting her go. "Now, let's get back to work before Felan decides to leave us behind."

They laughed, then started moving the planks onto the bridge, positioning them so they were in the right spot for the wheels to go across. As long as they held and didn't break, they would be able to get across the bridge safely. After that, they could focus on all the other problems.

"ALL SET?" ASKED FELAN. The caravan was lined up, ready to cross the bridge.

Ahna nodded. "Yeah, all good."

Felan snapped the reins, and the caravan started toward the bridge. As the horse stepped onto the planks, Ahna's chest tightened. No breath entered her lungs as she waited for the wheels of the wagon to go onto the planks as well. Once the front two wheels were on, the bridge sagged slightly, but it held. The horse moved slow and steady across the planks until the back wheels rolled onto the planks.

Ahna let out a sigh of relief.

It worked. It actually worked.

"You're on!" Scorcher called out.

"Shut up!" Felan spat back at him. "I'm trying to focus!"

Whoa. Why so hostile?

Ahna had seen Felan be rude before, but this had an added element. She couldn't tell what or why, but Felan seemed a little more on edge. She couldn't blame her, though; she would've been too. The bridge wasn't exactly the most stable.

Ahna and Scorcher waited as they watched her move across the bridge. Felan appeared to be very focused, so much so that she never looked down or back toward them, only forward.

When the wind picked up, the bridge swayed heavily from side to side. Felan let out a yell. The horse whinnied before it bolted across the bridge. The other horses were startled by the noise, and cries escaped from within the other wagons. Ahna had almost forgotten about the rest of the group since they were all inside the wagons, and now her heart was pounding through her chest.

"It's okay," she called out to the group. "Just a bit of wind. Hold on, and you'll be on the other side shortly."

Ahna hoped that they believed her, even though she wasn't so sure she did herself. She glanced back over to the bridge.

Felan had managed to get to the other side safely, which meant it was time for the rest of the wagons to move. Sticks was driving the second wagon full of kids, another wagon connected to it containing the rest of the group. Corinne was behind the third horse, driving the wagon with most of the medical supplies, behind which was another wagon carrying various other supplies: wheelchairs, crutches, cots, additional armor, and a barrel of food.

Ahna and Scorcher helped guide each of the wagons onto the planks before hopping onto the back of the last one. As they rode across the bridge, Ahna glanced down. A river of dirty green water coursed beneath them, splashing against jagged rocks. She couldn't imagine what it would feel like to fall down there, but she had a feeling that the cold water would be the least of her worries, if she managed to still be alive when she hit it.

Once they were halfway across the bridge with the final two wagons, Ahna heard the group shouting what she thought were cheers celebrating them getting across. When Scorcher pointed toward the area they'd just come from, though, she figured out the true reason for the noise.

Wallers.

At first, it looked like just a couple, but she quickly realized she was mistaken. A horde of at least thirty Wallers was sprinting toward them. Their screeching echoed through the forest, sending Ahna's heart racing.

How close are we?

Ahna peered back toward the rest of the group. The horse was near the edge, which meant they would be able to get onto the other side shortly. She let out a sigh of relief. Prematurely.

The wagon tipped slightly to one side as Ahna watched one of the planks slide out from under the wheel of their wagon. Scorcher was already up and starting to climb on the side of the wagon using the rope to guide him to the other side. Ahna gulped before following suit.

She gripped the rope, its coarse fibers digging into her calloused palm. Clinging on for dear life, she shuffled over the remaining planks of the bridge until she finally felt the hard ground beneath her feet. She had no time to celebrate surviving, though. The last two wagons were still on the bridge, and Wallers were closing in.

The Gray Wolves were already out of the wagons and readying their weapons, Sarah and Sticks joining them. Felan was perched on top of a large rock, peering through her scope at the incoming horde. Scorcher was focused on Corinne and the wagons.

"Just relax, Mom! You're gonna get across, I promise. Just don't go too quickly, okay?"

Ahna could hear the worry seeping through his voice, steady though it may have seemed. She moved to the other side, helping Scorcher with the wagon.

"Conserve your ammo, everyone," Felan called out. "Only shoot if necessary!"

This seems pretty necessary to me.

Ahna had no time to argue. The Wallers were already on the other end of the bridge. A few of the Gray Wolves shot arrows at them, sending them off the bridge to the river below. The screeches as they fell sent a shiver down Ahna's spine.

You sound almost . . . human.

"Almost there, Mom!" Scorcher yelled as the horse finally joined them on solid ground. The wagon was not far behind.

"I can't move them!" she yelled back. Ahna had never heard her yell like that.

Corrine kept glancing back and snapping the reins. The wagons were stuck.

Scorcher grabbed a handful of the Gray Wolves and the few Replacements who had escaped with them from Deliverance and began tugging on the wagon as Corrine continued to push the horse to go. It was working, but it was taking way longer than they had.

A shot rang through the air, and the horse cried out before racing forward. Corrine lost her grip on the reins as the front piece of the wagon snapped off and trailed behind the horse as it took off. Scorcher let out a grunt as he and the group tried to pull harder on the wagon. It was starting to fall back onto the bridge, and Wallers were nearing their position.

Ahna watched as arrows continued to fly through the air into the horde as they crossed the bridge behind the wagons. Some of the Wallers fell off the bridge, while others died in front of those trying to get across. They didn't let that slow them down, though. They were closing in. She didn't have time to think, just act.

Ahna grabbed the axe from Scorcher's waistband.

"I love you," Ahna said before sliding through the space between the wagon and the rope to get back onto the bridge.

"What are you doing?" Scorcher yelled. "Ahna!"

She didn't have time to explain her plan if she wanted it to happen. She kept moving, focused on the back wagon.

The bridge swayed from the movement of the Wallers as they clawed their way toward her, their screeching increasing in volume. Once she had reached the spot where the two wagons were connected, she planted her feet on the planks as best she could. Trusting in her footing, she let go of the rope.

It was almost like being on the raft with Scorcher back at the beach. Her body swayed side to side, water below her. The only difference was that if she fell now, she would most likely die. Ahna inhaled deeply before letting out the breath. She tried to push aside the cry of the wind, gunshots, and screeching of the Wallers and focus on the task at hand. Gripping the axe, she swung it down onto the connector between the wagons.

Splinters flew as she hacked away at it, each swing digging deeper into the wood. After a few hits, she felt it break loose. The axe slipped from her hand between the empty space of the planks beneath her feet.

"Pull now!" she yelled to Scorcher.

Quickly, she gripped the back of the wagon and hopped onto it. She felt it roll forward as Scorcher and the others pulled it onto the other side. Wallers climbed over the wagon that was still on the bridge, heading right for them. Felan was popping off shots as quickly as she could, while the others continued to fire their arrows.

Scorcher was hugging Corinne while the others readied their weapons to prepare for the incoming horde. Ahna tried counting the number of Wallers that were still climbing across the bridge, but she realized it was much higher than the numbers they had. There was only one way everyone would be safe from the Wallers.

Ahna rushed over to the rope connecting the bridge to the rocks and pulled out her knife.

"Ahna, what are you doing?" asked Felan.

Ahna hacked at the rope, watching the strands unwind beneath her blade until it snapped. The bridge sagged heavily, sending a good number of Wallers to their deaths.

Now the other side.

Ahna rushed over to the rock Felan was shooting from and began cutting the rope on that one. Felan jumped down to stop her, but Ahna pushed her aside. As she sliced into the rope the last time, she watched as it snapped and slid like a snake toward the ravine.

The group watched as their wagon plummeted toward the river below, accompanied by the screeching of Wallers. As it hit the rocks, the sound echoed around them. A horde of at least one hundred now stood, screeching, on the other side of the ravine.

That was close.

Chapter Two
Scorcher

"**D**o you have another problem we don't know about, or are you just stupid?" Felan was up in Ahna's face, yelling.

"I did what I had to, Felan," Ahna spat back. Their faces were almost touching as they shouted at each other.

"You better be glad there wasn't anyone inside the wagon, or I'd make sure you joined them."

That's it.

Scorcher felt his skin heat up before he stepped in, separating the two.

"Enough!" he said to Felan before guiding her away from Ahna. "Not here."

He pointed at the group standing behind him. Vincent was staring at them, tears streaming down his face, and others were visibly concerned. Coughs and moans sporadically escaped one of the wagons behind them, adding to the overall atmosphere. Hooves pounded against the dirt as one of the Gray Wolves appeared from the woods on the back of the horse that had taken off before.

Felan stared at him as if she could stab him with her eyes. Ahna looked upset too, for a reason he couldn't understand.

"Fine," said Felan, bumping Ahna's shoulder with her own as she brushed by her.

Ahna started to rebut, but Scorcher stepped in front of her.

"We need to get moving, Ahna. Another time, huh?"

She stared at him, her eyes narrowing slightly before she eventually nodded. "Yeah . . . another time."

As happy as he was to hear her agree with him, he couldn't shake the feeling that she was still upset.

What did I do?

Scorcher gathered Vincent and the others, guiding them back into the wagons. Once they had secured the horse back to the front of the wagon Corinne had been driving, they piled as many as they could inside. It wasn't as sturdy as before, but it would work. It would have to.

MORE TREES NOW LINED the road as they made their way back to the main highway and up a ramp. There was a split in the road, but they had no choice in which way to go since the road leading to the right had eroded and crumbled into the mountain.

"How much longer?" asked Baz.

"Yeah, my feet are killing me," Taz added.

They were so in sync that it was almost as if they were the same person. Scorcher could only tell who was who when they weren't in their matching Gray Wolves armor. He wasn't a fan of the fur-covered leather armor, with its metal plates in various spots around the suit. It struck him as somewhat obnoxious and way too hot. In fact, the heat inside the suit was mostly why he couldn't understand why they never took theirs off.

I'd hate to smell the inside of those suits.

The group hadn't stopped much since leaving the ravine. They wanted to get away from the horrible sound of Wallers screeching behind them. Scorcher felt like he could still hear them, which was absurd given they were miles away by now. Even if he could manage to clear his mind of that horrible sound, he'd never lose the image of their faces. They were slobbering feral beasts that were almost too humanlike for his taste. If not for the discolored skin and sunken eyes—and constant screeching—he'd have sworn he was killing normal people. They were far from normal, but then again, he had no clue what normal was anymore.

"I don't know," Felan said finally.

There was a shift in the group, murmurs transferring between them.

"What do you mean you don't know?" asked Ahna.

Felan brought the caravan to a halt. She glared at Ahna as she stepped down to her level.

"Exactly what I said, Ahna. Are you deaf now, too?" she asked, a small burst of air escaping her nostrils in a chuckle. Her hand hovered over the knife on her belt.

Ahna stepped toward her, her hand mirroring Felan's above her own knife.

Not again.

Scorcher started toward them but hesitated as he listened to Ahna.

"I heard you. It just doesn't make sense. You said you knew the way to find the rest of the Gray Wolves. These kids—heck, all of us—left the only place they knew as home to follow you. We did that because you promised you would lead us to them and they would help us take down The Delivery Company. Was all that a lie?"

Felan looked around. Gray Wolves and their own people were poking their heads out of the wagons. Others surrounded Felan and Ahna, listening, waiting for her answer. Her eyes darted side to side as if she were looking for the answer.

"It wasn't a lie," Felan said. "It just wasn't the whole truth."

There was a slight gasp from the group surrounding them. A patch of red was spreading on Felan's face, like iron on a fire.

"Then what is the whole truth?" asked Ahna, more relaxed.

Felan looked to the group again before answering.

"The Gray Wolves have grown, so much so that they finally settled down."

"Where?" asked Ahna.

"Out West."

"That's pretty vague," said Sticks, stepping more into the middle of the group to join them.

Felan nodded. "That's the problem. They used to bounce around from place to place, back when they were gathering more of the Rejected and anyone else who finally saw through the veil of corruption of The Delivery Company. Only reason I even know they've settled down now is 'cause I got word from another pack right before we hit Deliverance."

"Why not just ask the contact you talked to before and find out where they are?" asked Ahna.

That's a good question.

"Because they're dead," replied Felan. "Whole pack died in a Waller ambush."

Scorcher tried to push away the thought of being torn apart by Wallers. They had managed to keep that from happening so far, but just barely. He wasn't going to lose all of his friends . . . or his mom. Seeing her expression of sheer terror on the bridge, what he thought would be the last time he ever saw her, was enough to convince him to be more cautious from then on. He moved toward the girls, joining the conversation.

"If we're not careful, we'll face the same fate," said Scorcher. "You said we need to head west, Felan, so let's keep heading west. If you're confident they are out there, then we have to run into someone who knows where it is along the way, right?"

Sticks laughed. "How do we know she isn't leading us into a trap?" he asked. "Not that we'll have many supplies or people by the time we get there, if Ahna has anything to do with it."

Chatter erupted around them, arguments nocked on the bow of fear before flying across the circle at one another. Scorcher looked to Ahna, hoping she'd act as the leader she was supposed to be, but she did nothing. He could see her coming up with something, but the group was getting louder.

She's losing control of them.

"Everyone, stop!" Surprisingly, the crowd died down, allowing him to speak for a moment. "Ahna," he said, staring at her, "what's the plan?"

"Who died and made her the leader?" asked Felan, crossing her arms and cocking her head to the side.

"Seemore did," said Scorcher. There was an audible gasp in the crowd before they were silent again.

"We don't know that for sure," said Sticks. His voice cut like a dagger, sharp and deep.

Another gasp came from the others, murmurs following.

"Well, he's not here, is he?" asked Scorcher.

"No, he isn't," said Sticks. "A lot of people aren't here. And she's to blame." He pointed at Ahna. "That's why I don't think she ought to be the one to make decisions."

Scorcher's face heated up as he took a step toward Sticks, his fists balled up. "How about you just shut up and follow orders? You were great at that with Seemore."

Sticks swung his staff at Scorcher, who ducked and lunged toward him. Before he could make contact, Felan stepped in and held them both back.

"Chill out, both of you! I'm not having this kind of infighting in any group that I'm part of. Either stop this stupid childish arguing or I take my group and leave you all behind. Got it?"

Scorcher glared at Sticks, but they both nodded at Felan.

"Right then," she said, getting back up onto the wagon. "Ahna, since you're apparently the one to decide, what's the move?"

Please have an idea, or at least say something that won't make everyone upset with you again.

Ahna nodded as though she could hear his thoughts. She stood up straight, addressing the group.

"We continue heading west. Felan has information that will lead us to a group large enough to make a difference in our fight against The Delivery Company. If that's true, then we might actually achieve what we've been fighting for . . . what others died for. I know some of you are mad at me for what happened on the bridge," she said, and murmurs once again flowed through the crowd. "You're right to be upset—I am too—but if we hadn't lost that wagon, we might have lost much more." She pulled out the leather-bound book Seemore had given her and held it up in the air. "If this book is correct, then there's only a handful of facilities left around the country. The biggest one is out West, inside the last remaining major city. We take that down, we win. But we can't do that without the help of the bigger group of Gray Wolves, so unless somebody else has a better idea, I say we keep going. Felan?"

Ahna gestured toward Felan, and the group awaited a response. After a moment, Felan relaxed her arms and nodded.

"For once, an idea I can agree with," said Felan. "What are you waiting for? Let's move."

The group piled back into the wagons. Dirt merged into asphalt and they found themselves once again on the dilapidated highway heading west. Not more than a mile down the road, they watched as the trees parted to reveal a downhill stretch that opened up to a large open space. Framed by the mountains, they kept moving as snow slowly gathered on the tops of the wagons. Scorcher got excited before he saw the billboard bearing the logo of the stork beside the highway. Underneath that, on the side of the road right ahead, was another sign.

This one looked like a large piece of wood hung in an open space, framed by larger logs with a stone base. Hand-carved letters, faded by years of sun and damaged slightly, spelled out a message meant to be welcoming and comforting to many. It certainly wasn't meant for their group, though. Scorcher realized the caravan had stopped completely. He walked up to join Ahna and Felan near the front. They all stared at it. The base of it seemed to be newer than the rest of it, as though someone had taken the sign from somewhere else and put it there instead. He did think it strange that it was up this high in the mountains, given that they had been traveling through the state for a number of days already. The fact that they had still not made it out of the same state yet wasn't what surprised him, but what came after. Scorcher found himself reading the sign aloud in total disbelief.

"Welcome to Colorful Colorado, the original home of The Delivery Company." He stared at the rusted green sign with arrows slightly to the side of it. Next to the arrows, mostly chipped away with the rest of the paint, was the name of the upcoming city. While it was difficult to read the name fully due to the scratched paint, he could read most of the beginning.

Silver . . . something. That doesn't seem too far ahead.

Scorcher was going to read the altitude listed below the name when the thought hit him. "You don't think they're still here, do you?"

"No way," said Felan. A few others nodded and murmured in agreement.

A long deep tone echoed across the mountain.

Is that—

Smoke billowed from a source that was moving along the horizon. The speed at which it traveled was unlike anything he'd ever seen. They watched it for a few seconds longer before Ahna answered his question.

"I think that should answer your question, Scorch. If that's them, we need to move. Now."

The caravan jolted forward, the hooves of the horses a steady rhythm to the melodic whine of the wagon wheels. Scorcher could feel the dull pain in his feet with each step, but he couldn't take a break. There weren't many who could replace him, and with the other wagon gone, there was little room to sit and relax. He pushed through, trying to mentally escape from the snow-covered highway in the middle of a mountain range.

Warm thoughts, Scorcher.

He tried to imagine the feeling of warmth. His mind transported him away from the mountains, and he found himself returning to his secret beach. Sunlight seeped into his skin as he bobbed up and down on the raft. Ahna was lying on his chest, and they watched as birds soared over the calm water. The sails whipped around in the wind, their flapping a soothing rhythm. The birds then started to dive toward the raft, their calls louder than he'd ever heard.

As though the raft had been overturned, he felt the cold of the mountain engulf him again. Ahna was gripping his arm and pulling him toward her, crouching behind a half-rusted car. What he had once believed to be imaginary birdcalls altered into their true nature: whistles. And they were nearby.

"What's going on?" he asked, his eyebrows meeting near the middle as he looked around. "Where's the caravan?"

Ahna peeked above the car, then dropped down to talk to him.

"Elite up ahead. Bunch of 'em. Felan managed to get everyone else off the road and into the forest over there," she said, gesturing.

He tried to spot the wagons, but they were nowhere to be seen. At least he knew that if he couldn't spot the caravan, that meant the Elite couldn't either. Ahna spoke again, her tone softer.

"What happened? We all moved to get into cover, and you were just standing in the middle of the road. It was like you were sleepwalking or something. You okay?"

It didn't feel like a dream. It felt . . . real.

"Yeah," said Scorcher. "Just tired, I guess."

"We'll make sure you get some rest when we meet back up with the group." Her eyes were watering. Whether from the cold or otherwise, he wasn't sure. "Don't do that again, okay? I don't wanna lose you."

Scorcher nodded. "Don't worry. You won't."

As Ahna smiled, he felt a burst of energy flow through him. In that moment, he wanted nothing more than to kiss her. He was about to reach out and pull her toward him when he heard a voice call out.

"Where'd they go?" a boy shouted.

Footsteps accompanied the shouts, both nearby.

"You sure you saw something?" another asked, this one a girl.

If Scorcher had to guess, he'd say they weren't much older than he and Ahna. Of course, age wasn't important. He'd known plenty of kids almost half his age who were better fighters. It all came down to training. The Elite had plenty of that.

Scorcher pulled out his knife, and Ahna did the same. She peered through a hole in the car door.

"How many?" asked Scorcher.

"Just two," said Ahna. "Both armed and wearing pretty heavy-duty armor."

Scorcher thought for a moment, trying to come up with a plan. Two on two normally wouldn't have been a problem, but that was in the sparring circle with other Rejects. Besides, knives wouldn't cut it in a fight against guns. They had to play smart.

The two Elite stopped only feet away from their car.

"I know what I saw," said the boy. "There was a kid standing on the road and something else behind him that looked like a car."

The girl laughed. "A car? Now I know you're joking."

"I know people don't drive cars anymore, but that's what it looked like. It could have been something else. I just don't know what. I do know I saw a kid in the road, though."

"Sure he wasn't driving the car?"

The girl laughed again. Scorcher had to hold back a laugh himself. Even if they were trying to kill him, they were funny. The argument almost reminded him of how he and Ahna bickered.

"Look," said the boy, "I know I saw someone over here. We just need to find them."

Scorcher heard footsteps coming toward him and Ahna. His heart rate sped up, as though it were attempting to race the person coming toward him.

"It could've been a Waller," replied the girl.

The footsteps stopped, then moved back toward the girl again.

"Doubt that," said the boy.

"Every time we kill them, more come back. It's like they're sprouting up from the ground or something."

"That's impossible. Besides, we probably just missed a nest or something. We'll get it soon enough. That, or we'll finally move out of this frozen prison. Whichever comes first. I'm ready to get back to some warmer weather. Getting a tan makes killing Rejects even more enjoyable. Almost gives them a purpose."

The boy gave a dark laugh, pure evil. A whistle sounded through the trees, the low tone almost mocking the boy. It caught the attention of the two Elite.

"Train's getting back later than usual today," said the girl. "Must have run into trouble along the route. You think they brought some back with them?"

The boy laughed, but Scorcher could hear the worry behind it. He'd done the same thing when he was younger.

"I guess you never know, but I doubt it. What I do know is that I'm glad I wasn't given that position. That patrol is tough, don't get me wrong, but I don't know how much a train will help you if it runs out of fuel in the middle of the Wasteland."

The Wasteland?

Scorcher racked his brain for the reference, but there was nothing. Ahna had never mentioned it, and neither had Felan. He'd have to ask her and Wick about it when they got back.

"I get that. J-54 told me the last group that came back lost half their people to a horde of a thousand."

The boy scoffed. "He always exaggerates. There's no way there're that many Wallers out there. A few hundred maybe, but not thousands. Dean Tipper said they've exterminated most of them everywhere."

Ahna and Scorcher exchanged a look of surprise. They hadn't seen Dean Tipper since he escaped the destruction of the facility back in Deliverance. They'd figured he might still be alive but had no idea where he had gone. Now they knew he was at this facility . . . or at least had been at some point.

"True," said the girl. "I'm just ready for the day we get to finish taking out the Rejected. Those freaks are almost as bad as the Wallers."

"For real. They're so disgusting."

Scorcher's body heated up as he listened to them bash his friends and family.

You have no idea what we're really like. You wanna see a freak, I'll show you a freak . . .

Scorcher looked underneath the car, feeling around with one hand while he braced himself against it with the other.

"What are you doing?" Ahna whispered.

Scorcher touched cold metal and pulled it out from underneath the car. He held the slender pipe up, displaying his find to Ahna.

"Getting a different weapon," he said. "I don't want their blood on mine."

As he started to stand up, Ahna pulled on his shirt. He yanked away.

"Hold on, Scorch. You're gonna get yourself killed."

"Then you'd better help make sure that doesn't happen."

Before he could exit the cover of the car, screams echoed from down the road.

The Elite turned to face the barricade. Scorcher and Ahna peeked over the car to get a better look at what was going on.

Wallers again?

The screams intensified as Wallers descended upon the two Elite still at the barricade. The two who had been near the car sprinted back, guns at the ready. Shots rang out as they ran toward the barricade.

"We need to find the group," said Ahna. "This is our only chance without being spotted."

Scorcher argued with himself in his head before eventually nodding in agreement. He let out a sigh.

"You're right. Which way?"

"I don't know," replied Ahna. "They're in the forest, so let's just get into the trees and go from there."

Scorcher nodded, following her lead.

She moved with such dexterity and grace. It was so different from how she had been when they'd first met. He remembered that day very well.

She'd entered Tent City, a wounded animal, dripping blood from a fresh cut the entire path from the main gate to Seemore's office. When he helped massage her forearm, when their eyes met, he felt something. It was small at the time, and he didn't fully understand what it was until much later. After their time scrounging for leaves and the training where she'd kicked his butt, he knew he liked her. Had he not, she'd never have laid eyes on his beach.

No . . . Our beach.

Now, Ahna ran like a deer and fought like a bear. He didn't want to admit it, but she was probably better than him most of the time. Her short hair swayed side to side as she dodged the trees. It reminded him of how it had moved in the wind on their raft. He couldn't wait to go to the beach when they finally finished everything and could settle down. They'd make a bigger, better raft or even a boat and relax on the water. Waves would bob them up and down as they drifted off to sleep in the sunset. Scorcher smiled.

Soon. Then we'll have a normal life together.

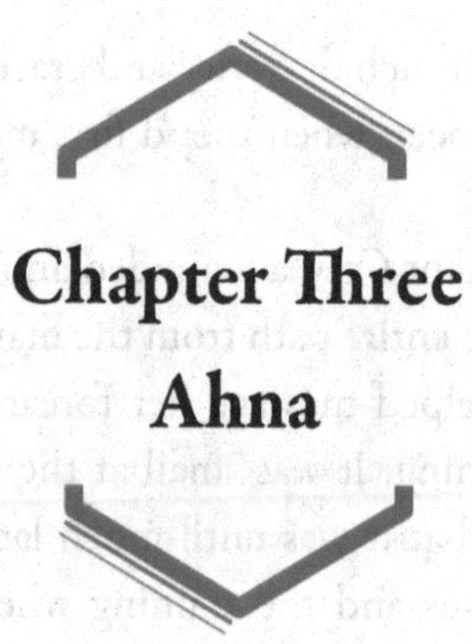

Chapter Three
Ahna

Ahna's heart raced as she ducked and dodged through the forest. Screeching rang out through the air behind them, adding to the stressful situation and reminding her how close they truly were to becoming Waller food. They needed to find the group before the Wallers did or there wouldn't be much of a group left.

Stupid trees. You all look the same.

Ahna had her head on a swivel, looking for any sign of the caravan or Felan's bright red hair. If nothing else, she figured she'd spot that fiery mane through the trees. Unfortunately, she had no such luck. She was about to pick up the pace and run deeper into the forest when she heard a cough.

Oh, yeah. Scorch.

She turned to see Scorcher, his face red from the cold, coughing into his elbow as he leaned against a nearby tree. His scars had become more accented by the contrast in his face. He had stopped wearing his helmet, so she had gotten used to seeing his face fully, scars and all. It was interesting how similar they seemed to the bark his hand was currently holding on to. Both the tree and Scorcher had been forever altered physically by their surroundings.

If only you didn't have to deal with the effects it had on your mind. Another reason trees are stupid.

"Where are we going?" asked Scorcher. He glanced around periodically. She could understand why.

"Honestly? No clue," replied Ahna. It didn't help to be dishonest with Scorcher. He was the only one she felt she could be completely honest with.

"That's encouraging," he said.

She could tell he was joking, but there was still a tinge of guilt and irritation from it. She forced a chuckle in response.

"Yep. I know they went somewhere this way . . . at least I think they did."

She looked around, trying to spot the caravan again. Nothing.

I guess this is what Seemore meant when he said something about seeing the forest through the trees. I'm ready to see something other than trees.

Scorcher grabbed her shoulders and pulled her down to the ground in one fluid motion.

"What're you—"

Scorcher put one hand over her mouth and pointed with the other.

Ahna turned her head to see what had him so spooked. Her eyes widened as she saw them walking not more than twenty feet away from where they were now crouched.

Wallers. Two of them.

Their teeth chattered as they scoured the area, swinging their heads from side to side. Ahna held her breath, hoping the

Wallers wouldn't smell or hear them as they sniffed the air and walked in their direction. She and Scorcher quickly crouched behind a nearby fallen log, but the cover provided would only work for so long. Once the Wallers came too close, they'd be spotted in a heartbeat.

Ahna let out a sigh as the Wallers quickly turned away from them and focused on another direction. They continued sniffing and grinding their teeth as they walked toward whatever it was they were now interested in, their backs hunched slightly. Scorcher looked at her, likely expecting an answer, but she didn't have one. She shrugged in response, and then they both moved to get behind another tree to observe the Wallers.

What are you so interested in?

Ahna couldn't wait any longer to find out. She followed the Wallers, moving tree to tree like a predator on the prowl, maintaining a moderate distance. Whatever they were heading toward had piqued their interest and now hers. She could hear Scorcher following her but kept her eyes forward. They weren't going to disappear.

After a few more minutes, they had traveled a bit deeper into the forest and farther up the mountainside. Ahna felt a cool breeze across the back of her neck and noted the dropping temperature. Her hair had grown a bit since she'd had it cut on their way out of Deliverance, but it was still short. She felt a little lighter now but sometimes missed the added heat across her neck when the weather got too cold.

Snow fell at a more consistent pace and continued to blanket the ground around them, dampening the sound of their footsteps. For once, she was thankful for the snow.

I hope the group was able to find somewhere to settle down . . . and that they aren't waiting for us to do it. Who am I kidding? If Felan had her way, she'd probably take the caravan and leave us here.

The Wallers jumped up and down, facing each other, and let out a screech. It was almost as though they were celebrating something, excited. Almost like they were human. Ahna stretched her neck to peer around them a bit more to see what they had been heading toward.

A pile of junk? Man, you freaks love your junkyards, huh?

The Wallers started moving some of the debris out of the way, revealing a large hole. They walked through it, dropping the debris back in place. Ahna's eyebrows rose as the cold wind entered her lungs through her smile.

They had created a doorway.

Ahna hurried toward the pile of debris, quickly looking side to side to ensure no other Wallers were in the immediate area. Once she felt safe, she continued on until she reached the makeshift doorway. After reaching the pile of debris, she started to lift the doorway, but the weight of the metal mixed with the wet snow proved to be too heavy.

Footsteps approached from behind, and she turned to see Scorcher. Snow covered his hair, almost making him look like more of an old man instead of a kid. It was a nice look, one she hoped she would see one day in the future. But first, they had to get through the day.

"I've got it," said Scorcher.

He pushed his sleeves out of the way, then gripped the large metal sheet. Ahna stared at him as he lifted the door, admiring his strength.

"You gonna go through or not?" asked Scorcher, straining a bit. She could see his legs shaking slightly as he continued to hold up the door.

"Yeah, sorry."

Ahna nodded her head, pulling her focus away from him and back to the task at hand. She slithered through the opening and held the metal up as best she could while Scorcher slid through to join her. After he caught his breath, they moved on through.

It was almost like a tunnel of debris, metal shards jutting out from every direction. It wasn't a very long tunnel. Light from outside was not far ahead.

They continued forward, keeping their footsteps quiet and watching for the Wallers. Ahna kept her hand on the hilt of her knife. As they neared the end of the metal tunnel, she saw a fence leaning to one side. Behind the fence, she spotted a sign that made her heart jump. It may have looked slightly different, but there was no mistaking the stork. She didn't need to guess because the wording was directly underneath it.

The Delivery Company.

"Jackpot," Ahna whispered to herself. She took off, sprinting toward it.

Before she knew it, she was standing in front of the threshold underneath the stork. She stared at the sign, its rusty form mirroring the state of the building itself. It felt like the stork was staring down at her, waiting to swoop down and take her away. A cold chill snaked down her spine. Exhaling, she stepped over the threshold and into the dark room ahead. There was a noise from farther inside the room. Once she crouched behind an overturned desk, she recognized the sound as the chattering of the

Wallers' teeth. As if that weren't enough, she could hear and feel them scratching the metal walls with their fingernails.

If you don't quit that, I'm gonna throw up.

Peering over the desk, she could see the Wallers, but just barely. The lighting inside the room was dim, almost entirely dark. If not for the daylight reflecting off the snow outside, it would have been completely dark. She tried to plan out her next move, think about how to take down the two Wallers she'd seen head this way, but she realized that she didn't know if any more were inside with them. She'd seen two, but she hadn't been watching that debris pile all day. She just needed a way to figure that out.

"Ahna! What are you doing?" Scorcher yelled from outside.

She tried to get to where he could see her so she could warn him, but he yelled again.

"Ahna!"

The screeching inside the room intensified. It was so loud she had to cover her ears with her hand and wrist.

Well, I guess we know there're more than two. Way to go, Scorch.

Ahna ran over to the doorway and waved at Scorcher, alerting him of her position.

"Scorch! In here," she called out to him. She figured it couldn't hurt now that the Wallers already knew they were here. She watched as the two she had followed started running toward her, sending chairs and other debris out of their path as they moved. "And hurry!" Ahna added.

She surveyed her immediate surroundings for something she could use: broken chairs, a few overturned desks, scattered debris. Nothing. She inhaled deeply before letting out a long slow breath, her fear transforming into adrenaline-infused confidence. She stared directly ahead, focusing on the Wallers sprinting toward her.

Scorcher appeared next to her, bow in one hand and an arrow in the other. Their eyes met briefly, just long enough for them to exchange a nod before a Waller leapt off an overturned desk and into the air. Scorcher nocked an arrow and let it fly, meeting the Waller on its decent and sending it off course and onto the floor.

Ahna gripped her knife, her fingers at home around the smooth wooden handle. Her eyes narrowed, focusing on the other Waller.

Get sliced, freak.

Ahna raced to the other as it ran along the wall around the debris. It let out a screech, baring its broken teeth, and swiped at her. She felt a slight burst of air as she dodged its nails and dropped into a crouched position. Eye level with the Waller's legs, she slashed through its knee. It felt like cutting into leather, but blood started to drip from the knife's path. Ahna dodged another swipe and thrust the blade into the Waller again, digging into its torso. That provided more of a show when blood splattered onto her.

The Waller screeched again and swiped at her, this time digging into her neck. Thankfully, the other attacks hit her armor, so she mostly felt the pressure instead of pain. It gave her just enough time to move away and send her leg into its torso. She aimed right for the spot she had stabbed. Spot on. The Waller stumbled back, gripping its fresh wound before staring her down. She felt a twinge as she turned her head, the pain in her neck sharp and throbbing. She reached to feel how bad the cut was and noticed scarlet staining her palm.

The Waller growled as its long teeth chattered, then flailed its arms as it ran toward her. The way it ran seemed too fast compared to what she remembered from the past. Ahna dashed sideways, spinning and pushing the Waller in the direction it was running. Then, in one swift motion, she brought her blade across the back of its neck. A screech was silenced as the head rolled to one side, then down to the ground. Ahna watched as the body followed shortly after, the arms twitching sporadically.

Yes! Take that!

She couldn't celebrate, though. A few feet away, Scorcher was grappling with the other Waller. A wooden shaft protruded from its shoulder, the arrow broken and still inside it. Scorcher held the Waller back with his bow, the string bending under the weight as the Waller attempted to bite his face off. They rolled side to side, taking turns being on top. Then Ahna saw the moment she'd been waiting for, her opportunity. Scorcher gained momentum, and the Waller was now on top again. Ahna flipped the knife so that her hand was gripping the cold metal. She exhaled, then launched it at the Waller.

The knife entered the Waller's head, and its body went limp, resting on the bow. Scorcher rolled it off of him, then pulled the knife out, wiping the blade across his pant leg. He held it out to Ahna.

"I think this is yours."

They laughed. It felt good to laugh, too. She hadn't realized how long it'd been, but her abs reminded her it had been quite a while. Once their laughter had echoed out of the metal room, it became silent. She wrapped her fingers around the wooden handle and returned the knife to its home on her waist.

"Thanks," said Ahna.

"I appreciate you helping with that one," said Scorcher. He gestured to the Waller, whose head was resting on a pillow of its own blood.

"You're welcome—"

"But," said Scorcher, holding out his hand to interrupt her. "We could've avoided this fight altogether if you hadn't run ahead without me."

You think that was the problem?

"No," said Ahna. "We could've avoided the fight if you hadn't shown up screaming my name like some lost child."

Scorcher's mouth hung open slightly. He was visibly surprised by that statement. She was okay with that, too.

"Someone has to make sure you're okay," said Scorcher.

"I thought you were supposed to be my boyfriend, not my father." Ahna could feel her skin heating up. "I lived a long time without someone to watch over me, and I think I can do it now."

"You don't think I know that? You're not the only one who didn't have a father growing up, Ahna. None of us did."

"You have a parent, Scorcher." She was almost as surprised at the use of his full name in private conversation as he was. "You don't have to act like mine just because I don't have one."

She felt bad immediately after saying it, but she couldn't let him know that. She turned her gaze away from him and stared back into the dark empty room. A moment passed before she heard Scorcher messing with a buckle on his armor. Then he appeared next to her, speaking low and firm.

"One of these days, your impulsive actions are gonna get somebody hurt or killed, Ahna. We're lucky that wasn't today with the wagon or in here."

"In case you forgot, my actions earlier saved your mom."

"They also destroyed all the extra medical supplies and a bunch of other stuff we need to help our group survive. I appreciate you thinking of my mom—I really do—but sometimes you have to think of the whole instead of the one."

Ahna couldn't believe what she'd just heard. There was no way he would suggest risking his own mother's life over some stupid supplies.

She tried to concoct a response, some sort of rebuttal, but failed. Adjusting her armor gave her an excuse to fidget while she stood there, waiting for him to continue critiquing her choices. Instead, his voice relaxed, and she looked back up to see the familiar sparkle within his emerald eyes.

"You're not alone anymore," he said. He spoke with a soft, warm tone, as though he were attempting to caress her with his words. His strong hand gripped her shoulder, and she didn't pull away. "Whether you're running into a Waller-infested building on the side of a mountain or whatever other crazy thing you haven't done yet, I'll be right here with you, always."

She stared into his eyes as a smile grew beneath them. Her mind relaxed, and she inhaled deeply, allowing her mind time to reset.

Maybe I was a bit . . . ambitious? Ugh. You're probably right.

"Scorch, I—"

Her apology was cut short when she spotted a faint blue glow behind Scorcher. It was almost mesmerizing. She couldn't look away.

"Yeah?" asked Scorcher. His eyes widened. "Ahna, what is it?"

Ahna gulped, her throat as dry as cardboard. When the blue light got close enough, she could finally see that it was moving with something else, something much larger behind it. The light didn't scare her, but what accompanied it did.

"We've gotta go," she said, her words almost inaudible. "Now!"

Screeching echoed through the room, penetrating her eardrums. A loud vibration joined it as a horde of Wallers stampeded toward them. She tried to run, but her body froze.

Without a moment of hesitation, Scorcher grabbed her by the hand and pulled her with him as they ran through the doorway back into the snow. As long as they got far enough away from the building before the Wallers made it out, they could hopefully make it back without being spotted. She knew it was a slim chance, but it was one they had to take.

Chapter Four
Scorcher

Ahna and Scorcher had spent hours walking and scanning the mountainside for their group when they spotted a silhouette of smoke dancing in front of the setting sun, rising toward the darkening clouds above. A slight smile spread across Scorcher's numb face, his lips barely moving from where they'd been frozen. Cold wind and snow swept across the canopy above, chilling him to the bone. His teeth had been almost constantly chattering for the last hour. He may have joked about being a Waller, but he couldn't waste what little energy remained on laughing. Even his legs had started shaking from overuse and cold, his toes frozen inside his leather boots.

I have to get these patched up soon. I cannot get my foot amputated. I know how that ends.

Each step dug deeper into the fresh snow. What had begun as cold and wet now felt like only a slight pressure against the sole of his boots. They had to get to the source of the smoke soon, even if it wasn't their friends. Smoke meant a fire, and fire meant heat. He'd have given almost anything to rest by a warm fire and thaw his limbs.

Ahna had been quiet almost the entire last hour. Whether because she was upset with him, focused on her own thoughts, or her mouth was frozen shut was anyone's guess. He hadn't attempted to talk to her either, given they had little to discuss besides which way to go the one time they'd ended up at a fork in the path. Scorcher thought back to their conversation—his lecture, more like—inside that abandoned building.

Was I too harsh?

He shook his head.

No. She needed to hear that. It's better it came from me instead of someone like Sticks.

As the path leveled out, an orange glow seeped through the trees, flickering beneath the smoke. Scorcher could make out the shape of a few tents and the wagons circled around the fire. He breathed a sigh of relief.

"I think I see them," he said. It was the first time he'd spoken in at least an hour, but he couldn't contain his excitement.

"I think you're right," replied Ahna. He could hear the excitement and relief in her voice, too.

They began walking much quicker and without care for the sounds they were making. They were close enough to the group that they could feel safe, or safer than they had roaming the side of an unknown mountain, anyway.

As they neared the caravan, another flame appeared closer to them. In the light of the torch, Sticks's eyes widened as he spotted them. Scorcher was surprised to see a smile make a home on Sticks's face.

"Wow. So you two are alive," said Sticks. The smirk faded as he gave them a good look up and down. "You both look awful."

"Wow, thanks," said Ahna.

"Yeah, man. We've had a long day," said Scorcher.

Sticks laughed. "Looks like it." He waved his arm as he turned to walk back toward the camp. "Come on, then. I imagine you want to get warm?"

They didn't need to be asked twice before they were already following him back to the fire. Without being close, Scorcher could almost feel the warmth and comfort of the flames. Wiping the snot dripping from his thawing nose, Scorcher continued to follow Sticks until they reached a collection of rocks and buckets next to the fire.

Scorcher felt a pressure envelop him. One smell of the strange, familiar combination of soap and vomit, and he knew it was his mom. Most people would hate that smell, but most people didn't have a mom who worked around sick kids all day. She hugged him for what felt like forever before finally letting go.

"I'm glad to see you both are okay," said Corrine. She hugged Ahna, then looked back at Scorcher.

You care about her almost as much as I do, don't you?

"I really thought I lost you," she said.

"If not for Ahna, you may have," said Scorcher.

"If only we could be that lucky," said Sticks, laughing. Corrine shot him a glare. "You know I'm kidding, Corrine."

You're intimidated by her, aren't you? Ha!

Corrine hugged him again, then guided him and Ahna to the ring of rocks and buckets around the fire.

"I'm glad you have each other then!"

Scorcher looked at Ahna, smirking as he raised his eyebrows. Ahna smiled in return.

"You can tell me all about it," Corrine said, "but sit down and get warm first. I don't want you dying from hypothermia."

Scorcher plopped down on the closest rock and closed his eyes.

Warmth blanketed his body. Pain awakened within his muscles, reminding him of their existence. The fight with the Wallers had been pretty intense, but he hadn't noticed until now how much of a toll it had taken on him. Combined with the heavy amount of walking through deepening snow and the mental exhaustion with Ahna, he would have loved to sleep for a whole day. Unfortunately, he knew that was never going to happen.

"Why are you both covered in blood?"

Scorcher opened his eyes to see Felan standing over them, her hair almost an extension of the flames.

"Don't worry, it's not our own," said Ahna. "Most of it, anyway."

Scorcher held back a chuckle.

"What?" asked Felan. "Did you two run into a small deer that thought you smelled like a potential mate and had to fight it off?"

She, along with a handful of Gray Wolves who were sitting nearby, laughed. The set of twin Gray Wolves had almost fallen over due to their excessive laughter, a usual overreaction on their part.

"Wallers, actually," replied Ahna. Her tone was flat, straight to the point.

The laughter stopped, the whole group suddenly intrigued.

"How many?" asked Felan. Her eyes were wide as she stared at Ahna, waiting for her response.

Scorcher watched Ahna as she turned her head toward Felan, narrowing her eyes.

"We killed two," said Ahna. The group looked a bit relieved before she continued. "But we didn't stick around to count the group running after us."

"There were more chasing you?" asked Sticks. He was suddenly on edge. "Are they just roaming the mountainside?"

Ahna tried to explain before the others could freak out any more than they already were.

"That's what we wanted to tell you all about. There's a building—not sure how far it is from here—that looks abandoned. Besides the Wallers, of course." She shrugged and moved on, her words flowing out like a verbal waterfall. "Anyway, this abandoned building had The Delivery Company logo on it, but this one looks a little . . . different—older, maybe? The building looks pretty decrepit, but there was a ton of stuff inside the room that we saw. It looks like it hasn't been used in years. There was a huge room with tables and chairs that could easily be cleared out to make more space for whatever we need. The best part is, it would keep us out of the cold."

Felan narrowed her eyes. "You're suggesting we go stay in some old Delivery Company–owned building that's full of Wallers?"

Ahna nodded, confident in her thought.

Felan chuckled. "You must be crazier than I thought. Scorcher, you were there. I hesitate to ask you since you're close and all, but what do you think?"

Scorcher could see how it sounded crazy. In fact, he thought it was somewhat crazy himself, but Ahna's ideas oftentimes ended up working out . . . mostly. Besides, it couldn't hurt to be on her side and have her hear him prove that.

As he looked around at the makeshift camp they had created, tent flaps whipping around in the wind, accompanied by coughs and moans of the children who were unable to sleep, he had his answer.

"I think it's our only choice," said Scorcher.

Felan seemed to weigh the options in her head before nodding.

"Okay, fine. But you said there was a group of Wallers inside there still. How many? A handful of us are sick or unable to get around very easily. Heck, besides them, most of the Replacements we took in from Deliverance can't fight to save their lives. Plus, you don't even know for sure where it is. That seems pretty risky if you ask me."

He wanted to argue with that, but she had a good point. With each passing day, more kids seemed to come down with something, and it was only getting worse. There were fewer each day who would be useful in taking down a horde, let alone an entire facility full of Wallers and eventually Elite.

"I wasn't asking," said Ahna. "Besides, it's a risk we have to take, Felan."

Scorcher raised his eyebrows, impressed. He continued watching Ahna as she spoke. He liked to hear her voice, especially after the lack of it the past few hours.

"Either we risk dying by a horde of Wallers or risk freezing to death and becoming possible food for Wallers. Either way, they are involved. At least we have the possibility of gaining shelter with one of the options. The wagons and tents will only work for so long."

Felan pondered the thought, then nodded.

"I hate to admit it, but you're right," said Felan. "Besides . . ." She paused, appearing to chew on the words that were about to come out. "We agreed you're in charge until we reach the rest of the pack out West. I gave my word, and I intend to keep it. So, when do we take control of the place?"

Ahna looked to Scorcher. He tilted his head back at her, hoping she understood that he wasn't going to make her decisions for her.

"As soon as we can find it again," said Ahna.

Sticks scoffed. "You don't know where it is?"

"Not really," said Ahna. "We found it not long after we saw the Elite, but we've been walking for hours trying to find our way back to you guys. There's no telling how far up, down, or around the mountain it is. I know it's pretty high up the mountain since we weren't far from the checkpoint. That should at least help us get close enough, right?"

"Maybe," said Felan. "After that, we hit it hard?"

Ahna shook her head. "Not quite. First, we need to scope it out. I won't have us running in full force without knowing the extent of the threat. We can't afford to lose any more than we already have."

She glanced at Scorcher, who smiled at her. She smiled back before turning to the group. He was proud of the progress she had made. No matter how small, it was still a step in the right direction.

Let's hope this continues.

"Speaking of, what happened with the Elite checkpoint? How did you all get out of there after we split up?" asked Sticks.

Scorcher spotted his mom walking toward one of the tents out of the corner of his eye. She was heading for the tent producing the majority of coughing and cries. That meant she might need something to boost her spirits before heading inside.

Scorcher stood up, giving Ahna the go-ahead to answer Sticks's question about their getaway while he left the group. Ahna's excitement faded into the background as he trudged through the deepening snow toward his mom.

For a brief moment, Scorcher felt as though he were walking home, as if he were inside the walls of Tent City. The thought of it made him laugh. For the longest time, he'd wanted to leave, to get out and see the world. He wanted to see the places he'd heard about in the stories of the few travelers who'd passed through over the years. Seemore had assured him that those places were no longer viable areas to live in, saying they were one of the few remaining cities outside of the Wall. Every time he'd heard that, he'd thought Seemore may be lying. Over the course of the past few months, though, he'd come to realize that the truth was far worse than Seemore had let on. At least Tent City had walls.

In the last few months since the destruction of Deliverance and their escape, he'd seen remnants of the past: craters where whole cities had once thrived, people living in conditions he'd never wish upon his worst enemy, and animals so mutated that he'd risk starvation over eating their meat. Living in Tent City wasn't glamorous, but it was simple. Nothing ever changed, besides the occasional additional Reject being brought in from the Junkyard. He only realized as they moved location day after day just how much he longed for that consistency. He glanced back at Ahna, watching as she used her arms to demonstrate a part of her story to the group around the fire.

You're the only good change that's ever happened to me.

Scorcher pushed the fabric aside as he stepped into the tent to find his mom.

He watched for a moment as she gingerly unwrapped a strip of fabric from the head of one of the Replacements. It was dark, the color ruined by the blood that had stained through. She dipped another ragged piece of fabric in a small bowl, wrung it out, then wiped the kid's wound. They winced, their cries of pain weakened. Corrine shushed them as she finished cleaning the wound and redressing it.

He felt as though he had been transported back in time to his childhood, watching her care for him and his wounds after the fire. Pain had plagued him long after the incident but had lessened over the years a bit. When he'd asked why he still felt pain all over after the scars had healed, she'd told him about something called fibromyalgia. It took him a long time to be able to say it correctly, too. Not that he ever told anyone what he had. It was always easier to just say his scars hurt. Nobody questioned that. She explained to him that the fire had caused the scars, but the trauma had caused his condition. He'd spent a number of nights crying himself to sleep, waiting for the pain to subside. Now he went days without it getting above a slight burning feeling, though he knew that was because of the salve they'd discovered. Sticks had been able to modify it further, but nothing ever got rid of the pain entirely. Some of the others he'd met who had the same condition weren't as lucky, though. He'd been reminded of that more and more over the last few months.

"Scorcher," said Corrine, noticing him standing near the entrance. "Come in, hon. Get out of the cold a bit, and I'll be right there."

He nodded, waiting as she redressed the wound and grabbed the bowl from the side of the cot. She hurried toward him, then pulled him back outside behind her. Once outside, she dumped the dirty water, which had become much darker after use in the tent. He shuddered. Corrine scooped up another bowlful of snow, then turned to face him. Her smile faded, moonlight carving shadows into the deep lines that had formed around her eyes and forehead. It astounded him how quickly she transformed from camp medic to concerned mother.

"Tell me the truth, hon," she said. "Does she know what she's doing?"

He was surprised to hear her ask that.

"Of course she does, Mom," said Scorcher. "Why?"

Don't you trust her?

Corrine looked toward the group, then back to him.

"I'm just worried, Scorcher. You two are really close now—I get that—but you have to admit that she's made some very questionable decisions. I mean, look at what happened earlier. We lost an entire wagon of supplies and food. We're lucky nobody else was inside it when it went down."

Scorcher felt the snow melt as it met his hot skin.

"I know what happened, Mom. I was there!" Scorcher quickly realized he had raised his voice and forced himself to calm down a bit. "I've already talked to Ahna about it. She knows she's made some mistakes."

Corrine smiled, giving him the look she always did when imparting her motherly wisdom upon him.

"I just don't want her to make a mistake with you, hon."

The tears in his mother's eyes reflected the moon and trees behind him. Whenever she cried, he had to fight to keep himself from joining her.

"She won't," he said. "Trust me."

Corrine gripped his shoulder, her strength less than he remembered. She was getting older a lot quicker these days. Everyone was.

"I trust you, hon. But Ahna," she said, pausing for a moment. "I don't see why Seemore chose her over you."

Scorcher smiled. "I do."

Corrine pulled away, looking at him for a moment. Then she nodded.

"Okay." The firmness had returned to her voice. "If she's going to continue to be in charge, she'll need your help, Scorcher. We all will . . ." She trailed off as she stared into his eyes, tears forming. She wiped them away quickly. "I need you to promise me something."

You're crying . . .

"Anything, Mom."

"I need you to promise me that you will do everything in your power to keep the group safe. What we're fighting for, it's important—not just to us, but to many more out there we don't even know. For once, it looks like we have a fighting chance." She glanced back at the tent. "But if we risk it all for the battles, we can't win the war."

You're worried about the group? I've always said I'll do what I can to protect them. I feel like that hasn't changed, but if you want to hear me say it, I will.

"I promise."

Pressure engulfed him as she wrapped her arms around him like a warm cocoon. After she pulled away from the hug, she wiped her eyes and smiled.

"I don't know what I'd do without you."

"Thankfully, you don't have to worry about that, Mom. I'm not going anywhere." He chuckled.

Scorcher walked back over to join the group around the fire, taking Ahna's hand in his as he sat down next to her. She smiled before finishing the rest of her story to the group.

One day, when our grandkids ask what it used to be like, we can sit around the fire and tell them this story. They will never believe it . . .

For the first time in a long time, he could relax. Scorcher closed his eyes, enjoying the crackling of the wood and heat from the fire as Ahna's voice faded into the background.

Chapter Five
Ahna

"Ahna, run!"

Scorcher's voice cut through the chilly mountain air. Ahna needed only one glance at what he was warning her of before she took off.

Powdered snow flew into the air as her feet pounded through the forest, as though tiny mines were exploding with each step. Her breath fogged in front of her face, sweat running down her back underneath the armor and fur. She dodged each tree, not risking a backward glance for fear she may not make it to her goal.

She spotted the rope up ahead. Held taut by the trees around it, the trap was set; she just had to get there before it got her.

She could hear its harsh breathing nearing her neck. The Waller was gaining on her, and if she slowed down, their plan would fail, and she'd be ripped to shreds.

Power through. Just make it there, and you'll be good.

Ahna took a deep breath, then pushed herself a bit harder. As she neared the trap, she smiled. Stopping right in front of it, she turned to face her predator.

The Waller was only feet away when it launched itself into the air, its fingers heading straight for her face.

She ducked and rolled to the side, hearing a loud snap and growl behind her. As she came to her feet, she shook the snow from her shoulders and smiled.

All right! It worked. Take that, you ugly freak.

The Waller hung five feet in the air, swaying back and forth as it screeched, fighting against the rope around it.

While Ahna watched the Waller roll about inside the trap, the others stepped out from behind the trees and bushes, gathering around her in the small clearing.

Sticks stabbed his staff into the snow as he stepped next to her. Felan swung her rifle over her shoulder as Scorcher caught up to the group, catching his breath. They all stared at the Waller, which writhed about within the ropes, attempting to reach out to them. Had they not been a safe distance away, Ahna would have been frightened.

Its eyes were a dingy yellow and almost protruded from their sockets. Where the nose should have been was nothing but a dark hole. Sharp teeth jutted out from its mouth, gnawing at the rope. Saliva poured from it as it attempted to break free from the trap. Because of its movement, Ahna almost didn't see what was growing on its skin: tiny blue mushrooms. They appeared almost iridescent, as though they reflected the sky. She recognized the blue light from before. For some reason, all the Wallers she'd seen in this new area had them. There were many along its body, so many that Ahna was mesmerized by them. She found herself staring at its body, not focusing on anything else. That became evident when Scorcher put his hand on her shoulder, breaking her away from her trance.

"Ahna? You all right?" he asked.

Ahna nodded, swallowing and clearing her throat.

"Uh-huh," she said.

"You had me worried back there," said Scorcher. There was strength in his voice, but his eyes echoed his words. When she'd first met him, she hadn't thought he could be worried about anything, much less her or her well-being.

"It didn't get me though, did it?" she asked.

Scorcher laughed. "No, I guess not. Next time be a little more careful, huh?"

Don't tell me what to do.

Ahna ensured her knife was safely snapped into its sheath on her waist.

"My staff," she demanded, extending her hand toward him, waiting.

Scorcher pulled it off his back and removed the makeshift sling he'd tied onto the ends of it before handing it over. Her fingers wrapped around it, finding their home in the grooves that had naturally formed over the past couple months of traveling. It wasn't as busy or ornate as Sticks's, though she hadn't expected that. She'd made sure it was a bit shorter than most she'd seen, too. The longer a staff was, the harder it became to control in battle. She needed as much control as possible. Besides, it was the first one she'd ever made, and carving a staff with only one hand was much more difficult than she had thought; however, the one thing she had learned in the last year was that nothing was impossible.

Felan took a step toward the Waller hanging in the trap and poked it with her rifle. It screeched again, clawing at her face.

"Be care—" Ahna started.

Felan smacked the Waller across the head with the butt of the rifle, and its screeching stopped.

"That's better," said Felan. "Can't hardly think with all that going on." She turned around to face the group, the Waller swinging silently behind her. "Anyone else notice something weird about this thing?"

"The mushrooms," said Ahna before anyone else could speak.

"Yeah, those weird mushrooms growing on its body," said Sticks, pointing his staff at the Waller. He was leaning against a nearby tree. Ahna hadn't even realized he was that close, and she almost jumped when he spoke.

"Exactly," said Felan. She reached toward its body and plucked one of the mushrooms off, which shriveled up in her hand and lost its color almost immediately.

Weird. I wouldn't think they would do that.

"It's not normal," said Felan.

"Nothing about these Wallers is," said Ahna.

Felan tilted her head. "What d'you mean?"

"It goes way further than just the mushrooms. Look at its body," said Ahna, moving closer to the Waller. She started to point at each part of it as she listed the different characteristics. "It's got sharper, longer teeth than the ones we've seen before. Its skin is rougher looking, almost like bark. And these things are fast—a lot faster than the ones we fought in Deliverance. If the trap were much farther ahead, it may have gotten me."

She didn't particularly like admitting that part in front of Scorcher, but it was true.

"What's your point, exactly?" asked Felan.

"Well—"

"Point is, they've adapted, evolved." Sticks had stepped away from the tree and was directly behind Ahna. "Something's happened to make them deadlier, more animalistic."

"What do you think that is?" asked Scorcher.

"No way to know for sure, but I'd guess the ones we fought before, back in Deliverance, were only the beginning, a prototype."

Scorcher narrowed his eyes. "You mean—"

A scatter of birds covered the canopy above, and their cries echoed through the forest. Everyone silenced. They all moved back behind the bushes, opposite the trap. The Waller was still silently swinging above them, directly in line with where the sound was coming from. Ahna crouched low and tightened her grip on her staff. She looked toward Scorcher, who nodded and smiled. She smirked, her eyes narrowing as she awaited whatever was approaching.

Leaves fell from the trees as the sound grew louder. Before they stepped into view, she recognized the screeching.

Wallers.

A sea of Wallers emerged from the trees, pouring into the small clearing. Three of them leapt onto the trap. Ahna thought they were attempting to free their friend . . . until they started tearing it to shreds. It was almost like watching vultures tear a dead deer apart, only much worse. The slurping and other sounds of them feasting on the Waller sent shivers down her spine, the hair on her arms standing on end. She couldn't take her eyes off the horde devouring their downed comrade. Thankfully, that kept them preoccupied while she moved to a better position. She was closing in on them when she felt something bend beneath her foot. The twig snapped, giving away her position.

Crap.

A pair of dingy yellow eyes met her frightened stare. The Waller shook its head violently and let out a screech, saliva spraying in all directions. Baring its teeth, it sprinted toward her. Ahna scrambled to get up and lost her footing. She felt the cold wet snow against her neck as she fell to the ground. She kicked her feet but had trouble getting up due to the slickness of the ground. The Waller leapt into the air, blocking the sunlight from above. Its wide eyes were almost excited as it dropped toward her.

Boom!

Blood spattered as the Waller's head exploded. Its body fell onto her legs, bits of it clinging to her fur.

She glanced in the direction of the gunshot to see Felan smile before reloading her rifle. The screech of the Wallers echoed through the forest as the group at the trap migrated toward Felan and the others. Sticks had his staff up, pointing at the group and swaying back and forth, waiting for the group to attack.

Ahna wiped off what she could and kicked the Waller away. A hand extended toward her.

"Can't fight from the ground," said Scorcher. His smile brought a welcoming warmth through her body. If not for the horde of Wallers heading toward them, she may have enjoyed the view a bit longer.

She grabbed his hand, and he hoisted her up, brushing some of the snow from her shoulders.

"Thanks," said Ahna. "Let's kill these freaks."

Ahna rushed toward the horde barreling toward them. She thrust the staff forward, feeling the weight of it in her hand. As it entered the body of an oncoming Waller, she could feel the resistance, vibrations running through the wood.

She pushed harder, twisting it as she brought it out and forced it back in. The Waller screeched and clawed at her. She dropped down, evading its claws, then swiped her leg under it, causing it to fall. As it went down, she jumped up and stood right over its chest. She brought the staff backward before launching it toward the Waller's face. The Waller went silent, lifeless on the ground.

Ahna smirked, but she didn't have time to admire her handiwork. Behind her, grunts and gunfire alerted her to the trouble.

Ahna turned to see Sticks and Felan going head-to-head with a handful of Wallers, about six still alive. Sticks twirled his staff, smacking two of them each second. Scorcher was grappling with one of them, smashing it into a nearby tree. A bow hung on his back, but he apparently preferred to use his bare hands. Snow fell from the branches with each hit, but Scorcher had it under control. Felan had been able to shoot those that were farther away, but she couldn't risk that any longer. They'd gotten too close. Instead, she started using the bayonet on the front of the rifle. That had come in handy far too many times in the last few months.

Ahna joined in on the fun.

She ran over to the group, directly behind one of the Wallers Sticks was fighting. As she tapped it on the back with the butt of her staff, it twirled around and bared its teeth at her, eyes wide. Before it could claw at her, she swiped the snow below onto its face, temporarily blinding it. She swung the staff over her head and onto the Waller's back. It bent slightly, and Ahna used her knee to bash it in the face before stabbing it with her staff. It let out a loud screech before she stabbed it again, and then she pulled the staff out and spun it. She landed one final blow across its face, hearing a crack upon impact. Its face went still, and its jaw dropped as its body fell straight into the snow.

Ahna's breathing became quick and shallow. Her heart beat as though it were attempting to escape her chest. She calmed herself, swallowing as she observed the others. They stood over their downed victims, which were all lifeless in a pool of blue-red blood.

They'd taken them all out. It hadn't been easy, but they'd done it. Like a rising tide, laughter swelled through them all.

"Did anyone else see that coming?" asked Sticks.

"Obviously not," said Felan. "Those freaks came out of nowhere."

"They're coming from somewhere," said Sticks. "The question is, where?"

Ahna stepped forward. "It could be the facility the Elite are from."

Everyone stared at her.

"That facility isn't near us," said Felan. "It's gotta be down the mountain a ways. We would have heard them working or practicing drills or something by now. Besides, a few Wallers making it up here makes sense, but that many in a short period of time? No way."

She wasn't wrong. It did seem a little unlikely.

"Maybe not that facility," said Ahna. "It could mean we're closer to the abandoned facility than we thought."

"That could be good," said Sticks. "As long as we don't get mauled by a hungry horde of Wallers tonight."

"I'll go a different route than usual while scouting tomorrow," said Felan.

She swung the rifle over shoulder, then pulled out a strip of fabric. She began to pull her hair back into the ponytail Ahna had gotten used to seeing and tied it up. As they cleaned off their weapons in the snow, Ahna walked over to the dead Wallers.

The bodies strewn across the ground suddenly reminded her of those on the battlefield within Deliverance. She stared at the Waller's eyes, permanently open. The longer she looked at the Waller, the more its face began to fade. Suddenly, it was morphing into the face of Rollin, then Raider, then Scout before finally becoming her own. She could sense something on her body, someone pulling on her. She whipped around and swung her staff.

"Whoa, careful!" Scorcher yelled as he ducked beneath it. He grabbed her by the shoulders and pulled her in close. "Easy, Ahna. Easy."

Ahna felt comfort in his embrace, the frightening feeling of death fleeing as swiftly as it had come. She felt herself relax into his body, warmth emanating from the skin beneath the fur and armor.

"Everything all right?" asked Sticks, who had run over to them. His staff was at the ready.

"It is now," said Scorcher.

Sticks lowered his staff, then strode away from them again.

"You okay?" asked Scorcher.

"Yeah," replied Ahna, pulling away from his body. She couldn't stay there for too long or else she'd risk a breakdown.

"What happened?"

"Nothing," said Ahna.

"It didn't seem like nothing," whispered Scorcher.

You wouldn't understand. You'd think I'm crazy.

"Let's get going," said Felan. She had already begun walking back toward the camp. "We don't wanna be out after dark, especially if there're more of those freaks out here."

Perfect timing.

"Let's go, Scorcher. Like she said, we need to get back."

"Okay," said Scorcher. "Whatever you say."

Ahna waited until the group had started walking back to make sure they were safe from another attack. When it seemed safe enough, she turned to Scorcher.

"Hey," she whispered.

"Yeah?" asked Scorcher.

"Thanks."

"What for?"

"For . . . everything," Ahna replied, reaching out to grab his hand.

He smiled as he took her hand in his own. "You're welcome."

Ahna sighed in relief. She didn't want to risk having him ask any more questions. She didn't need him to worry about her. They were already getting closer than she'd ever thought possible, but if they got too close, he might get scared and run away. She'd lost enough people already. She wasn't prepared to lose him, too.

Chapter Six
Sticks

Sunlight disappeared behind the mountain as they neared the camp. Colors of purple, blue, green, and orange streaked across the sky like paint across a canvas. It wasn't quite the same as fall, but Sticks had learned to appreciate the cold a bit more. For one, winter meant that people were lighting more fires, which meant he got to have the smell of a campfire pretty much every night. It had become the only thing he really looked forward to most days. Besides, it meant that he had survived another day, and that was always something to be happy about. Rollin had taught him that . . .

Not everything was great, though. As they got closer, he could see their makeshift tents, the doors flapping in the wind as though the fabric houses were trying to fly. The wagons were parked in a circle around the fire, which Felan had said would be helpful later on. Doubtful. He wanted to sleep in the wagon, but that wasn't a possibility. They'd lost one along the way, which meant there was no longer ample space; they'd barely had enough to begin with.

Sticks had tried to help create a mock Tent City multiple times, but there had been pushback. The Gray Wolves were opposed to setting up any other way. Apparently, they'd been doing this setup for years and were hesitant about putting down roots. He thought that was ridiculous but wouldn't argue with them. They may have been a team now, but there was still division within the ranks, and the numbers didn't favor his side. Besides, there were bigger problems to face than where they put the tents. They'd be moving them again soon anyway, according to Felan.

Felan seemed trustworthy so far, but he had reason to doubt everyone. With her, he had a strange suspicion that she was hiding something. He couldn't prove it, but he sensed it. Then there were the others. When they had gotten done with the mission, he'd wanted to know what happened to Seemore. He knew there had to be more information he wasn't receiving, but he'd find that himself. He had to be out there somewhere. There was no way he was gone . . .

Not like her.

Sticks rubbed the metal ring he now wore as a necklace. The metal had smoothed and become worn away in the spot where he'd rubbed it the past couple months. Every time he thought of her, he'd look down at it and smile. If for nothing but a brief moment, he'd be happy again. He'd see her face, that beaming smile, hear her bubbly laugh fill his head. He could almost picture her waving her arms and sailing over the smooth dirt of Tent City. He thought of the times they'd gone berry picking together, when he'd roll her down to the creek and teach her to fish. She hadn't known his feelings for her. Now she never would.

A sudden pop in his kneecap sent him tumbling to the ground, replacing the warm memories with cold, harsh reality. Snow fell onto him from the tree above as he bumped into its trunk, grasping it for support. The bark was rough beneath the white powder, scratching his palms.

"You okay, Sticks?" asked Vincent.

Where did you come from?

The kid had somehow snuck up on him.

"Yeah, fine," said Sticks. "Just tripped on a rock under the snow is all."

Vincent's face relaxed, his eyebrows lowering. "All righty then. You guys are back later than I thought you'd be . . ." He paused for a moment. "Everything okay?"

No, but if I tell you that, you'll go telling all the other kids.

"Yeah, just a little bit of a skirmish is all. Nothing to worry about."

Vincent nodded. "Okay." He paused again. "When are we gonna start our lessons?"

Lessons. Right. I had to say that, didn't I?

"I tell ya what. Whenever we get settled somewhere, you remind me, and we'll do those, okay?"

"All right."

Vincent forced a smile, but his eyes told Sticks that he wasn't happy with that answer. He couldn't waste time teaching Vincent how to build things when they had other things to worry about, though.

Sticks rubbed his knee, then walked on toward the camp. Flames flickered, illuminating his path, shadows of the group dancing on the deep snow as they made their way to the seats around the fire. The chairs were old buckets and logs. They didn't have the resources or space to carry real chairs. Besides, they didn't get a chance to sit around much; there was too much to do.

Sticks sat down on a bucket, pushing his cap up a bit to relieve some of the sweat that had built up on his hairline. Rubbing his hands together in front of the fire, he watched the others join him around it. Felan placed her rifle in her lap, careful to not get it in the snow, while Ahna wrapped herself in Scorcher's arms.

You two are getting pretty close, huh? Lucky you.

The warmth from the fire joined the heat already present in his face. His fingers wrapped around the ring again, his thumb moving back and forth across the cold metal. He kept his gaze on Ahna, watching her smile and laugh as Scorcher whispered something in her ear. She stopped laughing at whatever he'd just whispered, backing away from him briefly. At least they had each other.

If it weren't for you, I might still have her . . .

"You all are back!" Corrine almost shouted as she approached the fire. "How did it go?"

"Fine, Mom," said Scorcher. "Just a little bit of a fight, but nothing major."

"Fight? With who? You hurt anything too bad?" she asked, putting out way too many questions than needed after a long day.

"Wallers," said Ahna.

"There're more of them?" asked Corrine.

"Apparently so," said Felan.

"What does that mean for us?" asked Corrine.

"That's what we need to figure out still," Felan said.

Scorcher got up. "Nothing to worry about, Mom. Okay?"

Corrine looked at the group, worry evident in her glare. "Okay. But make sure you get to bed soon. Marie says there's going to be some bad weather coming our way."

"Did she say when?" asked Felan.

"Not sure. Tomorrow, maybe. Could be later. I don't really remember. She was talking too fast for me to keep up," she said.

Sounds about right.

Sticks laughed to himself, watching Corrine walk away from the group and back into the main tent. Marie had always been a fast talker. He enjoyed that, actually. It meant that he had to force himself to focus more, which could be a challenge sometimes. If he wasn't careful, he'd slip off into another world briefly while in a conversation or while in the middle of a task. Sometimes it was annoying, but other times it was a nice escape. He never appreciated it happening when there was a lot of work to be done, though. He hated when his mind made him not do things. It was annoying.

"Sticks?" asked Felan.

He realized he was doing it just then and focused his attention back to Felan. "What?"

"What are your thoughts on that?"

Thoughts . . . on what?

"Repeat the question. I wanna make sure I heard you completely before I answer."

Felan sighed. "Are the tents and wagons equipped to handle the storm if it comes tomorrow? Can they withstand a major storm?"

Honestly . . . good question.

They'd never been in this high of elevation or in a climate like this. Sure, he'd seen snow, but if the storm was really bad, he had no experience to know if the tents would hold or get blown off the mountain.

"Let me speak to Marie and figure out what sort of storm we're looking at, and then I'll let you know."

The group didn't look happy. Ahna and Scorcher were exchanging whispers. He hated when they did that. It felt like they were talking about him.

"If you two wanna add to the conversation, you can," said Sticks.

They immediately stopped whispering, Ahna's face turning red.

"It's nothing," said Scorcher. He glanced toward Ahna.

"Yeah, nothing," Ahna repeated. Scorcher put his hand on Ahna's leg, but she pushed it away before scooting farther from him.

Nothing . . . sure. Clearly, you're fighting, but I don't care. At least I know it's not about me.

"Anyway," said Felan, drawing their attention back to her. "We obviously have a bigger problem than just the weather. These freaks are showing up again. And not just one or two of them."

"We took care of them all," said Scorcher.

"That we know of," said Felan. She removed a strip of fabric and began to clean the stock of her rifle. It was almost mechanical, as though she could do it in her sleep. "If we saw ten, there're probably a hundred more out there."

"We didn't see any along the road here," said Ahna. She crossed her arms across her chest, holding her hands under her armpits for warmth. She rocked her body back and forth after moving closer to the fire.

That would've been a good point if they'd been talking about animals. Unfortunately for them, Wallers weren't. They were freaks that'd been created in a lab. The interesting thing about that was there was probably only a slight difference in Wallers' and their own DNA. Had he been in a different petri dish, he may have been one of them. He shuddered at the image of himself as a Waller, immediately purging the thought from his mind.

"That's because they don't come from anywhere other than facilities," said Sticks. "These things are made in the lab, and we know there's one nearby."

"Maybe the group we saw today followed us from Deliverance somehow," said Scorcher.

"Impossible," Felan said.

"She's right," said Sticks. "We all saw how different those things looked compared to the version at Deliverance. These are upgrades."

"You don't think they can multiply on their own?" Ahna asked.

I have no idea, but I sure hope not. If these things really are just multiplying on their own now, that's gonna be a much bigger problem. We already have enough going on as it is.

"Definitely not," said Sticks. "We need to make sure that facility you mentioned before isn't infested with them. If so, we can't just walk in without doing a bit of pest control."

"I was supposed to go hunting in the morning anyway," said Felan. "I can go hunting for Wallers instead if you want."

Sticks shook his head. "No. We can't afford that. We need the food."

"How bad is it?" asked Felan.

Sticks and Scorcher exchanged a glance. Sticks held his hand out to Scorcher, gesturing for the answer.

"Mom says it's getting worse every day. We have more people starving and sick than we have beds. If it continues at this rate, we may not have many to fight our way into the facility—if we can even get inside it."

"When," said Ahna.

"What?" asked Scorcher.

"When we get in it. You said if. You mean when."

Ahna was still crossing her arms. She had a stern look, one that almost reminded him of Seemore. He couldn't focus on that, though.

"Can't your mom take care of them?" Ahna asked Scorcher. Her tone was sharp. Something was definitely up with her and Scorcher.

"She's doing the best she can. You know that."

"Stop it," said Sticks. As much as he wanted to have them continue, he knew it couldn't happen right then. "Argue on your own time. Right now, you need to focus. People are dying."

Their mouths closed, eyes going wide. He had clearly caught them off guard by inserting himself into their argument, but he didn't care. He was as much a leader as they were, especially right now. They were acting like children.

"What about the data? The drives we've acquired so far. Anything from those?" asked Felan.

It seemed strange that she was more worried about the data than the people. Her wide green eyes reflected the orange flames as she leaned in toward the fire. He wished he had something better to tell her. She clearly cared about the data.

"Wick said there's no way to get to the data on those drives unless we get a stable power source and connection. If we plug the drives in and lose power, he said it might corrupt them."

"Corrupt them? What's that mean?" asked Felan.

"Like, ruin the data, basically," replied Sticks.

Felan withdrew slightly, glancing down into the flames.

"Then I guess that's what we'll do."

"What?" asked Ahna.

"Find a computer," said Felan. She stood up, slinging the rifle over shoulder.

"Where are you going?" asked Sticks. They had other things that needed their attention and had barely come up with a plan. He didn't like to leave things undecided. When plans didn't get fully fleshed out, they went wrong. People died.

"Bed," replied Felan. "I suggest you all do the same. We've had a long day, but it sounds like it's only gonna get worse tomorrow. I'm not gonna just sit by and wait for something to happen. I—we—have to find a way into their main facility . . . soon."

She turned toward the circle of tents and entered hers at the edge, vanishing behind the fabric door.

Sticks knew they needed to discuss other things, but he wasn't in the mood to deal with the feuding couple. Grabbing the edges of the bucket, he hoisted himself up to a standing position and took a second to balance himself.

"You leaving, too?" asked Ahna.

Can't stay here and listen to you two.

"Yeah," replied Sticks. "I gotta see about the sick. Probably gonna check in with Corrine before heading to sleep myself."

"Need my help?" asked Scorcher as he started to get up.

"I'm good, thanks," said Sticks. He took a step and almost fell, gripping the barrel, the flames licking his hand. He winced as he pulled his hand away, which was slightly burned.

Great.

"You all right?" asked Ahna.

"All good," said Sticks. "Just slipped on a piece of ice or some-thing."

Ahna's eyes narrowed a bit before she nodded.

"Okay. See you in the morning, then," said Ahna.

"Night," said Sticks.

Grabbing his staff, he trudged through the snow to his tent on the opposite side of the circle from Felan.

Lying on the cold, hard ground, he wrapped himself in his fur sleeping bag and stared up at the ceiling. A constant flap came from the tent doors as the wind blew past them. He rubbed his legs, which were starting to hurt again. It had been months since the pain had been there.

Why now? Why are you going back to before? Stupid legs.

After he rubbed his legs for a few minutes, the pain subsided a bit. As he rolled to one side, he felt the ring slide down his chest, resting next to his heart. He wrapped his fingers around it, gripping it tightly.

If you were here, maybe this wouldn't be so hard. Or at least I wouldn't hate everything so much . . . I miss you, Rollin.

A tear streaked down his dirt-crusted cheek before soaking into the course fibers of his pillow. Sticks kept his hand wrapped around the ring as he drifted off to sleep.

Chapter Seven
Scorcher

"Just listen to me for a minute," said Scorcher, grabbing Ahna's shoulder. She pulled away and turned to face him.

"What? What do you want to say that you haven't said already?" she asked, her lips pursed and eyebrows cross. This was the most upset he'd ever seen her.

"I-I just want to talk."

"Then talk, Scorcher. I'm listening."

He looked around to see if anyone was watching. They were too close to the tents. He didn't want anyone to hear their conversation. Some of the kids were terrible about eavesdropping. He knew that from experience.

"Not here," said Scorcher. "Come with me."

He pulled Ahna by the hand, but she pulled it away from him. Thankfully, she followed him as he led her into the tree line, out of earshot. It was his night for watch, so it was unlikely that anyone would walk in on them over here.

"What do you want?" asked Ahna.

"I wanted to talk to you," said Scorcher. "Without anyone else around."

"You got me," said Ahna. "What's your problem?"

Scorcher couldn't believe that he was about to say it, but he wasn't going to let it fester either. His mom had always said to talk things out with people before resorting to anything else. She had taught him a lot of things, but that was something that had stuck with him.

"You are," he said finally.

Ahna's mouth hung open. She huffed and crossed her arms again. "Oh really? I'm your problem?"

This was not going like he'd hoped, but she hadn't walked away yet, so that was a plus.

"I just mean that you're acting weird and—"

"Oh! I'm sorry. I didn't realize that how I act is bothering you," said Ahna.

"Shh," said Scorcher, holding his finger to his lips. "You'll wake the others. Keep it down."

Ahna chuckled. "Don't want that now, do we? Can't have me causing more problems, huh?"

That's not what I meant, and you know it. What's got into you lately?

"Ahna, please stop. I'm just trying to tell you what's bothering me and figure out what's going on with you."

Ahna breathed in as though she were going to say something, then stopped. Exhaling, she nodded. "Okay, fine. Go ahead. Talk."

Scorcher sighed.

Okay, Scorch. Just like you practiced . . .

"I feel like things are different than they used to be. I think back to our time on the boat, the beach, and all that, and it was so nice. Then, when we were fighting together, I was so proud of you for beating me. You were learning so quickly, and you impressed me . . . a lot." He took a deep breath. "But when the big fight happened and we had to leave Deliverance, you changed. You stopped smiling all the time. You stopped being spontaneous with me. You stopped being you."

He waited for a response for what felt like forever. Her eyes were watering, which made his stomach turn. Whether it was the cold or him, he was unsure.

"You think I'm the only one?" asked Ahna.

That's not what I thought you'd say.

"What do you mean?" asked Scorcher.

"I mean . . . it hurts, Scorcher. You used to be focused on me before, at least interested in hanging out whenever you could. Now? I see you trying to do almost anything but that. I feel like you don't want to be with me anymore."

Oh. I never thought about that before. Have I really been doing that?

"I'm sorry if that's what it looks like. That's not what I meant to do to you," said Scorcher.

"Don't." Her face was getting red, her tone sharper. "Just because you didn't mean to do something doesn't mean it didn't happen."

I guess you're right.

"I'm sorry, you're right. I absolutely want to be with you. I should've thought more about how you feel and how what I do affects that. I'll be more aware from now on. That's my fault."

Ahna smiled a bit. "It is. Thanks."

"For what?" asked Scorcher.

"For apologizing."

"You're welcome. Now what about you?" asked Scorcher.

Ahna raised her eyebrows. "What about me?"

"Aren't you gonna apologize too?"

Ahna moved closer to him, and his heart beat faster with each of her steps. As she neared him, she swept her hand around his neck, her fingers sliding through his hair. She pulled on his hair slightly, causing him to crane his neck down to her while she pulled his body toward hers. She met his lips with hers. The warmth from her mouth and nose felt nice in the cool night air. Each kiss was more passionate than the last. Suddenly, Ahna pulled away from him and stepped back, the scent of her hair still lingering in his nostrils.

"How's that for an apology?" she asked, smiling.

That wasn't an apology, but I'll take it. Maybe I should ask for an apology more often.

Scorcher was almost grinning from ear to ear. "That was . . . wow. Thanks."

Ahna laughed. "Don't say thanks after a kiss, Scorch. That's weird."

They laughed together for the first time in what felt like forever. Soon after, Scorcher led Ahna to his post in the shack they had found when they'd first set up camp there. Once inside, they sat together, watching the trees sway against night sky. Scorcher had done that many nights back in Tent City on his night shifts. It soothed his busy mind, allowing him to escape the craziness of the day.

Sometimes he would imagine what it must have been like before the war. He wondered if there had ever been a time when someone like him and the rest of his friends would have lived and played with the kids on the other side of the Wall. Corrine had told him stories of his grandparents and those who had lived before. She said they had lived in houses no different than Town

Hall. He had a hard time imagining that; it seemed like that would be too much space. They had lived in that tent for so long, he couldn't picture having his own room with real walls and a door—though he would've been happy to eventually have that, even if it was as small as the shack they were sitting in. He hoped it would be in a better condition, though.

The windows were busted out, shards of glass on the floor and around the edges. There was dried blood on a few of the shards. Inside, there was only one chair and a desk, which had been ransacked long before they arrived, its drawer busted and in pieces on the floor below it. They sat in the chair, which was big enough for them to share, but only slightly. It was a good thing they didn't mind being so close.

Overhead, the moon shone brightly, illuminating the branches of the evergreens that swayed in the wind. Ahna snuggled up next to him. He could feel a slight vibration from her body as she shivered, her teeth almost chattering. Scorcher pulled off his extra fur coat and placed it around Ahna before putting his arm around her again.

"Better?" he asked.

Ahna smiled. "Much."

She closed her eyes and laid her head back on his shoulder, the smell of her hair once again quickening his pulse. It'd been weeks since he'd felt this close to her. It was pleasant.

They sat in silence as owls hooted in the trees. Every now and then, one would take flight and spread its salt-and-pepper wings. It was so interesting to watch them soar around above the trees. He imagined what it must feel like to fly, to have the world beneath you and only the moon and clouds above. How nice it must've been to know nothing of the problems of the world.

How lucky they were. He wished sometimes that he might have that but knew it would most likely never come. If it ever did, it would be at a great cost.

Wind swept through the trees, sending a cold chill up his spine, but that didn't bother him. As long as Ahna was happy and they were together, that was all that mattered. At least for the night.

Chapter Eight
Felan

Snow streaked across her scope. The crosshairs landed on the Waller, its rotten skin now clearly in view. A cloud appeared in front of its face as it exhaled a toxic cloud, which would've been dangerous had she been there to inhale it. The Waller was trudging through the knee-deep snow. As it inhaled, she synced up their breaths. Her mind cleared, and she clicked off the safety. On her exhale, she steadied the gun on the rock in front of her and caressed the trigger with her index finger.

Air simultaneously escaped them both.

The familiar boom echoed down the mountain through the trees, a few birds scattering from their nests. In a split second, her hand had already pulled back the bolt, ejecting the shell, then pushed it forward again. Her eye never left the sight. She fired off another round, her ears still ringing slightly from the first. She reloaded again. It was still alive.

The Waller looked in her direction and grinned. Aiming right between the eyes, she fired off one final shot. The Waller's body sunk below the rim of her sight. She reloaded, then patted the side of the rifle's handcrafted stock.

Attagirl.

She smiled behind her scarf before her celebration was interrupted. Down below, she spotted a lump lying in a pool of red snow.

Not today, freak.

She started down the hill, slowing as she approached the body. As she neared the crest of the hill, more Wallers peeked from the edge. The early morning sun illuminated their silhouettes. There had to be at least ten of them. They were all packed together, a horde. One thing was certain: they were moving toward her, fast.

She looked around for another rock to mount herself behind but had no such luck. The best she had was a downed log barely sticking out of the snow.

That'll have to work.

She sprinted, diving behind it for cover, then dug out a bit of the snow to create a trench. That gave her a few more inches of cover before they were fully within view. Mounting her rifle on the log, she homed in her sight on the front of the pack.

"Good morning, freak," she whispered, clicking off the safety and pulling the trigger.

Skin scattered from the neck of her target like a firework. The horde behind it let out a collective screech and ran in her direction. She had already reloaded and fired off another round. It took one down, but it was already getting back up as she reloaded. She shot off another, this time aiming for its head. The wind must have picked up because it grazed its ear instead.

Shoot.

She continued to fire into the horde as the Wallers scurried up the mountainside. It was like shooting fish in a barrel—if the fish were undead and took multiple shots to kill. They weren't adept at dodging trees in the snow, so she had a slightly better advantage. Besides, she had the high ground. However, that seemed less helpful as the horde barreled through the snow. She narrowed her eyes and exhaled.

In that moment, her body took over. Autopilot.

As a breath entered her lungs, time seemed to slow, and it felt as though she were moving ten times faster than everything else.

They dropped one by one, clouds of snow popping up from the ground as they fell. The echoes were still catching up to her shots. As the last one dropped, she reloaded and scanned the mountainside for others. Seeing none, she clicked on the safety and slung the rifle over her shoulder. Scarlett circles scattered the side of the hill below. She approached them slowly, not wanting to repeat last time. She smelled them before she arrived, the odor of rotten flesh and feces permeating the air. Thankfully, she had a scarf on, which helped . . . somewhat. She'd never get used to that smell. Ever.

All over their bodies were the tiny blue mushrooms they'd seen in the group the day before.

I wonder if those things could be useful or taste good.

Her stomach rumbled at the thought of food. As uncomfortable as that was, she'd take hunger over agonizing pain any day. It'd been a while since the last instance, but it hadn't disappeared completely. She knew that. It was always lurking in the back of her mind, like a monster in the shadows waiting to strike.

Digging through the Wallers' pockets, she found some more ammunition, none of which worked in her rifle but would work for some of the others. Besides the ammo, she pocketed a silver necklace and a knife. That wasn't all they carried, but it was all she wanted. There was no need for dead rats or birds, especially when they'd been in the possession of Wallers for who knew how long.

As she finished searching the bodies, the wind howled through the trees. Snow swirled in a small vortex around her, chilling her to the bone. It was midmorning, but time didn't seem to matter on the mountain. It was freezing. All. The. Time. Her fingers had numbed after removing her gloves to search the bodies, so she slipped them back on and rubbed her hands together. Frostbite was nothing to mess with. She knew that firsthand.

A faint whistle pierced the air. It was a long deep sound unlike anything she knew.

Is that—

It went off again, repeating twice more before silence returned. The whistle echoed up the mountain, but she couldn't figure out the source. One thing she did know was that she had news for the group. Whether that news was good or bad, she was uncertain.

She pulled down her goggles and started back up the mountain. If she was quick enough, she'd be back to camp by lunchtime. The thought of food made her salivate. It'd been a while since their last feast, but she pictured the buffet in her mind as she hiked. Images of wild boar over the fire pit, pumpkins carved out and shaped into faces sitting around the wagons, and plenty of beer filled her mind. The memory of finding the two cases of beer from the store along the route produced a smile. The carbonation sometimes burned her throat after not drinking it for so long, though. And then there was the bloating. But those were the least of her problems.

AS SHE TOPPED THE CREST of the hill, she looked out at the sprawling tundra below. What used to be a city now lay mostly in ruins. No building was unharmed. Most were destroyed completely, reduced to rubble, though a few still looked to be sturdy enough to live in should the blizzard kick up again while down there. Thankfully, they didn't need to stay down below.

Chattering of the clan echoed around the corner as she hiked back down the path, past the old guard box and gate. A rusted car sat on the side on the road, buried in the snow. She'd searched it when they first arrived, but there was nothing inside besides a moldy stuffed animal and some magazines ruined by the rain and snow. Seeing that car had been a reminder of how lucky it was that they'd decided on wagons as their mode of transportation. Not that they'd had much of a choice, but finding gas between any of the major cities was almost impossible. While in the East, they'd had better luck. Ever since they'd gone West, it was a different world.

The land was barren for stretches at a time. There were dilapidated homes and charred forests whose ashes served as a distant memory of the war. It had taken them forever to travel certain areas thanks to bridges being destroyed, but thankfully they'd found that boat a while back. It had given them a slight reprieve from the growing cold and threat of Wallers. She would have loved to travel exclusively by boat if they hadn't had to abandon it on the dried-up lake. From there it'd been quite a trek. At least finding food for the horses was easy . . . mostly. If they lost any more of them, they'd be forced to abandon a wagon or two. That wasn't something they could afford—not when they had so much ground to cover. The new Tent City they'd created was meant to be temporary, mobile. They couldn't stay there forever.

Smoke from the fire pit blocked them from her view, but she didn't need to see who was behind it. She could hear him from a mile away.

"So there I was, a horde of those freaks just clawing their way through the debris we'd used to block the doors. Turns out, it wasn't enough. They came rushing in one by one, crawling past all the traps we'd set, only a few getting blown to bits. Before I knew it, they surrounded me. As they closed in, I did the only thing I could. *Bam!*"

Embers shot toward the sky as he struck the side of the flaming barrel.

One kid listening fell backward off his bucket and into a pile of snow. His imprint remained after sitting back on the bucket.

You always know how to scare the kids, don't ya?

"All right, Sticks. I think they've heard enough of your stories today," said Felan.

"But Felan," said the kid who'd fallen back into the snow. She could see then that it was Vincent. His eyebrows were still covered in white powder. He'd grown a little in the past few months, and she was still getting used to it.

"We've got work to do," she said, then looked to Sticks. "All of us."

Sticks smiled and got up, waving his arms at the kids. "All right, all right. You heard the boss. Let's get moving."

The crowd of children dispersed, the snow angel disappearing as the snow continued to fall. Felan moved to join Sticks by the barrel. Removing her gloves, she stretched her hands toward the fire. Its warmth did little to remove the numbing sensation of her legs, but at least she could feel her hands again. She'd thought she might have to pry her fingers from the trigger after that long trek down the mountain. Her body now felt less rigid, the warmth spreading.

"You gotta stop scaring them like that, you know?" said Felan, staring into the glowing embers below.

The oranges and reds reminded her of the season they had just spent traveling. Fires had once been lit for convenience but now burned out of necessity. Leaves no longer hung on trees, just as they no longer lived within the confines of safety. Everything was changing.

"It's just something to get their minds off everything," said Sticks.

"Their minds need to be on. All the time," replied Felan. "Everything requires our attention, now more than ever."

"What are you talking about? We took care of the horde already," said Sticks. "It's not like there're that many more around. We're alone on this mountain now."

Felan shot him a look. "Not anymore."

Sticks stopped smiling, his dark eyes locked with hers. "How many?"

" 'Bout ten."

"You sure?" asked Sticks.

"That's how many I took down, anyway. No tellin' how many are left," replied Felan. She watched as the embers danced in the barrel, the scent of pine filling the air. She longed to relax, to sit among the trees without wondering where her next meal would come from or the location of the next facility. If only. But she needed the data—not just for herself, but for everyone else. They were counting on her.

Sticks sat back down on his bucket. Orange flickered across his face, shadows dividing it in half. The lines in his face were growing deeper, longer, like sled tracks in the snow.

"We gotta move again, huh?" he asked.

"That was always the plan. Just doin' it sooner than expected," replied Felan.

"What about the weather? Half of us can't move on snow, let alone ice," said Sticks.

"I'm well aware of that. But if we don't go soon, none of us will move at all."

Sticks stood back up, stumbling a bit. Felan almost raced over to him before he regained his balance.

"Dang bucket got stuck in the snow," he said, feigning a laugh.

"Yep," replied Felan, forcing a smile in return. She didn't want to let on that she'd seen the bucket remain completely still.

His mobility had weakened exponentially the last couple months. Ever since they'd left The Delivery Co., he'd been stumbling periodically. It was only more recently that it had become noticeable to others. Marie had even mentioned something about it to Felan, but she'd told her to keep quiet. Sticks was one of the leaders, and people didn't need to know he was having trouble again. Not now.

"I guess I'll get the others?" asked Sticks.

"Yeah. Make sure you don't alarm anyone. Keep it casual. We can't worry anyone about what's going on. Not yet."

"You got it," said Sticks.

"One more thing," said Felan.

"Yeah?"

"You ever heard a whistle, kinda low in pitch?"

Sticks squinted his eyes, his thinking face. "Can't say that I have, no. Why?"

Felan shrugged. "Thought I heard one, but maybe it was nothing."

Sticks nodded, then turned to go back into the main tent. He turned back around about three steps after.

"You coming?" he asked.

"I'll be right there," replied Felan.

He hurried off toward the doors of the main tent, then disappeared inside.

Felan dropped to her knees, crouching beside the warm barrel. The heat surged near her, but she almost couldn't feel it. Leaning on the bucket for support, she gripped it as hard as she could. Pain surged through her abdomen. It felt like someone was attempting to wring out her guts from the inside. Her face scrunched up as she closed her eyes tight, waiting for it to stop. She hoped this time would be shorter than the last. It wasn't. If anything, it felt longer. She tried pushing back on her stomach, which didn't help. The pain continued. Fog gathered in front of her face as she exhaled in rapid succession. She'd figured out a while back that breathing out seemed to relieve the pain a bit, or at least keep her mind busy.

After what felt like a lifetime, the pain subsided. Her arm wobbled a bit as she pushed herself upright against the bucket. Catching her breath, she started toward the doors.

Snow fell, blanketing the green roof of the central tent. There were a couple kids playing tag around the rest of the tents, some throwing snowballs at the others. Behind the main tent, others were laid up in bed, some sick, others waiting for her to find a cure to their disease. So many kids; they all trusted her to lead them to a better world. One where they didn't have to fight off hordes of Wallers. One where The Delivery Co. no longer ruined the life of every child it created. One where the Elite weren't growing in number daily. One where children could just be children, no matter how they were born. One where they could just live, not survive. Was that really too much to ask?

She paused, gripping her abdomen, and allowed the pain to die down before heading inside. The sinking sun was a reminder of the time they had to make a plan.

Chapter Nine
Ahna

"Take the ones in beds and load them into that wagon over there. Marie will be inside, guiding you from there," said Ahna.

She pointed to the wagon on the far end, closest to the barrel containing the fire. The other wagons were lined up behind it, each containing different materials. Corrine had insisted that they space out the sick as much as possible while still allowing room for her and Marie to care for the kids while on the go. Along with that, they had to keep the guns and ammunition out of the snow, so that took up another slot. With the food supply being so low, that led to a bit of free space for the others who weren't sick, but there still wasn't enough space for everyone.

Ahna had volunteered to be one of the ones who walked along the side of the caravan. This was all her idea, so she thought she had to take some responsibility for it. She thought back to the captain on the ship, a storm raging and tossing its crew into the ocean. They were heading into a storm, so it only seemed right that she be at the front, ready to go down with the ship should the need arise.

There were torches on the corners of each wagon and in the hands of all those who had agreed to walk, so their path down the mountain would be illuminated, but only barely. Evergreens blocked the majority of the moonlight, which made it difficult to see too far into the forest.

Snow circled them as the wind howled through the trees. It had gotten worse since the morning, and at the rate it was progressing, they'd be lucky to find another shelter in time. They were putting everyone's lives at risk, but it was a risk they had to take. At least, that was what Ahna told herself. She had to be right, otherwise the death of all those kids would be on her hands. She couldn't live with that.

Once all the wagons were loaded up and packed which what leftover supplies they had, they abandoned the tents and started through the inches of snow, treading down the path of the mountain, hoping that somehow they'd find a place to hunker down for the storm.

Before getting too far from the makeshift camp, Ahna turned to take one last look at the tents they'd left behind. Snow had already piled up on their roofs, their doors flapping like flightless birds attempting to take off. They hadn't been there long, but she had started to like living on the mountain. It seemed that every place she'd been since being Rejected ended up abandoned or destroyed.

She thought back to Tent City, how only months ago she'd been an Eksider. Now she was leading the Rejected down a mountain in the middle of a blizzard, possibly toward their death. Seemore had given her big shoes to fill, and she was doing her best. She just had to hope that her best was good enough.

AHNA STUMBLED THROUGH the snow, each step feeling as though it were traveling through thick mud. Wind blew in the opposite direction, making it increasingly difficult for the horses to pull the wagons down the path while avoiding the edge. Darkness surrounded their ring of light as they traveled farther down the mountain. It had been only an hour or two, but it felt like days. It was getting progressively worse, snow melting in a constant hiss in the heat of Ahna's torch. With each bump and turn, groans escaped the back wagon. Ahna knew it was unsafe to move those kids, but it had to be done.

There was no other way.

She repeated that over and over in her mind as she trudged through the snow, her torch held high in front of her, staff slung across her back. She glanced at her other arm, the tissue around her wrist finally healed though badly scarred. She had taken the precautions and done the exercises and treatments that Corinne had suggested, so it was doing much better than it could have, all things considered. If Sticks hadn't found her in that Junkyard that day, she'd probably have been eaten by wolves . . . or Wallers.

A laugh escaped her. Ahna hadn't thought about the day she'd lost her hand in months. She certainly never laughed at that memory. It used to be the worst. She thought of the stares she used to get inside the cafeteria from those who hated her before, the looks she got when she first arrived at Tent City. Before and after losing her hand, she had been judged. It was almost like people weren't judging by ability or lack of, but instead by what they'd been taught to believe about the people marked as "others." Even the Rejected had that word, "Eksider." That was just their version of Rejected. When boiled down to their very core, people were people.

That was what she intended to fight for, what they would all risk their lives for. She was determined to bring an end to the corruption and deceit, no matter the cost.

Lost in her thoughts, she almost didn't notice the horse halting its steps, attempting to pull backward. It sensed something.

What is it, girl? What's out there?

Ahna met eyes with Felan, who tilted her head in the direction they were heading and pulled her rifle from her back, scanning the area. Ahna thrust her torch forward and crept through the blizzard into the darkness.

Evergreen giants swayed side to side, their creaking a haunting melody. Wind howled, her torch flame almost horizontal. As long as it didn't go out, she should be okay.

Snow crunched beneath her as she walked farther, the light of the caravan barely visible behind her. There were fewer trees as she continued, which was confusing. The forest had been dense for so long, it was strange to see any sort of clearing. That meant one of two things: there was a cliff or a building nearby. Either way, she had to be cautious. Wallers seemed to have an easier time in the darkness than the daylight. They had found that out the hard way when they lost the wagon. She couldn't let the memory shake her, though. Her mind was already racing, her heart attempting to keep up.

Crack.

Ahna dodged the large object falling toward her, rolling through the snow. She wiped the snow away with her nub as best she could while swinging the torch toward the source of the sound.

A branch. A big freaking branch. Wow, Ahna. Almost had a heart attack because a tree attacked you. Breathe, dummy.

She let out the breath she'd been holding and sucked in the cool air. After catching her breath, her heart rate decreasing, she saw someone walking toward her. It was hard to make out who it was through the snow. Whoever it was wasn't carrying their torch. Not smart in this kind of weather.

"Scorch," she called out. "That you?"

The figure paused for a moment, then she heard the terrifying sound of its screech before it raced toward her.

She could feel her heart pounding in her chest as she sucked in a horrified gasp. Directly in front of her was a Waller.

Thankfully for her, it was only one, but it had the slight blue iridescent glow like the others. If it was anything like those, it wouldn't be an easy fight, especially when she still had her staff slung across her back.

The Waller sped through the snow, mouth gaping, its claws aiming for her throat. She tried to move out of the way, but when she leapt sideways, she bumped right into a tree. Claws swiped at her again, hands moving so fast she could barely see them. Splinters rained down on her as she ducked beneath and slid to the side. As she stood back up, she spun to kick the Waller in the back. She felt the weight of the Waller through her foot, vibrations reverberating through her body.

Its maggot-ridden eyes stared back at her as its tongue swayed back and forth. It was barely fazed by her kick. The Waller ran toward her, then slashed at her again. She tried ducking again, only to feel her torch get knocked from her hand.

Darkness.

If not for the slight glow of the mushrooms on its body, she may not have been able to see the Waller at all.

Ahna pulled her staff around and gripped it in her hand. She watched the dim blue glow come toward her again but felt the attack before she'd expected to. The Waller slammed into her, knocking her back again.

What? Stupid glow is lagging!

She had little time to react before the Waller was slashing at her again. Its claws sliced through the fur on her armor, a violent barber forcing hairs to fly into the air around them. If not for the dense leather beneath, she may have seen her own flesh ripped to bits. With labored breathing and sore muscles, she brought the staff around and smacked into the blue glow.

There was a grunt, then a release of pressure from on top of her.

Phew.

As she stood back up, she felt a force slam into her again. Ahna soared through the air, this time slamming directly into a tree. Her staff fell out of her hand, lost in the darkness. Dim blue light was heading straight for her. She prepped herself for the impact, watching the blue get closer and closer. As it neared her body, she threw her arms up in front of her face and prepared to kick the Waller.

As if from nowhere, a flame appeared in the air and stuck into the Waller, who was mere feet away from her. Its screech cut through the night air like a knife as the flame engulfed its body. She watched as it ran around, attempting to get rid of the fire. It ran into a tree, which knocked the Waller backward. Able to see her staff in the newly lit area, Ahna snatched it from the ground and hobbled to her feet. She thrust the staff through the flaming body of the Waller, who crumpled to its knees. Its screech died down as its body fell, a hiss escaping the ground as the snow put out the flames.

Silence.

Ahna could feel her chest rising rapidly, her heart beating in her throat. She took a few deep breaths, using her staff to steady herself. The Waller was dead. It had done a bit of damage, but thankfully nothing a bit of salve couldn't fix. As long as they still had some.

Snow crunched in the rhythm of incoming footsteps. Accompanying the footsteps was a flickering orange glow, which illuminated his face.

Scorch. It's you. Thank the Creator.

He gripped a bow in his other hand, his leathery fingers wrapped tightly around the dark wood handle. In the flicker, every line and feature seemed more extreme, more detailed. His arms had grown over the last couple months, which she didn't mind one bit. He was one of the first people she'd met who'd been helpful within Tent City. Even with his tough facade, she knew his heart was kind. His actions reminded her of that . . . most days.

"Ahna," said Scorcher, his eyes wide and a grin stretching across his face. "You're okay."

Ahna smiled back. "Thanks to you, yeah. Nice shot."

Scorcher laughed. "Thanks. I've been practicing."

"I can tell," said Ahna, her cheeks warming.

"Gross," said Felan, stepping through the trees behind them. She carried her torch as well, though she didn't seem as excited to see Ahna alive as Ahna had expected. She couldn't admit she would've reacted differently had the tables been turned, though.

Felan looked over to the smoking corpse, its body mostly charred, the blue light fully extinguished with the flames. "This the only one?"

"Far as I know, yeah," said Ahna.

"Where did it come from?" asked Felan.

Scorcher moved to be next to Ahna. The torch helped to warm her a bit more, but it was his presence that made her feel better. That wouldn't fix her wounds, though. She'd need some salve as soon as they got somewhere safe.

"Not sure," said Ahna. She looked around for a moment before spotting the branch on the ground. "That fell, and then he came from behind, so . . ." She turned around and pointed. "That way, I think."

Felan nodded. "Then let's make sure there aren't any more of those freaks coming before we bring the group down this way. I don't want an ambush if we can help it."

Ahna and Scorcher nodded. Ahna slung her staff over her shoulder again and picked up her torch. It was slightly wet, but after a moment Scorcher was able to relight it with his.

Torches held in front of them, the three of them walked through the snow to the edge of the clearing. The firs and evergreens became denser as they continued around the mountain. Ahna thought they should be heading down, but it was hard to tell the direction in the dark. She would have to rely on the others for direction, as she usually did while traveling. She'd learn, eventually.

Felan kept an eye on their rear while Scorcher walked close enough to Ahna that she could smell him. The familiar fragrance of pine needles and campfire smoke filled her nostrils, and her heart skipped a beat. If there was ever a smell she would bottle forever, that was it.

After what felt like hours of walking, the wind had died down immensely. There was a slight clearing off to the side. Moonlight reflected off something metal in the distance.

Ahna kicked something hard and stopped to see what it was. A piece of metal with a broken screen attached to it lay on its side. She picked it up, examining it. It was familiar but badly damaged.

"Guys," she said.

Scorcher and Felan stopped. They both stared at the object in her hand, interested and cautious at the same time.

"What is it?" asked Felan.

"Is it a computer?" asked Scorcher.

Ahna shook her head. "Not exactly. It's the screen that goes on the inside of closets inside a facility."

Felan's eyes narrowed. "What's it doin' out here?"

"It looks old," Scorcher said.

"We were looking for the abandoned facility, right?" asked Ahna.

Ahna could feel the excitement building. If she was right, then she hadn't made the entire caravan up and move for nothing. If she was right, she hadn't risked their lives traveling in the dead of night in the bitter cold for no reason. If she was right, then it had to be really close.

Ahna sprinted toward the glint of moonlight in the distance, not caring about the pain in her body or the possibility that a horde of Wallers may have been waiting. After all, she was right. She had to be.

"Ahna, hold up!" shouted Scorcher.

"Yeah, wait for us," added Felan.

Finally, they caught up to her. Ahna only had to take a few more steps before she stopped dead in her tracks, putting her left arm out to stop them from continuing. She smiled as she held out her torch.

"I think we found it."

Torchlight reflected off the large metal wall towering above them. Bent in every direction, the doorway was badly damaged but still there. Large dents in the shape of different-sized bodies were pounded into the wall. To either side of the main door were guard boxes. A walkway through the main doorway led to another set of doors on the inside.

Ahna took a few steps forward, extending her torch. She spotted it flying above the doors.

The stork.

Chapter Ten
Sticks

Sticks stood amazed as he watched the younger kids enter though the doorway, their eyes and mouths open wide in awe. Their ignorance was something he envied. Those kids had never experienced The Delivery Co. firsthand. Not most of them, anyway. They only knew what it was like from the stories they'd heard or the battles they'd fought. They hadn't been strapped down to a table, cut open, manipulated, and mind-controlled. They had no idea what that place was capable of when fully functional.

As long as I'm here, you won't have to figure that out.

He waited by the door until the rest of the kids walked through, then walked over to the last wagon. Snow was already blanketing the tops of them. It was getting worse, just as they'd suspected. Rounding the corner of the wall, he heard grunts and groans—sounds of pain. Corrine and Marie were still busy unloading the kids who were too sick to get out of a cot. They grunted as they heaved each cot from the back of the wagon to the ground.

Hope you don't tip the kid out of the dang thing.

Sticks walked over to them, placing his hand above his eyes to shield the snow.

"Need a hand?" he asked.

Corrine jumped, almost dropping the cot.

"Dear! Sticks, you just about scared me to death. Can you make a bit more noise next time?" she said, straining to keep the cot level as Marie attempted to climb down while still holding on to it.

"We've got a few more in the back," said Marie. "If you think we have some spare hands inside, we could use all the help we can get. If these kids get too cold, they could get pneumonia or frostbite. Either way, they'd be cold toward us if we were let that happen."

Marie laughed at herself as she helped guide the cot toward the other one. Corrine forced a smile, something Sticks had seen many a time.

"I'll grab a few from inside and send them out to grab them all," said Sticks. "You two wanna join me inside and find the room we're gonna put them in?"

Corrine and Marie exchanged a glance before nodding in sync.

"Let's hurry. Like she said, they don't need to be out here for longer than they already have been," said Corrine.

Sticks led them back inside. Warmth enveloped his body. There was a group of Gray Wolves milling about the hallway not far from them. Sticks got their attention and pointed them outside.

"Go out there and help bring those kids in," he said. "Don't worry about bringing them in too far—just into this main area will be fine for now. Go on."

He waved his hand at them, and they ran out the door. Two other Gray Wolves pushed it shut behind them.

Felan's already put them to work. Nice.

A barrel in the middle of the room had already been lit and was providing a source of the heat. Thankfully, there was a slight hole in the ceiling through which the smoke billowed. Looking around at everyone's tired, weathered faces brought Sticks back to Tent City. To the morning of the attack when he led the group toward defeat. To the morning he was captured. To the moment his life changed forever. To the moment Rollin died.

"Sticks?"

The voice sounded as though he were underwater. A hand gripped his shoulder, bringing him out of his head.

"Sticks, you all right?" asked Marie.

"Fine," he said.

"Just checking. You weren't answering before, so I wanted to make sure," said Marie.

Marie looked at him for a moment longer before going back to Corrine, who was already moving miscellaneous junk around to make room.

The space they had entered was a large foyer made entirely of metal. There were a few desks strewn about, along with plenty of bent and busted chairs, but everything had some bit of wear and tear. It was unlikely anything was salvageable, but he knew he'd be the person to do it.

Ahna and Scorcher had been helping to unload while Felan cleaned her gun by the fire. Sticks made his way toward her, stopping to warm his hands by the fire. He watched the embers dance within, crackling and popping.

"This won't last long," said Felan. She didn't look up from her rifle, but he knew she was talking to him.

"I know," said Sticks. "I figure we've got the night. Come daylight, we should probably start looking for some sort of electrical source."

Felan dipped the cloth she had been rubbing on the barrel of the rifle in a dark substance, then continued to scrub. The firelight reflected off the barrel.

"It's probably in the back, on the main level," said Felan. "That's where they usually keep their generators. Far as I know, anyway."

I didn't see any generators while I was getting my tour with Dean Tipper. Course, he probably didn't want me to see it now that I'm thinking about it.

"How do you know?" asked Sticks.

Felan turned the rifle over and examined the stock. She picked off a piece of Waller flesh and rubbed that spot clean, then placed the gun back in her lap. She looked up at Sticks.

"I've studied blueprints of every facility we've come across. They all match up pretty well, give or take a few rooms or levels. The ones that have more money tend to be bigger, but not always. Anyway, they always had a generator room or some place they marked electrical on the map. It's gotta be there. It has to be."

It does have to be . . .

"Then let's hope this isn't the exception to the rule, huh?" he said.

Looking back over his shoulder, he spotted Corrine and Marie finishing up their makeshift hospital ward. Scorcher had made his way over to them and was talking to Corrine. Marie had a bandage in her hand, which she weaved back and forth between her hands as she wrapped it around a kid's wounded leg. That got him thinking.

I wonder if she could help with my problem.

"I'll take my watch tonight, but I'll join you in the morning to look for the generator," said Felan, standing and slinging her rifle over her shoulder.

"Shout if you need anything," said Sticks.

Felan nodded and then headed for the main door. She was tough, no question about that. He only worried about her motivations. She seemed like she wanted to help and everything, but he couldn't shake the idea that she wasn't fully invested in the group. He couldn't prove it, though.

Probably just overthinking it.

Sticks sat down next to the barrel, and the heat radiated into his back. It felt nice to finally be completely warm through the night. He'd gotten used to waking up in the middle of the night cold.

If we don't find that generator tomorrow, we'll all freeze.

Stretching, he felt a cold chill run down his spine. Settling in next to the barrel, he closed his eyes and drifted off to sleep.

"YOU GUYS HEAR THAT?" asked Ahna.

Sticks did. There was some sort of grinding metal sound and a slight screeching noise coming from down the hall. It was early morning, and the group had made it through a few rooms already, though nothing had come from it. Most of the rooms were damaged but in good shape overall. One thing struck Sticks as strange, though. None of them looked like the rooms he and Ahna had lived in while in The Delivery Co. before. Every living space had bunk beds, footlockers, and a larger shower area attached. It was almost like multiple people had shared each room.

The group crept down the hall in single file with their weapons at the ready. It was still somewhat dark this far into the facility. Not many windows were present the farther in they went.

As they neared the end, they discovered a large sliding door, which had been bent so badly that it was stuck in place. Sticks moved up to the doorway and peered through the crack.

Inside, he spotted what looked like a small laboratory. There were desks, broken test tubes and beakers, and a busted computer. The sound was louder now, but there was no sign of its source.

"Help me with the door," Sticks whispered.

Scorcher handed Ahna his blade and joined Sticks at the doorway. They each put their hands on opposite doors and counted down. On one, they pulled. Metal scraped, producing a loud scratching sound. Ahna and Felan covered their ears while Sticks and Scorcher continued to pull the doors as far as they could. Once they were wide enough for them to walk through, they let go, catching their breath.

"That should do it," said Scorcher.

They stood at the open doorway, hesitating.

"What are you waiting for?" asked Felan, swaggering into the room. She carried her rifle in her hands, the blade attached to the front of it. She didn't seem worried about the constant grinding and screeching that was coming from somewhere near the room.

Your disregard for safety is gonna get us killed one of these days.

Sticks followed the group inside, his staff now more of a walking stick than a weapon. He wouldn't be caught off guard if he had to use it, though.

Once they were inside the room, his head started pounding. Memories of lying on the table, bright lights and beeping sounds, and the doctor clicking his pen filled his mind. They were standing in a laboratory, but it was smaller than the one he'd been in most recently.

This can't be it. There's no way they only had this one lab.

While the rest of the group looked around the room, he focused on the sound. If he could find where it was coming from, maybe that would lead them somewhere. Sticks let out a long exhale, tuning out everything he could, focusing solely on the sound of the grinding metal. He put his hand to the wall to feel the vibrations, moving with them. Whenever they got weaker, he would go the other way. He circled the room a couple times.

"Sticks, what are you doing?" asked Ahna.

"Hold on," said Sticks, putting a finger up to Ahna to silence her. He focused again.

He realized the vibrations weren't the strongest in the walls; they were in the floor. Sticks started shoving desks and whatever else was in his way to the side.

"Move it," said Sticks, throwing scraps of metal to the side. He felt like he was in the Junkyard again and was on the hunt for something special.

"Move what?" asked Scorcher.

"Everything!" said Sticks, his voice on the brink of cracking.

The group hesitated a moment before joining in. They shoved all the objects and desks from the middle of the floor to the sides. It created a mound of junk, but Sticks wasn't interested in the room they were in. He wanted what was beneath. That was when he spotted it.

There you are.

A trapdoor was hiding beneath a rug that had molded long ago. Once they had that fully out of the way, they stared at the trapdoor.

"How did you know that was there?" asked Felan. He could hear the genuine surprise and interest in her tone. A welcome change.

"I didn't," said Sticks, chuckling after. "I just had a feeling. Turns out I was right."

"What do you think is down there?" asked Ahna.

He didn't know, but he was going to soon enough.

"Only one way to find out," said Sticks.

He lifted the trapdoor by its handle, flinging it back to reveal a chute with a ladder. Without a moment of hesitation, he spun around and descended into the dark hole.

When he reached the bottom, the sound of grinding metal and vibrations echoed like a swarm of angry bees. In front of him was another door, but this one had a biometric scanner on the wall adjacent to it and was shut completely. The red light on the biometric scanner was dimly lit.

There's power down here . . .

That was all he needed to know before moving forward. He didn't wait for the rest of the group to follow. He felt drawn to the door. He needed to know what was behind it.

A familiar sound joined the machine noises as Sticks neared the door: screeching. It was barely audible, but it was there. Sticks gripped his staff tighter, ready.

The door had a small porthole window at the top, near eye level. It was fogged over, dirty. Sticks used the sleeve of his jacket to rub away some of the muck and peered through.

Inside was exactly what he had expected to find upstairs, only larger. It was a laboratory that appeared to be twice the size of the one he'd seen at the last facility. There were no beds or dead patients rotting away on them. Instead, large vats stood in rows, extending the entire length of the room. Bodies floated inside each one, covered in the familiar green goo, but they weren't Elite or Replacements. They were Wallers.

Following the wires and tubes running from the vats, Sticks spotted the machine making all the noise. Sparks flew sporadically as it attempted to continue working. Every few seconds it would run before getting stuck again. While the machine was stuck, the lights inside the vats flashed. When the machine kicked back on, they returned to normal.

There's our generator.

Sticks heard a clatter of footsteps in the metal hall behind him as his friends finally joined.

"Why'd you go down here without us?" asked Ahna. "You could've been killed."

"Yeah, man," added Scorcher. "Not cool."

Sticks gestured to the door. "I think I found our power source."

Felan took a step forward. "Then what are we waiting for?"

Her attitude never ceased to amaze him. She was too cocky for her own good. One day that'd get her in trouble, but he was happy to have someone like that on the team. Ahna tried to be that way, but she didn't have the spunk that Felan had. He'd tried telling her that before, but she hadn't listened. Typical.

"Two things," said Sticks.

"Which are?" asked Felan.

"One, the biometric scanner here," said Sticks, gesturing to it on the wall.

"What about the other?" asked Scorcher.

"You don't hear them?" asked Sticks.

Ahna's eyes widened. He could tell she knew right away.

"Wallers," said Ahna.

She had good ears for someone who didn't like to listen.

Sticks nodded. "Exactly. Lots of 'em, by the looks of it."

Felan pushed past to get a look through the window. She backed away and pulled her gun from her shoulder, loading it.

"What are you doing?" asked Ahna.

"Taking care of problem number one," said Felan.

"You can't just shoot the scanner," said Ahna. "That's our only chance at getting in."

"Unless anybody happens to be an employee here, blasting the thing off the wall seems to be the only option," said Felan.

Scorcher tried getting in the middle of it. "Why don't we just take a minute to talk it out, huh?"

"Shut up," said Felan, not looking away from Ahna.

"Yeah, we can settle this," said Ahna.

Scorcher's mouth hung open for a second before he stepped away, resigning from the situation. As the two bickered, Sticks rattled his brain to think of something, anything they could do to figure out the problem.

Think, Sticks. Just think. How can we get past this? If we had access to an Elite, or maybe one of the workers, then we could just cut off their dead hand and place it on there. Obviously, that won't work. And it's not like we have the dean or doctor handy.

Then it hit him.

Sticks pushed past Felan and pulled Ahna by the wrist toward the door.

"Hey, what's your problem, Sticks?" said Felan.

"Yeah, let go!" said Ahna, fighting to pull her hand free from his grip. "What are you doing?"

Sticks yanked Ahna so that she stood right next to the scanner and forced her hand on to it, holding it in place. The red light blinked three times before turning green.

"Partial DNA match. Biometric identification complete. Welcome, Doctor," said a voice through a speaker above the doorway. A hiss escaped through the sides of the door before they heard metal click. The locks released; the door was open.

Sticks released Ahna's hand. Ahna stared down at her hand, then at him. Scorcher and Felan looked equally as shocked.

The door behind him slid open, and Sticks gestured to the opening.

"Ladies first," he said, smiling.

Felan walked by, pulling her rifle up and placing her eye on the scope. Scorcher followed, his blades in both hands, while Ahna stopped just before the door.

"How did you know?" she asked.

I didn't.

Sticks shrugged, then pushed her through the door.

"No time for questions."

A shot from Felan's rifle echoed in the lab as the group made it inside. After that, the screeching ramped up, hissing and scratching coming from directly in front of them. Thankfully, the flickering bulbs above produced enough light for them to see the incoming Wallers, but it was almost as though it were in slow motion.

Sticks pulled out his staff, crouching into his fighting stance. Sprinting forward, he threw all his weight into the staff as he thrust it though the body of the first Waller. Resistance pushed back as he passed through its flesh and bone, thick red blood pouring out onto the slick metal floor below. The Waller had been running so fast that Sticks had to put one foot on its torso to pry the staff back out. Once he had it removed, the Waller slumped to the floor. Just in time, too.

As he turned his head, he saw two more Wallers coming after him. Their teeth were long and sharp, jutting out at different directions like wires in the Junkyard. Prepping for the impact, he exhaled as he lunged with the staff on a horizontal, pushing into both bodies as they neared him. He felt the staff bend in the middle, almost cracking due to the force against both ends.

In order to save the staff from splitting in two, he pulled back. The staff quit bending, but that gave the Wallers more room to move. They closed in, and he spun to kick the one on the right while slamming the other with the staff. Midway through the spin, he felt it snap.

Crack!

It sounded almost as loud as a gunshot and felt worse. The room went black, then returned, hazy. Tears streamed down Sticks's face, mixing in with the dirt of the previous day. His staff fell, rattling against the metal floor before sliding away. Sticks gripped his knee, howling in pain.

"Oh god!" he shouted. "Ah!"

He couldn't help himself. The pain was more than he'd ever felt. It was worse than the nail in the Wall during their attack on the last facility. His body started shaking as he watched the two Wallers advance. In a split second, one of their heads exploded, the gunshot ringing in his ears. He heard Felan reload, then curse. The other Waller had been hit, but only grazed. It opened its eyes in a frenzied stare and charged toward him again. There was nowhere he could go, nothing he could do. His friends were fighting the others, his staff was across the room, and his knee was throbbing in pain. He accepted his fate and waited, holding his breath.

As the Waller approached him, Felan stepped in, smacking its face with the butt of her rifle. The Waller stumbled before bounding back. Sticks looked to the side to see Scorcher and Ahna fending off a handful of other Wallers themselves. Felan was his only chance.

"My staff," he cried out, hoping she could hear him.

Felan sprinted to the side and grabbed his staff, tossing it back to him. Sticks caught it and held it as tightly as he could, his knuckles turning white around its grip.

Felan and the Waller fought, trading blows. She ducked and dodged each of its swipes as best she could, but she wasn't fast enough. Bright red specks flew as the Waller slashed her across the torso. She dropped to her knees, one hand gripping her body, the other on her rifle. She was going to die.

Sticks exhaled, pushing the pain to the back of his mind. The lights flickered, his heart slowed, and his focus intensified. Raising his staff, he pulled it back and launched it forward. It went straight through the Waller's face, sending it tumbling back onto an overturned desk. Dead.

It worked. She's alive.

He smiled as the room around him blurred. He saw Ahna running toward him before everything went dark.

Chapter Eleven
Felan

"Stay still. I would rather not prick you."

Marie kept one hand pressed to Felan's side while the other threaded a needle through her skin. It felt unnatural to be out of her armor like this, but it was only her and Marie, so that helped.

She could feel each puncture, feel the thread sliding like a small snake burrowing its way through her skin. She shuddered at the thought. There wasn't time to worry about a small gash; the others were hurt. Sticks had looked rough when she'd last seen him. She had to know if he was okay.

"Where is he?" asked Felan.

"Who?"

"Sticks. He still in surgery?"

Marie pulled the last of the thread through and clipped it. Stepping back, she stared at the spot, admiring her work. She was weird about that sometimes. Her smile faded a bit when she answered.

"Last I heard, yeah. They're in one of the back rooms."

"Why aren't you in there instead?" asked Felan.

"It wasn't as bad as we initially thought, so Corrine can handle that. Besides, I knew you could use me. I hear you're quite the hero," said Marie. Her bright eyes were locked on Felan's, beaming through her thick glasses.

"I need to go. I have things to do," said Felan, pushing off the table. As she tensed up, she felt the stitches in her side pull a bit.

"Careful!" said Marie, moving to her side. "You bust those, I'll have to do it again. Not that I mind that, but it wouldn't be as pleasant for you the second time around."

"I can't just sit here and wait, Mar. We need to get things done. We found the generator down there but didn't get to hook it up. We need power by nightfall or we'll be in trouble."

Marie placed her hand on Felan's thigh, patting it.

"Scorcher's on top of it. He said he'd gather some people in the morning and clear out the room down there to get it set up. You don't have to worry about it."

Felan couldn't shake the feeling. Her mind was racing, her heart in sync with her thoughts.

"What if he doesn't know how to do it? What if he messes it up and we came into this shell of a facility just to die a day later than we would have? What if—"

"Felan," said Marie, her voice low. "Chill. Scorcher took Wick with him, so he'll take care of the technical stuff. He knows what he's doing. You trust Wick, don't you?"

With my life.

"Of course. It's Scorcher I'm worried about. He's a little preoccupied with other things most the time. I'm not sure there's room in his head for anything else."

"Are you referring to Ahna?" asked Marie.

"Well, yeah. I know you've seen them. One minute they're arguing about something trivial, and the next they're swooning over the way the other breathes."

Marie lowered her head for a moment before looking back at Felan.

"You're not . . . jealous of her, are you?" she asked.

Jealous of Ahna? What? Why would I be jealous of her? Scorcher's not that hot. I mean, he's probably the toughest guy in camp, but I'm tougher.

"Definitely not," said Felan.

Marie smiled, her eyes brightening behind her thick glasses.

"Good." Marie moved to grab something from a bag that had been sitting in a chair across the room.

Felan watched her as she searched. She moved with such precision, almost robotically. In fact, most of the time she worked she seemed mechanical. If she had to perform a procedure in her sleep, she probably could've. Felan would've placed a bet on her to do it, anyway. The only thing that reminded her that Marie was human instead of a surgical android was her nose ring. A small circle hugged the side of her nostril, reflecting the white light. It bounced up and down when Marie laughed, which happened a lot when she and Felan chatted. She was a good friend, the person Felan felt the closest to in the whole group. Ever since Marie had nursed her back to health last year, she felt a connection to her. Since then, Marie had been giving her a lot more attention, which was surprisingly nice. It felt good to have someone like her around.

Marie returned with a syringe of clear liquid. She flicked the tube a couple times, releasing the air bubbles, then turned her attention back to Felan.

"Ready?" she asked.

"For what? What's in that thing?" asked Felan.

"It'll help with the healing. Just an intramuscular injection, and you should be good to go."

"An intra-what?" asked Felan. Marie always used big medical words. She knew what she was doing, but Felan never said yes to anything until she understood it.

"That's just a fancy way of saying I'll inject it into your leg, right in the muscle. From there, the meds should travel through your bloodstream and get to work on the wound."

"It'll work on my side even though you're injecting it in my leg?" asked Felan.

"Yep! Blood travels around the whole body, not just one spot," said Marie, laughing.

Medical stuff is weird, but whatever.

"All right, go ahead."

Marie gripped Felan's leg again, pinching her thigh to grip some of her skin. It seemed a bit high, but Felan wouldn't argue with her on that. Besides, she'd seen plenty of people get shots, so it was probably normal.

Once Marie finished the injection, she tossed the syringe back in her bag.

"Am I good to go?" asked Felan.

Marie nodded. "Should be. If you have any issues with that wound, get a fever, or rip the stitches, you know where to find me." She smiled, pushing her glasses back up on her nose.

Felan lifted herself off the table and started toward the door-way. Her armor was near the door, so she started to put it back on, then stopped. Pain shot through her abdomen, stopping her in her tracks. The armor fell to the floor. Her knuckles whitened, and she gritted her teeth. Her body sunk to the floor as she held on to the doorframe for support.

Marie rushed over to her side.

"Oh god. Oh no. You okay? What's wrong? What can I do?" Her voice wavered, almost a stutter.

"Just . . . be . . . here."

Felan focused on her breathing, pulling in sharp breaths. She tried pushing on her stomach, applying any sort of pressure. She pushed in, hard, but it didn't help. The pain still coursed through her midsection. It was lower, too, as though someone were cutting her inside below the waistline. The seconds felt like minutes as she waited for it to go away. Marie rubbed her back as she waited for it to end, her hand on her back the only thing drawing Felan's full attention away from the fact that her body was revolting against her.

As the pain subsided, Felan's breathing slowly returned to normal. She started to gain her senses back and relaxed her body. A feeling of light-headedness came over her. On the floor below her was a small pool of bright red blood. Another drop dripped from her body. Her muscles had tightened so much that they had ripped the stitches.

Great. She just said to be careful, and I ripped them before leaving the room. This thing just keeps getting worse . . .

Before she could say anything more, Marie was helping her up to her feet.

"Come on," she said, her voice in a hushed tone. "Let's get you sat down. I can do the stitches from the chair instead."

Marie moved the bag to the floor, almost tossing it out of the way to make room. Felan put her weight on Marie's hand as she eased her down into the chair. Her body was weak, and she felt like she could go right to sleep. This thing, whatever it was, was tearing her apart.

Marie hurried to thread another needle and returned to her side. She placed her hand gingerly on Felan's rib cage, its cool temperature a stark contrast to her hot skin. She exhaled deeply and closed her eyes.

"Just relax, all right? I'll do my best to make you feel okay."

You always do.

Felan let her head fall back against the cool metal wall as she waited for Marie to stitch her back up.

Marie moved her fingers with such grace and care that Felan barely noticed when she had finished. Once she had put the supplies back in the bag, she crouched down next to Felan.

"How often has it been happening?" she asked.

Felan thought back over the past few months. It had gone away for a week or two. Those had been the most pleasant weeks of her life, current events excluded. But it had returned in worse condition than it had gone.

"I don't know," said Felan. Unfortunately, that was the truth. "It comes and goes."

Marie's voice hardened. "And you didn't think to tell me?"

Felan shrugged. "I didn't want to bother you. We've got too many kids laid up as it is."

Marie stood, pacing in front of her. "Too many kids? Sure, we have a lot of kids in some bad conditions and some that need my attention most the time. But these kids aren't you."

"What do I matter in the grand scheme of everything?" asked Felan.

"You matter to me—us. You're important to the group, and we can't afford to lose you. Especially not now."

What are you saying right now? Am I missing something, or have you been acting a little strange since these problems started? What am I supposed to say to that?

She said the only thing that she felt comfortable saying in that moment.

"How's it coming along with the data I recovered from the last facility?"

Marie visibly deflated. Felan watched her face sink and arms go limp at her sides. Her smile decayed into a thin line, returning to its resting position. Not what she had expected to hear.

"Fine," said Marie. She started gathering her supplies, tossing everything into the bag. That was very unlike her.

"Did Wick find anything yet? Any traces of a cure?" Felan asked, half expecting the answer to be positive this time around.

Marie grabbed her bag and zipped it up, cradling it like a newborn baby. "No."

She was being short with her. Felan had no idea why, but she didn't have time for games.

"Nothing at all?" asked Felan.

"It's encrypted."

"Did he say if there's a way to decrypt it?"

"No."

Felan felt warm as she inhaled deeply. There had to be a way to figure out the drive. After all the work she'd done, everything she'd gone through, she knew there was a way. It couldn't be impossible.

Felan stood as quickly as her body would allow and started gathering her armor. She placed it back on, wincing as the breastplate grazed her wound. Marie watched her, clutching her bag, glasses slightly foggy.

"What are you doing?" asked Marie, her words almost inaudible.

"Going to see Wick and sort this out. Once we get power up and running, we can focus on finding a computer. There's gotta be one around here somewhere. After that, we keep trying to figure out this data. And if the drive I got from the last place doesn't work, I'll go out and find another one."

Felan continued putting on her armor. Once it was all on, she felt a little more relaxed, more herself. Marie was the only person she'd ever been out of armor with, and that was becoming weird now too. She needed to get out of there.

"Why are you always going after the drives, Felan? Why can't you focus on what's going on in the world?" asked Marie. There was a bite to her voice now.

" 'Cause I won't be in the world much longer without a cure, Mar. I'll find the data I need to get the cure, even if I die in the process."

Marie threw down her bag of supplies. Felan took a step back, startled. Tears formed in Marie's eyes, her glasses getting foggy.

"Fine! Go ahead," yelled Marie. "Go out there and risk your life for a piece of prewar plastic. Spend your life chasing something you don't have instead of focusing on what's already in front of you. Whatever makes you happy, Felan. Because, apparently, that's all that matters!"

Marie stormed out the doorway, pushing past her. Her supplies were scattered on the floor, and the light flickered above. Felan sunk into the chair and sobbed into her hands.

What did I do?

Chapter Twelve
Scorcher

Scorcher peered into a massive hole in the side of the wall. Without light, there was no way to know what was in there, but judging by the number of bones and bodies, it looked like the Wallers had been living in it for a while. A pile of dead Wallers blocked the entrance to the hole.

Scorcher grunted as he picked up the body of a Waller and tossed it to the side. It was heavier than expected. He had to step to the side to avoid the dark goo that fell from its mouth as he moved it. The odor reminded him of the time they'd had a dead mouse in the Town Hall a few years ago. It had taken weeks to find the source of the smell, and by the time they did, it took days to air it out. He gagged at the memory.

"Found something over here!"

Scorcher turned to see the group of kids gathered in a cluster, all staring at something. When he approached, they parted for him to get through. He then saw the lever they were staring at, an arm of a Waller jammed inside its mechanism. Within the grasp of the dead arm was a blade that had been chipped away by the cog beneath it. That must have been the cause of the machine's grinding.

"Nice job, Vincent," said Scorcher.

Vincent smiled, his new front tooth poking its way back out to join its twin. A slight whistle accompanied every word with an *s*. Scorcher would have to get used to that for a while, especially given how much Vincent loved saying his name. Thankfully, it didn't bother him yet.

"Thanks, Scorcher. Only problem is that stupid freak's arm is caught up in it," said Vincent. "Want me cut it out of there?"

Vincent started to unsheathe his blade, but Scorcher stopped him.

"That's okay, I've got it. Thanks, bud," said Scorcher.

You're always trying to cut or shoot stuff, aren't you? I guess I was like that once.

He chuckled.

Clearing the space around the lever, he planted his feet and gripped the elbow part of the bone. He pulled as hard as he could and flew backward into the crowd of kids. Thankfully, they provided a somewhat-soft landing.

Click.

The lever fell into place, the remnants of the chipped blade flung from its teeth. The grinding sounds ceased, leaving them with a consistently smooth low hum. The kids cheered for him while they helped him to his feet.

"Way to go!" said Vincent. "Not the way I woulda done it, but still good."

"Thanks, kid. That's only problem number one."

"What's the other?" another kid asked; he was one of the smallest of the Gray Wolves. They had been together for a couple months, but Scorcher still hadn't learned all their names. There were so many, and he had spent a majority of his time with Ahna.

I wonder if she's still with Sticks . . . I wish she'd decided to come down here with me, but I guess I'll just have to tell her about it instead. I need to ask her about that scanner thing, too.

Vincent tapped Scorcher on the arm. "What other problems do we have, Scorcher?"

"Right," Scorcher said, nodding. "We took care of the machine noise, but this doesn't look like a generator. Am I right, Wick?"

Wick nodded. He'd been silently observing, as usual. Scorcher liked that about him. The kid was always lurking in the shadows, but he was a whiz when it came to technology. Scorcher wasn't sure if he was smarter than Sticks or not, but he wouldn't bet against either of them. In fact, he'd have paid good money to see a match of wits between them. They didn't have time for those kinds of games anymore, though.

"What we're looking for is something much larger, something that can crank out massive power. This is only a switch for it, most likely. However, it's highly unlikely the switch would be very distant from its source," said Wick.

"You saying we're close?" asked Scorcher.

"Very," said Wick. "Follow the connections, find the generator."

Scorcher looked at the group, their faces plastered with confusion. To be fair, he barely understood it himself.

"What Wick's saying is go look around for the wires and tubes that are connected to this thing, and we should be able to find what we're looking for. Go on."

He waved his hands at the group. The kids spread out, looking through the large laboratory. It didn't take long until one of them shouted that they had found something. Scorcher and

Wick joined them to see a long cable that was running from the lever to a doorway on the right side of the room. Scorcher tried turning the handle, but it was locked. He pushed against the door with his shoulder a couple times, which made the door budge slightly.

I guess I'll do it the hard way.

"Stand back," said Scorcher.

He backed away from the door and exhaled. His eyes narrowed as he focused on the spot next to the handle. Sprinting forward, he launched his entire body weight into a kick. His foot landed right next to the handle, which popped open as soon as he hit. He continued to fall through the air as his body followed the door inward. The metal floor caught his fall, but it hurt.

Wick strolled in behind him.

"I think we found it," said Wick.

Scorcher pushed himself up from the ground and dusted his body off. Once he stood up, he saw the big machine that whirred in front of them. The entire room was dedicated to this single machine, which chugged and buzzed. Weirdly, it was working, but they hadn't had power in the other rooms.

"Why is there only power running to the lab and not everywhere else, Wick?" asked Scorcher.

Wick stood statuesque near the hulking machine and studied it. He fiddled around with a few knobs and dials, then lifted a plastic cover, revealing a switch.

"It's on auxiliary mode right now," said Wick. "But I think if I can just switch it over to main . . ." He turned the dial to the right. Once it clicked, the machine revved. The sounds got louder and more consistent, almost too loud to hear each other.

"Did it work?" asked Scorcher, almost yelling.

"I don't know," said Wick. "Go find out."

"You want me to wait for you?" asked Scorcher.

"There's more for me to do down here. You go ahead," said Wick.

"What about the Wallers and stuff?"

Wick walked out of the room, Scorcher following right behind him. He continued to the lever, then stopped.

"If you can pull that to the other side, I think we'll find out," said Wick, gesturing to the lever.

"Whatever you say," said Scorcher.

He grabbed the lever and pushed it to the opposite side. There was a loud click, and the lights inside each of the vats turned off. The bubbles inside them stopped flowing, and the lab was mostly quiet. The overhead lights, however, stayed on.

"Problem solved," said Wick, smiling.

Scorcher laughed, then patted Wick on the back.

"You are one smart guy, you know that?" said Scorcher.

"I do," said Wick with a smirk. "Go on and check the rest of the facility, and I'll join you when I'm done."

"You're sure?" asked Scorcher.

"Yes, I'm sure."

"Okay. Just send the rest of the group up when they're done playing around down here. We'll need their help moving everything to the appropriate rooms," said Scorcher.

Wick nodded, then turned to go back into the room with the generator. It was still putting out a decent amount of noise, but it didn't seem to bother him. He was interesting. Smart kid, but strange.

Time to find Ahna and the others and tell them the good news. Let's see what this place looks like all lit up.

LIGHTS FILLED THE SPACE with a warm yellow hue, and Scorcher thought he felt a bit warmer than before, though he wasn't sure if that was his imagination or the heat finally deciding to kick on in the facility. As he walked through the main area again, he noticed that a lot of things had already been moved. Two Gray Wolves, Taz and Baz, were at the front gate, a pile of desks and other debris in front of them as a makeshift security barrier. They each had guns slung over their backs and were relaxing in the chairs behind the barrier, laughing at something.

Some security force. That would've never worked in Tent City.

That was one of the first times he had given any thought to Tent City in the last couple weeks. In the beginning of their journey with the Gray Wolves, he had spent many days talking about the fallout of their attack and going over all the possibilities of survivors and if Seemore was still alive or not. He liked to think he was, but Ahna disagreed. She'd told him she was sure because she had seen Seemore cradling a bomb as they abandoned the city before the attack. She'd claimed something about sister cities and a plan to restart a new version of Tent City for Rejects everywhere. That seemed like a nice thought, but he didn't think it would happen. The Delivery Co. was a dangerous group, and now it seemed like there was a lot more to them than he'd ever realized. He just hoped it wasn't too late to stop them.

He continued through the various halls. Most of the rooms off the hallway looked like the others before them. Each contained several bunk beds, footlockers, and standing wardrobes. The wardrobes were mostly empty or tipped over, busted. Some of the bunks still had mattresses on them, but they had grown black with mold. He had to hold his nose when checking in one of them. The facility had many rooms, but he hadn't seen anything other than bedrooms and what looked like training spaces.

One of the larger rooms he went through had a large circle painted on the ground and metal stands on either side for people to sit. There were weapon racks on the walls and shrapnel and broken pieces of weapons strewn along the floor. The facility seemed to put a lot of importance on training, more so than he remembered Ahna talking about. She had told him some stories of the inside and what being a Replacement was like. So far, this didn't match up to her stories.

Scorcher continued through the halls, roaming around until he found his way back to the main area.

There were a few more kids out playing tag. They jumped over dead Wallers and armor riddled with holes as though they were normal pieces of furniture. He felt his chest tighten. He felt bad for those kids. He thought back on his childhood and playing tag in Tent City, remembering how being "it" was the hardest thing he had to do. Now he felt like he was always "it" and was chasing an impossible enemy.

Corrine was exiting a room as he continued past the gate toward another hallway. Her face lit up when she saw him. She raced right toward him, arms outstretched.

"Scorcher, honey, you did it! Thanks to you, we have power," she said, pulling him in for a hug. He struggled a bit, feeling a bit grown for her long hugs now.

"Thanks, Mom," said Scorcher, escaping her grasp. "Glad to know it worked. But it wasn't just me who did it. How's Sticks? Is he okay?"

Corrine nodded. "He'll be good to go soon enough, just needs to take it easy. He's lucky he didn't break anything. Between you and me, hon," she said, leaning in, "you need to watch out for him. I think he's getting worse. He won't admit it, but he couldn't hide it from me. His tests don't lie."

Getting worse? Oh no.

"Is he . . . dying?" asked Scorcher. He'd had no idea Sticks was in such bad shape.

Corrine laughed. "No, dear. It's just . . . just make sure he doesn't overwork himself for a bit, okay?"

"Okay," said Scorcher, nodding.

"Thank you, hon," said Corrine. "I'd love to stay and chat, but I've got a whole ward of sick kids who need my attention. I've gotta go, but I'll see you later, okay?"

"See you later, Mom," said Scorcher. Before she got too far away, he asked, "You know where Ahna is?"

Corrine turned around. "Last I heard, she found some sort of control room. It's up the stairs, toward the back of the facility." She pointed in the direction he needed to go, then continued back inside the room.

As he turned to head down the hallway, he spotted Marie. She was walking so quickly that she almost bumped into him.

"Hey, Marie," said Scorcher. "How's Felan?"

"She's fine," said Marie, her tone sharp. "She's always fine, all by herself."

"What are you talk—"

"Sorry, Scorcher, but I need to go." She pushed past him. "Your mom probably needs my help with something."

Marie stormed off, leaving Scorcher behind, his mouth hanging open.

What's gotten into you? You're never like this . . .

Scorcher made his way down the hall until he reached an intersection. The hallway went both left and right, but there was a staircase leading up. Before he headed up the stairs, he spotted Felan coming from the right and waved to her.

"Hey! I was just asking Marie about you. How's it—"

"Apparently, Ahna found the control room," she said, cutting him off. "Where is it?"

Scorcher didn't want to pry, but she seemed in a mood, just like Marie. Felan's eyes looked a little red and puffy, too. She must have been up all night or something.

"Up the stairs, I think," said Scorcher. "That's what Mom said, anyway."

Felan pushed past him. "Great. Let's go see what she found."

Scorcher followed her up the stairs, still surprised at her attitude. She and Marie were both in really weird moods. He didn't understand, but he'd never really understood girls anyway—except Ahna. But she'd been somewhat different than usual recently, too. Everything was changing besides him.

They entered the control room, which had beeping coming from various buttons that flashed yellow and red. It was unlike any machine he'd ever seen. Ahna turned around to face them, smiling.

"Check it out!" she said, gesturing to the large computer behind her. There was a big screen up on the wall, but it was still dark. Large metal boxes with buttons and dials surrounded it. It took up most of the wall.

"What have you found out so far?" asked Felan.

"Well . . . nothing," said Ahna. "But we only just got power recently. It's been making a bunch of weird noises since the power came on, and some of the lights that were flashing red are now yellow. That must mean something, right?"

Felan pushed her aside. "Let me see what we're working with."

Ahna stepped next to Scorcher, and they watched Felan mess with the buttons and dials. She seemed to know what she was doing, though Scorcher had no idea how any of that worked. He was fine if he had to beat the machine to death, but bringing it to life was not his specialty.

Scorcher held Ahna's hand while they watched Felan work. He liked having her hand in his, the way their fingers intertwined. It felt comfortable, natural. Holding her hand, however, made him think of the scanner incident the day before. He wanted to ask her about it but didn't want to make her upset. She hadn't wanted to talk before they went to bed either. Something had bothered her about it, so he wanted to give her time. The last thing he wanted was to cause problems.

A loud beep rang through the room.

"Yes!" Felan shouted. Her thin lips turned upward into a smile, all traces of her anger vanishing.

The screen on the wall flickered. It took a moment for the entire screen to light up, but when it did, they all went silent.

The screen displayed a map. They recognized the spot where they were and the mountain they had just descended. But the thing they were staring at was another building, one that was bigger than the one they were currently in.

"What do you think that is?" asked Scorcher.

"Whatever it is looks big," said Felan. "Maybe it's abandoned, too. Maybe they have more resources or weapons." She was getting excited.

The map flickered again before beeping, and red dots appeared all over the map. Some were stagnant while others moved, a handful moving at a quick rate from the west toward the bigger building before slowing to a halt. Scorcher pointed to the dots on the screen.

"What are those?" he asked.

Ahna walked up to the screen to get a closer look, then turned to face them. Her smile faded.

"Designations," she said.

"What do you mean?" asked Felan.

"Yeah," added Scorcher. "Designations for what?"

Ahna swallowed before continuing. Scorcher could see the fear in her eyes.

"The Delivery Company gives all Replacements a designation when we—they—are born. Mine used to be A-9. Everybody inside their facilities has one."

No way . . .

Scorcher's eyes widened.

"So that means all those dots are—"

"People," said Ahna. "A lot of people."

Chapter Thirteen
D-72

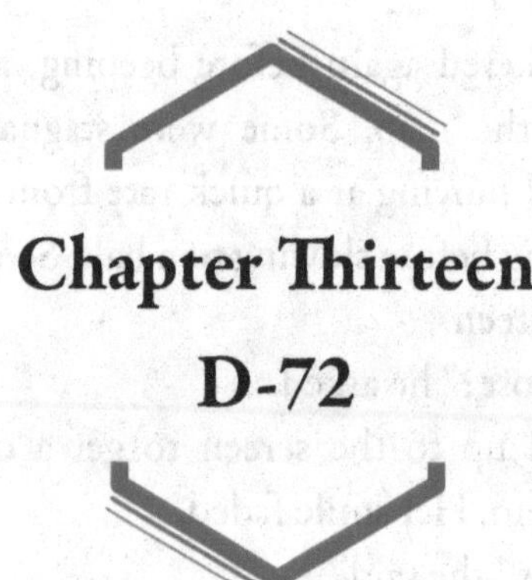

Apart of the map that usually remained dark now flashed yellow in the far right corner. Pulling his feet off the desk, he put his drink down and sat up to get a closer look. It looked almost like some of the other facilities on the map. It was quite a bit smaller, though, so it was hard to tell. He rolled his chair over to the filing cabinet and yanked on the drawer. The handle ripped right off and went flying across the room.

Oh man. Not again.

He got up to grab the handle and pulled open the small drawer of the side table next to the desk. Grabbing the container of glue, he applied the usual amount and reattached the handle to the cabinet drawer. It wasn't perfect, but it would do . . . until next time, anyway. He felt bad about it, but it wasn't his fault. They just hadn't made those handles for people of his size.

Digging around inside the filing cabinet, he found it: the list of icons and their corresponding coordinates on the map. He fumbled through the pages, looking for the area where the indicator flashed. The bulb was flickering in that spot when he looked at it again.

Must be old. I'll take care of that later.

After he searched every page, he almost gave up. Then, in the back of the file, he found an additional page that had been ripped out of its spot and stamped "closed." He checked the icon against the one flashing, then double-checked. His eyes widened when he realized it was an old facility.

I wonder what this means. Is it back open? Are we going to get transferred to this one? Oh!

A smile spread across his face as he thought of the possibilities.

Maybe it's a surprise. Either way, I should make sure with him before I raise any sort of alarm. Don't want to ruin the surprise if so.

The smiled faded as he thought back to the last time he'd gone to the dean with unsolicited news.

Maybe I should ask the lieutenant for his opinion. He always knows what to do.

He grabbed the page and headed out the door. The office was just down the hall, so he didn't have to leave his post for long. Besides, not much happened there anyway. It was mostly a place for him to rest between training sessions.

Lieutenant T-3 was typing on a computer, his back to the doorway. His helmet was on the table, right next to his shock baton. Seeing that made him gulp. Those things were no joke, especially when used outside of training. Nobody had to stop hitting you if there wasn't an instructor around.

Clearing his throat, he knocked on the doorframe. The clicking stopped. T-3 turned around, and his eyebrows rose when he spotted him in the doorway.

"What is it now, D-72?" asked T-3, his exasperation evident. He used that tone a lot when D-72 had questions or concerns, which was why he tried to limit the times he came into his office.

He couldn't help when he had questions, though. He just didn't understand things a lot of the time. It took him a little longer than the others.

"Sorry to bother, sir. I just, um . . . I just—"

Staring at the shock baton, he found himself struggling to speak.

"Out with it. You're wasting my time," said T-3. He brought his hands to the table, one of them resting only inches away from the baton.

D-72 gulped, then took a deep breath. "There's some strange activity on the screen, sir."

T-3 tilted his head slightly. "Strange how?"

"Well, there's an icon flickering, sir."

"They tend to do that, D-72. Or have you forgotten?" His hand inched closer to the baton.

"No!" said D-72, his voice cracking. He calmed himself quickly. "I mean no, Lieutenant, sir. But the flickering is in an area that I've never seen before. I checked the registered icons, like I'm supposed to, and then I found this."

He handed the page he'd found to T-3, who snatched it from his hand. The paper cut his hand on its way out, but he kept his groan silent. T-3 scanned the page quickly before tossing it back to him.

"Nothing to worry about, D-72. It's just an old training facility. A rat or one of those dumb Wallers probably triggered a sensor is all. It's been abandoned for years."

D-72 nodded. "I just wanted to make sure, sir. You know, in case it was some of the Rejected or something. Thought I would tell Dean Tipper if it was important. But since it's not—"

T-3 put his hand up, silencing him. "Wait a second, D-72. Actually, now that you mention it, I think that would be a wonderful idea."

"You do?" asked D-72. He didn't understand the sudden switch in decision but knew better than to argue.

"Yes. In fact, I would go alert him of it now," said T-3, smiling. "And be sure to tell him your theory, as you told me. Off you go."

"Yes, sir," said D-72. He picked up the paper, saluted, then exited the office.

D-72 hurried into the hall and headed toward the command center.

Turning the corner, he heard the dean's voice before he saw him. In the middle of the hall was a cowering Elite, his helmet in his hand.

Dean Tipper.

Knowing better, D-72 neared them slowly so he didn't interrupt and make the dean more upset.

"Do you really expect me to believe your story, Sergeant?" asked Dean Tipper, his voice raised. He carried a gun on his hip, always loaded from what D-72 had heard in the mess hall. Someone had told him that they had seen Dean Tipper shoot an Elite for something small. Some rumors were that he had said he wanted to see the outside world, while others said he had hit Dean Tipper in the face. Rumors never seemed to make much sense. What did, though, was that Dean Tipper was an angry man with a short temper. He was not to be messed with if you wanted to eat that day. D-72 knew that firsthand.

"Well, sir," said the sergeant, "it's a complicated matter. You see, the train is supposed to be fitted with the hydrogen batteries along the route, then return here for the loading of the cargo."

"I'm well aware of the process. Get to the point," said Dean Tipper.

"Um, right. Sorry. As I was saying, there's usually a stop along the route to refit with the batteries. However, due to an incident, they had to bypass that stop to return here."

"What do you mean they had to bypass the stop?"

"It was too risky, sir."

"What was the risk?" asked Dean Tipper, his hand resting on his pistol.

The sergeant took a slight step back. "There was an attempted attack on the train, sir. A band of Re—"

Dean Tipper backhanded the Elite across the face, the sound echoing slightly in the metal hall. The Elite stumbled back into the wall before regaining his footing. Dean Tipper hovered over him.

"Don't give me excuses, Sergeant. I want this matter resolved, or I'll see to it that everyone involved in this incident is never involved in anything again. Understood?"

The Elite nodded.

"Good," said Dean Tipper, backing away from him. "Now go."

The Elite placed his helmet back on his head and hurried away. Dean Tipper turned and spotted D-72 standing behind him. Their eyes locked.

D-72 stood, frozen in place. He swallowed before forcing a slight grin, hoping that would help his situation.

"What do you want, soldier?" asked Dean Tipper.

"I . . . uh, well, sir, I . . ." D-72's thoughts scampered around in his head like a rat looking for food.

"Don't make me wait. Why are you out of your post?" asked Dean Tipper.

Lieutenant T-3 said to tell him, so just tell him. It must be important if he said to do it. Just tell him what you found. Maybe he'll be proud of you for catching it. Maybe you'll get a promotion and not get pushed around anymore.

D-72 straightened up, his body akin to that of a small bear. He was much larger than Dean Tipper, but he knew that size didn't always match skill. That was what they taught in the ring, anyway.

"I think I have some important information, sir," he finally spat out.

Dean Tipper raised his eyebrows. "Really? A lowly soldier has important news for me? Well then, by all means, go ahead, soldier. I can't wait to hear it," he said, smiling.

Really? Wow. I didn't think you'd be this excited about it. I'm glad I came to tell you now.

He flashed the paper in his hand in Dean Tipper's direction.

"I spotted some strange activity on the map, sir. There was an alert that I've not seen before, and I think it might be them, sir. I think it's the Rejected, and—"

Dean Tipper slammed his hand against the wall.

"Enough!" he yelled.

Oh no. What did I do? I thought you said you wanted me to tell you what I found, but now you're yelling at me.

Dean Tipper came toward him, stopping only inches away.

"What's your position, soldier?" he asked.

"I monitor the map, sir."

"And do you know why you monitor the map, boy?"

"Because I'm good at it?"

Dean Tipper laughed. Each laugh felt like a swipe of sandpaper in his brain. D-72's face scrunched up as he tried to understand what was happening.

"You really are as clueless as they said in your report, aren't you?"

Clueless?

There was no time to respond as Dean Tipper continued.

"You are in the map room to hide your embarrassing amount of stupidity," he said, then looked at the designation on the front of his armor. "D-72, you are not there because you are 'good at it.' You are a fool who just happens to have the best stats in the fighting ring. If you weren't such an asset to our fighting efforts, you'd be tossed out with the rest of the brainless. You're nothing more than a dysfunctional brain wrapped in a suit of muscle. If you ever step out of line like this again, I'll see to it that you join the Rejected, in which you are, it seems, obsessively interested. Do you understand me?"

His heart pumped like pistons in the Meat Maker, feeling as though it were going to beat right out of his chest. Air became thin as he attempted to catch his breath. He felt as though he were watching his own body standing in front of Dean Tipper, unable to speak or move.

"Boy!" shouted Dean Tipper. "I asked you a question. Answer me!"

Dean Tipper's hand connected with D-72's face before he could react, and he fell to the ground. His vision blurred, and the shadow of Dean Tipper hovered above him. His words were loud but muffled, as though he were speaking underwater. After he finished yelling, he left.

Look around for something, anything . . .

D-72 rocked back and forth on the floor. He looked to the ceiling.

Lights. There're lights . . . flickering slightly.

Then he looked to the side.

A door with a security latch, which rotates counterclockwise to open and clockwise to close. It's heavy and made of metal—modified steel, to be exact. There is one on each side, just like the one that leads to the central control room.

Slowly, he stopped rocking. The intensity of the lights above dimmed.

In . . . out . . . in . . . out . . .

He felt his breath slow, his heart rate decreasing, and saw the surrounding area with a bit more clarity. Returning to his feet, he hurried back down the hallway.

He didn't stop at his post but instead rushed past. The hallway felt longer, wider. Sprinting down the hall, he bumped into a few Elite who stumbled back, but his pace didn't slow.

When he reached his bedroom, he flung his bed aside and dug around inside his footlocker. Finding the stone, he gripped it tightly in his hand, the once sharp edges rubbed smooth.

D-72 moved his bed back in place and climbed under his sheets. With the covers pulled up, it was like being in a warm cocoon. The pressure from the blankets was comforting. As he became more comfortable, he allowed his mind to slow, his heart rate to return to normal, and his emotions to regulate.

When his thumb ached, he knew he'd spent too long rubbing the stone again. He stopped rubbing and wrapped his fingers tightly around its smooth round body.

I'm no fool. I know something is happening there, and I'm going to prove it.

Chapter Fourteen
Ahna

Ahna had studied the book by moonlight over the last few weeks as the caravan weaved through the country. So many landscapes had been decimated, their once thriving beauty stripped away. Craters now housed small lakes, and trees—while plentiful in the mountain regions—had been burned down in many places. The pictures they had seen in history class reminded her of just that: history.

Nothing in that book had prepared her for this. Nothing had prepared her to see the silhouettes burned into the decrepit buildings, to watch kids writhe in pain before dying because of lack of medication, to make decisions that directly affected the lives of others. In fact, the book, and the facility, had prepared her for nothing.

Seemore had written so many great plans, so many details about what to do in certain situations or events, but he hadn't seen what it was like beyond Deliverance. What he'd expected, or thought he knew, was wrong. There was no other way for Ahna to describe it. He had given her hope of a world that was thriving beyond their plot of land, hope that there would be a place for them to build Tent City 2.0 and to avoid The Delivery Co., to rebuild and start anew. But there would be no starting anything new until they took care of the old. There would be no Tent City 2.0 as long as The Delivery Co. existed. In fact, there would be no semblance of a free world as long as the eyes of Dean Tipper loomed over her shoulder. The pressure was building, and she felt it with every step, with each eye that stared at her, waiting on her decision.

"Ahna?" asked Scorcher.

"I know," she said, slamming the book closed and turning her attention to the group. They were all standing around, wasting time. Time was a commodity they couldn't afford to waste. "We can't just stay here and worry about what's going to happen. As of now, it's probably safe to assume they have no idea we're here. Right, Scorch?"

Scorcher nodded.

"And if that's the case," Ahna continued, "then we have the advantage. But not for long. We need to gather information, form a plan, and then execute that plan. With no changes once we begin," she said, shooting a look toward Felan.

Felan crossed her arms, leaning back on the large frame of the computer.

"How do we get inside? That place looks huge."

It was. In fact, based on what she could tell, the facility on the map had to be at least twice the size of the one in Deliverance. But size didn't matter. At least, she hoped it didn't.

"We don't need to worry about how big the walls are, Felan. What we need to focus on is getting through them and what is waiting for us on the other side."

"We don't exactly have the numbers for an all-out attack, Ahna," said Scorcher.

He was trying to be polite, but she knew he was angry at the way their last mission had gone down. She was too, but she couldn't dwell on it. People died, but if she didn't focus on the future instead of the past, more people would be killed.

"I'm aware of that," said Ahna, her tone more biting than she had intended. "Which is why gaining as much information as we can is the only way we can win."

As she said the word "win," she hoped she sounded surer of herself than she felt. She had accepted the role given to her but still felt that she had big shoes to fill. She couldn't let them down—not again. If they failed this time, there would be no next time.

"So, what's the plan?" asked Felan, her arms still crossed. Something was up with her, but Ahna had no time to worry about her personal life.

Ahna cleared her throat, then picked up her staff. Its grip had become familiar, its weight like that of a companion who constantly walked by her side. She had carved more into the shaft on their travels, so it was a little more ornate than her original idea. She'd even let Scorcher carve his own design on it. He had chosen a snowflake. When she'd asked why, he'd said it was because she was unique, different from all the rest—like a snowflake. She smiled at the thought of those days traveling, but her smile faded when she snapped back into the reality of the moment.

She pointed the staff toward the map, using it to guide everyone's eyes across the landscape as she spoke. "You see the building we're in?" She watched them nod, then moved on. "That's here. I'm pretty sure I saw a tower nearby, with some sort of dish or something on top. I think that's in this area here," she said, circling a spot on the map not far from their current location.

"Why do we need to find a tower? How will that help us?" asked Felan.

"I was thinking that maybe we can get a good vantage point, scope out the area from a little higher up. Also, I'm thinking it could be a sniper's nest for you, Felan."

"Oh. Cool. On it," said Felan. She flashed a toothy smile. The very mention of her being able to snipe at the Elite from on high seemed to excite her. Ahna had never seen her smile like that before. It was a strange but welcome change from her usual demeanor.

"What about me?" asked Scorcher.

"You're in charge of seeing what we're dealing with on the ground. Specifically, we need you to get close and see what's going on down there. Scope out the perimeter, see what sort of numbers we're dealing with. There were dots moving toward the facility before. Maybe there's something to that?"

Felan pushed off the wall and walked right up to the map. A chuckle escaped her as she turned around. She pointed back up to the map at the spot where they had seen the large number of dots huddled together.

"I know what it is."

What are you talking about?

"What is it?" asked Sticks. He had been mostly silent during their meeting but for some reason was interested in the answer. He usually wasn't that silent. Something was up.

Felan smiled. "It's a train."

Like those big metal boxes that traveled on those tiny strips of metal we saw while crossing the country? They move that fast?

"Really?" asked Ahna.

"I knew it!" Felan clapped her hands in a celebratory mood.

"What makes you so sure?" asked Scorcher.

"I heard what I thought could be a whistle. A sort of long, low tone echoing through the woods," said Felan.

"I didn't hear that," said Ahna.

"It was while I was hunting those freaks. It was faint, but I knew I heard something. Now it makes sense. And it was traveling from the west, right?" she asked, awaiting the response with wide eyes.

"Yeah," said Ahna, nodding. "Why's that matter?"

"You don't know about the Railroad?" asked Felan.

Ahna and the others shook their heads.

Why would I know about that? I didn't even know what a rabbit was a few months ago . . .

Felan grunted before calming down.

"You know how you had Tent City, right?" asked Felan.

"Yeah," said Ahna, hesitating slightly.

"The Railroad is like that but much larger. It's this big underground city on the West Coast, a safe haven for Rejects from around the country. I even heard that they have medicine and other stuff from before the war. Who knows what else they have or what they are capable of," said Felan.

This could be better than Tent City 2.0. They could help us bring down The Delivery Co. for good.

"How do we find them?" asked Ahna.

Felan shrugged. "Don't know."

"If we figured it out, we could take the train to reach them?" asked Ahna.

"Maybe. It'd get us closer, at least," replied Felan.

Ahna nodded, her lips pulling in slightly as she pondered the plan she had originally stated. She had said something about not changing, but they hadn't fully fleshed it out yet, so she didn't feel bad for making a slight alteration. Besides, she was the one who'd created the rule.

"Slight addition to the plan, Scorcher. While you're down on the ground, see what you can find out about the train. Look into why it's there, what they are using it for, and how we might be able to use it."

Scorcher nodded.

"When should we get started?" asked Felan.

"As soon as possible," said Ahna. "Maybe in the morning so we don't have the added challenge of darkness during it. Besides, they'll see a torch walking toward them, and that will give us away."

Felan nodded. "Morning it is. If we're done here"—she slung her rifle from her shoulder to her hands—"I need to make sure she's ready for the expedition."

"You're not going that far," said Scorcher.

"I wasn't very far last time I saw a horde either. I don't think those freaks care about my personal space," said Felan.

"We're done, yeah," said Ahna. "Go clean your rifle, and let us know what you find tomorrow after getting into the tower. Same for you and the train, Scorch."

Ahna turned to stare at the map while the group shuffled out the door. She watched as the dots meandered around the facility like an army of ants in a colony. She imagined holding a giant magnifying glass over them, letting the sunlight burn the colony to the ground. She chuckled at the thought.

A hand touched her on the shoulder. She jumped slightly, startled. Her grip had tightened on her staff but loosened when she turned to see Scorcher. His face looked tight, like he was clenching his jaw. He did that sometimes. Usually, that wasn't a good thing.

"Hey, Scorch. What's up?" asked Ahna.

He checked over his shoulder before answering. Sticks was still in the room, fiddling with a part of the computer near the door. He seemed lost in his own world, much like he had been through most of the meeting.

"Can we ... can we talk for a minute?" he asked, his voice less solid than usual. It sounded like he was asking Corrine for something rather than her. She felt strange, her stomach tightening at those words.

Talk? About what? Why did you phrase it like that? Are you upset?

"Uh, yeah, sure. What did you need?" asked Ahna.

"I'd rather talk to you"—he glanced back toward Sticks—"in private. Can you meet me at the guard box in a bit? Maybe at sundown? I think that will be a better place."

You want me to come out there just to talk? Are you thinking about breaking up with me? Did I do something wrong? Oh god. What did I do? Was it the train thing? Maybe I shouldn't have sent you to do that . . .

"Ahna?" asked Scorcher. "That good with you?"

Ahna gulped. "Yeah, sure. No problem. Meet at guard box, got it," she said, nodding as though her head were a buoy in an ocean.

The corners of his mouth traveled upward slightly before he turned to exit the room. She noticed that Sticks had disappeared, which was strange given that she hadn't heard him leave.

In the silence that arrived with their departure, she let out a sigh. Things were getting bigger, more involved—not only in the situation with the facility, but in her personal life, too. Sarah had mentioned to her that when boys said they needed to talk, it wasn't good. She didn't want things to get worse; she wanted them to get better. Talking was bound to lead to trouble, so she did what any respectful person would do in a stressful situation regarding a close relationship: she avoided it.

AHNA MEANDERED THROUGH the corridors, cries from the hospital wing sporadically sailing through the air. The Gray Wolves had seemed like they would be so helpful in the cause, and many of them were, but they had a lot of kids in worse shape than she had originally realized. It was always so rough to see their faces, hear their cries. Many of them had known life as merely a pain-filled journey toward death. So many diseases, disabilities, and ailments, and no treatments or cures. When she'd heard Seemore talk about the possibility of such things, she'd been filled with hope, ambition, and drive. Her balloon of hope had been deflated entirely upon discovery of the reality of the country.

During their travels, she had searched for a sign that something, anything was improving. She had found no such thing.

What she had found were ruins, shells of buildings that had once housed hundreds of people reduced to rubble. Animals had taken up inside abandoned areas, some more dangerous now than before the war. Marie had told her it was because of something called radiation. Apparently, they used to use radiation on people before the war, too, as a sort of treatment. Ahna couldn't imagine how, given the number of deformed animals she'd seen and eaten the past couple months.

Her stomach growled at the memory of food, regardless of the fact that it had been barely edible.

We need to find more food and supplies. If I'm hungry, those who are sick are probably starving.

Ahna stopped in front of the scanner, her eyes fixated on the small box attached to the wall. She'd seen them before, but they hadn't seemed important. They'd served as a way to access a door, nothing more. Until now.

Ahna stared at her hand, her eyes trailing the river of calluses on her palm. Each one held a story of resilience, perseverance, and strength. Her hands had been so soft and clean before she'd been Rejected. She hadn't used weapons, dug into the earth, or carried rough wood inside the facility. She hadn't used her left hand for literally everything before. She recalled something Corrine had told her one day while patching up a gash on her finger. *Hands of the oppressed plant the seeds watered by their oppressors so that their children may reap their reward.*

She stepped up to the scanner, her heart rate rapidly increasing as she moved closer. She let out a long sigh before placing her palm on the glass. The scanner buzzed as it read her data. The red light blinked three times before turning green.

"Partial DNA match. Biometric identification complete. Welcome, Doctor," said a voice through a speaker above the doorway, just as it had before.

It must be a mistake. Why would it—

"I thought you might be down here."

Ahna yanked her hand away from the scanner and spun around.

Sticks was standing in the doorway, one hand on his staff, a smirk on his face. What caught her attention, though, was his legs.

You're wearing braces again . . .

"I know, I know," said Sticks, moving toward her. "You don't have to stare. It's not like you haven't seen them before." He fumbled a bit before stopping next to her.

She could smell the scent of smoke as he neared. He must have been stoking the fire before coming down. She thought that maybe a piece of firewood had fallen on his leg or something. She was worried. She hadn't seen him in braces for months.

"Sorry, it's just—wait. What are you doing here?" asked Ahna.

"I knew you'd be here."

Ahna's eyes shot toward the floor, darting back and forth between her feet.

How did you know that? I didn't even know I'd be down here until I was. That's weird.

"What happened to your legs? Did you drop a piece of wood on them or something like that?" asked Ahna.

"Something like that." He pointed to the scanner. "You tried it again, didn't you? Wondering why it opened the door for us?"

Ahna nodded. "Must be a malfunction," she said. She clenched her hand into a fist, her nails digging slightly into her palm. Though it had been slightly painful originally, there were now small lines that had grown accustomed to their presence.

"It's working fine," said Sticks.

"Then why would it welcome me? Obviously, I'm not the doctor," said Ahna, a slight chuckle following.

Sticks raised his eyebrows. "It doesn't have to be a perfect match for the scan, just close enough."

Close enough? Why would it be close enough?

"What are saying, Sticks?" asked Ahna.

"You remember the letter you got on your birthday? The day of your Rejection?" asked Sticks.

Of course I remember that! I—

"How do you know about the letter?" asked Ahna.

Sticks smiled. "They put me in your old room while I was being held prisoner. Turns out, you aren't the greatest at hiding things."

"What does the letter have to do with this?" asked Ahna.

He was dancing around the point, and she didn't want to wait any longer. Besides, she had to go soon.

"I did some digging and put a few facts together. Conspiracy, mostly . . . until yesterday. When I put your hand on the scanner, I honestly had no idea if it would work. I just knew it would prove my theory one way or another. And it did," said Sticks.

"What facts? You're still not answering my questions, Sticks."

His eyes narrowed slightly before a smirk crept across his face again.

"You're different, Ahna. Haven't you realized that by now?"

"No different than most people here. We're all a little different."

Sticks shook his head. "No, Ahna, we're not. Not like you. I remember you telling me that there had to be a reason Dean Tipper hated you, more than just the nameplate thing, right?"

Ahna nodded.

"Well, based on everything else I knew, the stories I'd heard from Seemore, and the letter, it just made sense."

"What did?" asked Ahna.

"You weren't a normal Replacement, Ahna. In fact, you weren't a Replacement at all. You were an original. That's probably why Dean Tipper hated you so much."

This is insane. You're insane.

"What do mean by original?"

You were created by the doctor himself, from his DNA. Doctor Sundry is your biological father."

Ahna's heart skipped a beat, her thoughts buzzing inside her head like a hive of bees.

Surely, Sticks had made a mistake. Surely, he had made all that up. She didn't have a father. She was a Replacement, just like everyone else. She felt different at times, sure, but everyone was different in their own way. Then again, Sticks didn't usually lie to her. He was rough around the edges, had almost killed her when they'd first met, and was a terrible teacher when it came to sparring, but the one thing he wasn't was a liar.

"I don't understand," said Ahna, her words barely escaping her mouth. "What does all this mean?"

Sticks gestured toward the hallway. "I'll explain it as best I can again, but let's walk. I need to move around a bit. You good for that?"

So much to process. I need to know more.

Ahna nodded. "Lead the way."

Chapter Fifteen
Sticks

"How long have you known?" asked Ahna.

I never really knew, just had a hunch.

"A while," Sticks said. "Just didn't have a chance to prove it until now."

He led Ahna down a hallway he'd not yet been down. Lights flickered above, casting shadows of the debris ahead. Damaged desks, busted pipes, and fragments of the wall were piled in a semiblockade in front of them. It looked too organized to have fallen there or to have been placed by the Wallers. It was thought-out, meticulous, strategic.

Why would they block this hallway? What were they protecting?

Sticks stopped, holding a palm in the air toward Ahna. "Hold up."

"What is it?" asked Ahna. She readied her staff.

He admired her shorter staff, with its ornate designs and similarity to his own. Her ability to wield it so readily and her skill with it during battles had proven useful beyond his expectations. He envied her sometimes. If she'd had both her hands, she would've proven even more deadly. That would never happen, though; he knew that. She had been appalled at the mention of him building her a bionic hand; she wouldn't hear the idea fully and didn't want it mentioned again. He wouldn't force it, but after being given the ability to use his legs for the first time, he'd witnessed what a difference it could make. He stared at his braces, a slight burst of air escaping his nose as he chuckled to himself.

You know, I don't want you either . . .

Sticks edged closer to the barricade of debris. Nearing it, he smelled them before he saw them. It was as though his nose had smacked him in the face attempting to escape from the pungent odor pervading the air.

"Ugh!"

His face squished as he held his nose and stumbled backward. One of his braces caught on a broken pipe and sent him tumbling toward the floor. He felt Ahna's hand slip under his arm. As her staff hit the metal floor, he felt her other arm against him, bracing his back. He let out a small sigh of relief from not face-planting on the metal floor.

Stupid braces. What's wrong with me? Really? Now? In front of—

"You okay?" asked Ahna, her worried eyes darting between his.

"Yeah," he said, grunting as he recovered his balance. "Uh, thanks."

Ahna's face contorted slightly, accentuating a small dimple he had never noticed.

"What is that?" she asked, covering her nose with her arm.

"Elite," said Sticks. "But don't worry, they're dead."

They both laughed a bit before he walked back toward the barricade.

"What are you doing?" asked Ahna.

What does it look like?

"We need to get past here."

"Why?"

"They died protecting something," said Sticks. "Don't you wanna see what?"

He gripped the side of one of the broken desks and pulled, the barricade barely budging. It wasn't going to be easy, but he hoped whatever lay beyond would be worth it. If not, at least he wasn't alone.

ANOTHER SCANNER WAS the only thing keeping them from getting through a final doorway, this time a double-door system. Cracked glass hung like a spiderweb between the portholes of the doors. They were cloudy, as though someone had painted over them, a dark gray film blurring their view of what lay beyond.

"What are you waiting for?" asked Sticks.

Ahna tilted her head slightly, her eyebrows moving in opposite directions. It was kinda cute when she got confused; it didn't happen that often anymore. Also, it reminded him of Rollin whenever he would blabber on about the latest invention he was working on or about some interesting fact that went over her head.

Rollin had been smart; she just hadn't seemed to care about the technology and science stuff. Not like him. But she'd always listened. She'd even asked questions to make him think she was interested. He'd later realized she did that so that she could hear him talk more about whatever thing it was he was passionate about that day. She'd told him so one night before Ahna had showed up. Before they'd started to rebel. Before—

Before everything changed.

"Your hand," said Sticks, returning to the moment. "Or did you forget you can open most any door inside here?" He laughed.

"Oh, yeah," Ahna replied, chuckling. "I keep forgetting."

She placed her palm on the scanner, which did its usual routine before opening the double doors. Beyond the doors was a large open space outlined by suits of armor and weaponry.

Yellow lights burned above them as they walked into the room. The walls were intact and barely damaged at all, it seemed. A white line separated the two halves of a large circle etched in the middle of the room. Chain-link fence ran along the edges of it, benches placed behind each side. Between the fencing and benches, Sticks noticed a thin transparent line that seemed to reflect the light from overhead.

Is that glass?

He walked over to the fencing and extended his hand, knocking on the invisible barrier. It felt like high-grade plastic but looked like glass. There were a few spots within the panel of plastic that splintered out like a spiderweb. Inside each web was a small bullet. Sticks's mouth hung open.

No way. This can stop bullets? That's—I mean, I knew they existed, but I've never seen one. It's so cool!

"Ahna, come over here! Look at this," said Sticks, gesturing to the plastic panel. He had never seen anything like it before, only heard stories. Sure, there was metal that could stop a bullet, but it would have to be really thick. This looked thin enough to break with his bare hands.

"What is it?" asked Ahna. She stopped near the fencing, then realized what he was pointing at. "Is that—"

"Nope, not glass. Plastic or something similar."

"Whoa."

"I know. Crazy, right?" said Sticks, tapping it with his staff.

He couldn't get over how genius it was. If they had been able to use something like it in Tent City, there would have been no way that anyone could have—

Oh, yeah . . .

He felt himself deflate slightly, as though someone had cut the string that was holding him upright. It had been days since he'd thought about that moment. Every time he did, it didn't feel right. It was almost like a dream, a nightmare. Some nights he awoke to damp blankets, his sweat staining the bed, his breath rapid and shallow. Many times he was able to wake up before it got too bad, but other times . . .

"Sticks? You okay?" asked Ahna.

He raised his head slightly, smirking.

"Of course. Just thinking."

"What about?"

Nothing. Everything.

A story he'd heard popped into his head.

"Did you know they used to have panels like this in schools?" he asked.

"What schools?"

"Prewar schools. You know, the ones that actually taught people like us with the other kids."

"Oh," said Ahna, her brow furrowing slightly. "Why did they have these? They look like something you'd see for the military or something."

"Right?" replied Sticks. "I don't know the whole story, but I heard they started putting them in classrooms between the door and the kids."

"Why?"

"To protect them—for defense."

"Defense? In a school? Weird," said Ahna. She shrugged, clearly done with that, and began scouring the remainder of the room, moving toward the edges. "You know, that's only the first thing we found. Think of what else we might find here."

He could hear the excitement in her voice as she bounded toward the large metal boxes that lined the wall opposite the doorway. He hurried to join her in case they ran into any more stray Wallers while searching. That was the last thing they needed, especially now that he was in an old pair of barely functioning braces.

The boxes were twice their size and had front hinges on either side. Sticks thought they looked familiar but couldn't place how or why.

"You think this will do something?" asked Ahna. Her hand hovered over a button at the top of a pedestal that stood next to the box on the end of the line.

"Worth a shot, right?" replied Sticks.

Everything was worth a shot now. They didn't have time to waste worrying about things, and if they took enough risks, they were bound to have something good from them eventually. At least, that was what he told himself every day.

The click of the button sounded like a bone snapping, causing Ahna to jump back after pressing it. A brief silence followed.

Sticks and Ahna exchanged a confused glance before a hiss of air sputtered in their direction. Metal roared at them as the boxes began to open, small sparks soaring from their hinges. Smoke billowed from the surrounding pipes. Ahna stepped back, stumbling a bit. What lay at her feet looked like a prewar electronic device. She picked it up and gave it to Sticks.

"What do you think this is?" she asked.

Sticks took it, examining it further.

It was rectangular and had buttons on one side. A chip in the casing on one of the corners revealed a strand of wiring within. Its front side had small holes all over, something that reminded Sticks of those he'd seen in the ceiling of the other facility.

Is this a speaker?

He pressed a bunch of the buttons, but that did nothing. He hit the one on the very end, which was slightly bigger than the rest. Static played from the device, now accompanied by the cacophony of clinking cogs and grinding gears. Barraged by the smoke and noise, Sticks and Ahna retreated from their positions.

Once they were far enough back, they stood side by side, their eyes opening in sync with the boxes in front of them. Dark smoke billowed from the teeth of the boxes, as though they were metal beasts regurgitating their prey—if they preferred their prey in a glass tube and covered in goo.

There were five tubes in total. Each of them had a distinct green glow that Sticks recognized from the lab he'd been taken to upon his capture within the Deliverance facility—all except the third tube, which was empty and broken. A bloodstained vignette outlined the shattered glass of the tube, no light within.

The rest of them were on, and bubbles bounced around inside the tubes as electricity flowed through the connected pipes. The bodies inside bobbed slowly up and down. Something was off, though. Unlike the bodies in the tubes he'd seen in the lab before, there were no differences whatsoever between these. In fact, they all looked . . . identical.

The static transitioned into the voice of a man, but Sticks couldn't discern his age. What he did notice was that the voice was eerily familiar.

"H-hello," he said. His voice was shaky but stern in tone. "If you have opened these, that must mean one of two things. One, we successfully avoided the seemingly inevitable catastrophic annihilation that comes with war. Or two, I'm long dead, and this is playing because you are a rat that has managed to learn how to press buttons. I'm going to speak as though it's the first. As you know, we tend to think positively in stressful situations. Calms us."

We? Us?

"Where was I? Oh, yes. Should the subjects remain in good shape, you must continue the work. It is imperative. One of the subjects, Subject Three, is doing exceptionally well. The reason is unclear, but if we can figure that out, it could be our key to moving forward. We are on the brink of a breakthrough; I can feel it." A siren erupted in the background of the recording. "There isn't much time to explain, but if you are able to continue, please do. I know the pressure from the president and the dean is weighing on you. I know they said the facility is doing great things and that project Deliverance will help all of humanity, but they're lying. I can't prove it, but something isn't right. That's why I have done this. That's why we must push through and finish our task.

We must finish it before it gets into the wrong hands. I think if we are able to do that, then we may be able to sa—"

A gunshot echoed through the room from the device, followed by a howl of pain. The man on the recording must have dropped the recording device to the ground afterward because everything became more difficult to understand. There was a stampede of footsteps and murmurs of voices before another gunshot. Everything drowned in the sea of sirens until static returned. Then . . . silence.

Ahna and Sticks stared at each other, then at the tubes in front of them. Sticks felt his body relax as the sound of the water in the tubes soothed his mind. Their constant bubbling reminded him of the creek that flowed by Tent City. He'd spent many days resting his legs while listening to the creek and the music of the birds overhead. He had never realized how simple times were then. It had been only months ago but felt like another life—a life to which he longed to return.

"What does all that mean?" asked Ahna. Her words brought him back from the warm woods of Tent City, back to the cold chrome room. She was looking at the device and the tubes, waiting for his response. She was smart and usually knew what she wanted to do, so it was weird that she'd asked him for his opinion on the matter. It was nice to be asked.

His mind was busy, his thoughts a blizzard on the verge of an avalanche. He pushed those thoughts to the back of his mind and took a deep breath, focusing on the task at hand. "It means this is only the tip of the iceberg," he said. "It means there's more to this plan than us."

Ahna's eyes widened. "We need to figure out the rest of the plan. But how?"

"We need to look for some sort of information, documents or files, something. Maybe a computer? I don't know what, but there's definitely more here. There's gotta be. If they left this behind, there's no telling what else we could uncover."

Ahna nodded and narrowed her eyes, a smirk crossing her face. Sticks could tell she was excited. With her, excitement could be dangerous.

"Let's get looking then."

Ahna bounded away, scouring the desks and debris scattered around the space. Sticks watched as she flung large pieces of metal and other scraps aside, her eyes darting from one place to the next. It was like watching a young deer playing in the woods after discovering the leaves in fall. He chuckled before pocketing the device still in his hand.

If I were going to hide something important, something worth protecting, where would I hide it?

There were few places within the room that hadn't been overturned by Wallers, rats, or Ahna. He scanned the walls, floor, and ceiling, hoping to spot an abnormality in their design. He thought there may be something behind a panel or hidden away.

If I were gonna hide something, that's what I'd do.

He didn't make it far in his search before Ahna called out.

"Sticks! Come quick."

His knee twitched at the sudden movement, causing a slight pain to shoot through his leg. He winced but pushed through it.

When he approached Ahna, she didn't appear injured.

"What? What's wrong?" asked Sticks. His elbow was already bent, and he was ready to jab something with his staff at the first sign of trouble.

"Look!" said Ahna, flashing a remote in his face. "What do you think this is?"

How do you not know what so many things are? Didn't they teach you anything?

"It's a remote of some kind," said Sticks.

"What does it do?"

"Let me see it," said Sticks, holding out his hand.

Ahna dropped the remote in his palm. He examined it and pressed a few of the buttons.

"Nothing, apparently." He tossed it back to her. Ahna caught it easily. Her agility was improving. He felt a sense of jealousy creep up. "Keep looking. And if you find any cables or pipes that still look functional, try to—"

That's it. The pipes.

"Sticks?" asked Ahna, but he was already walking away from her.

As he approached the tubes, he observed their setup. Each tube was stationed in its own base and connected to the inner frame of the box. Inside, he could see the bubbles coming from the bottom of the liquid. Following the pipe from the bottom and up the back of the tube, he could see where the pipe connected. From there, he followed it down the side of the wall until it disappeared through the wall.

"What are you looking at?" asked Ahna, now closer to him.

Sticks ignored her and hurried to the place in the wall where the pipe entered. At either side of the pipe, about two feet on both sides, were thin lines that continued to the floor. Sticks wedged the point of his staff into the line of the metal and pried it open. A sliver of light escaped through the crack.

"We're looking at a door," said Sticks, smiling. "Now help me open it."

Ahna crammed her staff into the other side of the metal panel, and they pushed in sync.

"All right," said Sticks. "On the count of three. One, two, three!"

As they put their body weight into their staffs, screws shot out from the wall like bullets, falling to the floor behind them. The panel creaked as it started to fall toward them. Sticks tried to get out of the way, but his staff got caught on part of the remaining wall. Ahna plowed into him from the side, sending them both to the floor. The metal panel fell just inches away from them, clanging loudly. He could feel the vibrations before it settled.

"You okay?" asked Ahna. She was already returning to her feet.

"Yeah," replied Sticks. He struggled to get up. His staff was still in the new doorway. Ahna extended her hand to him. He let out a sigh before taking her hand and getting to his feet. "Thanks."

"No problem," said Ahna. She jumped onto the metal panel and picked up his staff, tossing it to him. "Catch."

Sticks caught the staff, then used it to walk over the panel and into the room they'd uncovered.

That's it?

He had expected to find something a bit more extravagant, more mysterious. Instead, there were only a few desks, most of which had been stripped of their drawers, each with its own computer, and piles of paper strewn along the floor. At the far end of the room was a large computer, not unlike the one upstairs in the control room. Unfortunately, its screen was bashed in. A rusty pipe protruded from within, the obvious cause of the damage.

"Why would they hide this? It's just a bunch of computers," said Ahna. She started clicking the buttons on the keyboards of each one. "A bunch of broken computers."

Yeah. Why would they hide this?

"Hey, check it out!" said Ahna. He heard the clicking of the keyboard before he approached.

"What'd you find?" asked Sticks.

"Messages. A lot of messages."

"Who from?"

"A bunch of people. Looks like some of them are from before, then there's a gap of a bunch of years, then they start again. The weird thing is, they're all to the same person."

"Who?"

He didn't have to wait for her answer because he spotted the name on the screen. Multiple messages from multiple different years, some as far back as before the war. It seemed impossible, but he knew what he saw was real. All the messages were addressed to the man who had been on the recording.

Dr. Sundry.

Chapter Sixteen
Felan

Felan's eyes darted side to side, like those of a cheetah on the prowl. While the coast seemed clear, she strolled toward the boxes that sat at the end of the cafeteria line. They were usually closed, but someone had left one cracked. Unlocked.

Sweet.

Taking one last glance around the room, she slipped her hand into the box and retrieved a stick of meat before putting it in her pocket. She could feel her stomach rumble at the thought of devouring it as soon as she was out of the facility. Hunger was becoming a normal feeling, but she didn't want to risk getting stuck in the snow with nothing to eat. After the last time, she didn't like to take any chances.

Felan smiled as she stuck her hand back into the box. She needed to get as much as she could before anyone noticed. Lucky for her, nobody was around.

"What are you doing?"

Marie. Shoot.

"Hey," she said, the word lingering as she tried to concoct an answer. "I'm . . . going to the tower. It's, uh . . . part of the plan."

That's the truth, so it's fine.

"Was stealing part of the plan, too?"

"I don't know what you're talking about," said Felan, shrugging. She did all she could to act confused, but she was a hunter, not an actress.

"Come on, Felan. I know you better than anyone. I know you're lying. Besides, I saw you take it."

"If you saw me take it, then why did you ask?"

"I wanted to see if you'd tell me the truth first," said Marie. "Good to know I can't expect that. Not that I did anyway."

Felan pursed her lips, exhaling through her nose.

"Fine. Yeah, I took a meat stick from the box," she said. Her voice then sped up. "But I missed dinner last night, and I'm starving. Besides, I'm gonna miss breakfast and don't know if I'll be back in time for lunch, so I wanted to make sure I was equipped. That okay with you?"

Marie took a moment before nodding.

"Okay, fine. Next time you need something, though, just ask me. You know I'll give it to you."

Felan scoffed. "As long as I give you something in return, you mean?"

Marie's eyes widened, her mouth opening as though she were going to yell, but she quickly closed it, staying silent. Then her calm demeanor returned. "Just don't do it again, okay?"

"Got it, boss," said Felan. She started toward the exit.

"Hey," said Marie.

Felan turned, waiting for her to say whatever it was she needed so that she could finally get going. "What?"

"Stop by the hospital wing next time you're able to. I want to make sure you're not going to lose your stuffing," she said, chuckling slightly at her own joke.

Felan nodded. "Sure."

She needed to go, to get to the tower and back before it got too late or the path was blocked or something, but she couldn't let herself leave before making sure she hadn't burned her only bridge. She turned back toward Marie.

"Thanks again for the grub . . . and not snitching," she said, her voice barely audible.

"Like you told me a long time ago: snitches get stitches," said Marie. "We don't have any stitches to spare." She chuckled.

Felan smiled slightly before turning back toward the gate. If she was going to die out there, at least she knew she hadn't completely lost a friend.

Felan pulled up her hood as she stepped out of the door into the biting cold of the morning.

ICE-COLD WATER SPLASHED against her face, shocking her body awake. Before she took her first breath of the morning, she felt the pain. Chains rattled, pulling her back toward the wall as she tried to stand. Coarse brick grated her already scarred back, and a laugh echoed through the room as she winced in pain. A tear streaked down her dirty face, her vision cloudy. But she didn't need clear vision to recognize her captor. His face, his voice, his . . . everything would remain burned into her memory forever. He was a scar only she could see.

"Time to wake up, girl," he said, pouring another bucket of cold water on her.

The smell of fish and trash that accompanied the nearby river now clung to her body, causing her to feel nauseous. She'd had noth-

ing to eat for days, though, so she wasn't even sure she could purge anything more from her body.

Felan spat what little water had gotten into her mouth back at the man in front of her. As soon as a drop hit his shoe, she felt his hand land against her cheek.

"I guess you're awake then, huh?" he said, laughing and rubbing his hands together. "I'm excited for today. Aren't you?"

Felan shook her head, though she couldn't tell if it was actually moving or if she was only imagining it. Her eyes were level with the whip that hung on his waist, the metal tips on the end stained from use. She shuddered at the thought.

"Why not? You've been such a big help so far. This will only further demonstrate that. Besides, we have a feeling that this could be the day for discovery. Because of you, we can improve the future children."

Every ounce of energy had vanished from her body, and nothing felt real. Even the air around her felt thin, her vision still hazy, as though she were in the clouds. Felan tried to speak, but it came out as nothing more than a grunt.

The man laughed.

"Don't worry. We'll make sure you're remembered for your contribution to the success of our project. As you know, sacrifice births greatness." He clapped his hands before smiling. "Let's get you cleaned up for your big day."

He pulled out a ring of keys, and she heard the metal click before her arms dropped to her sides like two heavy pieces of rope. He then unlocked the clasps around her ankles. The sudden relief from the pressure was amazing. Air passed over parts of her skin she'd not seen in forever. But when she looked at the spots where the clasps *had been, she wished she hadn't. She turned her attention away, back to the man.*

His back was turned while he searched through a bag on the side of the room. Her eyes darted between him and the door, her breathing becoming rapid. The door was open for the first time in days. If she was going to escape, this was the moment. She couldn't afford to wait for another chance.

Adrenaline pumped through her veins as she pushed herself up from the ground. She used every bit of strength she had to get up, feeling each joint pop as she stood, but she had done it. All she had to do was make it through the door. If she could do that, she would be free. She started toward the doorway, pushing through the exhaustion and pain. Only a few more steps. A few more steps, and—

She felt the familiar sting of the whip before she heard the crack. Her knees buckled, and she met the metal floor with her face. Her body went numb, but she heard the crack of the whip at least a couple more times, accompanied by his screaming. She rolled over enough to look at him one last time as he pulled back his whip. As he flicked it forward, she shut her eyes, waiting for it to strike.

A loud crack echoed through the room, her ears ringing from the sound. Her eyes shot open to see the man stumble backward, the whip slip from his grip, the metal tips tapping against the floor. His eyes widened as he tried to speak before falling back against the brick wall. His body slumped down, chains on either side, in the exact spot where she'd been living for months. Seeing him lying there sent tears streaming down her face.

A warm hand gripped her shoulder. She tried to pull away but had no energy left to fight.

It was a woman of unknown age. She had a revolver on her hip and a band of bullets across her torso. Her curly black hair was bundled in a tattered bloodred bandana. Various bits of armor lay mismatched across her body, a walking collection of trophies from downed foes. She smiled as she extended her hand out toward Felan.

"Don't worry, kid. I've got ya."

Felan took her hand, leaning on her for support as she stood upright. The woman picked her up and carried her past the motionless bodies in the hallway, through rooms she'd never seen, and out of the building—out into the world. Sunlight hit her skin for the first time in months, and she felt . . . free. She smiled, then breathed in her first breath of her new life.

A CLOUD FORMED IN FRONT of her face as she exhaled, the trees dancing in the wind around her. Her hands finally regained their feeling as she released her grip from the nearby branch, the blood pumping back into her fingers. The pain had finally subsided enough to allow her to continue, but if it returned as frequently as it had been the past month, then the trip was going to take much longer than expected.

Trudging through the snow, Felan dodged each low-hanging branch on her way up the mountainside. Though faint, she could hear the sound and murmur from below. The facility was already hard at work, its hive of worker bees constantly buzzing around. She wanted to run in and gun them all down, take the data she needed, and get out. Obviously, that was not how it would go down, but she liked to imagine it could.

The tower's important. At least, it better be. If not, I'm gonna take advantage of my time away from everything.

Her stomach rumbled.

Just wish I'd gotten more before Marie caught me.

The thought of Marie made her uncomfortable. She pushed her from her mind, focusing on the task at hand. Each minute she wasted out in the snow was another minute closer to dark. With the number of Wallers they had seen before, she didn't want to risk being alone against a horde. If the horde didn't kill her, something else would do it for them. She imagined freezing to death would be the easiest way to go, though she wasn't keen to find out.

As she stepped into the clearing, the silhouette of the tower blocked the sun. It stood at least thirty feet tall, a large round ball near the top of a skinny body. It almost reminded her of a boy she had met a long time ago, lanky with a big head. That made her chuckle.

Felan approached the bottom of the tower and peered upward at the head, craning her neck to see it fully. A nearby ladder had given her hope that she would get to the round building at the top easily. Unfortunately, she was wrong. The ladder had been torn down almost completely, with only remnants remaining. Because of that, she was going to have to climb the side of the tower.

She wasn't known for her climbing, but she could manage. That wasn't what bothered her, though. She tightened the strap that ran across her body so that her rifle clung to her back. After a deep inhale and a mumbled prayer, her fingers wrapped around the cold metal body.

Each time she had to move a hand, her heart skipped. Ice and snow covered most of it, which made for a more difficult climb. She was careful to avoid the pieces of metal that broke formation, the jagged pieces that came toward her like striking snakes. The last thing she needed was to impale herself on one of them, or worse . . .

She glanced down.

Oh god . . .

The thumping in her chest echoed in her ears like a war drum. Her fingers tightened around the pipes, her body going stiff, paralyzed. She tried to do something, anything to fight it, but nothing could pry her attention from the vision of seeing her body fall through the air onto the icy rocks below. A sudden gust of wind sailed through the clearing, and she felt the tower sway.

No. No, no, no. Not today. Not like this. This can't be how it happens.

As the wind continued, Felan tried to calm herself as best she could.

Inhale . . .

Exhale . . .

Once she felt like she could continue, she turned her attention to the head of the tower. Gritting her teeth, she dug her foot into an intersection of pipes and pushed herself upward. She focused only on the pipe ahead. There was nothing but her and the pipes above. With every step up, she released a breath, pulling in another as she prepared for the next. She moved in a rhythm, as though she were a machine.

Snow battered down on her, but the amount that hit her face decreased as she neared the top. As she saw the lip of the head, she smiled, but not for long. She wouldn't celebrate until she was inside, safe. Felan pushed herself forward. There were only a few pipes left to grasp. Then only the lip.

She reached up to grab it, relieved that she had made it up without falling, happy to know she wasn't a pile of broken bones on the mountain snow. But instead of a metal floor, as she'd expected, she felt something more like leather. No, not leather. Cold, stiff fingers.

She flung herself away from whoever or whatever was trying to grab her, her feet slipping. Time slowed as she flung her arms to grab something to keep from falling. Her eyes were wide with terror, no breath entering her body. The snow seemed to freeze in place as she tumbled down. It seemed as though all the sound had been removed from the world, including her own screams. As her body hit one of the pipes, she heard a small pop, then felt herself turn. She was headed straight toward the ground face-first. She awaited her fate, happy to know she hadn't died without making things right. Then the world stopped its approach. The wind returned, and with it the numbing cold. Halfway down the tower, her body hung from a pipe by her rifle strap. She cried tears of relief, her screams still echoing around her.

She tugged at the strap, loosening its grip around her neck just enough to allow her to breathe. After she caught her breath, she laughed. It was the only thing she could do. Why, she had no idea. She patted the butt of the rifle and smiled.

"Attagirl," she said, chuckling again.

Once she felt herself returning to normal, she looked up toward the head of the tower again, expecting to see someone peering back down at her. The owner of the hand must have been curious to see her fall, right? But there was no one there. It was as clear and quiet as it had been. That struck her as weird.

If there's no one up there, then whose hand was that? Or was I just imagining things? I guess there's only one way to find out. Besides, I can't go back to the group and tell them that I gave up because of some stupid imaginary hand. They'll never think of me the same way again.

After building up the courage to climb the second half of the tower for a second time, she continued upward. This time was much easier because she had indentions in the snow from her previous path to follow. She was still wary of whatever had touched her, but she had no plans of letting go again. If she had to, she would kill whatever it was for causing her to almost die.

As she neared the top for the second time, she yanked a piece of ice from one of the nearby pipes. She counted to three, then tossed it up into the opening of the shack. It hit something before rolling around on the metal floor. She waited a moment for whatever was up there to react, but there was nothing. After waiting a moment longer, she pushed herself up and over the lip into the building.

As she lay on the floor, finally inside, her eyes locked with another pair. She gasped before realizing that the eyes staring at her never blinked. In fact, they probably hadn't blinked in years. She got up from the floor and dusted the snow from her jacket. The body on the floor looked as though it were frozen in place, its hand conveniently right at the edge of the opening where she'd entered. She let out a sigh.

"You really got me, man, you know that?" she said, laughing as she shook her head.

Peering around the inside of the building, she figured it wasn't much larger than the control room back at their facility. Before doing anything more, though, she rolled the body out of the way with her foot and closed the door that was lodged behind it. It was almost immediately warmer and much quieter. She could finally think. She searched for anything useful, hoping to find something that would justify almost losing her life.

A bookshelf against the wall caught her attention as light reflected off a small metal box. When she picked it up, there was a clinging inside. The cover of the box was heavily obscured by dust and grime. Felan wiped it away with the sleeve of her jacket and stared at the drawing of a large gray animal on the front, a man with a rifle perched with one leg on the animal, a wide grin across his stupid face.

"Tranquilizer bullets," Felan read aloud. "Guaranteed to make your hunt easier or your money back." Both *guaranteed* and *easier* were underlined, a line leading to a small message scratched on the side that said *open to interpretation*.

Below those words were smaller weird-looking words, almost like someone had been shaking as they wrote them. Felan continued reading aloud, sounding out what she didn't understand right away.

"The company is not liable for the use of their bullets on animals smaller than el-i-pa-hants, including humans."

Felan narrowed her eyes.

What in the world is an el-i-pa-hant?

She put the half-full box into her bag before continuing toward the table of wires and debris.

"Whoa."

Wires were strewn across a variety of computers and other equipment on a table that spanned the width of the room, a large window above it. She examined the materials on the table, moving the pile of wires out of the way as best she could before spotting it.

A microphone? Is this—

Felan rummaged through the equipment until she came across the body the mic was attached to and smiled.

A radio. A real-life radio. Cool.

She spent a few minutes untangling the wires and figuring out which one connected to which device. After she got that out of the way, she flipped the switch on the box. Nothing. She flipped it back and forth again, thinking that would change the outcome. When it didn't, she ran her fingers along the wires from the back of the unit and followed them to the end.

Wow. Really?

The plug was sitting on the floor directly below the outlet. She examined the outlet, making sure it looked like it wouldn't electrocute her, then hoped she was right as she plunged the plug into the holes.

After a sigh of relief, she returned to the box on the table.

"You'd better work now, okay? I didn't climb up this stupid tower for nothin.'"

She flipped the switch. Nothing.

"Ugh!"

Felan cried out before punching the wall next to her. She winced, realizing her stupidity. As she looked at the wall she had hit, she noticed a light switch in the off position. Her eyes narrowed. After massaging her injured hand, she reached to flick the switch on. Once she did, she was surrounded by lights and sounds.

Who says anger doesn't get things done?

The purr of the electronics coming to life filled her with delight, and she smiled wide.

Static buzzed in the box, a collection of lines and numbers illuminated within the rectangle on the front. Success. She found the dial on the side of the box and the button on the body of the mic and did what she could remember to make it work. She had to search for another voice, cut through the static. That turned out to take longer than she'd expected.

While she listened for any sort of change in the static, she looked out the window at the trees below. Just beyond the line of trees, she could see the facility and part of the train. Seeing the train caused her heartrate to spike.

If we could steal that, we could ride it all the way out West. Hopefully the Railroad is still there. If we make it to them, maybe we'll have a chance. Maybe I'll have a chance.

She turned the dial until the static cut off and a sound played through the box. It was some kind of beeping, the length of each one changing slightly and at random intervals. She had no idea what it meant, but Wick might. She listened to it for a moment, imitating it as best she could, attempting to sing back what little she could remember.

"I sound so dumb," she said, laughing at herself. "But maybe it means something. It has to."

She opened the door, the snow blowing inside the room. Staring down at the pipes below, she gulped. Lying on her stomach, she inched out of the opening until she felt her foot touch the pipe below. After she put her weight onto it and didn't fall, she relaxed. One foot after the other, she descended the tower, singing the notes from the radio over and over. She couldn't risk forgetting them, not if it meant saving herself and the others. Of course, she had to make it back to the others first, make it down without falling.

Focus, Felan. You've got this.

She glanced at the ground below, gasping as her grip tightened around the pipes. She gulped.

Just don't look down.

Chapter Seventeen
Scorcher

"You all right, man? Ya look tired," said Vincent as a set of armor swallowed him whole. His hair sprung through the opening like the top of a carrot in spring.

"I'm good, bud. It's nothing," replied Scorcher.

Like usual. Everyone else gets her attention, and I get . . . nothing.

"Well, maybe you can sleep on the ride there," said Vincent.

Scorcher's brows rose. "Ride? We're walking to the facility, Vincent."

Vincent sighed. "But why? We have the carts and horses."

"And they will hear our carts and horses from a mile away. So we gotta walk. Got it?"

"Got it."

"Good. Now hurry up and finish getting ready. I gotta check on the rest of the group. When you're done, meet us at the front, okay?"

Vincent nodded before attempting to force himself into a tight pair of armored pants. Scorcher chuckled and then exited their room, heading toward the main gate.

It was early enough in the day that not everyone had gotten out of bed yet. Coughs and moans were as frequent as ever, though, and that wasn't bound to change anytime soon unless they were able to gather supplies on their mission. He didn't expect that to happen. Then again, he had no idea what to expect. The facility was far enough away that it would take them a while to get there but close enough that they could walk without worrying of tiring themselves too badly. Walking for months helped in that a bit, too.

Near the front gate, Scorcher spotted the others: two Gray Wolves and Sarah.

Sarah volunteering for the mission would have surprised him when they'd first met. After using a machete to cut through a small horde a couple weeks ago, though, she'd proved herself useful. Just as long as she didn't use her new skills to hurt him if he and Ahna ever broke up.

I wonder what she's up to . . .

"Hey, Scorcher," said Sarah. "You didn't sleep at all last night, did you?"

Why does everyone want to know how I did or didn't sleep?

"I'm good, thanks. You ready?" he asked.

Sarah flashed a knife at him, smiling. "Yep. Ahna even let me borrow the knife she snatched off that guy back in Kentucky. The custom wooden handle should make it easier to slash some Elite throats."

She slashed through the air, showcasing her excitement. The two behind her backed away quickly, which Scorcher thought was a smart move. She may have killed a few Wallers, but she wasn't the least clumsy person in the group. He didn't want anybody losing a limb. The hospital was already full.

"What about you two?" Scorcher asked the Gray Wolves.

They both nodded as they voiced their readiness. Each was wearing a full set of leather-and-fur armor, the emblem of the wolf on the breastplate. In addition to the armor, they both wore a helmet, which was unusual, but he understood the need for it. He could've used one himself, but he didn't like the feel of it. Besides, he didn't want to mess up his hair. If there was one thing he loved about his appearance, it was his hair.

"Okay, good," said Scorcher. "You know, it's hard to tell who you are with the helmets on," he added, chuckling, hoping to cover up the fact that he was unsure to whom he was talking.

"We get that a lot," said one.

"True, Baz. That's why I always keep mine on," the other said.

"Me too, Taz!"

They high-fived. Then their eyes widened as they pointed behind Scorcher, and they doubled over, laughing hysterically.

"What's everybody laughing at?"

Vincent had finally made it. Scorcher stifled a laugh when he saw him. His pants were barely up around his waist, and the breastplate was hanging around him despite the ties on both sides being as tight as they could go. Along with that, he had a blade on either side of his waist, and the shield on his back threatened to send him to the ground if he stood the wrong way.

"They're just being dumb," said Sarah.

"Yeah," said Scorcher, smiling and hoping that Vincent wouldn't catch on. "You sure you want to bring that shield, bud? It's a little much, don't you think?"

Vincent nodded. "Yep! Gotta be prepared for the worst, right? That's what you always say, anyway."

Man, I've gotta start watching what I say around you.

"You're not wrong, but I don't think you need all that stuff. We want to be quick and silent. I doubt all that gear will help you any. Don't you agree?"

"I guess," said Vincent, slouching slightly, his tone lowered and soft. "I'll go take it off and be right back."

He started back toward their room.

"I'll help you," said Sarah, smiling. She joined him on his walk back. "That okay with you?"

"Yeah," said Vincent, perking up. "Thanks."

Sarah flashed Scorcher a quick smile and a nod before escorting Vincent back to their room. Scorcher waited with Baz and Taz, listening to them tell each other jokes and laugh to themselves the entire time. Once Scorcher spotted Sarah and Vincent, he stood up and tightened his armor.

"That's enough jokes, guys," said Scorcher. The boys stopped laughing. "Grab your gear and quiet down."

They followed his orders. It was strange how quickly they went from goofball to soldier, but he wasn't going to complain. As long as they did what they were told.

"All good," said Sarah. She and Vincent stopped just short of the group.

"Great," said Scorcher. "Now listen up. This isn't a run-and-gun mission, okay? We're going to get as close as we can to the facility without getting spotted, gather what information we can on their security and firepower, and get out of there as quickly and safely as possible. Everybody understand?"

They all nodded.

"Good. Then make sure you use the bathroom and are back here in two minutes. We don't have time to waste if we want to make it back by dark."

The group dispersed. Scorcher sat down on the chair behind one of the barriers and carved into the handle of his bow. The design was getting close to how he wanted it but wasn't there yet. He'd been able to get some of it done the night before, thanks to Ahna not showing up, but not as much as he would have liked. He'd spent too much time creating scenarios for why she hadn't shown and what could have happened. It wasn't something he enjoyed doing, but he had no choice in how his mind worked. He could push the thoughts aside sometimes, but not then.

The group trickled back in, everyone in their gear.

"All right, everyone," said Scorcher, standing up. "Stay close and stay quiet. Follow that, and everything should go smoothly. Let's get going."

Scorcher stashed away his carving knife and thoughts of Ahna. Those things needed to disappear until the mission was over. Focus was crucial if he was to ensure the safe return of the group.

No risks this time. No changes. No repeats.

THE WAY DOWN THE MOUNTAIN trail had been less treacherous than he'd originally planned for, which was a pleasant surprise. Although, that added safety had unfortunately also added time to the journey. For most of the walk there, the group had moved as one, Scorcher the head of the snake, the rest flowing behind him in a fluid motion. Vincent had done surprisingly well given he wasn't usually stealthy either. Scorcher planned on making sure he knew how proud he was of him when they returned.

Poor kid needs all the encouragement he can get.

Sounds of the mountain slowly became drowned out by the cacophony within the facility. As they approached, he could tell it was much larger than the one they'd destroyed before. In fact, the walls of the facility stood at least twice as high as the ones he knew from Deliverance. The nearby trees seemed dwarfed by their existence. Reflections blinded him slightly, the sun now on the other side of the facility. They didn't have much time to observe—not that they needed it. It was evident as they arrived that it would be impossible to get inside the facility without major firepower.

Just a quick thing. Get in, look around, and get out. Nothing more.

Scorcher crouched low, then traced a quick circle in the air with his index finger. The others crouched low and fanned out, each moving behind a different tree. He hadn't expected any less, but it was nice to see things work the way he'd planned. He slid behind a large maple tree, his leather almost blending in with the brownish-gray bark.

I wonder if that's why the Gray Wolves use this type of armor.

Firs and thick-leafed maples were scattered around the facility. Trees like the fir offered much less coverage, but they were able to stay hidden enough to get within close range of the walls. The main entrance was not too far off, but Scorcher's hopes of getting in were dashed when he spotted their security system.

Automated turrets sat on both sides of the opening, their long barrels pointing right in his direction. The turrets seemed to be fitted with a glass-like shield in front, with a hole through which the barrel extended. In addition to the turrets, guards were stationed nearby, though they seemed to be out of their exoskeleton armor, assuming they had any. Scorcher didn't intend to find out. They each held a large gun and were outfitted in heavy armor similar to what he'd seen inside Deliverance, though they looked different. He got so caught up trying to take everything in that he almost didn't hear the murmur of voices coming from his right. They were somewhere near the tree line, which meant they were close enough to warrant caution.

Scorcher clicked his tongue, mimicking a squirrel. He'd figured out that the sound was unlikely to be suspicious after using it back near Deliverance. Squirrels used to roam freely all over the place, but he hadn't seen one in a long time. Watching them chase one another up and down trees and leap from limb to limb made for an afternoon of entertainment. Nothing was entertaining about that moment, though. After he gave the signal, he knew his friends had prepared their weapons, ready to strike. Scorcher waited as the voices approached them—close enough that he could hear two people talking. Though, it was difficult to tell what they were saying exactly because their voices distorted, as though they were speaking through a radio or megaphone. It became easier as they continued toward Scorcher's position.

"What do you think about the new orders?" asked a boy, probably close to Scorcher's age based on the tone.

"I just go wherever I'm told, man," replied a girl. "East, west, up, down, doesn't matter. If we were told to go to the moon or the bottom of the ocean, I'd go."

"I mean, yeah, same," he said. "But . . . don't you ever have thoughts of your own? Do you ever wonder if we're doing the right thing?"

"No," she said, her tone harsh. "Thinking for yourself is how you end up one of them. I don't plan on having some illness I can't get rid of, or worse. As for doing the right thing, Dean Tipper knows what he's doing. The man is a genius, and we're lucky that he decided to come here. We needed his guidance, especially with the new plan."

Their footsteps sounded much heavier than Scorcher would've expected from a couple soldiers. It almost sounded like there were at least ten of them. Peering around the edge of the tree, he realized why. They were wearing exoskeleton suits.

No way. How did they build more? And did they get bigger?

Scorcher thought back to the suits he'd seen and fought against inside Deliverance. Those had been big, but not compared to the ones these Elite wore. The new ones made the Elite stand almost ten feet tall. They were massive. It looked like they would've been able to rip the tree he was hiding behind up from its roots and throw it like a toothpick. He shuddered to think what they could do to him.

"You're right," replied the boy. "Sometimes it just feels like he's leading us right off a cliff or something, you know?"

"You just don't understand him," she said. "He defeated the Rejected in the East. Now we're going to do it here and, eventually, in the West. Once we have them all wiped out, the world can go back to the way it was before the war. Nobody will be sick or disfigured. We'll just be normal."

"What about the Wallers? We'll still have them to worry about," he said.

"No we won't, stupid. The Wallers can be wiped out easily once we take care of the Rejected. Dean Tipper already said that we have a weapon that will rid the entire country of them whenever we're done. After that—"

Crack.

"What was that?" the boy asked, stopping midstride to turn in Vincent's direction.

Vincent was shaking. His eyes were wide as he stared back at Scorcher, terrified. Scorcher's mind raced, weighing his options.

If I attack them, I'm dead. If I don't, they kill Vincent. If they find Vincent, they'll send out the rest for us. We can't let them find the others. They can't find us, or else—wait.

Scorcher picked up a rock that was lying next to his feet. He waited until the two Elite were closer to Vincent, their backs to him. He'd spotted a No Trespassing sign in an area near the wall. He hurled the rock as hard as he could at the sign, hoping it would hit. When the rock met the metal, it sent a clang across the clearing.

"Over there, toward the gate!" the girl said, pointing toward the sign.

The two Elite raced back toward the main gate, moving faster than he would have imagined the suits would allow. They shot something toward the sound, and a loud boom echoed into the trees. The main doorway into the facility opened, and Scorcher could see an armored Elite standing over two other Elite, one motionless and the other looking to be badly injured. The two outside in the bigger armor suits stomped around, and it looked like the Elite he had seen in the doorway had disappeared. This was his chance.

With that diversion, Scorcher clicked his tongue again, calling the others toward him. Once he knew they were going to be safe, he retreated from his spot near the gate, giving up his view of the Elite and the doorway that had just opened to the inside.

Rip.

Scorcher felt a stinging pain in his upper arm, his run halted briefly as turned to see his attacker. A piece of his shirt flapped in the wind, the bloodstained strip of fabric hanging from a sharp broken branch. He wanted to go back and grab it, but he didn't have time to retrieve it if they wanted to get out of there alive.

Once they were all together, they remained low and raced swiftly though the trees. When they were out of earshot, Scorcher glanced over his shoulder to ensure they hadn't been seen by the Elite. He breathed a sigh at their absence.

"I'm so sorry, Scorcher," Vincent said. "I didn't mean to—"

"Don't worry about it, bud," said Scorcher, cutting him off. "We have to go. Quick and quiet feet, everyone. It'll be getting dark soon, so stick close to me. Understood?"

They all nodded.

"Good. Let's go."

Scorcher moved past them, leading them back toward the facility, chasing his shadow through the trees as the sun set behind him.

Chapter Eighteen
D-72

D-72 grazed the stone in his pocket with his fingers as he hurried down the hall. His eyes darted away from any and all who looked in his direction. He couldn't risk being stopped—not if he wanted to follow through with his plan.

Dean Tipper's voice rang through the halls, but he couldn't focus on the message. His mind raced back to the day before, Dean Tipper hovering above him, ready to strike. He smacked himself in the head as he walked.

Get. Out. Of. My. Head.

It still hurt occasionally when he did that, but the pain was minimal compared to that of what was inside. He noticed another Elite staring at him as he walked, so he quickly lowered his hand back inside his pocket. The smooth body of the stone soothed his busy mind, allowing him to focus on what was ahead: the exit.

As he neared the doorway to the outside of the facility, he pressed the button on the side of his chest plate, and his armor tightened to fit his body. The suit had been specially made for him due to his larger size. Even though he'd been made in the same lab as the others, he was still different, and they never let him forget it.

Two Elite stood on either side of the doorway, one blocking his exit, hand outstretched.

"Hold it, soldier," he said. "Where are you going?"

Don't panic . . .

He swallowed, his throat suddenly dry.

"Outside," said D-72.

The Elite laughed.

"Not without special orders, you're not."

D-72's mind raced to come up with an excuse. The memory of yesterday flashed in his mind once again.

"Dean Tipper gave me orders. Secret mission."

The Elite looked at each other, whispering their conversation so he couldn't hear them. Finally, they stopped.

"We know about you and Dean Tipper," said the one. "Lieutenant said you told the dean quite a story. Did he enjoy his story time?"

They both laughed.

"Are you in love with those freaks so much that you made up a story to go find them? Are you a giant freak just looking for your own kind?"

They laughed again, tears coming from their eyes.

Their laughter cut through him, scratching into his brain. Every joke, every laugh, felt like they were attacking him. Heat radiated from his body, sweat forming on the edge of his hairline and under his armor. His breathing quickened, and the room blurred slightly.

"Yeah! D-72 wants to kiss one of those freaks and have stupid little Reject babies!"

"Just imagine how ugly and dumb they would be! They'd probably fail all their tests just like him!"

They high-fived each other, their laughter now a sea of muffled sounds. D-72's nostrils flared as his eyes narrowed. His mind went blank, and he saw himself as though he were watching it all from outside his body. The Elite had no time to react.

D-72 gripped their heads, one in each hand, and pulled them toward each other so fast that it was like cracking eggs. The crack echoed in the hall. As the guy stumbled backward, D-72 grabbed the other and slammed her into the wall. Her body slid down the wall into a slump, motionless. The other was trying to get up, but he kept falling, blood trickling from his ear. The Elite was almost able to grab his gun before D-72 pulled him by the ankle, his armor scraping against the metal floor. His fist connected with the Elite's face, and blood poured from his nose. He pulled his fist back again and thrust it toward the Elite, who was attempting to block the incoming attack.

Boom.

Vibrations echoed through the floor near the doorway, the door to the outside sliding open on its own. Two Elite in Mega Armor ran toward the entrance, weapons hot, searching for something. A burst of frozen air hit D-72, and he snapped back into the moment. The Elite was cowering on the floor below him, arms in front of his swollen face. D-72 shook as he realized what he had done.

What did I—I can't stay here. They'll kill me . . .

He stepped away from the cowering Elite, leaving him behind as he headed toward the exit. He couldn't look back—not unless he wanted to get caught. The two Elite outside were still looking for something but had made their way around the perimeter of the wall. This was his only chance at getting away before someone caught him. He took it.

He sprinted through the doorway, and snow pelted him in the face, blurring his vision. He didn't need to see much other than the trees in front of him, and that was what he focused on. The tall firs and pines that stretched across the mountainside were the only thing he knew anything about. Trees were big, tall, and strong, and nobody ever made fun of them for it. He liked that about them.

As he entered the forest, he wiped his face with his forearm and glanced over his shoulder. The Elite were heading back to their post. They hadn't seen him. He'd made it out.

Now . . . where is that facility?

He pulled the map from his pocket and held it out in front of him to get a better look. He tilted the map left and right, rotating it multiple times. There were few markings on it, and the ones that existed were faded at best. Sighing, he stuffed the folded map back into his pocket.

How am I supposed to—what's that?

A small strip of fabric was flying from a nearby branch. It looked like a small flag as it waved in the wind. Walking up to it, D-72 noticed a spatter of blood. He pulled the fabric off the branch, looking at it closely. It felt warm—too warm to have been out there that long, anyway. Then he spotted something moving through the trees in the distance. It was a person, and they were running away. He stuffed the fabric in his pocket with the map and took off in their direction.

"HOW MUCH LONGER?" ASKED the smallest of the group, his hair sticking up in all directions. He slouched as he walked at the rear of the group. The torch in his hand swayed as he struggled to keep it above him.

Yeah, how much longer?

"Just over the ridge, bud," said another boy, who was holding his own makeshift torch. A scarred pattern ran down one side of his face. He looked older, probably close to D-72's age, though it might have been the scarring that made D-72 think that. A large rip in his shirt revealed a cut on his shoulder.

You're the one who lost the fabric. What were you all doing so close to the facility?

"It woulda been sooner if we'd taken the shortcut I suggested," said one of the two with a helmet on.

"Yeah," said the other helmet kid. "Why didn't we take the shortcut?"

The taller boy turned to the pair.

"Because I'm not going to lead you down a path I've never been on and have us die, okay?" His voice was strained but firm. He was obviously the leader of their group.

"Fine, fine," said the pair, crossing their arms.

Crack.

"What was that?" asked the taller boy.

D-72 launched himself behind the nearest tree, holding his breath. He could hear the group walking toward him. He balled his fists, waiting for the moment to come.

"Must've been nothing," said one of the kids in the helmets.

"Yeah," said the boy after a moment, "I guess so. Let's get moving. We don't want to freeze to death before we get back."

The light from the torch moved away from him, and he let out a breath. He waited a moment before following the group up the hill.

With the darkness came a cold D-72 had never felt before. He'd been outside a few times, but never in this weather, and not without a suit of Mega Armor. Those things had kept him warm and safe. He had his own armor, but it was nothing compared to Mega Armor. His suit wasn't weatherproof. It protected against incoming bullets and blades when it was powered on, and that was helpful, but being bulletproof wouldn't help him not freeze to death. He hoped he wouldn't even need that, but if so, he'd be ready. There would be more of them when they got there, provided he was right about them. So far, so good.

Following the group in silence, he did what he could to stifle his footsteps as he trailed as far back as possible while keeping them in view. It was proving to be much more difficult to move in the forest while under the blanket of darkness. The dim light from ahead provided minimal guidance, but he knew they were still there. That was all that mattered.

After walking for a while longer, the group stopped at the top of the hill. More light was ahead of them, so he must've been getting close. When he glanced over his shoulder, he spotted a dim light twinkling like a star in the distance. They had walked a good distance, but thanks to the elevation the facility remained visible. He never thought he'd be so relieved to be this far away from there. It had been his home until mere hours ago, and now he had nothing. He was following a random group of kids he assumed were Rejects and hoped they would lead him toward their hideout in the abandoned facility. If that was true, he'd have a chance at getting back on Dean Tipper's good side and maybe even getting a promotion. He could provide proof that he was right, that he wasn't making up a story. He could show the dean that he wasn't stupid.

When he looked back up the hill, the group of kids had vanished.

What? How did you all—ugh!

He'd followed them for hours and had gotten so close only to lose them at the last possible moment. He couldn't let that happen, especially since he didn't want to freeze on the side of the mountain and get eaten by feral Rejects or something. That was not a way to go.

When he approached the top of the hill, a building appeared in front of him.

There it is. The abandoned facility. Just like on the map. Everything is exactly like I thought it was. This is great.

He let out a chuckle.

And they think I'm always wrong!

Dim yellow light escaped through a few windows in the facility. A few bodies lay to the side of the entrance, but they looked frozen, like they'd been there for days or longer.

There's light on inside, yet they called me crazy. Who's crazy now, huh?

D-72 felt himself heating up, his heart racing as adrenaline pumped through his body. He hadn't been this excited for something since Adoption Day the year before . . . the incident. Pushing the button on his chest plate, he waited for the armor to tighten up around each limb. Electricity should have buzzed through the suit as it powered up, but none came. There was no movement in the suit. He pressed the button again. Nothing.

What's going on? Did the battery die already?

He pushed the button over and over, hoping it was just slightly frozen. When nothing happened, he let out a groan and gave up on that option. He'd have to rely on his brute strength when he got inside. Hopefully that would be enough. Besides, he didn't need to be bulletproof with a bunch of Rejects. He would just walk up to them and take them out one by one. It was going to be easy. They probably didn't even know what a gun was.

Click.

Metal pressed into the back of his head. His heart leapt into his throat, and his eyes darted side to side, looking for the quickest route away from there. Before he could take a step, he felt the metal press harder into his skin. A voice came from behind him, loud and firm.

"Hold it right there."

Chapter Nineteen
Ahna

"Have you seen Scorcher?" asked Ahna. "I've been looking for him everywhere."

Marie looked up from her clipboard and shook her head, her glasses sliding slightly down her nose.

"Last I saw, he was heading out with a group this morning. They should have been back a while ago, though."

I know.

"Thanks, Marie. If he—they—aren't back soon, I'll need some supplies to send out with a team in case they got injured on the way back."

"Don't have to twist my tibia," said Marie, laughing. "Whatever you need, you'll get." She smiled before pushing her glasses back up her nose and continuing down the hall.

Ahna continued to look around the various rooms within the facility, but Scorcher was nowhere to be seen. Sarah and Vincent were gone, too, so they must have gone with him. The mission should have taken them a few hours to get there, get what they needed, and get back. It couldn't have taken all day. Something must have happened.

Ahna pictured Scorcher's body lying mangled in a mound of snow on the side of the mountain. The thought sent a chill down her spine, goose bumps on her arms causing the hair to stand up.

When she approached the hospital wing, she forced a smile before entering. She couldn't let Corrine know she was worried.

"Ahna! So good to see you in here," said Corrine. She was bandaging a wound on one of the kids in a bed. "What brought you in? Are you sick?"

Ahna shook her head. "Just checking in to see how things are going. How are supplies?"

Small talk, Ahna? Really?

Corrine shrugged. "We're low, but we've managed to slow the usage by repurposing some other materials. It's amazing what you can do with some leaves and a bit of adhesive."

She chuckled, but Ahna could tell it was out of desperation. Supplies were dwindling. That had been a problem for months, but she needed to continue looking around inside the room without worrying Corinne.

"That's resourceful," replied Ahna. "You think we'll be able to make it through this weather without having to scout for more?"

"To be honest, I'm not sure," Corrine said.

As Corrine continued speaking, Ahna weaved through the rows of kids on beds and in chairs, each dealing with something completely different, but all coughing sporadically. They were visibly ill, which for some of them meant closer to death.

Her wrist had stopped causing her pain, most days, but when it returned, it did so in full force. Marie called them phantom pains, but the name it was given didn't change how badly it hurt. She experienced searing pain most of the time, but other times she was lucky and it was only minor, like a beesting. When it was at its worse, she felt transported to the day Sticks had found her in the Junkyard. The smell of trash and iron would come back to her, filling her senses.

Sticks's shadow would loom over her, the sun beaming from overhead. With as much as she had been bleeding, she would have attracted the wolves . . . or the Wallers. She knew there would have been no chance of surviving past that day had she not been Rejected at that exact time. Sticks could have killed her, but he hadn't. In fact, he'd done the opposite. Even though it had taken her longer than she'd admit to realize, she knew he was a nice guy. His rough facade was something he had to develop over time, but she figured she would have done the same. She hadn't been born into this life, but once she was forced into it, she felt like she had changed a bit herself. Of course, she hadn't undergone near as much as Sticks in her lifetime, but she hoped that wouldn't be necessary.

"Ahna?" Corrine was suddenly right next to her, her soft hand on Ahna's shoulder. She leaned in, her brows moving down over her tired, worried eyes. "What's going on with you?"

Besides the constant worry that every time I'm given the chance to make a decision it ends up getting someone killed? Or the fact that I may have ruined the one relationship I've managed to have with someone who may or may not be a frozen corpse because of a plan I came up with?

"Nothing."

Corrine rubbed Ahna's shoulder before removing her hand. She opened her mouth to respond, but a violent cough erupted from one of the kids across the room. Corrine rushed toward them, leaving Ahna relieved, able to escape.

A burst of cold air sent a shiver down her spine as she entered the main area. Chatter echoed through the metal chamber, a sea of murmurs and excitement. The door was open, and a small crowd had gathered in front of it. More were joining every second, attempting to see whatever was going on outside.

What are you all so excited about?

She started toward the doorway, her hand hovering over the hilt of her knife on her waist. She didn't have time to get her staff, so she hoped that would be good enough.

Barreling through the crowd, she made her way into the opening. Once she stepped outside, she saw the cause for excitement.

Sarah had a gun pointed directly at the face of a massive Elite, whose hands were up and to the side in a defensive manner. Baz and Taz stood on either side of him, guns drawn. For someone his size, he looked abnormally terrified. That was understandable, though. Ahna figured she would be too if there were a ring of kids surrounding her with guns, no matter how big she was.

The Elite towered over most of them and looked bigger than most of the Elite she had seen back in Deliverance. She almost didn't recognize the uniform he was wearing, but she was close enough to see the stork logo branded on the chest plate in its usual location. While the basic concept of the old Elite armor was there, everything else was different. She couldn't believe the build of the armor. It was almost as though someone had taken the original armor and sent it through an upgrade machine or something. It looked similar to the exoskeleton she'd seen Sticks wearing before the battle in the last facility.

Is this the armor all Elite are wearing now?

At the moment, that wasn't important. What mattered was the reason they'd brought the Elite back to the base and why Scorcher wasn't with them.

"What are you all doing?" asked Ahna.

Sarah looked at her quickly before returning her attention to the Elite. The gun was shaking slightly in her hands. Whether that was due to the cold or her nerves wasn't clear.

"What needs to be done, Ahna."

Scorcher stepped out from behind the Elite. Hearing his voice gave Ahna a feeling of relief, but it was quickly dashed by the tone it carried. She couldn't believe how he was speaking to her, especially in front of everyone.

"What's with the guns, Scorch?" said Ahna. She examined the Elite quickly to double-check her assumption, and it seemed correct. "He's not armed."

"Trust me, he doesn't need a gun to kill us," said Scorcher.

The Elite mumbled something, and Scorcher smacked him over the head with his bow. There was a crack as Ahna saw the wood split into two and hang from Scorcher's hand.

Oh no.

"Now you've done it!" Scorcher pulled out a knife and lunged toward the Elite, but the Elite was quick to react. Scorcher went flying, landing in a pile of snow. Ahna stepped between the Elite and Scorcher, who was coughing heavily but otherwise looked okay.

Boom!

A gunshot echoed through the trees, and a high-pitched whine rang in Ahna's ears. She turned around to see Sarah drop her gun, her eyes wide as the Elite stumbled to the ground. Baz and Taz stepped back to avoid the Elite landing on either of them, and Sarah was frozen in place. The Elite hit the ground, inches away from Sarah.

"Oh god!" screamed Sarah, stepping away from the body.

"Way to go, Ahna!" Scorcher yelled, standing up and moving toward the body. His tone was much harsher than before, but his voice was slightly raspy. He cleared his throat before continuing. "Look at what you did."

Ahna inhaled sharply through her nose, her nostrils flaring as she narrowed her eyes.

"What I did? You're the one who brought an Elite the size of a tree back to our base. What were you thinking?"

Her heart was racing.

"I was thinking he would've made his way inside and killed the others if I hadn't had the group surround him."

"That worked out well, didn't it?"

"Contrary to what you might think, I'm very capable of making decisions—ones that don't end up with people dying!"

Ahna's mouth hung open, her vision blurring behind a pool of tears.

"Shut up, both of you!"

Ahna wiped her eyes before Felan stepped out from behind a tree.

"He's not dead," said Felan. Slinging the rifle over her shoulder, she walked over to the Elite and knelt beside him. She pulled a thin metal tube from his body, showing it to the group. "He's knocked out."

"How?" asked Ahna.

"You mean I didn't kill him?" Sarah asked, her eyes wide.

"No, you didn't kill him, Sarah," replied Felan. "As for how, Ahna, I found these little babies in the radio tower I scouted earlier today."

"What are they?" asked Scorcher.

"Tranquilizer bullets. Apparently, they can put big animals to sleep. Figured it would work on this walking boulder, too." Felan chuckled as she pocketed the metal casing of the tranquilizer bullet.

"Wait a minute," said Ahna. "Radio tower? That's what that is?"

If that's true, we might be able to find more people after all. Maybe we actually have a chance.

"Yeah," said Felan. "And it still works. At least, I think it does, anyway."

"This could change everything," said Ahna.

"I know."

Scorcher cleared his throat again. "Can it change the fact that we have to carry this guy inside now instead of letting him walk on his own?"

Why are you being so rude today? What did I do to you?

"Taz, Baz," Felan said, then motioned toward the group of onlookers. "And the rest of you. Get over here and help carry this flesh mound inside."

A handful of Gray Wolves moved, some more hesitant than the others, and gathered around the Elite.

"Where you want him to go?" asked Taz.

Felan looked at Ahna, raising her eyebrows.

"Uh . . . put him in the old storage room. The one down the hall from the hospital wing," said Ahna.

"You sure?" asked Baz.

"Yeah," said Ahna.

I think I have to be.

"All right then," said Felan, her voice raised. "You heard her. Let's take this sack of flesh inside. And be careful not to let him fall too hard. We need him alive." She turned toward Ahna, her voice suddenly lower. "He does need to be alive, right?"

Ahna nodded.

"Yeah, we need him alive!" she shouted to the group again. "Let's get moving before he freezes to the ground and becomes a permanent iceberg out here."

On the count of three, the group moaned as they lifted the Elite up. They managed to get him a few inches off the ground, which was enough to move him over the threshold of the entrance. As they carried him in, Ahna followed them, walking next to Sarah.

"You okay?" asked Ahna.

Sarah forced a smile, nodding her head quickly. Ahna had seen her do it enough times to know her next answer was a lie.

"Yeah," said Sarah. "I'm good. What about you two?" She cocked her head in the direction of Scorcher, who was slightly ahead of them with the group, keeping the Elite's head from hitting the ground.

"Good," said Ahna. "All good."

She thought repeating it might help her believe it.

It didn't.

"THAT'S NOT HOW YOU tie someone up, you idiot," Baz said, pushing Taz aside. "Let me do it."

"I'd rather . . . knot," said Taz. They both laughed and high-fived before Felan shut them down.

"Get back to tying him up, or I'll make sure you both get firsthand experience with it. Understand?"

They nodded, a laugh still bubbling under their puffy cheeks. They had grown on Ahna over the past couple months, but they needed to be kept in line every so often. She was glad she didn't have to be the one to do it. She had enough to worry about.

"Sorry, Scorcher," said Felan. "You were saying?"

"I was just asking what you think we should do with him. Do you think he's worth keeping around or that he might be a spy or something?"

The dim light from the hallway cast a shadow on his face in a way that made it look almost normal. Ahna had never thought of the scars as negative, but it was interesting to see what he looked like without them, even for a second.

Why am I thinking about that right now? You've been rude for no reason, and I've only been trying to help you. I don't care how hot you look right now; you can't do that.

"He's not a spy," said Ahna, her tone flat.

"You sound pretty certain of that," said Scorcher.

He moved enough that the light now focused mostly on his eyes, which burrowed into her skin. She looked away, toward the Elite.

Now tied up on a wooden chair, he looked a bit more normal. His armor was in a pile on the side of the room, so he was only in a casual outfit. The Elite wore T-shirts and stretchy jean material when not training so that they were always ready to jump into a suit of armor or move quickly. His outfit had clearly been handed down from the biggest previous Elite they could find, but it still looked almost tight on him.

"I am," said Ahna. She walked to the side of the Elite, pointing at the designation on his shirt. "See his designation? The *D* means he works with distance-based missions or maps. Those jobs are given to the Elite who can't or aren't good enough to make it through the more intense training, which means he can't be a spy."

Scorcher's eyes narrowed as he crossed his arms. She could tell he was genuinely convinced and intrigued.

"You can tell all that from the letter and numbers?"

Sarah was holding back a laugh in the corner, so Ahna knew she would be outed if she didn't do it herself. She chuckled.

I tried.

"No," said Ahna. "I picked up this piece of an old map and a candy bar wrapper that fell out of his pockets on the way here. Spies don't eat candy or carry physical evidence of their knowledge. At least, I don't think they do. I just thought it'd be fun to mess with you."

Sarah finally let out her laugh, and Felan chuckled, too.

"Was it?" asked Scorcher, obviously upset at himself for believing her story.

"Yeah, actually," said Ahna.

Felan kicked off from the wall she had been leaning against and approached the Elite. She put her hands on her knees, staring him in his face, his eyes shut and mouth hanging open. She turned to face the others.

"So what're we supposed to do with him?" she asked.

I didn't think about that . . .

"Well," Ahna said, "we can figure that out."

Scorcher scoffed. "You didn't have a plan when you brought this thing inside our base?"

God, Scorch. You don't gotta be so mean. What's your deal?

"I—"

Before Ahna could answer, the door to the storage room opened. Sticks stood in the doorway, catching his breath.

Sticks? What are you—

"Guys. There's . . . a . . ." Sticks said, struggling to get more than one word out at a time as he spoke.

"Waller? Another Elite?" asked Felan, her rifle already in her hands as she started toward the doorway.

Sticks held his hand up, shaking his head. Felan backed up, returning her rifle to her back again. She stared at Sticks, waiting for a response.

"Well?" asked Felan, clearly annoyed.

He took a second to catch his breath. "We—Wick and I—found something pretty exciting. At least, I think it could be."

Ahna's eyes widened as she grinned and headed for the door.

"Where do you think you're going?" asked Scorcher. He sounded more surprised than upset.

"You heard him," said Ahna. "They found something, so I'm going to check it out. Don't you want to do that, too?"

Scorcher nodded.

"Well, yeah," he said, gesturing at the Elite, who was almost falling over from his own weight. "But we're kinda busy right now."

"It doesn't take five people to guard an unconscious tied-up Elite, Scorch," said Ahna. She thought about just walking out but really wanted to smooth things over with him. "But if you wanna go instead, I'll stay here with him."

Scorcher stared at her for a moment, and she could see him contemplating it. Sometimes, when he was thinking, she noticed he pulled his lips into his mouth and bit down on them. She'd always thought that was a weird thing to do, but she figured she had things herself, though she didn't know what those might've been. He'd never mentioned anything negative about her. In fact, he almost never mentioned anything negative about anything.

"No, it's fine," said Scorcher. "You go ahead. I'll stay here while you hang out with Sticks . . . again. I'm used to it now, anyway."

"I'm sorry, man," Sticks said. "I—"

"All due respect, *man*, just go. I really don't wanna hurt you right now."

Sticks started to push past Ahna, but she blocked his path into the room. Things were getting out of hand. The last thing she or the group needed was for them to fight and potentially hurt each other, especially with the Elite being inside the base. She needed to stop them before one of them ended up in the hospital, or worse.

"I'll meet you in the hallway, Sticks," said Ahna, guiding him back out the doorway. Then she turned around. "I don't know why you're so upset with me or Sticks. Why are you being so childish?"

"You're the child, Ahna," said Scorcher, his voice getting louder. "If you—" He stopped himself, inhaling deeply. Crossing his arms, he leaned against the wall next to the Elite and exhaled. "Just go. I'll hang out here. One of us should follow through with what we say we're going to, right?"

"You—fine," said Ahna. Too many thoughts were racing around for her to decide on anything better, so she headed through the doorway.

I can't believe you're telling me—if it weren't for—I'm gonna—

"Have fun, you two," Scorcher called out.

Ugh! You—you're such a jerk! Out of my way, Sticks.

Ahna barreled past Sticks, only slowing her pace after realizing she had no idea where she was going. She stopped and waited for Sticks to catch up, which took him longer than expected. She understood then why he was so winded when he arrived. Even his movements were not as fluid as they used to be. Something was wrong with him, she just couldn't tell what it was exactly.

"I don't know what's gotten into him recently," said Ahna. "Sorry."

"You shouldn't apologize for him," said Felan, appearing from around the corner. "He's being a jerk. He deserves to be stuck with that stupid Elite by himself. Maybe they'll bond." She bobbed her eyebrows up and down on the last word, chuckling. Ahna's face suddenly felt hot.

I'm the only one who gets to say those things. Not you.

Ahna turned her attention back to Sticks, trying to keep herself from punching Felan straight in the face.

"What did you find?" asked Ahna.

Sticks smiled. "Follow me."

Chapter Twenty
Sticks

"Candle Wick! What's crackling?" asked Felan.

Wick rolled his eyes and huffed. He was walking over toward the computer with a stack of papers in one hand. Sticks noticed his leg dragging behind him a bit more than usual. Dark bags hung beneath his eyes.

Did you work all night?

"I told you to stop calling me that," said Wick. He plopped down in his scooter, adjusting it with the handlebars. They'd been able to find some spare parts in the debris to make him a chair with an electric motor, that way he could get around the workshop area a bit easier. Whether or not it would be helpful when they left the base remained to be seen. Sticks would carry him out if he had to, though. There was no way he'd risk him getting hurt because he couldn't run by himself. He wouldn't let that happen again.

"Why do you think I still do it?" Felan asked, laughing as she slapped him on the back.

She seemed like a totally different person with him, almost like they were siblings. Sticks knew that wasn't true. Wick had told him how Felan had brought him into the Gray Wolves when he was practically still a toddler. She'd raised him and made sure that he never got picked on by anyone except her. Sticks never would've guessed she could care for someone in that way. In fact, he couldn't remember a time he'd seen her be caring at all. The only person she was kind to in the whole group was Marie. With the exception of the past couple days, they spent a lot of time together.

Everyone's been a little on edge the past few days . . .

"How're things going with the drive?" asked Felan. She sat down on a stool next to the desk, her elbows resting on a pile of papers.

"Slow and steady. They had a lot of stuff on there, but most of it was encrypted. I've been able to decrypt some of it, but it could take another couple days."

"We don't have a couple days. The longer we wait, the more behind we get. I need—we need—to get those files decrypted sooner than later if we want to get rid of it."

"Get rid of what?" asked Sticks.

"The, uh . . . the facility. Obviously." She fumbled around, sending a blizzard of papers to the floor.

"Felan!" Wick yelled. He tried to maneuver so he could bend over to get the papers off the floor, but Felan kept his chair from going anywhere.

"My bad, my bad. I'll pick 'em up. You just focus on the files, all right? Don't go all berserk on me, geez."

Wick huffed before returning to the computer. It was the only computer they'd found that worked besides the one in the control room. Apparently, it was pretty slow. The last time Sticks had asked about the files they retrieved from the last facility, Wick had told him it'd be faster to build a time machine and talk to whoever created them. Sticks had never planned on having a partner in his workspace, but Wick was different.

"Oh!" said Wick, turning toward Sticks. "I've been waiting to tell you. We've had a development in the implant project. I was able to remove the microchip without damaging anything important. As long as we have the right tools, I think we could replicate it. Or, at the very least, modify this one. But we'll have to wait and see."

"Implants?" asked Ahna.

"He didn't mention it?" asked Wick.

Ahna shook her head.

"It's nothing," said Sticks. "What about our recent discovery? Everything ready?"

Wick nodded. "Should be fully functional. You didn't tell them what we found?"

"I wanted to show them first," said Sticks.

"Always keeping secrets. That's gonna come back to hurt you one of these days," said Wick. "That's why I'm an open book."

Felan laughed. "You don't talk to anyone besides us."

Wick shrugged. "I have to trust you first. Then I'll tell you anything and everything you want to know."

"We know," said Sticks, chuckling again. "Let's go before he starts telling us about his rash again."

Sticks started through the doorway they'd uncovered earlier that day with Ahna and Felan behind him.

"You know, that was a pretty rough time for me, actually," said Wick, his voice trailing as Sticks led the group through a dark hallway toward the secret building. He hated leaving Wick talking to himself, but he did that enough that he probably wouldn't notice they were gone until he finished his story.

"YOU'VE GOTTA BE KIDDING me," said Felan.

Sticks shook his head. "Why would I joke about something like this? Besides, Wick said it was functional."

"Is its function to get us killed?" asked Felan.

"What's the matter?" Ahna asked. "Scared?"

Ahna had become riskier and more outspoken in the time since he'd first met her. She hadn't gotten herself killed yet, but she kept the option open. Her dangerous streak was starting to grow on him. He used to hate having her around, but now he didn't mind it. She could be useful, even if she took risks when she really shouldn't.

Felan scoffed, turning her head to the side. "Scared? Nope. Untrusting of a contraption that's been here since who knows when? Yeah."

Sticks could understand where she was coming from. When they first found it, he had his doubts, but Wick had assured him that it would work. Once he got inside the machine itself, he knew Wick was right. The only thing he wasn't fully confident about was the wires. Machines he could work with, but he couldn't do a thing about gravity.

"Trust me," said Sticks. "I wouldn't have told you about it if I didn't think it'd be useful."

"How'd you find this place?" asked Ahna.

"What is this place?" asked Felan.

Sticks pointed to the sign that hung at an angle on the edge of the platform.

"Mayflower Mill. At least, that's what it used to be called. When Wick and I were moving things around, I saw some light coming through the wall. Once I stripped the plywood and stuff off it, I found that doorway leading back here."

"It's a whole other building," said Felan.

"Was a whole other building," said Sticks. He gestured toward the dark hallway to the side. "Most of it looks like it was destroyed by some sort of rockslide or something. Found a few dead Wallers in a pile of debris down there, but that was it. The only thing that seems to be working is this thing."

"That makes me feel better about it," said Felan, stepping back from the tram.

"What exactly is it?" asked Ahna. She was already opening the door to the cart.

"Wick called it a tram. We found some old book called a manual. It said they used to carry people and other stuff all the way from here down to the mines."

Ahna's eyes widened. "Mines?"

Before Sticks could respond, Felan interrupted.

"You want us to get in that rusty bucket thing . . . and ride it down there?" She gestured toward the open sky, her face contorted as if she'd eaten a whole lemon.

"Eventually, yeah. We just need to make sure the end of the line is clear. If so, we think we could transport everyone this way. Apparently, it can hold tons of metal and rock. I think it could fit a few of us in each car. Besides, it'd be quicker and easier than going down the mountain, not to mention it would put us right by the facility."

"No way. Not happening."

"Why not?" asked Sticks.

"I'm not risking the lives of the group by cramming them into some hundred-year-old soup can on a wire. There's no way that's safe. Not safer than my wagon, that's for sure."

"Actually, Wick said—"

"Speaking of Wick, he probably could use a hand in there. Let me know when you're done playing around out here. We've got other problems to worry about."

She exited back through the hall they'd entered. Sticks wanted to call after her and explain his plan.

"What's this do?"

Before he could answer Ahna's question, there was a loud metal crunch, and the motor of the tram kicked on behind him. Metal ground as the machine awoke from its hibernation, its yawn rattling the platform beneath him.

Oh no. This isn't . . . Did you just . . .

Ahna was already hopping into the cart, waving back at him as it lurched forward. She squealed with excitement. Sticks felt his heart jump.

"See you at the bottom!" Ahna called out, her head disappearing behind a blanket of snow.

Sticks rushed, as fast as his legs would allow, to the edge of the platform. Peering down, he spotted Ahna. Thankfully, she was still alive, smiling as she sailed through the sky toward the ground below. Originally, he'd planned on scouting out the area where the tram ended before taking it down there, but that was now impossible.

Why do you always do this kind of thing?

There was one other cart still left nearby. Sticks sighed before opening the door and hopping inside.

"This better not get us killed."

He pushed the button, sending his cart forward toward the edge of the platform. He felt a pull on his pants as he tried to sit down. They were caught in the door of the cart. He opened the door quickly before the cart cleared the edge of the platform and moved so his pant leg was free. When he slammed the door shut again, he heard a snap.

What was that?

He peered over the edge of the cart to see a screw skydiving underneath him. The door was now at an angle, squeaking slightly as the cart carried him toward the ground. Sticks mumbled a quick prayer, hoping he wouldn't end up like the screw. A gust of wind caught the cart, causing him to swing side to side. His grip on its edges tightened.

Stay still . . . Don't freak . . .

Sticks inhaled, filling his lungs with the biting cold air as snow drifted overhead, the cart bringing him closer to the ground.

"JUMP!" YELLED AHNA, standing a few feet below him. Her arms were outstretched as she looked up at him.

The cart continued on the track, about to make the turn back up the mountain toward their base. He didn't have much of a choice if he wanted to see what was down there. Plus, he couldn't let Ahna discover it after he'd been the one to find the tram. He needed something to make the group think he was useful again. He took a deep breath, pushed the door open, and jumped.

Sticks groaned as he landed on something soft but hard at the same time. The door to the cart landed right beside him.

"Get off!" yelled Ahna, her voice muffled slightly by his jacket and torso.

She pushed him away and stood up, brushing herself off. Sticks struggled with his footing as he tried to stand. There was a slight pain in his knee and an ache throughout his body. The cold had been causing him to feel sore in certain parts of his arms and legs. As if he needed anything else to worry about.

Ahna extended her hand, and he took it, pulling against her to finally stand. Once he was upright, he brushed the snow off his jacket.

"Nice jump," said Ahna, chuckling.

"Nice catch," said Sticks.

They laughed.

"Now what?" asked Ahna.

"Well, I guess we find this mine."

Ahna smiled as though she were plotting something evil. "Where do you think it is?"

Sticks pointed at a tree standing a few feet away. The bark was wrapped around a metal sign, as if the tree were consuming it. The words on the sign were faded, worn away from years in the elements, but he could still make out the ones at the top.

"Old Hundred Gold Mine," he read aloud. "Arrow's pointing that way." He pointed toward an opening in the earth. The entrance would have been impossible to find if they had come from any other direction.

"You think we'll find gold in there?" asked Ahna.

Sticks chuckled. "Let's hope that's the worst thing we find."

Ahna sprinted toward the opening to the cave, Sticks trying his best to keep up. A throbbing in his kneecap returned, a constant reminder not to be too risky. There was only so much he would be able to do from a desk, and he needed to be out, fighting for their cause. There was no way he'd let himself fade from the front line.

Once he reached the opening, he spotted Ahna. She was crouched down, touching something near the ground.

"What are you doing?" Sticks called out.

As he reached her position, she turned, extending her hand forward.

"Check it out," said Ahna. "Cool, huh? Looks just like the one we saw on the Waller the other day."

Sticks nodded, examining it closely as he took it from her.

Dim blue light pulsated from the center of his palm, as though he held the beating heart of an alien creature. The mushroom felt abnormally warm for the weather, its leathery skin a stark contrast to the soft hairlike particles protruding from its top. He'd never seen anything like it, besides on a few of the Wallers. Those never glowed like the one in his hand, though. Blue light continued to flash as they stepped farther into the cave, sending shadows onto the wall. Sticks smiled.

It almost looks like those shadow puppet shows back home.

His smile faded as a memory of sitting around the fire with Rollin flooded his mind.

You used to love those . . .

Chapter Twenty-One
Scorcher

"*This should be far enough,*" *said Scorcher. They'd finally found a spot away from the rest of the group. Privacy was hard to come by most days. He cleared out a spot with his feet, moving broken limbs and debris from the area before placing the blanket on the ground. Once they'd smoothed it out, they lay down, finally able to relax from the day's trek. As he lay there, he noticed his breath was clouding in front of him. Winter was right around the corner.*

"There it is! See it?" asked Scorcher, pointing straight up.

Ahna strained her neck toward the sea of stars and shrieked.

"Ah! So cool! What'd you say it is again?"

"A shooting star," replied Scorcher.

"Where does it get shot from?"

Scorcher laughed. "Nowhere. They just used to call 'em that."

"Why?"

"No idea."

"I bet it's 'cause they look like a really shiny bullet."

"You know, you might be onto something there."

Scorcher wrapped his arm around Ahna, her cheek rubbing up against his shoulder as she nestled into her usual spot near his neck.

Scents of pine and lavender filled his nose. It reminded him of the trees back home. If he closed his eyes, he almost felt like they were there.

He could feel the waves move the raft up and down, the breeze gently sail across his skin. He could hear the birds calling to each other from the nearby canopy before chasing one another across the water. The only thing he couldn't feel was the warmth of the sun that would send them into an afternoon nap. Thinking about the warmth, he felt heat against him as Ahna moved in closer.

Her eyes stared into his own, the heat from her face radiating onto him. He could feel her heart beating against his chest.

"You know what?" she asked, her voice low.

"What?" asked Scorcher, mimicking her whisper.

Ahna inhaled deeply and put her hand to his face. Her fingers fell into the grooves of his scars, as though they had been molded for her hand. She gripped, the pressure and warmth soothing his cold face, and smiled. A sky full of shooting stars would pale in comparison to the universe contained within her eyes.

"I love you, Scorch."

He thought he'd freak out the first time he heard someone say that to him. He thought he'd need to take a while to figure out what to say back. But he was surprised, and relieved, to realize he'd been wrong. There was no need to figure out anything. He'd never been more sure of how he felt than in that moment.

"I love you, too."

Their eyes closed as their lips met. The warm beach had been replaced, a cold clearing in the woods now the place he'd return to forever in his mind. A place he and Ahna could share.

Their very own starry night.

CRACK.

Scorcher shot up from his chair, rubbing the sleep from his eyes and readying his knife.

He relaxed his grip when he realized it had been the leg of the Elite's chair. Splinters scattered across the floor beneath the Elite as he stirred in the chair, finally waking up. Scorcher sighed as he dragged his own chair next to the Elite and sat down, waiting for him to fully open his eyes.

"Wh-wh-where am I?" he asked, his voice slightly slurred. Felan's tranquilizer bullet must have been pretty potent.

Scorcher stared, moving the overhead lamp so that it shone directly in the Elite's face. His eyes were glazed over, still adjusting to the bright light in his face.

"You don't need to worry about where you are," said Scorcher. "You need to worry about where you'll be if you don't tell me what I wanna know."

The Elite struggled in his chair like a bear tangled in a fishing net. His groans intensified as he became more aware of his surroundings.

"Let me go!" he yelled.

"Shut up!"

Scorcher threw his chair across the room, the sound echoing through the room. The Elite stared at him, his eyes wide.

"Now," said Scorcher, his voice almost a whisper. "Tell me why you were following us."

The Elite looked side to side, clearly looking for a method of escape. Scorcher knew there was no way out other than the door behind him. He wouldn't let him leave anyway.

"I-I was trying to find the dot," he said. His voice had lowered. It almost made him seem smaller.

"Dot?" asked Scorcher.

"On the map. I saw it flash. That means there's activity. I-I tried to tell them, but . . . nobody believed me. So I came to find out for myself."

"That doesn't answer my question," said Scorcher. "We could've been heading anywhere, but you chose to follow us. How did you know we'd be going to this facility?"

The Elite shrugged as best he could. "Rejects are the only ones who'd be dumb enough to use this place."

"How dare you—" Scorcher raised his hand.

"No, I just mean that it's so close to the facility and hasn't been used in so long that it wouldn't be anyone else! That's all, I swear."

The Elite was almost shaking, which was surprising given his intimidating size and strength. There was something unusual about him that Scorcher couldn't quite figure out.

Let's find out if that's all . . .

Scorcher relaxed and retrieved the chair he'd thrown, sitting down opposite the Elite. He stared at him for a moment, watching as he mouthed words under his breath. His eyes were darting around the room as he muttered whatever he was saying, his shaking dissipating. Once he had calmed down, Scorcher tried to speak in more of a conversational tone, hoping it might help the Elite feel more inclined to answer. Besides, he realized he may have overstepped when he felt the dent in the side of his chair from its encounter with the wall.

"You said it had to be Rejects here. How do you know we're them?" asked Scorcher.

The Elite swallowed, staring at the light as it swung slightly above his head.

"Your scars."

Oh. Right . . .

He found himself touching his face at the mention of them but lowered his hand immediately. Scorcher leaned in.

"Okay. Let's say we are the Rejects you were looking for. What now? What was your master plan?"

The Elite shook his head. "Didn't have one."

Scorcher hadn't expected that answer. Not that he'd hoped for the guy to tell him every detail, but he'd half expected something more than he'd gotten. He thought over his options, weighing whether or not to resort to force again. But that hadn't worked before. He didn't like it, either. It felt unnatural, and he didn't want to become someone who used violence to get what he wanted. That was exactly what they were fighting against.

Scorcher leaned back in his chair, crossing his arms. He spoke to the Elite as though they'd known each other for years.

"Let's pretend your story is true."

"It is," said the Elite.

"If you really had no plan, then why did you come looking for us? Why did you run away from the facility?" A memory from earlier ran through his mind. "And why did you beat up one of the guards on your way out?"

Panic flashed in the Elite's eyes as they began to shift and dart around the room again.

"They were—" His breathing became shallow and quick. "It was the only way out."

Scorcher felt the panic coming from him as he spoke, his own heart rate beginning to increase. Something was really upsetting the Elite, and he intended to find out what and why.

"You had food, shelter, and constant protection. Why give that up?" asked Scorcher.

He was genuinely interested. Before now, he'd never heard of an Elite running away, let alone had the chance to talk face-to-face with one who wasn't trying to kill him. He figured that might not have been the way it went down had Felan not put him to sleep . . .

"Elite aren't all the same, you know."

Scorcher tilted his head, his eyebrows coming together. "What do you mean?"

The Elite stared at him. "Just 'cause I wear the armor, doesn't mean I am them."

"It kinda does, though."

"You think I had a choice? I didn't sign up for that," said the Elite.

"No. You were just lucky enough to be born into it," said Scorcher. "Or unlucky, I should say."

"I don't support them. Never did."

"You support something every minute you allow it to continue," said Scorcher.

The Elite raised his voice. "Have you not been listening? I told you, I'm not one of them anymore!"

The Elite rocked back and forth in the chair again, much harder than before. The ropes were starting to slip. Before Scorcher could calm him down, the back leg of the chair snapped in half, sending him toward the floor. Once he was on the ground, he was untangling the ropes, flinging them off. He was free.

Oh no.

While the Elite muttered more words to himself, Scorcher pulled out his knife and sprinted to open the door.

"Baz, Taz! Get over here now!" he yelled. "And bring your guns!"

He didn't have time to see if they'd heard him or not because the Elite was already standing up. The storage room seemed a lot smaller now that he was no longer in the chair. Scorcher stood firm between him and the doorway, flashing the knife. The Elite looked at him and shook his head.

"You think that will help you?" he asked, brushing the splintered wood and dirt from his shirt.

"You don't want to find out," said Scorcher.

"Do you?" asked the Elite.

Not really . . . Where are you guys?

He shot a glance toward the door, but Baz and Taz still hadn't arrived. He wouldn't be surprised if they showed up after he'd been beat to a pulp. He gulped at the thought. The Elite started toward him.

"Stand back," said Scorcher. He could hear the panic in his own voice and tried to hide it. "Or else."

The Elite stopped. Nodding his head, he held up his hands and took a step back.

"I won't fight you," said the Elite. "If you talk to me instead. We have a deal?"

I'm supposed to be the one in charge, not you. Then again . . .

Scorcher lowered his knife. "Okay, fine."

The door opened behind him, and Baz and Taz ran into the room with their guns drawn. They pointed them at the Elite's face.

"Don't move, big guy!" said Baz.

"Unless you wanna look like Swiss cheese!" added Taz.

"That would be a Bries," said Baz.

They both cackled like hyenas until Scorcher raised his hands to silence them.

"Put down your guns," said Scorcher.

They looked at him, clearly confused.

"But, Scorcher, we thought you said—"

"What I'm saying now is to put down your guns." He waited for them to follow his order before continuing. "Good. Now head back outside the room and stay near the door. And stop making stupid jokes at times like this. One day that'll get you killed."

Taz looked at the Elite with his eyes squinted, then looked back toward Scorcher.

"He playing some sort of Elite mind control game on you?"

Baz nodded his head. "Yeah! Is that what's going on here?"

They were both in shock at their ridiculous revelation. Scorcher shook his head and pointed at the door.

"Get out."

"Scorcher, we ought to—" started Baz.

"Now."

They both gasped, overdramatic as usual.

"Just so you know, if you turn evil," said Taz, "I got no problem shootin' you."

He narrowed his eyes and pointed at Scorcher, Baz following his lead as they walked backward through the door, shutting it behind them.

Scorcher turned back toward the Elite.

"Okay," said Scorcher, his voice calm. "You wanted to talk?" he asked, shrugging his shoulders. "Let's talk."

Chapter Twenty-Two
Felan

Wick sat at the computer, mumbling to himself as he typed away. Clicks from keyboard reminded Felan of the clocks they'd seen in the old museum back East. She loved that museum. So many fun figures of humans, stuffed animals, and old artifacts to look at and touch. It was like having her very own time machine to the prewar world, a world that seemed so much easier and more interesting than her own. People had machines that could fit in their pockets that allowed them to talk to and see other people no matter where they were. If they had that technology again, she'd be able to reach Elaine. She always knew what to do. Now that she led the biggest group of Rejects in the country, she had some firepower behind her, too. All they had to do was find her, and they'd get the help they needed. Not just in the fight against The Delivery Co., either. They had to have medicine there, or at least more information that could be useful in finding or creating it, if they didn't already have some themselves. But she had more to worry about before then.

The facility down the mountain was huge, much bigger than those she'd seen so far, anyway. Based on what they'd uncovered, it was mostly Elite, too. That struck her as odd, but then again, the whole company was based around a flawed system of ideals. Every night she lay down, she felt the reminders of their research-fueled brutality. She often wondered how things would have been if they'd used their resources and knowledge for good, but that train of thought often derailed into rage and sleepless nights. She couldn't afford to lose any more sleep than she already had—not if she was going to fight for those who couldn't fight for themselves.

Felan watched Wick work for a moment, the clicking in different bursts, rhythmic. The sounds of his typing were almost soothing. Many nights she had seen him doing the same thing when she'd returned from a night out with the others in some of the cities throughout their travels. No matter how many times she asked him to join them, he never did. He was always reading or working on whatever computer or electronic device he could get his hands on. It had been that way since the day he'd joined the group. She hadn't thought she would be as thankful as she had become for his introverted habits.

"Decided not to go, huh?" asked Wick, talking to Felan's reflection in the computer screen.

How did you see me?

She grabbed the stool next to him and plopped down, watching him work. She noticed the reflection of the room behind them on the screen, realizing he had seen her that way. Much simpler than she'd thought.

"I don't trust machines that have been sitting around for hundreds of years," said Felan.

"Don't blame you. I figured you'd end up not going anyway. It's a little . . ." Wick smiled. "High off the ground."

"How did you—"

"Don't worry," said Wick, a smirk plastered across his face. "I won't tell anyone." He turned his attention back to the computer screen, where a long bar had just finished filling up with a weird vomit-green color. "Ha!"

"What are you so excited about? That stupid bar?" asked Felan. She couldn't understand how or why he was so interested in something so minimal.

"This 'stupid bar' means we have finally finished downloading the decrypted information on the drive we uncovered from Deliverance."

Felan's eyes widened. "Well?" she asked. "What are you waiting for? Let's see what we got!"

She could barely contain her excitement. They'd traveled through some rough stretches of the coast, struggling to get by just to reach that facility. They'd been told that it was one of the few remaining facilities still in operation in the eastern part of the country. That meant the information held within it had to be useful to her . . . and the group, she had to remind herself.

Wick pushed the "Enter" key on the keyboard, and a box appeared on the screen, showcasing a long list of files, individually named and sorted into folders. She'd seen Wick working on them enough that she could tell that they had uncovered a decent amount of information. The only question was if it was useful.

Wick's face twisted as he squinted and leaned in toward the screen. He clicked through a number of the folders, opening multiple documents in succession before closing them. She watched him repeat the process over and over for a while, waiting for him to tell her everything she was looking for was on the drive.

He slammed the mouse down and flung himself back into his chair.

"Ugh!" he growled, his nostrils flaring as he crossed his arms.

"What? What's wrong? Did we lose the files?"

Her heart sped up in anticipation of the news—news she'd hoped would be positive, but she was beginning to think her hopes were incorrect. Wick gestured toward the screen.

"There's nothing to lose," said Wick.

"What are you talking about? I thought I saw a bunch of folders on there," said Felan.

Wick nodded. "You did. Most of those folders were just copies of mundane documents pertaining to the inventory and scheduling of various parts of the facility. Besides those, it looks like backups of the system. Unless . . ." Wick's eyes widened, and he leaned in again, a smile spreading. He began laughing as he clicked through a few of the files and started typing an assortment of letters and symbols.

"Unless what, Wick?" asked Felan. Hope once again ignited within her mind as she awaited his response. Watching him work was almost more stressful than fending off a Waller attack. At least she had skills to contribute when it came to the Wallers. She couldn't fight a computer virus to save her life . . . which was exactly what she was hoping to accomplish, for her own life and everyone else's.

Wick chuckled and clapped his hands. "They thought they were clever, and they were, but not clever enough for Wick!"

Felan laughed. He only talked in third person when he felt the most invincible. She wouldn't complain, though. Seeing him happy was always a welcome sight. It had taken a while for him to become comfortable around the group after they'd originally found him. After he latched on to her like a pet, she couldn't shake him. Recently, though, she felt like the roles had reversed when it came to some things. Whenever he doubted himself, she'd remind him of that. Thankfully, he didn't need the reminder often.

"Elaborate for me, huh?" said Felan.

"Oh, right," said Wick. "You know how I said they had files labeled as backups on here?"

She nodded.

"Okay, so, people would normally create a backup of the files on their computer, and it would be named as such. This computer seemed to have multiple backups, which isn't unusual for someone as anal-retentive as I assume Dean Tipper to be. But the interesting thing was the size of the backups when I looked into them against the others."

He bobbed his eyebrows up and down. Felan shrugged.

"You're starting to lose me," she said.

"Sorry. Basically, I say all that so you know how important this next bit is. Most of the files were within a small range of one another, all fairly sizable, data wise. However," he said, pointing his finger in the air, "there was one that didn't match up. It was labeled like the rest of them, but it was much smaller than the rest. This specific backup folder lives up to its name in a different manner, though." He clicked on the folder, opening the files, then clicked on one of the documents. His tone lowered, suddenly serious. "I saw the mention of a possible plan of distribution with some hypothetical data that was problematic. What's even weirder is that it wasn't for the facility we destroyed."

Felan could sense where it was going: downhill, fast.

"Spit it out, Wick."

"The facility mentioned is located in Colorado, the one at the bottom of this mountain. And the numbers provided, if correct . . ." He gulped before he continued. "Are astronomical."

She tossed the information around in her mind, attempting to comprehend what he was telling her.

"Are we talking about them shipping out food or weapons? If so, maybe we can—"

"No," said Wick. "We're talking people."

Exporting people? How? Why?

"What does this mean for us?" asked Felan.

Wick pointed to the document on the screen, a blinking section of green highlighting a handful of white text. Felan leaned in to read it as he read the words.

"You will have thousands of soldiers, built for war, at your disposal. This should aid in the annihilation of all Rejected and those who attempt to fight against our cause. The Delivery Company has been improving our society since the beginning, and we aim to continue to do so for the foreseeable future. Yours Truly, Dean Tipper."

Felan and Wick exchanged a terrified look.

"Does this mean that facility down there is—"

"An Elite factory? Most likely," said Wick.

There's no way we'll be able to take on that many Elite—not unless we reach the rest of the Gray Wolves.

"We need to find Elaine, fast," said Felan. "There's no way we can take them on alone."

Wick sat back in his chair and shrugged. "How do you suppose we do that? You already said you don't know for sure where they are. It's not like they're broadcasting their location for us to hear."

He laughed, but that triggered a memory within her mind. Her eyes widened.

The radio tower!

"Okay," she said, feeling the adrenaline rush through her body as she stood up from her chair. "This might sound crazy, but I think you might be right."

Wick tilted his head to the side. "About what?"

"Broadcasting their location! Maybe that's what it was. That song could be a clue or a sign or something," Felan said, almost yelling.

"Song?" Wick perked up, a grin on his face. "Explain."

He was clearly interested. Felan recalled her time in the radio tower, attempting to sing back the tones she'd heard pour from the small speakers. As she finished, he asked her to repeat it as best she could while he typed out something on the computer. When she finished again, she could see that he had transcribed a series of letters that formed a handful of possible words.

Not just words. A message.

"What was it?" asked Felan.

"What you heard was something called Morse code. It was used during many of the wars as a way for soldiers to communicate, but it was also used on ships and many things as a form of communication. It's quite an interesting tool for getting messages over long distances, too, even before the days of the internet. Man, I wish I could have seen the full extent of the internet before the war. I hear it was pretty cool. Of course, it was littered with a lot of trash, too. Apparently, people posted images with stupid captions. They were called memes."

Wick laughed, but Felan didn't have time for his lectures.

"I appreciate you wanting to live in the past, but we're trying to save the future. What was the message, Wick?"

"Sorry," Wick scoffed, clearly offended at her lack of interest in his knowledge. She would have to remember to ask him to tell her about it one day later on. But not today. He turned back to read the message he'd typed out on the screen. "After eliminating the obvious incorrect choices, it looks like just two words: Union Station."

"Union Station?"

"You know it?" asked Wick.

"Oh, I know it," she replied, nodding. She'd heard the name over and over for years. She couldn't believe how stupid she'd been in not guessing it before now. "You don't?"

Wick shook his head. "Surprisingly, no. Is this good news or bad?"

"Both?" said Felan, chuckling. "Good news is that we're heading in the right direction. It's definitely out West."

"And the bad news?"

"It's a little farther than we thought."

Wick leaned forward in his chair. "How much farther?"

"California."

Wick's mouth hung open. "That means—"

"Yeah," said Felan, nodding. "We're gonna have to go through the Wasteland. Guess we're gonna need that train for sure, now, huh?"

Chapter Twenty-Three
Ahna

*S*cratch.

Vibrations skirted up her arm as she scraped the blade against the wall of the tunnel. She was unsure whether the hair standing up on her arms was due to the vibrations or the cold, though. Her leather-and-fur armor became less and less effective as they traveled deeper into the tunnel. Even Sticks had a sporadic cold chill, which was surprising given that he was the one holding the torch.

Not that you'd admit to being cold, anyway.

Ahna chuckled as she continued marking the wall as they went. Even though it had been a straight path so far—and Sticks had made sure to mention that fact—she didn't want to risk it. She'd been thinking about what Scorcher had said, all the events that had happened so quickly over the past few days and months. Most of the issues they'd faced were due to her choices as the one in charge. Even Sticks was limping slightly now due to jumping from the tram cart. She knew she hadn't pushed him out of it, but he wouldn't have had to jump if not for her impulsive behavior.

Can't believe it took me this long to figure that out. Better late than never, right? When we get back to camp, I'll have to tell Scorch how much I appreciate him helping me.

Her stomach gurgled slightly.

Well, maybe after we eat dinner.

"You hear that?" asked Sticks. He was crouched behind a large rock, the torch held low and to the side while he peered above it.

Ahna laughed. "Funny, Sticks. I know it was loud, but don't act like you aren't hungry, too."

Sticks shushed her, signaling her to crouch near him. "I'm not talking about your stomach, Ahna."

She waited for a moment for him to quit joking around before she realized he wasn't.

"Oh. Sorry," she said, joining him by the rock. She was appreciative of the minimal heat radiating from the torch. Sticks faced her, speaking in a whisper.

"See anything?" he asked.

Ahna peered over the rock into the darkness of the tunnel ahead. Without his torch in front of her, she found it almost impossible to see much at all.

"Same rock and dirt we've been looking at," she said. "It's probably nothing."

She felt something touch her hand and jumped up. Her scream bounced off the rock walls around them as she drew her knife and started slashing in the direction of whatever had just touched her.

"Ahna, hold on!" said Sticks. He held his staff up in front of her, breaking her enraged fury of slashing and allowing her to calm down and return to the moment. When she looked over at

Sticks, he appeared to be holding in a laugh. Not a second later, she knew she'd been right because he let out a loud laugh as he pointed down.

"Look!" he said, struggling to form his sentence between each heave of laughter. "You just tried . . . to murder . . . a rat!" He continued laughing.

Ahna felt her blood rush through her as she stared at the beady-eyed sack of flesh waddling in the middle of the tunnel. As she attempted to move out of its way, a yelp came from beneath her shoe. She let out a yelp in response. Sticks quit laughing almost in sync with the final yelp of the rat. Ahna looked down to see the aftermath, knowing full well what to expect. After all, she had felt its fur and flesh cushion her step. The sound of its carcass deflating beneath her replayed in her head. She gagged. Ahna wiped the residue from the bottom of her boot, then turned back to Sticks. He was stiffing a laugh.

"Don't tell anyone about this or I'll squash you like that rat," she said, attempting to be intimidating.

Sticks smirked.

"Sure thing," he said, imitating zipping his lips together. "I won't say a word . . . oh Great Stomper, Vanquisher of All Rat-Folk."

He laughed again, and Ahna pushed him forward. She wanted to keep them on track, but she also didn't want him to notice her holding back a laugh.

Great Stomper . . . I like it.

Sticks continued to guide them through the tunnel while Ahna marked the side with her blade. She occasionally found herself having to scrape her boot against the ground. She was hopeful that the residue would be completely gone by the time they got back. Nobody needed to smell day-old rat guts. She almost gagged again at the thought.

"CHECK IT OUT," SAID Sticks.

He swung the torch to the side, bathing a small metal sign in the orange glow. Though it had been badly damaged, by multiple elements from the looks of it, Ahna could still read most of the message printed on the top half. She read it aloud, as if that would somehow change what was written on the sign.

"This mine is property of Project Delivery. No trespassing. Under federal government regulations, all those found doing so will be charged with a felony." Ahna gasped before reading what someone had crudely added in paint directly underneath it. "Or shot."

She looked to Sticks, who bobbed his eyebrows up and down before sighing heavily.

"Sounds like someone really wanted to keep people out of this mine," he said.

Ahna nodded. "Yeah, but why?"

"Good question. Another thing I'd like to know is what Project Delivery is."

"Probably just what they used to call The Delivery Company," said Ahna.

Sticks looked somewhat surprised by her answer. "Okay, okay. No need to show off your fancy education," he said jokingly.

Ahna chuckled. "Don't feel bad. Not everyone can be of average intelligence."

They laughed again, and the soreness in her abdomen was a welcome stranger. She'd gladly take that more often, especially given the circumstances.

"I feel like we need to get back to the group soon, too. I know you're hungry." Sticks chuckled before continuing through the tunnel.

They didn't get much farther before Sticks tumbled to the ground, dropping the torch. He caught himself before his face hit the rock underneath him, but the torch rolled to the side.

"You okay?" asked Ahna, rushing to him.

"I'm fine," said Sticks, pushing her away. He got himself up but struggled more than usual to do so. He gestured toward the torch a few feet away. "Grab that, will you?"

Ahna walked over to retrieve it but felt her foot get there first. Before she could bend down to pick it up, it rolled again, this time into a small puddle of dirty water, extinguishing itself. Expecting total darkness, she gripped the handle of her knife and waited for something to strike. After a moment, she realized that she was still able to see Sticks, barely. Instead of the orange flicker, though, there was a dim blue light. And it was coming from the area straight ahead. Sticks met her wide eyes with his own before they joined together in the middle of the tunnel and journeyed forward toward the blue light, its luminosity increasing with each step.

"WOW," SAID AHNA, HER eyes wide.

An ocean of blue light poured over them as the tunnel melted into a larger cave opening. Over every surface, from the floor to the ceiling, blue mushrooms sprouted through the rock. In fact, there seemed to be very little actual rock to look at because of the density and number of mushrooms. As they walked deeper into the room, Ahna could see that the mushrooms were moving slightly, almost bobbing up and down. With the addition of the blue light, their dancing made her feel like she was on the ocean, only at night.

Scorch would love to see this. Maybe I'll bring him back here before we have to leave.

As she thought of the beach, Ahna swore she felt the breeze against her face. She shook her head, telling herself that was impossible. They were however many feet below the surface. Unless . . .

Does air flow inside caves and mines?

She pushed the thought aside and bent down to pick a few of the mushrooms from the floor, gathering as many of them as she could fit in her hand.

"What are you doing?" asked Sticks.

Isn't it obvious?

"Getting a new light source," said Ahna, smirking. "We might need one moving forward."

Sticks nodded. "Good idea . . . for once," he said, chuckling. "Let me know if you need a—if you need help."

You remembered. Huh.

Ahna plucked another mushroom from its roots and felt cool air caress her cheek.

"Sticks?" asked Ahna. "Do you feel a breeze?"

Sticks turned toward her, then tilted his head slightly. "No. Do you?"

Ahna thought she may have imagined it, but it happened again. A breeze drifted across her skin, this time bearing an odor she couldn't place.

"Yeah," said Ahna. "Come here. Tell me if you feel it."

He walked over to join her and stood, waiting. A moment later, she felt it again. When his eyes widened, she could tell he'd felt it too.

"See?" she asked. "There's a breeze in here. Weird, right?"

"Yeah," said Sticks. "It is weird. But why would there be a—" He suddenly stopped speaking, his mouth opening wide as he gasped. "Get up, Ahna," he said quietly.

Ahna glanced in the direction he seemed fixated on and realized why he had become so silent. Air escaped her. She hadn't imagined the dancing of the mushrooms, the way they bobbed like buoys in the ocean. However, the ones in front of them moved quite a bit more than those she'd seen at the opening of the room. She hadn't thought twice about it, but she wished she had. Attached to the mushrooms below her was the source of the breeze, or breath, as she would now classify it: a Waller.

She looked around the rest of the room, wondering how many more she'd missed, and realized how bad it truly was. The mushrooms had deceived her with their natural beauty, acting as a camouflage for those feral beasts. She counted five more in total. Her lungs filled deeply as she struggled to think of a plan. She turned to Sticks.

"You thinking what I'm thinking?" she whispered.

"Get the heck out of here as quietly as we can? Yeah," replied Sticks.

They backed away, Ahna feeling as though she were attempting to walk a tightrope with each step—a tightrope that would end with her being ripped to shreds if she fell. As they crept through the remaining portion of the room, she could finally hear the collective sound of their breathing echo around the chamber. She'd never get over the dichotomy of the serene nature of the ocean and the vicious Wallers drowning in the illusion.

Sticks stifled a groan as he caught himself against a large rock near the exit on the other side of the room. A high-pitched clink echoed slightly around the room as a screw fell out of his braces onto the hard rock floor. Ahna drew in a deep breath, awaiting the imminent chaos. She felt her heartbeat attempting to accompany the melodic clang of the loose screw, which had finally slowed its roll across the cave floor. Ahna and Sticks waited a moment longer. Surprisingly, the room fell back into the silence of sleeping Wallers. Sighs escaped them both simultaneously, relief entering her with the next breath.

Ahna looked at his braces and knew they couldn't leave the screw behind. She held out the handful of mushrooms she'd collected to Sticks, whose titled eyebrows led her to whisper her plan.

"Take these. I'm gonna get that screw," she said.

She shoved the mushrooms into his hands, and he gave in, taking the bundle.

"Are you crazy?"

"Aren't we all?" asked Ahna, smirking.

She turned away before he could fight her on it, before she could change her mind. As though she were back outside the main gate of Tent City, she stealthily stepped back into the middle of the room. Between each step, she waited for the next exhale from the Wallers. She kept her own breathing in sync. When she reached the location of the loose screw, she sucked in a deep breath, holding it as she bent down to grab the screw, which was only an inch away from the face of a sleeping Waller. She gripped the screw but froze on the way up.

An eye was staring straight at her.

Don't move, Ahna. Just stay really, really still . . .

Her heart and lungs felt like they were going to explode as she stood, statuesque, shaking slightly. She watched as the eye traveled up and down her figure, then blinked. A wet eyelid trailed back across the eye, leaving a slimy residue in its path. Then it blinked again, the eyelid traveling slower than before. Ahna felt her lungs collapsing with each blink of the Waller, knowing she had mere seconds before she'd have to let it out and breathe again. She didn't dare move, not even her mouth.

The eyelid parked at the bottom of the eye. The Waller had fallen back asleep.

Ahna let out a stream of air, dots of light dancing within her blurred vision. She sucked in as much air as she could to refill her lungs, then tiptoed back to Sticks. After they exchanged the mushrooms for the loose screw, Sticks put it back into place as quietly as he could. He pulled on the brace to ensure the screw was secure before they continued out of the room.

As they moved deeper into the cave, the blue light from the mushrooms illuminated their path. They just had to figure out where that path led.

Chapter Twenty-Four
Sticks

A spiderweb of tunnels snaked away from the center of the open area where they stood. Continuous dripping echoed from one of the tunnels, though Sticks couldn't tell which one. Everything looked the same once they'd gotten so far. When it came to the forests, he felt right at home, but when he was forced to navigate beneath the trees, without the sun, he felt completely lost. Not that he would admit that to Ahna, however. Besides, she was supposed to be their leader. Now was her chance to prove it.

At least this way I won't have to take the blame for whatever happens.

"Which way?" he asked.

Ahna peered down each tunnel as though she were expecting to see a sign flashing with the message, *This way! Obvious choice here!* Then she said something he'd never expected to hear come out of her mouth.

"I think you'd probably know better than me. What do you think?" she asked.

He was genuinely surprised by her response. He'd fully expected for her to jolt down one of the tunnels headfirst without a concern for their safety or at least have a choice already made. He knew it was no surprise to her that he found her leadership questionable. He'd voiced his opinion a few times already.

Maybe you're finally learning. It's about time.

Sticks looked at each of the tunnels once more. None of them looked especially exciting, but he used his senses. He'd heard the dripping from somewhere, so he focused on it, just like he used to do with animal footsteps in the woods.

I guess it's not as different underground as it is above, huh?

He pointed to the tunnel on the far right, the source of the dripping.

"That one," he said.

"You seem confident about that," said Ahna. "How are you so sure?"

"I'm not," replied Sticks, a smirk across his face. "Sometimes the best decision is the one that gets made."

He grabbed one of the mushrooms from Ahna, then started off down the tunnel as he held it out in front of him.

I'm not gonna trip again. Once is embarrassing enough.

"HOLD UP," SAID STICKS, slowing his pace as they neared the exit of the tunnel. There was a glow just beyond the opening, only it was different than the one they'd seen in the room before with the mushrooms. The one in front of them wasn't blue or changing in brightness. It looked familiar, warm. He spotted a glint of light reflecting off something on the ceiling of the tunnel near the exit.

Pipes.

Metal pipes snaked along the top of the tunnel toward the opening ahead. At the crossroads of two pipes, he spotted the source of the dripping noise: a small leak from the seams. While he would have suspected such a thing from rusty old pipes, these were not that at all. In fact, they looked much newer than most anything else he'd seen. It struck him as strange, which sparked a curiosity within him. Sticks followed the pipes through the end of the tunnel, the light ahead growing brighter with each step.

Before he made it much farther down the tunnel, he felt a slight shock reverberate through his skull. He winced, gripping the wall. It was gone before he knew it, but it had made sure he could tell it was there. As he waited for it to return, he focused on catching his breath.

"You okay?" asked Ahna.

Sticks nodded. "All good. Just choked on my saliva." He forced a chuckle.

"I get that," replied Ahna, laughing. "I hate when that happens."

He waited until his heart stopped racing and his lungs returned to their normal rate of inflation. Running his fingers over the remnants of the implant in his head, he exhaled deeply.

I'll have Wick look into it when we get back. Stupid thing hasn't done this since we left Deliverance . . .

They continued down the tunnel until they reached the end. Sticks stopped again, his mouth hanging open as he stared at the fence now creating a barrier between them and the area beyond. What lay beyond that thin metal spiderweb would prove to be useful . . . if they could get to it.

Boxes, crates, barrels, and other various containers littered the cavern floor. Most of them looked sealed or clasped shut, except for the barrels. The wood that had been used to create them all looked to be from another region, nothing like the fir and pine they'd been traveling through the past month or so. It was all stained a similar shade of dark brown as well, though some had been scraped and scratched.

Probably rats. There's no way those Wallers found their way inside there. Unless it's unlocked . . .

Sticks pushed on the handle of the gate, but it didn't move an inch. Not that he was surprised. He handed the mushroom he'd been using back to Ahna and pulled out his knife. He pulled his arm back to strike the handle.

"What are you doing?" asked Ahna, breaking his focus.

"I was gonna stab the thing," he said, letting out a burst of air and gesturing to the gate handle with his knife. "Until you interrupted me."

Ahna chuckled. "You think that's gonna open it?" she asked.

Judging by the look she gave him, he knew the answer.

"No," he said. "But I'm out of other ideas unless you know how to pick a lock like this."

His laugh was cut short as Ahna thrust the pile of blue mushrooms into his hands and pushed him aside. She pulled a small, skinny piece of metal from her hair. He'd seen her wearing it plenty of times but had no idea why she was removing it for this situation. Sarah wore the same kind of metal in her hair, which had made Sticks believe it was some kind of weird uniform piece from the facility that they'd never gotten rid of. He figured out that it may be useful when she inserted it into the lock and jimmied it around.

"Don't just stand there. Help me," said Ahna.

Sticks joined her at the gate and shrugged. "What am I supposed to do?"

"Rotate the handle a bit. Then, when I tell you, thrust upward with all you've got. You think you can do that?" she asked.

Sticks nodded. There should have been no question that he could handle such a simple task, but he wouldn't argue with her. Too much to do, not enough time.

He gripped the cold metal handle, moving it up and down at her direction. She continued to move the metal piece inside the lock mechanism.

"Now!" she barked.

Sticks thrust his weight into the handle as he pushed it upward. The handle moved completely, causing him to stumble forward through the gate. He threw his arms in front of him and tucked as he approached the ground. Sticks let out a grunt as he landed on his forearms. Ahna chuckled.

"Smooth, Sticks," she said. "Need a hand?"

She extended her hand to him, which he gripped. She helped him to his feet, and he dusted off his armor and coughed, sending the dirt and dust out of his mouth. Now that they were through the gate, he had a chance to look around at what was inside the room.

Guns and staffs sprouted from the mouths of barrels, their condition surprisingly pristine. While some looked older than others, they had all been there for a while. That was obvious by the water stains and small mold spores growing on the edges of certain planks. Mold wasn't the only thing they all had in common, though.

"Look who they belong to," said Sticks, pointing at the barrel containing the guns.

Ahna gasped when she spotted the stork logo.

"The Delivery Company?"

Sticks nodded. "Yep. Looks like they stored some of their goods here."

He could see Ahna's eyes circling around as if she were accessing folders in different areas of her memory.

"Why would they have all of this underground, especially in a place so close to Wallers?"

"Good question," said Sticks. "They'd need to have a way to get to it all without having to fight off the Wallers every time, right?"

Ahna nodded.

He meandered through the maze of crates and barrels, looking for answers to their questions.

The pipes must lead to the facility. That means, as long as they weren't put here too long ago, they could lead us right to—

Sticks stopped in his tracks, gasping.

"Ahna, over here!"

She rushed over to join him, and they stared at the large metal door in front of them, eyes wide with excitement.

The doorway stretched about twenty feet across and ten feet high. There was a small window in the center of the metal, but there was no sign of a handle or other method of opening it. On both sides, lights illuminated the entrance and the surrounding area. Another biometric-type scanner was affixed to the wall to the right, slightly newer looking than the ones they had seen in the abandoned facility. Sticks pulled out his knife and crept toward the door, Ahna following behind him. Once they reached the door, he paused.

"Hold up," he whispered, peering through the small window in the center. Dimly lit by the warm bulbs overhead, the room was practically empty—at least empty enough they didn't need to worry about anybody shooting at them right away.

The room wasn't large. The floor was comprised of metal grating, the walls adorned with some sort of nozzles. He couldn't tell what for, but it didn't look like a shower. A small screen hung from the back of the room above another doorway, inactive. Next to a door on the opposite end was another scanner, just like the one keeping them from getting inside.

His voice returned to normal as he turned back to Ahna. "No sign of Elite."

"Then why don't we see what's inside?" asked Ahna, a smile stretching across her face.

Sticks shrugged. "Up to you. You're the leader, remember?"

She nodded, then walked over to the scanner on the wall next to the door. "Think this works the same as the other facility?"

"I don't see why not," replied Sticks. "Either it'll open the door or it'll destroy your hand in a massive explosion. Either way, it'll be interesting."

Ahna glared at him, her look of anger melting into one of worry. "You don't think it'll actually do that, do you?"

Her eyes widened, and Sticks immediately felt a twinge in his chest.

Oh, shoot. I didn't think that would get to you . . .

"No, definitely not," said Sticks. "It was just a joke. It will probably open the door like before or not work at all. Nothing to worry about."

At least, I hope not.

Ahna exhaled before placing her palm on the scanner. It took a second before the box whirred to life, and they heard the familiar beep as it scanned her palm.

"Ow!" Ahna jumped as she pulled her hand away from the box.

"What's wrong?" asked Sticks. He felt his body fly into fight mode, ready to swipe anything that came close to them.

"It pricked my hand," said Ahna, holding her palm out toward him. A small red line ran through the middle of it.

"Why would it do that? None of the others did," said Sticks.

"I don't know!" said Ahna, gripping her hand.

A red light emitted from the box on the wall, and they heard a voice speak from within it.

"Partial match unacceptable. Please try again."

Ahna huffed. "I'm not giving you any more of my blood."

"But it's thirsty," said Sticks, chuckling.

"Ha ha, very funny," said Ahna. "That hurt, you know."

"Looks like it."

"Well, I'm not doing it again. Why didn't it work?" she asked.

Sticks shrugged. "Maybe they've upgraded since last time, or maybe it was a fluke. No way to tell for sure."

A sound of forced air and metal rattling came from behind the door. Sticks shushed Ahna and gestured at the crates behind them. They hurried to hide behind them, crouching low. The door opened, revealing a pair of Elite.

No way . . .

Sticks had to keep himself from audibly reacting to what he saw. Their armor was upgraded heavily from the last time they'd faced off against the Elite in Deliverance. It fit their bodies more efficiently, allowing for more movement and simultaneous-ly guaranteeing more coverage and protection. On top of that, he could see blades attached to the underside of their forearms and small boosters at the back of their feet. There was no mistaking the design. It was an upgraded version of the prototype he'd built for them while under their control.

Ahna looked at him, her face frozen in shock, and he felt as if he were staring at a reflection of himself. He could tell that she recognized the armor suits, too. She didn't have to say a word; her eyes pierced straight through him. His thoughts raced as he watched the upgraded Elite scour the area. Once he saw how they had used his designs, he knew he had to find a way to fix it, fix everything.

I helped them . . . I helped the enemy. Just like before . . .

Sticks swallowed, wiping away the sweat that had started to streak down his forehead.

If we lose, it's gonna be all my fault.

Chapter Twenty-Five
Felan

"Hold it steady, Felan," said Elaine.

Her voice was soft and smooth, like the clouds that skated across the sky above them.

"I'm trying," replied Felan, huffing. "It's heavy."

Felan gripped the rifle as best she could, attempting to hold the butt against her shoulder. The cold numbed her fingers, making it difficult for her to keep it from slipping. Elaine stepped to the side and held the barrel up for her while she placed her other hand on Felan's shoulder.

"Oftentimes, when what we carry is heavy, we need only to ask for another to lend a hand," said Elaine. Her smile sent a warmth through Felan's body. She smiled back, nodding.

"Thanks."

Elaine nodded. There was a rustle in the leaves nearby, and she placed a finger to her lips. She made a slight shushing sound, then listened for a moment until the rustling returned.

"You hear that?" she whispered.

Felan nodded, keeping her mouth shut. She heard the crunch of the compacting snow beneath heavy steps. Whatever it was moved closer, heading straight toward them. Harsh breathing accompanied each step as it approached their position.

"There," said Elaine, pointing downhill and to the left.

About twenty yards away, Felan spotted a dark coat of fur and antlers moving between the trees. Its head bowed as it ducked beneath a low-hanging limb and continued through the snow. The wind changed direction, and the deer stopped, sniffing the air. Felan looked to Elaine, her eyes wide. She knew their scent would be carried downwind if it blew in the right direction, and she didn't want to spook the deer. She held her breath as it continued sniffing for a moment longer. Once it lowered its head and moved forward again, she released her breath.

Elaine moved in to whisper in her ear.

"Are you ready?"

That question was something Felan had asked herself for so long before that day. Now that she was with Elaine, she finally knew the answer. She swallowed, nodding.

"One hundred percent," replied Felan.

Elaine smiled. "Steady your aim and take the shot."

Her command eased Felan's mind as she moved the deer into her sights, swaying slightly as she struggled to keep it steady. She watched it walk toward a tree, then start to rub the bark with its antlers. After a deep breath, the sway of the gun disappeared, and she was able to focus on the task in front of her. She clicked the safety off. The world went silent as she exhaled again, her finger caressing the trigger. Once the deer stopped moving and the crosshairs landed on its neck, she squeezed.

Felan rocked backward into the tree behind her as the gunshot echoed through the trees. Her breath returned, the smoke clearing to reveal the deer lying on the ground only inches from where she'd shot *it. Her smile quickly vanished as a cry escaped the deer and clawed at her brain. Had she not seen a cloud of air escape with each cry coming from the deer, she'd have sworn it was a human.*

Her heart raced as she watched the deer twitch. She was unable to take a full breath. No part of her would move, as though she'd been frozen to her spot. She felt Elaine's hand on her shoulder and the muffled voice speak to her. The words became clear as Elaine repeated herself.

"Reload, Felan. We can't let it suffer."

Felan felt her hands move, watched as she went through the motions of reloading her rifle. Each step was perfectly executed, just like practice. She raised the gun to her shoulder once more and pulled the trigger. Silence enveloped them, the cries of the deer carried away on the breeze. Felan snapped back into the moment, her heart and head throbbing as the cold returned to her face. She wiped away the tears that had trickled down her cheek and stood up.

"Well done, Felan," said Elaine.

Felan nodded. She started to walk down the hill, then stopped.

"Does it ever get easier?" asked Felan.

Elaine's smile faded. She shook her head.

"No," she replied. She paused, looking toward the deer and then back to Felan. "It never gets easier, but we can always get better. Sometimes you'll have a choice. But I want to make sure you're ready for the moments you don't."

Felan nodded, her body starting to relax. Elaine reached into her bag and pulled out a thick strap.

"Hand me your gun."

Felan handed the rifle to Elaine, who started to attach the strap to either end of it.

"What are you doing?" asked Felan.

"I made this a while back, but I wanted to wait until this moment to give it to you," said Elaine. She finished attaching the strap to the rifle.

"Why?" asked Felan.

"To lighten the load and to remind you of today. This way I can help you even when I'm not around." She handed the rifle back to Felan.

"Thanks," said Felan.

"You're welcome, Felan. Besides," continued Elaine, "it might just save your life one of these days."

Felan smiled as her fingers ran along the smooth strands of string, colorful and ornate. She stared at the silhouette of a deer standing in front of a setting sun, a perfect depiction of their day together.

FRAYED STRANDS STRETCHED out from the setting sun as Felan stroked the strap with her thumb. Her calloused fingers continued along, following the outline of the deer to the spot where the tower had damaged its body. Felan chuckled to herself, a cloud appearing in front of her face as she sat behind the broken glass of the guard box.

I guess you were right. You did save me. One day soon, I'm gonna thank you for it, too.

Felan turned her attention to the mountainside below.

The trees danced in the breeze as the snow continued to fall. Each day welcomed more snow and colder temperatures than the last. Wick had mentioned the possibility of harsher weather coming but was uncertain of the time frame and full probability. Not that she fully believed him. She couldn't see how people could predict the weather. Mother Nature was unpredictable.

And unfair.

Wick had told her about how, prewar, people used to predict weather for everyone in their city. Of course, they hadn't had massive amounts of radiation affecting their weather patterns. Though, Wick had said they had a problem with something called an ozone layer. She didn't fully understand it, but apparently it was a layer in the sky that helped keep weather in somewhat of a pattern. She didn't argue with him, either. He usually knew what he was talking about. Besides, she didn't really understand all the words he used anyway. It was always easier to let him talk and try to piece it together afterward.

Crunching behind her alerted Felan to someone's approach. Before she turned to see who it was, she smelled the cooked onions and deer. She used to love that soup, but it had gotten old fast.

Steam clouded Marie's glasses as she stepped into the guard box, extending the soup to Felan. Felan gripped the cup in her hands, the warm container a welcome addition to the cold interior. Marie smiled, pushing her glasses back up her nose.

"Thought you might be hungry," said Marie.

Felan felt her stomach rumble as the scent of soup continuously flowed through her nostrils.

"You thought right," said Felan. "Where's the—"

"Inside."

Marie tapped the top of the container. Felan removed the top to the soup and saw it inside, just as Marie had said. Surrounding the spoon was an abnormal amount of meat, much more than she'd seen in the usual portions. Felan smiled.

"Thanks. What's with all the meat, though? This looks like double the usual amount."

Marie shrugged. "I gave you mine."

Why would you do that?

"But you need to eat, too, Mar. You can't just skip meals," said Felan. "It's not healthy."

Marie crossed her arms. "I know what's healthy, Felan. Besides, I didn't skip the meal, just the meat. I thought you'd be happy to get a little extra. Sorry I was wrong."

Marie started to turn around, but Felan gripped her shoulder.

"Marie, wait," said Felan.

Marie stared at her, her glasses slightly foggy again. Felan's voice became soft and low.

"I appreciate you bringing me the soup and giving me your portion of the meat. It means a lot. I guess I was just worried about you not getting enough."

Marie smiled slightly, one hand gripping Felan's shoulder.

"I have enough," said Marie. "Trust me."

Her heart beat fast, each throb leading into the next, her thoughts racing a mile a minute. She looked into Marie's eyes, noticing the small details she'd never seen before. Her glasses helped to increase their size, which only helped her look even cuter. Felan smiled.

"Marie, I was thinking—"

Shouts interrupted her, and Felan felt her cheeks flush as she was forced to pull her eyes away from Marie's. She turned to look in the direction of the shouts, which had come from the woods below. Two silhouettes appeared, outlined by the sun behind them. Sticks and Ahna were running up the hill at full speed.

With a Waller behind them.

Felan swung her rifle up to its familiar position, the butt resting in its home on her shoulder. Marie's words fell into a muffled murmur as Felan switched off the safety and placed the crosshairs between the eyes of the Waller. She had no time to determine the wind direction or distance because the Waller was coming up right behind Sticks and Ahna. Judging by their faces, they knew it was going to get them.

Felan fired off a shot, her hand gripping the bolt and pulling it back to reload the rifle before she took another breath. Her sight never left Ahna and Sticks, but the Waller had disappeared. Upon a quick movement downward, she spotted it in a pool of blood behind them, motionless. Ahna's face was frozen in awe, which made her chuckle. She switched the safety back on and lowered her rifle.

"You should have seen the looks on their faces, Marie. Hilarious." Felan started to spin back around to face her. "Sorry for the interruption, Marie. Like I was saying, I thought maybe we could—"

Oh . . .

A trail of footprints led from the guard box back to the main entrance of the facility. Marie had vanished. Felan's posture sagged, her head lowered toward her chest as she exhaled deeply.

Never mind.

Chapter Twenty-Six
D-72

D-72 circled another spot on the map, which was now more circles than not. After he looked it over, he sat back and crossed his arms. Scorcher looked at the map, then at him. He seemed shocked at the number of circles, but D-72 couldn't understand why.

Scorcher finally sat back to face him again, still processing the information. He shook his head.

"No way," said Scorcher. "You must be lying so that we get scared or something."

That's ridiculous. Why would I do that? I don't want to scare you. I'm not a scary person. If anything, I feel like I get scared by people more than I scare them. Is that a bad thing? Should I be worried about that? I mean, my size should be something that keeps me from being scared. I don't know why I'm like this. If people didn't scare me, I wouldn't freak out and end up hurting them so easily. If she hadn't scared me, then maybe I would've had a family instead of ending up—

"D-72?"

Uh-oh. Was he talking to me again? His face looks mad. His eyebrows look like fuzzy caterpillars in spring. I miss those. I wonder if they'll be out again. I should go look for some again. That's always fun.

"D-72!" shouted Scorcher.

D-72 felt his body tense up, but he tried to put his focus entirely on Scorcher going forward.

"Sorry," said D-72. "What?"

Scorcher sighed before grabbing the map and thrusting it toward him. "You circled all these spots," he said, pointing at each circle before landing on their current abandoned facility. "And somehow they are all around us. Are you trying to scare us with this information?"

D-72 shook his head. "No. Never. You said circle where they have units, so I circled."

"How do I know that you aren't lying?" asked Scorcher, his voice raised slightly.

I followed orders. I followed orders. I followed orders. I followed orders. I followed orders.

The lights above started to become brighter, a buzzing sound growing with the brightness. It was starting to grow too much, as though he had a hive of bees in his head. He couldn't take all the noise.

"D-72?" asked Scorcher.

"I followed orders!" D-72 yelled. "I followed orders! I followed orders!"

Scorcher raised his hands and stared directly into D-72's eyes. "It's okay," he said, his tone soothing. "It's okay."

D-72 slowly lowered his voice until he repeated it for one last time, almost inaudible.

"I followed orders."

"I know," said Scorcher. "You've done a good job of that so far. It's clear you follow orders very well. That's probably why you came up here to us, right?"

D-72 nodded.

I have many more things I excel at, too, but nobody ever wants to know that. Nobody really wants to know me at all. They all do what you do; everyone yells at me and tells me what to do. Then they freak out when I get upset because of what they did. It's their fault, not mine. It's not my fault that other people make me upset. I'm good at my job. I'm a good person.

"That's what I thought you'd say." Scorcher paused, leaning back. "What's your name?"

Why are you asking me for my name? You've been saying it multiple times already. Is this some sort of trick? Why are you still teasing me?

"You know it. D-72."

Scorcher shook his head. "No. Not your designation, your name."

D-72 tilted his head, scratching his nails against his pants as he rocked slightly in his chair.

"Is that not it?" he asked.

Scorcher shook his head and laughed.

Are you laughing at me? I thought you were being nice. What's going on?

"No. They aren't the same thing at all."

"How are they not?" asked D-72.

Scorcher seemed a little surprised by his question. It didn't help that he answered his question with more questions.

"What do you like to do?" asked Scorcher.

"What do you mean?"

"What do you like? Like, what are you good at? Do you do anything in your free time?"

Free time? I don't do anything other than what I'm supposed to do. I'm good at many things, though.

"I'm a good fighter."

Scorcher laughed but stopped quickly after D-72 scowled at him.

"That's good. What else?" asked Scorcher.

"People call me big. I guess I'm good at that."

Scorcher covered his mouth, most likely in an attempt to hold back a laugh, which D-72 appreciated. It was clear he was trying to not upset him further. The questions he was asking almost felt like he wanted to know him a little. It felt good to be asked those things.

"Being big isn't something you can necessarily say is something you like to do . . . but you would say you're good at using your size against others, right?"

D-72 nodded.

"Okay. So you're a big guy who likes to fight," said Scorcher. "I'll work on your name ideas a bit later, but first . . ." Scorcher sprung up from his seat, jarring D-72. Scorcher walked over and opened the door, smiling. "I have an idea."

D-72's eyes narrowed. "What idea?"

"You said you're good at fighting. I want to see how good."

"OW!"

Scorcher picked himself up from the floor and dusted off his chest. He shook his head and stretched his eyebrows toward the sky, his eyes wide.

"You okay?" asked D-72.

I don't want to hurt you. You are not very big and didn't get the same training that I did. It seems very unfair.

"I'm fine. Good hit."

"Thanks." D-72 smiled.

Nobody has ever said that in a serious way before. Usually, it's always followed by a laugh or something.

Scorcher leapt toward him, catching him off guard. D-72 moved sideways just in time, reaching out to grab Scorcher's arm as it passed by. The look on Scorcher's face quickly confirmed his suspicions. He had moved much quicker than he'd thought. He wasn't finished.

D-72 didn't let Scorcher wriggle for more than a second in his grip before flinging him down to the ground again, adding a chop to his back on the way down. Scorcher grunted as he smacked into the floor.

D-72 laughed. It was the first time he remembered laughing at something like that in a long time.

A foot swept under his legs, causing him to stumble to the floor. Scorcher then slid out of the way and chopped him on the back, mimicking his previous move.

"Bigger you are, the harder you fall. And you fell hard," said Scorcher, laughing. He extended his hand toward D-72. "Let me help you up."

D-72 grabbed his hand and started to regain his stance. Before he was all the way up, Scorcher flung him to the side, tripping him again. His face met the floor, and he heard popping in his ear.

"Ugh!" he groaned.

D-72 balled his fists and huffed as he pushed himself back up from the ground.

"That's two all," said Scorcher. "Not so bad myself, huh?" he asked, gloating. "Maybe next time you won't be so—"

D-72 slammed into Scorcher with his shoulder at full speed. Scorcher's feet dangled in the air as D-72 ran faster and flung Scorcher across the room.

Metal clanged, steam burst from a pipe, and glass shards went flying as a nasty goo seeped from the tube Scorcher now lay under. D-72 saw red liquid joining the green, and his eyes widened.

A boy rode into the room on a scooter and started yelling.

"What are you doing? Do you know what this is? Who is—" He stopped when he realized it was Scorcher under the tube. "Scorcher? Are you okay?"

A groan escaped the rubble.

"Scorcher?" asked D-72, moving toward him.

The boy on the scooter cut him off, heading toward D-72 instead. His voice seemed to amplify the closer he got.

"Don't come near my friend! Why did you do that? You monster! That was a good guy you just hurled into a very important work of science, too. Now we might never know how it worked! Stupid Elite. What were you thinking?"

I'm sorry. I'm so sorry. I didn't mean to hurt him. I didn't mean to hurt him. He tricked me. I thought he was helping me . . . It's not my fault.

As the boy got closer, he started waving his fist toward him.

"Get out of here! Go! Get out, now!"

D-72 backed away from him and turned to run as soon as he could get out.

The hallways all looked the same, metal with lights blinding him at every turn. Nowhere felt safe, no matter where he went. He kept moving forward, bumping into people and objects, until he finally ran into a door. Without a second thought, he opened it and went inside, shutting the door behind him.

Finally. This feels good. Focus on that. Just focus on what's here. Nobody can hurt me in here.

Tattered clothing and darkness surrounded him. A warm fuzzy piece of cloth fell over his shoulders, as though someone were comforting him in their embrace. He scratched into his pants, his fingernails following the indentions already created. As he scratched, he counted for as long as he could, focusing on nothing but his breathing and the numbers.

Eventually, he would have to come out of the small dark place. Until then, he would stay safe, wrapped in the arms of another unwanted, forgotten scrap.

Chapter Twenty-Seven
Ahna

Ahna peered through the crack in the doorway and watched as dust particles danced above Scorcher's head in the fluorescent light. Shadows exaggerated the scars on his face, drawing her attention to them even from afar. She felt it strange, considering how long it had been since she'd taken any time to look at them. When they'd first gotten together, he wouldn't let her see them. Most days since then she barely noticed them. She had become more interested in the person they'd made their mark on. After seeing the bandages wrapped around his body, she hoped he wouldn't be adding any additional scars to his collection.

Scorcher rustled in his bed, which meant he was awake.

I should probably stop staring and go in. I'll never hear the end of it if he notices me out here first.

Ahna pushed the door open and strode inside.

"Wow. You look a lot better than I expected," said Ahna. She forced a laugh.

Scorcher moved to face her, trying to laugh with her. What came out instead was a groan.

"Say that within reach and I'll have to make it so you're in the bed next to me." He smirked.

Ahna raised her eyebrows. "More efficient if we just shared one, right?"

Scorcher's eyes widened. "Maybe I should do it after all."

They both laughed again, but the laughter quickly melted into an awkward silence. For a moment, during the laughter, it almost felt like they'd returned to normal. She missed normal.

Ahna moved to the edge of the bed. She reached for his hand, his coarse sandpaper palm a stark contrast to her own. His fingers slid between hers, surprisingly warm. She wouldn't complain about that, though. Her hands and feet had always been abnormally cold growing up. Scorcher used to joke about her being only three-quarters as cold now. She'd always laughed at that joke even though she'd never found it funny. She did that for most of his jokes. The fact that he had so many only made it a little more difficult. Thinking of some of them in this moment made her chuckle.

"What?" asked Scorcher.

She felt his hand almost pull away. Her laughter dissipated as she gripped his hand tighter.

"I miss this," said Ahna.

Scorcher tilted his head, eyebrows scrunched toward the middle. "Miss what?"

"This," said Ahna, shaking his hand slightly.

"Holding my hand?"

"Not just that." Ahna shook her head. Her tone softened. "Being with you, nobody else around—alone, together."

His fingers tightened like a boa constrictor around hers, each cut on his hands a small monument to all the things they'd been through. All those Wallers, the countless nights of patrolling, the sacrifices they'd made to get to where they were. But she wouldn't trade those moments for anything. It certainly hadn't been easy getting here, but she had help. She had Scorcher.

"I don't think you can be that, Ahna. Kinda goes against the meaning of the words, doesn't it?" asked Scorcher.

Ahna chuckled. "Would it kill you to pretend to be dumb sometimes?"

Scorcher gestured to his bandages, red now soaking through the top layer.

"Clearly."

Though he was joking, Ahna could sense his worry. She'd seen him training harder the last few weeks, pushing himself to his limits. When he broke a toe a while back, she wanted to yell at him, tell him how much he was putting at risk by acting so careless. Instead, she'd helped splint it and taken care of anything he was supposed to do that would require more time on his feet so he could heal faster. She wasn't sure if that's how that worked, but it made her feel better to at least pretend it did.

"You have to be more careful from now on, Scorch," said Ahna.

"I was," said Scorcher, wincing as he tried to move. "Turns out they train those Elite a bit better here. He's not such a bad guy, either."

"What makes you say that?" asked Ahna.

"Had a nice talk with him before he ended up trying to use me to remodel the metal walls. I'll have to make sure to watch for his tell next time we spar. Won't let him get me with that again, I know that much."

As he was talking, Ahna couldn't help but stare at the bruises scattered over his body. A few more and he'd be more bruised than not. If he had been any unluckier, she wasn't sure that he would even be there to talk to. She couldn't let him be so care-less going forward. He was one of the key people for the attack, and there was no way it would succeed without him. They need-ed him, but so did she.

"I'm starting to worry about you. When I was talking to Sticks—"

"Of course you were," said Scorcher. He shuffled in the bed, moving away from her.

His demeanor mirrored that of the cold winter night beyond the window.

"What's wrong?" asked Ahna. She knew that he and Sticks had been fighting before, but surely it was something more. If not, she hadn't realized how petty he was.

"I don't know," said Scorcher. "Why don't you go ask him?"

"Ask who?"

"Sticks."

The name escaped Scorcher's mouth as though he were spit-ting out a moldy piece of meat. Ahna's jaw clenched.

"What's Sticks got to do with this?" she asked. She was gen-uinely interested to hear his response.

"Exactly, Ahna," said Scorcher. The way he said her name made her face heat up. "What's Sticks got to do with anything?"

"He's a part of the group—a big part of it. Besides, he's also our friend," said Ahna.

Scorcher raised his eyebrows. "Just a friend, huh? Sure that's all?"

"What are you trying to say?"

Ahna could feel herself transition into fight mode. Her blood rushed through her veins, her heart racing.

"You're smart, Ahna. What do you think I'm saying?"

She let her words flow without a second thought.

"Look, Scorcher. I don't know what your deal is with Sticks, but you shouldn't include me in it. Whatever you two have going on, whatever this is, has to stop. It doesn't matter who is the strongest, smartest, has the best staff, or whatever you're arguing about this week. Instead of worrying about things that don't matter, you should focus on what does: us. The group needs you to help take care of them, which isn't likely to happen when I've gotta take care of you. You need to be more careful, Scorch. Whatever's going on with Sticks needs to stop, today. Got it?"

Scorcher's mouth hung open. He was stunned, something she'd not seen him display before. Through the anger, she felt a bit of pride. If nothing else, she'd gotten a genuine reaction out of him. Finally, he nodded his head in response to her question.

"All right," he said. "As long as you promise me the same thing."

What's gotten into you?

"Sure," said Ahna. "Nothing's going on with me and Sticks. It never has, never will. You should know that by now. If not, you should at least know me by now."

Scorcher scanned her body before landing on her eyes. Anger had been replaced with something much deeper, something almost solemn.

"It's hard to know you as well when you don't spend time with me anymore, Ahna."

"What are you talking about? We're always together."

"Name the last time we spent time alone, just the two of us."

"Okay," Ahna said.

This should be easy. I know we've been together a lot recently. I've just gotta think of one time . . . just one time. What is that one time, though? What about—no, that doesn't count. Oh! There was . . . wait. Never mind. Why can't I think of something? Why can't I think of something . . .

"You can't, can you?" asked Scorcher.

Ahna tried to remember something, anything to use as an example. She couldn't. Ahna shook her head, her eyes tearing up.

"I'm sorry, Scorch. I don't know why I didn't realize it."

Scorcher shrugged. "You weren't avoiding me on purpose?"

"No," Aha said quickly. "You really think I would do that?"

"I was starting to," he said.

I've never seen you be this open before. I must have really messed up . . .

"I never want to avoid you. I might not want to be around you because of a stupid joke you made or something," said Ahna. They both laughed. "But I'd never avoid you completely. Trust me."

Scorcher nodded, smiling. "I do."

Ahna smiled, feeling the last bit of worry escape her body in a sigh. The red stains scattered across his side caught her attention again.

Wow. I can't believe I almost forgot about that.

Ahna moved toward the desk beside the bed and dug through the drawers. She tossed aside what was left in the collection of junk before she finally felt the cloth rub against her fingertips. It wasn't the softest, but it was clean. That was all that mattered at the moment. Pulling her knife from her waist, she pinned the bandage between her knees, holding the end in her teeth. She cut a strip of the bandage, spitting it onto the bed next to him before returning her knife to its sheath.

"No way," he said, waving his hands in front of him. "Not gonna happen. It's still healing."

"Exactly. And it won't heal correctly if I don't change out the bandage. Unless you want to get an infection."

"You just spit on it."

Ahna chuckled. "You've seen my spit before. Relax."

Ahna watched Scorcher toss the idea around in his mind, his eyes darting from the bandage to her face. Finally, he let out a sigh.

"Fine," he said. He moved so that he was fully upright in bed. "But if you make it worse—"

Ahna put her hand on his shoulder. "Relax," she said, her tone hushed. "I've got this."

They stared into each other's eyes, their breathing in sync. When she could sense that he felt ready, she moved the blanket so that she could access the bandages fully.

Ahna guided her hand over the strips of fabric, still warmed by his skin. Once she found the edge of it, she pulled it off gingerly, unwrapping him like a present in one of the stories she used to hear about Christmas. She'd always wanted to have that experience, opening presents near a tree surrounded by her new family. It seemed so nice, so magical.

For now, I'll just have to settle for unwrapping you . . . not that I mind.

Ahna smirked at the thought of Scorcher covered in wrapping paper under a tree.

"Watch it!" Scorcher cried out. He jerked away.

"Sorry! What happened?" asked Ahna.

"You scraped my insides! That's what happened," said Scorcher.

His emerald eyes burned as he stared into her. She knew he was in pain, but the way he looked at her in that moment made her feel as though she were the one who'd been wounded.

"I—" She took a breath. "Won't happen again." She paused, her voice now stern. "Sit still for second."

"Where are you going?" asked Scorcher.

His voice was almost inaudible due to the hum in her head. Ahna got up and walked over to open the window, a sense of relief escorted on the cool breeze. As it sailed over her skin, she felt a shiver down her spine. The hum disappeared, and she watched the trees outside wave back at her. A snowflake landed on her nose, melting immediately. She was reminded of why she'd come to the window in the first place and cupped her hand. She collected the deposit of snow that had accumulated on the windowsill outside and brought it back in, leaving the window ajar until she could return with an empty hand. Once she reached Scorcher, she sat back on the bed and looked him dead in the eyes.

"Breathe in."

She kept her tone warm, soft. His eyebrows relaxed as he slowly sucked air in through his nostrils.

Now's my chance.

Ahna pushed her hand to his side, feeling the snow melt entirely as it hit the warmth of his body.

"Ah! Ahna, what the—"

"Relax, you big baby. It's just water," said Ahna playfully.

"No, it's ice-cold water. That's much worse."

"Water is water."

Scorcher sighed. He stared at her, his head tilted slightly with his eyebrows raised. Ahna looked back at him for a moment, waiting for him to say something. When his lips didn't part from each other, she had to break the silence.

"What?" asked Ahna.

"Aren't you gonna finish taking care of me? Or were you just gonna leave after making a mess?"

"You're already a mess without my help."

They laughed, and Scorcher gave her a push. Ahna pushed back, which made Scorcher pull back with a wince.

"Careful," said Scorcher, his tone harsh.

"Sorry," said Ahna. Suddenly, she thought she was losing all hope of him forgiving her. She tried his method of making a stupid joke. "I think I forgot you were hurt for a second."

"You know," said Scorcher, sitting up in the bed, "if you're not careful, you're gonna get me killed one of these days." He smirked.

"Maybe it's for the best," said Ahna, smiling.

"At least give me a warning before I go, huh? Wanna make sure I get to eat something good beforehand."

Ahna shook her head. "Well, you're not dying today," she said, resting her hand on his shoulder.

"How can you be so sure?" asked Scorcher.

"Because I've gotta make sure you make it through the doorway of the facility first. I can't let you get out of this mission and leave us to do it without you. Wouldn't be fair to everyone else. After that, though, all bets are off."

"How kind of you."

"I know. Consider it a gift."

"Pretty terrible gift."

"It was the best I could do. I figured this would be better than a rusty spoon or a dead rat."

"How big's the rat?" asked Scorcher.

They laughed until her stomach ached.

"Shut up and sit still."

Scorcher nodded, the smirk still present on his face.

The bandage was barely attached to his torso, hanging down like a streamer they used to use to decorate the halls for Adoption Day.

Wow . . . I haven't thought about that in a while.

She pushed the thought away, focusing instead on what was in front of her: Scorcher. Ahna gripped the bandage near where it clung to his body.

"This is gonna hurt."

Chapter Twenty-Eight
Sticks

Wooden walls stretched toward the sky, flames licking their bare bodies. In the shadows, silhouettes of soldiers marched into the small makeshift city of the Rejected. Metal armor covered his body, carefully crafted to deploy destruction on anyone who stood in his way. It moved well, more efficient and agile than his braces ever could have allowed. He smiled.

Screams pierced the cool night air as they battered down the entrance to Tent City. Sticks gestured forward, shouting for the Elite under his command to search and destroy. As long as he had Lawrence or Seemore—whatever his real name was—he didn't care about the others. He had orders, and he had to follow them.

Metal clashed, sparks flashing like lightning in a storm of chaos. Fire spread around them, its orange glow illuminating more of the town. Tent flaps waved in the breeze, most of their inhabitants either fighting or fleeing. Sticks watched as the scene unfolded, his eyes peeled for any sign of Seemore. He had no doubt he'd find him there. The only question was where.

An arrow skimmed past his ear, close enough that he felt the feather brush against his skin. He turned to see Scorcher smirking in the shadows, bow in hand. Another arrow was already within *his grasp. Behind him, Sticks heard a footstep brush the dirt and turned, ducking as he did so.*

A staff swung above his head, barely missing him. It gave him just enough time to react. He lunged forward, putting all his strength into the strike. The blow landed with such force that Raider flew backward, breath escaping him. Sticks moved toward him, blade extended from his forearm. As he knelt beside Raider, he pushed Raider's shoulder down with one hand, pulling back the blade.

"Please," Raider pleaded, gasping for air. "Please don't do th—"

Sticks plunged the blade into Raider, watching as his eyes widened. He could feel the resistance lessening as he held Raider down and retracted the blade. From the side, a swift motion brought pressure onto his head. A second of pain surged before transitioning to fury.

Sticks watched from the corner of his eye as the staff returned for a second swing. He was ready. Catching the staff midswing, he yanked it from who he now realized was Scout. He snapped the staff in two, tossing it aside and focusing on Scout. It was clear that without the staff, he would have no chance. Sticks laughed at that fact.

Swiftly, Sticks sprung over to Scout and slashed him with the blade. It took mere seconds for Scout to stumble, falling to the ground mere inches from Raider. The two of them lay there, barely breathing, clearly fighting for life. Sticks watched as their chests slowly stopped rising, their pace becoming slower with each breath.

Before heading to find his target, Sticks walked over to make sure they were not going to get up again. As he stood over Raider and Scout, he heard his name come from them both, in unison.

"Sticks," they said, barely a whisper.

It was eerie, as though he were hearing a ghost call his name. The hair on his arms stood up as they repeated themselves.

"Sticks," they said again. "Sticks . . . Sticks . . ."

It was starting to get louder, more urgent. Their voices were starting to melt into one, suddenly sounding nothing like them. Their lifeless eyes stared into his own as his name was yelled out one more time.

"Sticks!"

"STICKS!"

Metal walls and a familiar face stared back at him when he opened his eyes. It felt like he was still there, Raider and Scout staring at him, their never-ending stare. Light poured into view, almost blinding him. Thankfully, as his vision returned to normal, he realized the blurry shadow staring at him was only Wick.

"Finally," said Wick. "I leave you for a few minutes and you fall asleep. I know you haven't gotten much rest since coming back up, but we don't have time for naps anymore."

"How long was I out?" asked Sticks.

It felt like he hadn't just slept but had instead traveled through time. The hair on his arms stretched toward the ceiling, making that feeling even more concrete.

"Not long," said Wick. He paused. "Who are Raider and Scout?"

How do you know about them?

"Why?" asked Sticks.

"Just wondering. You said their names while you were dreaming. I haven't heard you do that before. It was interesting."

Why are you watching me sleep?

"Sorry, guess I was tired," said Sticks. He quickly changed the subject. "We still good for the Waller hunt today?"

Wick smiled, holding up a small box with a group of animals on it. "You bet. Got these from Felan."

Sticks looked closer at the box in Wick's hand. "What are they?"

"Tranquilizer bullets. You know, the kind of stuff that puts large animals to sleep without killing them?"

"Okay . . . and?"

"And I thought we could use them to capture our Wallers. I know it's not quite as ingenious or sophisticated as some mechanical trap, but it will definitely get the job done."

"How long will it keep them knocked out for?" asked Sticks.

Wick shrugged. "Long enough, I guess. No idea."

"What happens if it isn't very long?" asked Sticks.

"We'd better be prepared for that, then." Wick handed him the gun and tranquilizer bullets.

Sticks gulped.

The thought of a Waller waking up in the middle of the transport back and eating him alive was not one he preferred to linger on any longer. Loading the rifle, he focused on the task at hand.

"You sure you'll be all right up here without me?" he asked.

Wick nodded. "Sure. It's not like I haven't done it before," he replied. A chuckle followed.

"Makes sense," said Sticks. "Just checking."

Wick's eyes narrowed slightly. "You need someone to go with you?"

"Nope!" Sticks laughed it off. "I don't need anybody. All good."

"Whatever you say," said Wick.

Slinging the rifle over his shoulder, Sticks started for the doorway and stuffed a handful of extra bullets into his pocket. If he was going to make it out with a knocked-out Waller, he needed to make sure he wasn't going to run out of bullets. He wasn't too worried about it, though. After they had talked the plan through, he felt confident.

"Also," said Wick. Sticks paused halfway out the door.

"Yeah?" asked Sticks. He turned to face him.

"I got a reading from the radar showing a spike in numbers down there. Not sure if it's Elite, Wallers, or both. Figured you should know."

"Thanks."

"No problem," said Wick. "Be careful out there. If you end up a Waller, I won't hesitate." He made a gunshot gesture with his fingers and fired off a couple shots while making sound effects with his mouth.

"You're a terrible shot, Wick. You couldn't kill a Waller if you had it tied down at point-blank."

Wick laughed, Sticks joining in.

"If only I were as fearless as you," said Wick. "Good luck down there. See you when you get back."

Sticks waved before crossing over the threshold of the door. Wick waved back, smiling, before he headed back to work on the computer. Once Sticks made it outside the room, silence amplified the thoughts that had begun to sprout in the back of his mind—thoughts he wasn't used to having.

Maybe I should have asked for someone to go with me . . . Too late now.

SALIVA DRIPPED FROM the tip of the Waller's sharp teeth like a melting icicle. As the Waller sniffed its surroundings, its head jerked side to side. Sticks held his breath, waiting for his moment to strike. He could hear his heartbeat, a low, rapid thumping. It was almost in sync with the marching in the distance near the facility.

Those Elite better not hear this rifle or I'll have bigger problems.

The Waller carved a path through the snow as it headed straight for its next meal. A small piece of meat hung suspended from a tree about ten feet from the cave entrance. That piece of meat was directly in Sticks's crosshairs.

As the Waller neared the bait, it snarled. It sounded almost like a purr, which Sticks thought strange. He'd not heard a Waller make that sound before. The sound was clearly one of joy. When the Waller reached the meat, it started swiping at it with its long nails.

You look like one of those kids hitting the piñata on the poster. Only uglier.

Sticks stifled his laugh, not wanting to give away his position.

The poster had been hanging halfway peeled off the wall of one of the many dilapidated houses on the route out of Deliverance. An animal, which Wick had later confirmed was called a llama, was hanging from a rope on a tree. Its body was covered in bright colors, as if it had rolled around in a rainbow. A group of kids circled around it with sticks raised toward the sky in a victorious pose while candy trickled down like a waterfall onto their joy-filled faces. Meanwhile, the decapitated head of the llama lay on the ground, battered by the barrage of feet.

There's definitely no candy inside that hunk of meat.

Sticks rested his body against the tree that he had been hiding behind and tightened his grip on the rifle. He took a deep breath, a trick he'd learned from watching Felan practice. Once the meat was fully within the grasp of the Waller's sharp nails, Sticks fired off a shot.

His shoulder was thrust back, and a grunt escaped him. He had forgotten how much recoil happened when using the rifle. Returning his eye to the scope, he landed the crosshairs on the Waller, which was now lying on the ground. The chunk of meat was in its hands, but there was no sign of movement.

Did you die? Or do these things just knock you out that quickly?

Sticks smiled, slinging the rifle back over his shoulder, and headed toward the Waller. He hadn't planned on things being this easy but wouldn't complain about the results. If anything, it gave him more time to enjoy being away from the others, cramped inside the old rundown facility.

Snow continued to sprinkle over the landscape, the morning sunlight reflecting off the trees. While autumn was his favorite, winter was a close second. He'd always thought of snow as a white paint that could blind people to the defects of their surroundings. It had a way of making the ugly places a little more beautiful and calm. He hoped to one day have the opportunity to sit and watch the snow fall without wondering if he and his friends, and the rest of the world, would do the same. That day couldn't come fast enough.

Sticks walked down to the Waller, slowing his pace as he neared its body. The Waller's chest rose and fell like a boat on the water. Its eyes were still closed; it was most likely knocked out cold, asleep. He breathed a sigh of relief.

You made this easy on me, you know that? I really thought it would—

A crack penetrated the air behind him.

Sticks swung around, ready to fire off another shot. He almost fell, a slight pain in his knee from the rapid twisting motion.

Wow.

Sticks lowered his rifle and huffed as he stared at a large branch now implanted in the snow at the base of a tree.

Really? Dumb tree and your branches falling off. Almost gave me a heart attack.

He laughed and turned back to deal with the Waller on the ground.

"Now how I am gonna get you back up—"

A low snarl made the hair on his neck stand at attention. Sticks froze, only his eyes slowly rising to look toward the source of the sound. He gulped.

All right, Sticks, nice and slow. Just have to make sure it doesn't get too close.

Sticks inched his finger toward the trigger, and his other hand gripped the body of the rifle. He watched the Waller sniff the air like the one now lying beneath him. Sticks had no idea why they did that; there was nothing to smell. From what he could tell, he wasn't giving off any big scent. It hadn't noticed him yet, but he couldn't risk moving too quickly.

It continued moving toward him, slowly but unwavering in its course. Another crash happened to the side as a mound of snow fell from a tree, and the Waller turned its attention in that direction.

Now's my chance!

Sticks raised the rifle, put his eye to the scope, and pulled the trigger.

Click.

Time stopped when he realized what had happened.

No . . . How did I not reload? No!

In the silence, the click echoed around them. The Waller's head snapped back toward him, fully aware of his presence. It let out a loud shriek and bolted toward him at full speed.

Sticks fumbled as he pulled back the bolt of the rifle and pulled the previous shell from the chamber. He reached into his pocket for another tranquilizer bullet and thrust it into its spot before pushing the bolt forward.

It stopped halfway.

"No!" Sticks yelled.

He pulled the bolt back again and pushed down on the shell that had gotten stuck halfway going in, then slid the bolt forward again. Once it was fully in, he raised the rifle back to face the Waller, but the Waller was already there.

Sticks pulled the trigger and felt the gun sway heavily. The Waller had pushed it to the side just in time, and he had missed.

"Get back!"

Sticks jammed the butt of the rifle at the incoming Waller's head. There was a crack before it shrieked at him, tripping over the body of its unconscious comrade. Sticks questioned reloading the rifle but knew he didn't have the time. He had to fight.

I've fought a bear . . . I can do this!

Sticks bent down and gripped a handful of snow. He compacted it into a ball and launched it at the Waller as it was standing back up. It was caught off guard and almost fell back down. Sticks ran toward the Waller with the rifle gripped securely in his hands.

He put all his strength behind it as he thrust the barrel into the Waller's chest. The Waller cried out as it swatted the gun away, blood slowly dripping from the spot on its chest. Its eyes widened as it stared at Sticks and shrieked.

Before he knew it, Sticks found himself on the ground, the Waller on top of him. Claws swiped at his face but caught his forearms as he blocked the incoming attack. Sticks struggled to get it off him, to somehow stop the Waller from ripping him to shreds, but had lost that opportunity.

Each swipe cut deeper into his arms, blood soaking through his shirt. He tried to bring his knees up, kick it from underneath, but it was in the perfect position to prevent that from happening. Sticks tried everything he could think to do. Nothing worked. He fought as hard as he could to stay alive, but he was beginning to tire, fast. Even the pain that had surged through his body faded as his body went numb in the snow. Another few swipes and he would have to accept the fact that he was going to die.

At least I'll be with Rollin again . . .

Then, for some reason, the Waller stopped.

What's going on? What's happening?

Its eyes widened, and a shriek escaped its mouth. It was staring at something, but Sticks couldn't see what.

Another Waller?

Suddenly, a large body slammed into the Waller. It happened so fast that Sticks couldn't tell what it was, but it had taken the Waller with it. Sticks was free to move. When he tried to push himself up, he moaned as the pain that had once diminished returned in full force. His arms were torn up, but he didn't have to see much of the damage due to his shirt—or what remained of it, at least.

Shrieks from the Waller motivated him to push through the pain. He had to go before he became prey to whatever predator had the Waller making those sounds.

If I don't get out now, I never will.

Sticks pushed himself up, propping himself against the Waller he had knocked out before. He was relieved to see that the bullets worked for a long time. Once he was finally able to see the fight, he couldn't believe his eyes.

No way . . .

Sticks gasped as he watched D-72 smash the Waller into a tree, pulverizing it. Silence blanketed the area for a moment while Sticks stared in awe.

How did you . . . Where did you . . .

Even his thoughts were scattered as he watched D-72 wash his hands in the mound of snow by the tree. When D-72 saw that Sticks was watching him, he smiled and waved. D-72 hurried over to him, extending his red-stained palms.

Sticks took his hand, wincing as D-72 pulled him up to his feet. Once he was standing, he took a moment to catch his breath.

"You need this?" asked D-72, pointing to the unconscious Waller.

Sticks nodded, still trying to piece together how the Elite had even appeared. D-72 slung the Waller over his shoulder like a sack of potatoes. Sticks couldn't believe the level of strength he had just witnessed, nor the fact that he had managed to be there without Sticks noticing.

"How did you—" Sticks stopped when he spotted it again, now understanding why it had fallen. "The branch. That was you?"

D-72 nodded and frowned.

All the footsteps he'd heard on his trek down the mountain earlier now made more sense.

"You've been following me the whole time, haven't you?" asked Sticks.

"Sorry," said D-72, nodding again.

"You have nothing to apologize for," said Sticks. "But how did you know I was coming here?"

D-72 looked nervous, his eyes shifting toward the ground.

"I . . . I was listening to you and Wick talk. Sounded danger-ous. Wanted to help."

Sticks smiled. "You did help. You're a good person, D-72."

D-72 looked up again, his eyes wide, and gave Sticks a big smile. "Really?"

"Really," said Sticks, smiling. "Thank you."

"For what?"

"For saving my life."

Chapter Twenty-Nine
Felan

"All right, everyone, listen up!"

Felan was perched at the top of the stairs so that she could see the entire group below. Ahna stood near her, Scorcher and Sticks down below. The rest of the kids gathered at the foot of the stairs, most in their full armor. When she saw that she had their full attention, she continued.

"Thank you for showing up ready to go today. As you know, it's super important for us to be able to practice this trip as many times as we can. This will not only help us avoid confusion on which way to go but will also cut down on the time it takes us to get there and back in case of an emergency. Before we head out, does anyone have any questions?"

A few murmurs came from the crowd, but there seemed to be very few people who needed further clarification. She was happy about that, especially considering she'd expected most hands to shoot up immediately.

One hand raised in the crowd, another one shooting up right after that one. Felan sighed.

"Yes, Baz?"

Baz did a quick victory gesture at Taz, who lowered his hand following a loud groan. He was clearly disappointed to have not been called on, but she didn't have time for their petty games.

"What about all of them?" asked Baz, basically shouting his question.

"All of who?" asked Felan.

Baz gestured to the makeshift hospital space.

"Those who can't really do anything for the attack. The ones in the hospital, people with all sorts of disabilities that don't let them do anything. What are they supposed to do?" he asked.

There were a few others in the crowd suddenly talking and getting riled up by the growing concern for their friends who couldn't go on the expedition. Some were actively arguing with Baz because of his comment, too. Before Felan could say anything more, Ahna stepped forward.

"Everyone can do something, Baz. Being differently abled doesn't mean you can't do things. It just means that you do things differently," said Ahna. Baz grimaced at her calling him out like that, but the crowd seemed to like what she'd said. When they quieted down, Ahna continued. "Those who are unable to join in the real attack are to be transported to the wagons outside and driven down the mountain so they'll be out of harm's way. At no time will we risk their lives by forcing them to do something that they are unable to do. For those who have any sort of mobility impairment, Scorcher has agreed to build ramps and other devices to allow everyone to do the most that they can with what we have available. While this mission is underway, Marie and Corrine will be working with the others who feel comfortable helping to care for any needs of those in the hospital. As you can understand, sickness waits for no one. Everyone will be taken care of, I promise."

The crowd cheered.

Bold words, Ahna. But making promises hasn't really worked out for you so far, has it?

Felan raised her hands to signal the crowd to silence themselves.

"Now that you know everything, it's time for our first trial run. Everyone, make your way to your spots in an orderly fashion," announced Felan. "When you hear the signal, the timer will start."

Felan waited for the group to head down the stairs before she followed. They headed for the tram cars, while others created a barricade for the doors or handed out what few guns they had available. Every time she thought they were one step ahead, it seemed they got pushed back two. She only hoped that by practicing they would have a leg up on the enemy for once.

We sure need it.

As they got into the tram cars, Sticks went to the lever and awaited the signal. Not long after, a loud whistle blew, and the tram cart lurched forward. Felan took a deep breath, getting into her zone.

Before the cart reached the bottom, Felan felt a surge of pain travel through her abdomen. It was as if it her stomach knew when she needed to focus and decided to not allow it. She gripped the side of the cart, waiting for the pain to pass, and focused on her breathing.

Come on . . . come on! Hurry up!

She pleaded with the pain in her mind as the cart neared the end of the line, where she would have to get out. When it didn't listen to her, she sucked in a deep breath and jumped out of the cart onto the snow below.

When she stood up, she took an extra second. The pain finally subsided, but it was staying longer each time it came.

I don't have time for this. Not today, not ever.

Felan sprinted past the rest of the group toward the cave. There was no time to waste. She would have to prove to herself and the others that she was totally fine, no issues. If the pain returned, she'd have to power through until they made it back from the run. There was no way she would allow her body to take her away from what she needed to do. Felan forced herself to focus on the task at hand, keeping herself from thinking of her pain and how frequently it was showing up.

If I don't focus on it, it doesn't exist.

"HOW DID WE DO?" ASKED Felan.

She plopped down onto the chair next to Wick, her muscles relaxing.

Wick looked at the computer monitor. "Faster than last time. Not by much, though."

Felan scoffed. "Every second counts, right?"

Wick nodded. "If we can shave another minute off, I think we might improve our odds by 10 percent."

"Math? Really?" asked Felan.

"Math saves lives," said Wick.

Felan laughed. "You think it's possible for us to get it done that quickly? Can we improve our chances by that much? For real?"

Wick smiled. "Absolutely."

Felan got up from the chair and started out the door.

"That was a quick visit," said Wick. "The numbers inspired you to do it again, huh?"

Felan stopped and turned back to face him. As she spoke, he was riding his scooter over to her.

"Not at all," she said, smiling. "I have to go check in with Ahna, make sure the boss is happy." Suddenly, she felt another slight twinge in her stomach. She fought through it, forcing a chuckle to hide the fact that she wanted to groan.

"Everything okay?" asked Wick.

Worry filled his eyes as he looked her up and down, his voice low. She couldn't look back into his eyes—not if she wanted him to believe her.

"Yeah, totally fine, thanks." She turned to exit again, finally relaxing her face from the fake smile.

"Just make sure you don't overdo it, Felan. We need you around, you know," said Wick.

Felan smiled and continued through the doorway without responding.

She couldn't turn back to face him before leaving. She couldn't let him see the tears forming in her eyes.

D-72 WAS STANDING BY the fire barrel when Felan walked into the room. His massive body almost blocked the flames from view. His size still amazed her; she'd never seen anyone that big before, besides maybe the guy who had been with Dean Tipper in Deliverance.

Maybe they're related.

Felan made her way over to join him next to the barrel, making sure nobody else was around for their talk. She paused behind him and waited a moment before she silently stepped up next to him.

"I hear you saved Sticks from being shredded like paper yesterday."

"I helped a friend." D-72 continued to stare at the fire, warming his hands over the flames.

Friend? Huh.

Felan looked him up and down, trying to figure him out. She realized quickly that nothing about him stood out other than his size. In fact, she figured he was probably the most boring person she knew, besides when he got angry. That was always exciting.

"That's pretty nice of you, especially considering you're one of them," she said. When she put emphasis on the last word, D-72 turned his head toward her.

"I am not one of . . . them," he said. His face twisted as though the word were a sour lemon. "Not anymore."

Felan watched his reaction, looking for a sign that he was lying. She waited for something to show, but it didn't. That surprised her.

"You think you're on our side, then?" asked Felan.

She walked around to the other side of the barrel. Light flickered on D-72's face, the shadows enhancing the space between his large features. What was interesting, though, was how innocent he looked. She'd always thought that people of his stature carried themselves in a way that made people aware of their strength. D-72 behaved like a big child—a big child who would break you if you stole his toy or made him upset. She had only known one or two others who reminded her of him, but she didn't know them very well. They certainly didn't have his strength.

"I am on your side," said D-72.

Felan stared at him, his eyes welcoming her glance. He was focused on her, too.

"Saving Sticks certainly helps prove that point," said Felan. "But one good deed doesn't make up for all the bad you've probably done while with them. Just know I'll be watching you when we go on this mission. Don't try anything, understand?"

"What would I try?" he asked.

"You've switched sides before. What's stopping you from doing it again?" asked Felan.

Her tone had gotten harsher than she'd intended, but she couldn't help it. She wouldn't have anyone hurting her friends, her family.

D-72 looked behind him, then back at her. She could see the conviction in his eyes.

"People here care about me. Almost everyone is nice to me now, so I am nice to them."

Felan chuckled. "There are more important things in this world than being nice."

"You're right," said D-72. "But that is the first step."

Wow . . . maybe you are smarter than you let on.

Felan walked back around the barrel and tapped him on the arm as she walked by.

"I'll be watching you."

"Thank you," replied D-72.

Felan almost stopped, confused by his response. Her threat had gone unnoticed. She was beginning to think there may have been more to him than she'd ever thought. Maybe he wasn't so bad after all. He'd saved Sticks from the Waller, but she'd need to see him do something for the group before she believed he truly was a part of it. She began to think of a way to give him that chance.

Chapter Thirty
Scorcher

"Do you remember your first mission outside Tent City?" His mom finished cleaning the last of his wounds before applying the new bandages. The way she applied the fabric was as gentle as always, somehow never hurting no matter how bad the wound. However, this time, something was different than those others. Even when they were in the middle of a battle, or if she was sick, he'd never seen her hands shake like they were now.

"Of course. Why?" asked Scorcher.

What made you think of that right now?

She chuckled, finishing the adhesion of the bandage and placing a pea-sized amount of salve on the irritated skin around the fabric.

"What was it that you went out to do again?" she asked.

I haven't thought about it in a long time . . .

"I . . . It—"

It suddenly felt as though he had been dragged deep underwater. Scorcher struggled to catch his breath as images from that day flooded his mind. The sunrise over the hill, squirrels foraging for their breakfast, a staff in his hand that took a few years to grow into, bloodstained hands, cries echoing through the forest . . . While he may have forgotten almost everything that happened that day, he wouldn't—couldn't—forget the face. When Scorcher walked up to him, calling out to what he'd thought could be a new friend . . . He could see that it wore clothes, played with an old broken toy it must have gotten out of the Junkyard.

It was so small, young . . . just like me. I didn't want to hurt it, let alone kill it. How was I supposed to know it was a Waller?

Scorcher blinked, bringing his attention back to his mom. He pushed the memory away, trying to force it back into its mental hiding spot. It didn't need to come back out from that place in his mind. He wasn't ready to deal with that again, especially not with everything else that was going on.

"We were doing some recon around the facility, trying to see if we could spot a weak point in the Wall."

"That's right. Seemed like a simple enough job, didn't it?" she asked.

"Yeah, it did. Everything seems simple at first."

It never ends up that way, though.

Corinne nodded, adding a hum of agreement. "You were so beaten up when you came back. When Seemore carried you into our home, I was so worried, so mad, so—I thought that I had made a terrible decision in raising you there. Allowing you to grow up fighting and training, then giving the okay for you to be one of the key people to go on runs outside the walls was . . . hard."

Her voice gave no indication of the tears that had already wet her cheeks. Scorcher hated seeing her cry; it was the only time he felt like he might do so himself. He forced the feeling back, his voice stern but soft.

"I always came back, Mom. Always."

He grabbed her arm gently. She wiped away what tears remained under her eyes and forced a laugh. Then she took his hand in hers, her grip tight.

"I know, sweetie."

"What's wrong, then?" asked Scorcher. "It's not like I've changed that much. If anything, I know more than I did before."

Corrine squeezed his hand again before letting it go, taking a step back from him and scanning him with her eyes. A slight smile formed, but her eyes still looked worried.

"You're so grown up," she said. "When I look at you, I don't see my baby boy anymore."

"I'm glad," said Scorcher. "I'm not a baby; I'm a man."

It felt weird to say it like that, but that was exactly how he felt. Of course, he had been the man of the house for years. However, he hadn't really called himself a man aloud before. That felt somewhat strange.

"You are," she said. "A man with many responsibilities. A man with more than just himself to look after now, too." She raised her eyebrows, and Scorcher could tell what she was referring to. "One day, you'll have a family of your own to look after. I don't mean everyone in Tent City, even though I know you think of them as family, and they are. I mean you and Ahna . . . and one day, hopefully, kids of your own. I just—I want you to be able to have that experience, live the life that I fought to give you, the life that you deserve. You deserve so much more than I've been able to give you. I guess I just worry that everything is getting a little out of hand and putting that in jeopardy."

Scorcher tried holding in all the feelings that were surfacing while she spoke. He listened to her speak, all those emotions swelling from deep within. When he couldn't hold them back any longer, tears trickled down his face. Scorcher lunged forward, his face burrowing into his mom's shoulder for the first time in a very long time.

Corrine's arms wrapped around him. The pressure eased his erratic mind; he felt calmer, safer in the embrace. She started humming the song she used to sing when he was little. The melody flowed around the space, and he could feel the vibrations in her chest while she hummed. One hand held his back while the other stroked his hair. Scorcher hadn't realized how long it had been since that last happened, but he welcomed the return of the ritual.

Scorcher felt his body and all his emotions align with the ending of the song. As she hummed the final note, he sniffed and wiped away the tears remaining on his face. He couldn't let his friends see that he'd been crying.

I'd never hear the end of that.

Thinking of all the jokes he'd be the center of made him chuckle. A sense of joy returned, and his mom held his shoulders while she looked him in the eyes.

"I'm glad to see that some things haven't changed." She smiled.

Scorcher sniffed again, finally finished purging the negative feelings from his face, and nodded in response. "I told you, I'm still me."

She nodded. "And I'm so happy you are. I love you, Scorcher."

"I love you too, Mom."

They hugged. She lovingly rubbed his back before letting him go again.

Scorcher walked toward the exit of the tent.

"Scorcher?"

He stopped near the flap, turning slightly back toward her. "Yeah, Mom?"

She hesitated for a moment before continuing. "Just . . . be careful, okay?"

Scorcher smiled. "I always am."

The bitter cold slapped him in the face as he pushed through the flap and exited the tent. He needed to get some rest. They were going to begin their attack in the next couple days, and he needed all the rest he could get beforehand. The first time they'd hit Deliverance hadn't gone well, and he was determined to make sure that didn't happen again.

Scorcher yawned once he finally reached the front his tent. He wasted no time once he got inside, heading straight to the bed.

Can't take down an evil corporation without a proper night's rest.

Chapter Thirty-One
Ahna

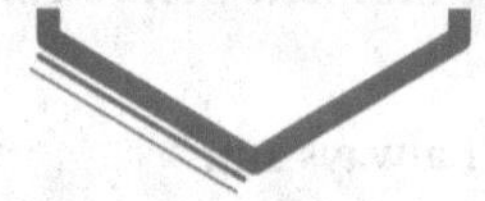

Clutter added to the claustrophobia Ahna was currently experiencing. She needed to get all the boxes of supplies out there before they piled up too high and toppled onto her, suffocating her to death. There was so much work to do, so many things to decide if they were going to fully take down The Delivery Company.

Why did I sign up for this? Well, I mean . . . I didn't actually sign up for it, but I went along with it. I could have walked away, just disappeared and lived on my own. Why didn't I do that?

A laugh from the main area somehow cut through the door and into her room. Ahna smiled, imagining the sort of crazy games Baz and Taz were up to out there. Her window gave her a good vantage point of a wagon as well, which was being loaded up now that the snow had died down a bit. Marie was lugging a box out to the wagon, Felan showing up to help her carry it the rest of the way.

Those two seem really close. That's nice.

A horse whined as Felan hurled the box into the back of the wagon, and Ahna felt her heart drop, the air in her lungs escaping with it.

CORINNE CALLED OUT to Ahna as she clung to the edge of the wagon, which teetered on the cliffside, the bridge about to fall behind her. Ahna struggled to breathe, to think at all. She called out to Corrine, telling her that she would help her, to just hold on. Corrine told her that it was too late, and the wagon started to topple backward into the ravine below. Ahna reached out to grab the wagon and felt a pull. Suddenly, she was on the wagon too as it fell down the ravine toward the rushing river below.

As the wagon hit the river, Ahna plunged beneath the rapids. Her body bounced between rocks below the surface, and she fought to get back above. Her limbs wouldn't move, and her lungs felt as though they were going to collapse at any minute. Suddenly, when she thought all hope was lost, she felt a hand grip her shoulder and pull her out of the deep, dark water where she was about to drown.

A WAVE OF CALM WASHED over her as Scorcher pulled her into his chest. Ahna coughed, catching her breath, and slowly returned to her senses. Scorcher's arms wrapped around her in a warm embrace. Ahna wanted to smile, but something within the confines of her mind fought that instinct. When she felt like she had finally gotten back to normal, Ahna finally blurted out, "I can't let it happen again, Scorch. I won't."

Her tone was sharp, direct. What she'd just experienced was more than enough reminder to focus on what was important.

"Let what happen?" asked Scorcher.

His voice was soft, soothing. Unfortunately, it wasn't soothing enough for what currently ran through her head.

"The bridge," said Ahna. "Not just that, but everything else, too. All the times people have either died or almost died because of my decisions. I know I haven't been the best leader, Scorch, but—"

She got choked up and paused to allow herself to calm down. Scorcher pushed a strand of hair from her face to rest behind her ear. He rubbed her earlobe as he spoke. He always knew how to ease her mind.

"You can't dwell on the past, Ahna. What's done is done. Instead, you can focus on the now. Even the smallest change in the present can improve the future. And that's what we're fighting for, right? Change. I know you'll do what's right when you're given the opportunity. You have been and will continue to be a great leader. I'm sure of that."

Ahna pushed herself off his chest so that she was sitting up facing him. She stared into his twin pools of emerald as they reflected the light behind her.

"But how do you know?" asked Ahna.

Scorcher smiled and shrugged, as though his answer were the most obvious thing he'd ever said. "I know you."

Scorcher leaned in and kissed her, pulling away shortly after and admiring her for a moment.

"Believe me," he said, "when the time comes, you'll do the right thing. You always do. And when it's all over, I'll be waiting to celebrate our win with you."

He smiled, and Ahna felt the hair on her arms stand.

"Thanks, Scorch."

"Any time, Ahna," said Scorcher. He started back toward the supplies, then paused and turned back toward her. "Ahna?"

"Yeah?"

"I appreciate you."

"I appreciate you."

In that moment, time slowed just enough for Ahna to feel like nothing else was going on. They had been intimate before, kissed many times, but hearing him say that made her feel truly . . . loved.

It was a welcome respite from what was to come. Like most good things in the world, it didn't last for long. A thought of the upcoming mission crept in, forcing her to return to the real world, to focus on everything standing in their way of having more moments like this. But Ahna didn't want moments. She wanted days, months, *years*. It would take a lot of work, but she was willing to do whatever it took to get there. She had a feeling that he was, too.

As they packed up materials and organized boxes, Ahna couldn't help but wonder about what Scorcher had said. In all their time together, he'd never let her down. She'd done that so many times, and she couldn't understand how he was still around. Of course, she had nowhere else to go either—nobody did. That was what she was fighting for, what they all fought for: independence. Some nights she'd lie awake, wondering what she would do in a world where she was free to do anything without fear of The Delivery Co. or another antagonizing force coming for her. Whenever Ahna questioned if fighting for freedom was worth it, she thought of all the headstones she'd seen by the waterfall near Tent City.

All those kids died for something . . . I've gotta help make sure of that. I mean—

She looked over at Scorcher, who was carrying multiple boxes out the door, smiling.

We will make sure of that.

Ahna continued prepping, checking the ammo and weaponry, and ensuring her personal armor was in good shape. In the midst of preparation, she was reminded of something she used to hear from one of her teachers back in the facility, a phrase that had stuck with her since she'd first heard it.

Focus on you, Ahna. Control what you can, forget what you can't.

That was exactly what she planned on doing.

Chapter Thirty-Two
Sticks

"Is it ready?" asked Sticks.

Wick reached into the bag that hung on the side of his mobile scooter and handed the remote to Sticks, shrugging. "As far as I know."

"That's not very reassuring," said Sticks.

Wick shook his head. "It's experimental. We haven't tested it much before now, so there's no telling whether or not it will work."

Sticks nodded. "Good point." He turned the remote over in his hand, examining it fully.

It was about the size of a small walkie-talking and just as boxy. The paint around the exterior was chipped, the metal dented slightly. He didn't care how it worked—only that it did. And knowing he and Wick had created it, he had no doubt that it would. Now he had to see it in action.

"All we do is press this button, and it should attack whoever is in sight, right?" asked Sticks.

Wick nodded. "That's the idea. I still don't understand why you didn't want to ensure control over the subjects. Doing it this way means we can't guarantee our own safety."

"Safety is never guaranteed," replied Sticks. "Besides, I'm only allowing the Wallers to create a distraction. I'll control where they go, but what they do is all their fault, not mine."

Wick raised his eyebrows, tilting his head. He hesitated before saying, "I guess you'd like to see it in action then, huh?"

"That'd probably be a good idea," said Sticks.

"When do you want to test it?"

Sticks smirked. "The sooner the better."

Wick chuckled. "I figured you'd say that."

Wick rode away from the desk, turning his back to Sticks as he drove his mobile scooter toward the back room.

"Where are you going?" asked Sticks.

"Toward the test subject," replied Wick. He was already reaching the door at the other side of the room.

You had it ready to go?

Sticks laughed before quickly catching up with Wick.

You know me too well.

"THIS BUTTON HERE?"

Wick nodded. "That's the only one. Just press that, and it should send a signal to the implant. From there, we'll see what happens," he said.

Sticks's finger hovered over the red button on the remote. Before he pressed it, he took another look through the transparent pane separating them from the two Wallers below. They had been able to use some of the bulletproof protection from the training room to create a safer environment from which to view the test. Sticks still felt his heart rate increase as he stood only feet away from two Wallers.

Slobber dripped past their bladelike teeth and shredded lips onto the metal floor below. The two Wallers had originally attempted to attack the plastic barrier upon their entrance, but to no avail. That made Sticks feel a bit better about the whole situation, though he never fully trusted anything he hadn't made with his own two hands.

Sticks looked to the one that had the implant in its temple. It was picking at a piece of the wall, bending the metal back from its place. Its teeth were clicking together as it did so. The other Waller was scratching at its body, some of the skin peeling slightly under its long sharp nails. A cold chill snaked up Sticks's spine as he watched them.

It's almost like watching real people . . .

He shook his head, clearing that thought.

They're not real people. They're monsters.

Before he could convince himself otherwise, he pushed the button on the remote. The Waller who'd been picking at the piece of wall began to shake. It gripped at its head for a moment before going still, then stood and turned toward the other Waller, letting out a shrill howl.

Arms spread wide, it launched itself at the other Waller, who had clearly not expected the incoming assault. The one with the implant tore into the other, its sharp nails ripping the other's clothes and skin. As the one struggled and fought back, it was able to free itself briefly. It ran right toward Sticks and Wick, its face slamming directly into the transparent barrier.

Its blood and other bodily fluids splattered against the hard plastic, streaking across the area where its body had hit. In a flash, the other Waller was once again on top of it. The Waller with the implant gripped the head of the other and began to slam it repeatedly into the barrier. Sticks felt his heart rate increase, as if it were attempting to be in sync with the rhythm of the assault only inches away.

Crack.

A spiderweb shape formed across the plastic barrier after the Waller's head imploded against it one last time. The Waller with the implant didn't seem to notice the other was dead as it began beating its body. Then it turned its attention to Sticks and Wick, hitting the spot where the crack had formed. The web grew with each impact of its fist. Wick gasped. He turned to Sticks.

"Hit the button, Sticks! Quick!"

Sticks fumbled with the remote before finally hitting the button again.

The effect was immediate. A foot away, the Waller that had been attempting to attack them stumbled backward over its lifeless companion, falling to the floor. It sat on the floor for a moment, its breathing labored, clearly tired. Its hands gripped at its head, and it rocked back and forth.

"What just happened?" asked Sticks. He was still trying to grasp the situation, his mouth dry and his heart slowly returning to normal.

"Carnage in its most primal form," replied Wick.

"That was insane . . ."

Wick nodded. "That was only one Waller. Imagine an entire horde equipped with these implants."

Sticks inhaled deeply before letting out a long sigh.

"I don't know if I want to . . ."

They stared at the Wallers behind the barrier, the one still rocking back and forth slowly while the other lay in a pool of its own blood. The dead Waller was almost indiscernible, a pile of flesh rather than a clear figure.

"I can understand your hesitation after what we just witnessed," said Wick, "but there's not much of a choice anymore. We either do this . . . or end up on the other side of this barrier."

He pointed at the lifeless Waller on the floor. Sticks shivered at the thought of dying like that. But he wasn't worried about himself as much as the others. They'd fought so hard, come so far, yet nothing had changed for the better. Everything was going downhill, fast. If he didn't do something drastic, it would only get worse.

It has to be worth it . . . right?

"We'd better get to testing it more, then. What's next?"

Chapter Thirty-Three

D-72

*S*unlight blanketed his skin as beads of sweat formed within his brow. Summer was just around the corner. Although, he didn't need the sun to alert him to that. The roar of the crowd behind the gate worked just as well. It happened every year, without fail, and his favorite part was coming up soon.

He dug his feet into the well-worn earth and pulled the stone from his pocket. The smooth stone felt cool in his palm, its weight almost making him feel more grounded. After taking one last glance at the gate, he forced a smile.

"Next year. I'm sure of it."

As that familiar phrase left his lips, he pressed the stone into the bark of the tree, adding yet another parallel line to the existing collection.

He stared at the tree for a moment longer. When he first began marking the Adoption Day ceremonies he had to watch from afar, he never expected it to be for long. As he was constantly reminded, "Families have a choice" and he was not that choice. At least, not yet. The more he stared at the lines, the more he saw a family. Each line stood for his potential father, mother, brother, or sister that would one day be his. He just had to wait a little longer.

While he waited for the huddled masses to finish their departure from the ceremony, he tossed the stone into the air. Each toss soared higher, as though he were attempting to eventually hit the sun. His goal was the top of the tree, but the last time he tried to throw it that high he left with a crabapple-sized knot in his head. He would have to work his way back up to that one day, but for now he was content to have fun by himself. Most days didn't mind being alone.

With all the time he had left in the day, he decided to make a game of it. A loose branch hung suspended only a few feet up from where he stood. Beyond that, a bird's nest. One wrong move, one miscalculation and the stone would knock into the nest forcing its inhabitants to fly or learn to do so quickly. That was something he wanted to avoid. After shooting at the gun range, he had no doubts that the branch would be an easy target.

Air flowed through his nostrils as he took in a deep breath and planted his feet on the ground. On the inhale, his arm pulled back, the stone grasped within his fingers. He counted to three in his head and picked up his front foot to give him a bit more momentum on his upcoming throw. As he exhaled, his foot slammed back into the earth while his arm swung forward to release the stone.

"Look who we have here."

D-72 felt a hesitation and the stone soared past the branch. He held his breath, watching as it struck the trunk of the tree directly next to the nest. Air escaped his lungs as though he were a deflating balloon. A thumping within his chest seemed like it was attempting to rise into his throat, its rhythm quickening. He turned around to look at the owner of the voice, the one responsible for throwing off his concentration which almost killed a family of birds.

When he turned to face the one responsible, a flash of sunlight bouncing of the boy's armor blinded him. D-72 took a step toward the owner of the voice, a taller Elite with another on either side of him.

"What do you want?" asked D-72. The pounding in his chest a constant war drum in the background of his mind.

The Elite in the middle smirked before taking a step toward D-72.

"Just doing our patrol around the perimeter, that's all. Enjoying your day off?"

D-72 took a second to collect himself, sucking in a deep breath again.

"I was."

"What were you doing?"

The Elite behind added their own questions to further echo the one in the middle, clearly the leader of the trio.

"Just trying to get some fresh air, relax outside for a bit."

The Elite walked past him, every muscle in his body tightening as he stopped right behind him. D-72 turned to see the Elite running his fingers down the lines carved into the tree. Heat radiated from his face again, but he held himself back from reacting. There was no use in trying to start a fight over something so small. He had to be careful.

"Would you look at that?" The Elite chuckled as he bent down. Somehow, his stone had somehow ended up within a couple feet of the tree. "This is a pretty nice-looking rock, isn't it boys?" The other two Elite nodded, laughing. "Maybe I should keep it."

Seeing the Elite's dirty fingers wrap around his stone caused a spike in his heart rate. They were allowed to do a lot of things within the walls of the facility, but he couldn't stand them extending their power beyond there. He finally had something of his own, something that nobody else knew about, and he wasn't going to let it be taken away.

"Give it back."

The Elite chuckled again.

"Finders, keepers."

D-72 stepped toward him, his jaw clenched and hands balled up into fists. The two Elite that had been laughing behind their leader slid to the sides of him, awaiting orders. D-72 stopped a foot away from the main Elite, their eyes locked.

"It belongs to me. The only reason it's on the ground in the first place is because you interrupted my throw."

"What were you trying to throw it at?" The Elite turned the stone over in his palm before turning his gaze toward the sky.

"Just tossing it up and down, that's all."

He wasn't about to talk to the Elite any longer than he had to. Besides, the crowd exiting the gate had already begun to dissipate. There was no point in staying to watch anymore. He just wanted to get the stone back and head to his room, not start any trouble.

"Oh? That's all, huh?" asked the Elite. His minions chuckled behind him.

D-72 nodded. He was biting his tongue, fighting back any urge to escalate the situation. But before the Elite continued speaking, a small squawk called out above.

"Well, well, well. You hear that, boys?" The two nodded as the leader continued. "Sounds like a baby bird crying for help. Maybe we should give it hand. This rock seems like it might give it a nice boost."

D-72's jaw clenched. Pain in his palms paled as he focused his full attention on the Elite.

"Don't."

The beating within his chest felt as though his heart was trying to escape. He waited, sweat building on the outskirts of his forehead as he watched the Elite weigh his options.

Surprisingly, the Elite extended his hand toward him.

"Fine," said the Elite, his tone almost playful. "I won't throw the rock at the bird, okay?"

D-72 stared at the stone, his stone, now basking in the sunlight within the palm of the Elite's hand. He didn't have to beg and, better yet, he didn't have to fight them to get it back. Why the Elite listened to him was a mystery. Regardless, he was just happy to get it back. Seeing the Elite willing to give him the stone made him feel as though maybe not all of them were as bad as he had experienced so far.

"Thank you," said D-72.

He reached out to take the stone from the Elite, but it was pulled away at the last second. In one swift motion the Elite pocketed the stone, turned around with his gun drawn, aimed at the tree, and pulled the trigger.

D-72 squinted as the ringing in his ears echoed within the cavern of his mind. The laughter and words of the Elite, and all other sounds, seemed muffled. It was as though his ears were underwater.

Splinters and feathers rained down from above. There was no more branch, no more nest, no more bird.

Suddenly, he felt as though he were no longer in control of his body. Brief flashes of action bookended by darkness filled the moments that followed.

Finally, his senses returned. D-72 sucked in a shaky breath as he surveyed the scene. He was standing in the same spot he had started, but everything was different. Scarlett-stained leaves scat-

tered the bodies of the Elite lying motionless around his feet. A cool breeze drifted across his damp skin, cooling hot face.

Slowly, he began counting, continuing until his breathing returned to normal. His grip loosened on the object within, revealing the stone, his stone again in his possession. His thumb rubbed against its course body, a streak of dark red in its wake.

HIS THUMB CONTINUED its familiar path down the red river in the stone. D-72 focused on that repetitive motion and closed his eyes. Air flowed in and out, his heartbeat in its normal pattern, and the room felt almost quiet. For a moment, he could relax.

Knock, knock, knock.

D-72 sighed. He was happy to have had a moment of peace. Moments were all he could hope for anymore, anyway.

"One second," he called out.

Before the door opened, he tried to figure out something, anything, to do. His helmet lay next to his chair in the corner of the room and a mountain of dirty clothes near that. Those seemed like two good potential options for looking like he was working on something. Standing around didn't sit well with many in the group and he didn't want to appear to be lazy. Even if he felt that what he was doing was helpful for himself, they wouldn't understand. Nobody ever does.

Sarah stepped through the threshold, stomping her feet on the mat near the door. Snow flew from her boots, which helped him to see that she wasn't adorned in her usual armor. Instead, multiple layers wrapped around her body. Her face was almost hidden behind a thick scarf that was stuffed into her jacket. Looking at her made him feel a bit warmer, as if he were bundled up too.

She swiped the stray hair off her cheek and smiled.

"Hey."

D-72 hesitated. In thinking of something to do, he realized he'd never actually decided to do either of them. He'd have to think of something else if necessary. Sarah was the last person he wanted to think of him as lazy.

"Hey." The word came out, but just barely. He swallowed, trying to get any remaining saliva in his mouth to coat his suddenly dry throat. Hydration was something he tried to be on top of usually, which made this sudden sensation strange.

"Sometimes I hate the snow," she said, shaking the remaining snow from her coat. She didn't get it all though. Snow still sprinkled throughout her dark hair, reminding him of the night sky. "You been out there yet?"

D-72 shook his head. He didn't want to speak again until he was sure his throat was back to normal.

"Well, we got the fire going and I was—" Sarah paused, her head tilting slightly as one eyebrow stretched the ceiling. "Are you okay?"

Why are you asking that? I know that's not why you came in here. Nobody just comes to check in on me.

D-72 swallowed again. His throat seemed to be back to normal. Besides, he couldn't stand there and not speak. That would be just as weird.

"Fine. Why?"

Sarah's eyes narrowed slightly as she took a step toward him. She stopped in front of him and pointed at his hand.

"You're rubbing that stone again."

Suddenly, within his chest there was a heavy drop, as though his heart were stone as well.

"What are you talking about?"

D-72 went to stuff the stone in his pocket, but Sarah gripped his arm, stopping him.

"It's okay," she said, smiling. "You don't have to hide it."

His heart beat heavy in his chest, his mouth once again drying up like a desert. Contrary to her cold hand against his upper arm, there was a warmth spreading within. Her eyes stared at him with a feeling he didn't see often from most anyone. Her words, and glance, seemed genuine, real. When she removed her hand from his arm, she kept it suspended in the air with her palm facing up.

"Can I see it?" she asked.

Nobody has ever asked that before.

"Why?"

"It seems important to you," she said. "Plus, it looks cool."

She laughed at herself, a laugh that wasn't directed at him. Something he wasn't quite used to yet.

D-72 stared at the stone, then back at Sarah. She was being patient and seemed interested in it, more than most anyway. No matter how kind she seemed, though, he couldn't shake the memories of the previous stranger that held it. He had to be sure nothing would happen to it. Or him.

"I can't let you hold it," he said.

The spark in Sarah's eyes, as well as her smile, faded. She lowered her hand.

"Oh." She looked away from him and turned around to leave. "That's fine. Whatever."

A voice in his head told him he was making a mistake. Sarah was clearly not going to steal the stone or use it to hurt him. He knew that.

"Wait."

Sarah paused and turned to face him, waiting.

D-72 swallowed. Sweat had appeared on his palms so he wiped them clean as best he could.

He held out the stone.

"Here."

Sarah's eyes widened. She slowly walked back and stopped. Looking at the stone in his hand, then back at him, she paused her hand above it.

"You're sure?"

That's a good question.

D-72 nodded, waiting for her to take the stone from his hand.

Sarah rubbed her hands together, as though the stone would feel the cold. Seeing the caution she was taking with it, with him, he knew he had made a good decision. As she lifted the stone from his palm, he suddenly felt lighter. It was as though she had removed a piece of him. In truth, she had practically done exactly that.

She treated the stone like a small, wounded bird. Her fingers traced each small crack until they reached the red river. There, she paused.

There was a crescendo on the drum within his chest. He had no idea what he was going to tell her when she asked how the red stain appeared. He wasn't sure he wanted to. Suddenly, he felt he had made a mistake. It took everything in his power not to reach out and snatch the stone from her hand immediately. He had to restrain himself, wait to see what was to come from her hesitation.

Sarah looked up and smiled. She held the stone out toward him, the sparkle returning to her eyes.

"It's beautiful."

D-72 smiled.

His fingers found their home around the stone, gracing her palm as it retrieved it and returned it to his pocket. A sense of relief joined the added weight. He was complete again.

Sarah almost started out the doorway before spinning back to face.

"I almost forgot," she said, laughing. "We got a nice fire going at the front and a few of us were hanging out. I wanted to see if you might want to join us. If you weren't busy or anything."

You came here just to ask me to hang out? Nobody's ever done that either.

D-72 nodded.

"Sure. Sounds like fun," he said.

Sarah smiled, then quickly covered the smile with her scarf.

"I'll save you a seat."

Sarah headed out and all the energy in the room seemed to go with her. She was different from the others in camp. Of course, she hadn't grown up in the world that they had. No. Instead, she was raised in the sterile forest under a fluorescent sun. A world different than anyone outside the control of The Delivery Co. could imagine.

His world.

They were the same, he could sense that. Throughout their short time together, he felt that she could too.

Heat filled his face again. Only this time, it wasn't rage. It was something different, something he hadn't felt in a long time. Happiness.

It's nice to have a friend.

"ALL I'M SAYIN' IS, if I had to choose between a Waller and you," said Taz, giving a dramatic pause to look around at the group before looking back at Sarah. "I'd choose the Waller!"

Smiles, laughter, and jokes accompanied the crackling of the fire in the center of the group. Sarah had saved him a seat near her. It was barely big enough for him, but he was thankful, nonetheless. After everything that had happened, it was still hard to believe how welcoming they all had become, how comfortable it felt to be with them. Sometimes, he felt that it was too comfortable, though. He'd never had the opportunity to sit around and joke with anyone back in the facility. They were always moving, training, eating, or sleeping. There was never just . . . peace.

"Looks like you're gonna get your chance now, Taz!" Baz said, pointing behind Taz.

All eyes were glued on Taz as he pulled out his gun and spun around in the snow, tripping over the stump he had been sitting on and faceplanted in the snow. Laughter erupted again around the circle. D-72 couldn't help joining in, especially when Taz stood back up with a face full of snow and dirt.

As the sounds of the crowd died down and he was shuffling to get more comfortable on his seat, a small pressure pushed down on his shoulder three times in quick succession.

D-72 turned, staring right at the gap-toothed smile of Vincent who had somehow snuck up behind him during the cacophony of voices.

"Come with me," said Vincent. He waved his arm then walked away from the group.

Didn't give me much of a chance to decide if I wanted to or not, did you?

D-72 chuckled as he stood to leave. He tried to get away unnoticed, but he felt a hand grip his arm before he was out of the circle completely.

"Where you going?" asked Sarah. Firelight danced in her eyes as she stared up at him, waiting for an answer.

D-72 tilted his head toward the tree line where Vincent had gone. "Vincent asked for me to go with him somewhere real quick."

Sarah smiled. "Oh! Yeah, cool. He asked if you were gonna be here earlier. Make sure he doesn't go running off by himself."

He nodded before starting off toward the light of Vincent's torch.

When he arrived, he could see that it wasn't exactly the best-looking torch. It was just a stick that Vincent had tied some fabric to before he stuck it into the fire. He was resourceful, that was for sure.

D-72 pulled back the branch that hung low enough to smack him in the face as he neared Vincent. Shadows danced across Vincent's face, making him appear somehow older. A large grin, with a missing tooth and all, erased any lingering thoughts of age. Sometimes he wished he had gotten to experience those little things of childhood. Or even, to experience a childhood like Vincent had at all.

"You came," said Vincent, almost surprised.

D-72 chuckled. "Of course, I did."

Vincent pulled a log over as best he could, dropping it with a muffled thud into the snow again.

"Have a seat," he said. "Please."

D-72 raised his eyebrows and narrowed his eyes slightly.

"This isn't another one of those tricks where you are going to have me close my eyes and when I open them I'll be covered in spiders or something, is it?"

Vincent laughed hysterically, wiping his eyes when he finally calmed down. He took a few deep breaths and shook his head at D-72.

"Man, that was hilarious! I totally forgot about that. Thanks for reminding me."

He let out a chuckle again, D-72 doing the same.

"No problem," said D-72.

As much as he hated to admit it, it was a little funny. Though, it was not an experience he would like to repeat any time soon.

"What did you want?" asked D-72. A cold chill crept down his spine. "And why did we have to leave the fire?"

Vincent rummaged around in his pocket. Once he turned around, he stared at D-72 with a huge smile again. The smile seemed different than his usual, though. Instead of laughter behind it, there was something D-72 had only seen in the eyes of families on Adoption Day.

Why are you looking at me like that?

"Back in Tent City, where I'm from, we had this waterfall." Vincent must have seen D-72 tilt his head in confusion because his eyes narrowed slightly. "Wait. You ever seen a waterfall?"

Seen one? I've never heard of one.

D-72 shook his head.

"But you know what it is, right?"

D-72 shook his head again, adding a shrug.

"Wow." Vincent looked like he'd had the air knocked out of his lungs. "I never met anybody who didn't know what a waterfall was."

He scratched his head then his eyes grew wide. Tossing the torch to D-72, Vincent returned to his previous spot. With arms raised, Vincent began to move as if he were performing.

"Imagine a river." He waved his hands in an up and down motion, simulating waves. He paused quickly, tilting his head. "You do know what a river is, don't you?"

D-72 laughed. "Of course."

"Okay, good. Where was I? Oh, right," continued Vincent. He cleared his throat and assumed his performative stance again. "Imagine a river. Usually, a river runs on the ground, through trees and mountains and stuff, right? Well, if the river is running through a place that's higher up and it doesn't have any place else to go, it has to go someplace." He paused. "That's what it does. It goes down." Vincent sweeps his arms through the air and in an arching motion before slapping the snow beneath him. Then, he ran his fingers through the snow. "That's why it's called a waterfall. And at the bottom of it, a big pool of water happens. Sometimes, there's even fish and stuff in there which is kinda cool. I like watching them swim around." Vincent's fingers swam through the snow as though his hands were fish. After a moment, he paused. A cloud appeared in front of his face as he took a deep breath, then stood.

Vincent's hands encased something hidden in his grasp. Because of the imaginary fish, D-72 hadn't realized that Vincent had grabbed anything. That was the second time the kid had managed to skirt his observational skills. Either he was slipping or Vincent was much sneakier than he realized. If he had to guess, he would bet on the latter. Vincent never ceased to amaze him. If nothing else, he was certainly entertaining.

Vincent looked down at his hands then up at D-72, his playful personality taking a backseat. Instead, his tone became warm and soft. Shadows continued to dance within the valleys of his face, the flicker illuminating his watery eyes. D-72 wanted to ask if everything was okay, but before he could speak Vincent kept going.

"The waterfall that I was talking about before, the one where I'm from . . . it was the same place as the cemetery. All my friends and family, even people I never met were buried there. I used to be scared of it back when I was little, but after one of my best friends died I started going there every day. I would visit him and talk to him, tell him all about whatever was going on. I know it seems weird, but it was really nice to have someone to talk to. Besides, Seemore always said that everyone who died could still hear us if we really wanted them to. And I did."

Vincent paused, using his forearm to wipe the tears from his eyes. Whatever was in his hands remained hidden while he did so. He cleared his throat, then extended his arms toward D-72.

"Here."

Vincent's hands opened like a blooming flower, revealing a large, round stone. White specks scattered its midnight black body. It looked smooth already, except a few spots in the middle. Light from the torch splashed across lettering that had been etched deep into the stone, painted a similar white to the sur-rounding specks.

"For me?" asked D-72.

Vincent nodded.

D-72 retrieved the stone from Vincent's hands. It was as smooth as he imagined, practically equal to the one in his pocket. When he held it, its beauty became even more apparent. His thumb caressed it without hesitation. Even though it was new, it felt familiar.

His smile faded as his thumb ran across the grooves etched into the stone.

"Why is this word carved into it?"

Vincent moved closer and touched the lettering.

"I know everybody calls you D-72, but I misheard you the first time you said it. Since then, that's what I called you in my head. I know you have a designation, but I feel like you deserve a name."

D-72 looked down at the stone again, then back at Vincent.

"This is my new name?"

Vincent nodded. "If you like it, yeah."

D-72 smiled and nodded. "I do. A lot."

Vincent smiled wide as he wrapped his arms around D-72. He squeezed tight, then jumped back from him as he released.

"Let's go tell the group then, huh?" he asked.

D-72 held out his hand, gesturing toward the path they'd come down.

"Lead the way."

The buzz around the fire had died down with it, but every-one was still hanging out. They were just doing their own thing instead of all together. It was almost peaceful.

Baz and Taz were still going with their ridiculous banter, Felan was polishing her rifle while listening to Marie tell a story of some medical mystery, Sarah was sharpening her knife, and Ahna was showing Scorcher some sort of drawing in a book.

Vincent walked up with D-72 following close and stood up on a log. He raised his arms as he spoke, once again assuming a performer's stance.

"Attention, everyone."

He waited, but it was clear that most of the group hadn't heard him. Most likely due to Baz and Taz cackling at each other's dumb jokes. D-72 felt an urge to help, but Vincent said it again, only much louder.

"Attention everyone!"

The gang paused what they were doing and looked up at Vincent. His face beamed with pride having clearly gained their attention.

"Thank you," he said, continuing. "I know you all have a lot going on, but I think this is important."

"What are you going on about now?" asked Taz.

Sarah smacked him in the arm and he winced before apologizing.

"Sorry," he said. "Continue."

Vincent nodded at Sarah then continued.

"As I was saying, this is important. Some of you might not know this, but in Tent City we all gave ourselves names if we didn't like what we were given. That's always been a big part of who we were. Well, my friend here hasn't had a name for a long time." He gestured toward D-72. "I thought that it was time to change that. Everyone, I would like for you to meet my friend. Introduce yourself, pal."

Vincent put his hand on D-72's shoulder, their eyes locked. Vincent nodded and cocked his head toward the group as he pat D-72 on the shoulder.

D-72 stared down to his hand, rubbing his thumb across the four letters etched into the stone still in his grip. He cleared his throat, took a deep breath, and stepped forward.

"Hi, everybody," he said, swallowing the lump in his throat before continuing.

"My name is Dune. It's nice to meet you."

Chapter Thirty-Four
Scorcher

Her hair felt smooth against his rough fingers, the scent of pine sweeping upward, entering through his nostrils. Even though it had become a normal aroma in the past few weeks, it always made him smile. Thoughts of Tent City, the beach, and their many adventures together filled his head. They allowed him to escape from the constant threats to their safety, if only for a moment, and focus only on them, together.

Her chest rose up and down like a buoy, each exhale a light ocean breeze. Her body twitched, and she moved slightly before returning to her calm state. Colorful beams through the small window above illuminated her hand, drawing his attention to it.

Scars marred the skin on the back of her hand. Each marked a success or failure, but all represented her progress. Scorcher thought back to their early days: sparring with her in the circle, her face the first time she tried fresh game meat after a hunt, her hesitation to attack and lack of confidence.

That didn't take long to get rid of, did it?

He chuckled lightly, watching her hand move up and down with her torso.

I only worry you may have grown too much . . .

As though she could hear his thoughts, Ahna stirred. She wiped her eyes, yawning, then stretched as she looked around the room before her eyes landed on his. She cocked her head to the side, squinting.

"Were you watching me sleep?" she asked.

Scorcher shrugged. "Uh . . ."

"Don't be weird, Scorch," she said. "Besides, I don't mind. I always sleep a little better when I know you're there. That way, if anyone tries to kill me, you'll fight them off . . . or die in the process, giving me extra time to wake up and fight. Either way, I appreciate your sacrifice."

"Gee, thanks," said Scorcher.

They laughed. He let it continue as long as he possibly could, soaking in the happiness and calm joy. He knew it wouldn't last long, but it felt good, especially considering what was coming. Unfortunately, Ahna cut it short.

He watched as she covered the rest of her body in yesterday's clothes, then the armor. The morning sun was just beginning to take the place of the moon, casting a warm glow inside the room. She paused what she was doing, smiling as she stared at him. He felt a shiver run down his spine.

"What?" asked Scorcher.

Ahna shook her head. "Nothing. It's just . . ."

"Just what?"

Her chest plate rose slowly before descending again. "The way you look right now, in the sun, it's . . . I wish cameras were still around. I never want to forget this moment."

You're being weirdly sentimental today. Are you worried about the mission?

Scorcher smiled. "Don't worry," he said, getting up and walking over to her. "There will be plenty more moments like this, and better, in the future. You won't forget the ones that matter, anyway."

Ahna smiled, nodding. "You're right. I guess I'm just worried about today. What if it doesn't go well? I don't want to mess everything up again."

Scorcher placed his hands on her shoulders. Staring into her eyes, he lowered his tone, keeping it firm but comfortable.

"You won't, understand? You've had us run the route multiple times. In fact, I could probably do it blindfolded if I had to."

"Scorch—"

She was clearly not in the mood for jokes, so he switched gears quickly.

"Okay, okay," he said, moving one hand to her face and lowering his voice to almost a whisper. "My point is, you've put in the time and the work to improve as a leader. The group trusts you, I trust you, and now it's time for *you* to trust you. But if you need any more reassurance, know this. I'll be there with you the whole time. Whatever you need, I'll make sure you have it. When I told you I'd always be there for you, I meant it." He paused for a moment, his heart almost beating out of his chest. "I love you, Ahna. I'll always love you. No matter what."

Scorcher closed his eyes as he leaned in. He gently guided her face toward him until their lips met. He felt her relax as he held her in his arms, returning the kiss. Warmth enveloped them, whether from the heat of the moment or the sunlight now pouring through the window, he was unsure. When they pulled away from each other, Ahna touched his face as he had hers.

"You'd better keep your promise. If you get yourself killed, I'll bring you back just to kill you again myself."

They laughed again, then Ahna finally finished getting dressed and headed out the door. Watching her leave, fully dressed in her armor, brought Scorcher back to the reality of their situation. His stomach turned as he began to put on his own armor.

I'm tired of wearing this. I'm tired of constantly having to run. I'm tired of fighting.

Scorcher placed his helmet over his head after blowing a tuft of hair from his eyes. Gripping the handles of his blades, he slid them into their sheaths on his waist. Noises from the hallway and main area meant the others were ready, so he started for the doorway. Then he hesitated. Filling his lungs with one deep inhale, he turned to look around the room, soaking in the last moments of calm before the storm.

I wish we could just run away from all this, go back to Tent City or create our own. Just . . . live. Maybe one day we can.

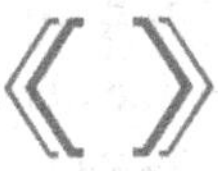

SCORCHER SCANNED THE small circle of kids gathered around Ahna in the early morning sun. The scene reminded him of the morning in Tent City right before the attack. They had all been so young, so inexperienced.

So unprepared . . .

Raider's and Scout's faces entered his mind. The image of them on the ground outside the facility, motionless, sent a shiver down his spine. Not a day went by that he didn't regret not having been able to save them. As much as he longed to go back, to set things right, he knew he couldn't. He pushed the thought to the back of his mind, forcing himself to focus on what he could do for those who were still alive.

There was a major difference in the group that stood around him now versus the group that had fought that day in Deliverance. For one, they had more people now than before—about three times as many people, in fact. Numbers alone helped their odds, so he was grateful for that. Besides that, they'd been training for months in the time that they weren't traveling or sleeping, though sleep seemed to happen rarely for many most days.

Standing in the middle was one of the biggest differences from before.

Ahna.

He couldn't believe how much she'd improved over the past few months. Even though they'd had some rough times—as a group and as a couple—she seemed to have finally learned from those mistakes. Of course, he knew he'd made his fair share of mistakes, too. Ahna seemed to learn a little bit quicker from hers than he did from his, though. Even his mom had told him that he needed to try to be more like her now. That always made him laugh, but he could see why she'd said it, especially as he looked at her now. Ahna looked confident as she stood in front of them, directing them on the mission details. She spoke with such a calm, comfortable command.

I can understand why Seemore chose you. He saw what you would become instead of what you were.

He smiled, feeling a little guilty for doing so in such a heavy moment, but he couldn't help it. It didn't last long, though. Before he knew it, Ahna had signaled to the group to enter the tram cars, and Sticks moved into his position by the handle.

As Scorcher followed his group into the head car, he ensured each of the others were inside before shutting the door. Cold wind stung his face as it entered the eyes of his helmet. He blinked as many times as he could to send the water from his eyes away, then took a seat with the group. A tug on his pants worried him for a moment before he realized it was only Vincent.

"What is it, bud?" asked Scorcher. He tried to pay attention to Vincent as much as he could while also making sure everything ran smoothly behind them.

"Are you scared?" asked Vincent. His voice cracked.

Scorcher knew it wasn't his age but his fear that had caused it. He wanted to lie, but he knew Vincent would know. Besides, he'd learn one day that life was almost always scary.

"Of course I am," said Scorcher. "But sometimes the bravest people are the most afraid."

"Does that mean I'm brave?" asked Vincent.

"The bravest kid I know," replied Scorcher.

Vincent's eyes grew wide, and he smiled as he latched one arm around Scorcher and hugged tightly.

"All right," Ahna yelled behind them, "off we go!"

Sticks pulled the lever on the platform, and the cart lurched forward, swaying back and forth as it moved. Vincent's grip tightened as the rest of the kids inside the cart gasped. They'd run the route a few times before, but it never seemed to get easier for them. After a moment, they relaxed a bit. They sat quietly, some of them pulled inside their suits of armor to stay warm on the ride down. The farther down they got, the more it seemed to snow.

The kids started to tilt their heads back, sticking out their tongues. Scorcher followed their lead, letting snowflakes melt one by one on his tongue. For a moment, he felt like the kid he should've been. He hadn't realized how much he'd been forced to mature the last few years.

It seemed like age didn't matter when you lived outside the Wall; all that mattered was that you lived. Numbers just helped people know how long you'd survived.

AS THE CART NEARED the final part of the track before the turn back up the mountain, Scorcher stood up and began the demounting process. He opened the door and waited for them to reach the spot where they'd placed the landing pad. Once he spotted it, he turned to the kids. He spoke quickly, to the point.

"We're almost down. This part is important, so listen careful-ly. I know that we've done this plenty of times, but that doesn't mean you don't treat it like it's the first, understood? You can still get hurt, so we need to be careful. Careful, but quick. Got it?" He watched them all nod their heads in agreement, then ges-tured toward himself. "All right, you know the drill. One by one, let's go."

They all moved closer to him, just like they'd rehearsed. As one got to the front, he picked them up under their arms and helped them stand on the edge of the cart. Then, after counting to three, he dropped them onto the landing pad below. They had to move quickly so that they had everyone off safely before the next cart started their turn. Once he'd dropped Vincent onto the pad, he drew in a breath and hopped out of the cart.

Once he hit the pad, he gathered the kids who were strug-gling to get up and guided them over to the side. They stood silently, watching the rest of the group do what they'd just done, until everyone was down. Once Ahna joined them, she silenced the group's murmurs.

"I know you're excited, but this is the real thing. We need to move quickly and quietly. On my command, we keep our mouths shut and feet moving. Got it?"

They nodded. Ahna shot a quick glance at Scorcher before waving the group toward her.

"Let's move."

BLUE LIGHT GUIDED THEM all the way to the end of their path, each hash mark on the wall indicating another portion of the journey complete. As they neared the end of the tunnel, the familiar fluorescent glow welcomed them. The gate remained open, just as they'd left it, and the door was within view. Scorcher's heart raced as they moved closer to it; they were only a few moments away from the attack.

Deep breaths, man. Don't let the kids see you freaking out.

He followed his own advice as best he could until his body relaxed. Ahna guided the rest of the group toward the door and positioned them. She stood near the box, ready with the vial of the doctor's blood, and Scorcher moved in front of the door, Vincent by his side.

"Ready?" asked Ahna.

Vincent looked up to Scorcher, who knew from Vincent's rapid breathing that he had to say something before they went inside. The more he freaked out, the bigger chance he'd mess something up. They couldn't afford to let that happen. Not again. Scorcher leaned down quickly, one hand on Vincent's shoulder.

"You've got this, bud," said Scorcher, his voice low. "I'm right here with you."

Vincent forced a smile but remained jittery. After a few seconds, though, his shoulders slowed their up-and-down movement. Thankfully, he had managed to slow his breathing enough that Scorcher could no longer tell if he was freaking out or not.

That'll have to do.

"Ready," replied Scorcher. He smiled at Ahna, who returned one quickly, before facing the task at hand.

Pulling his blades from their sheaths, he felt the blood rush to his hands. His grip tightened as Ahna dripped the blood from the vial onto the scanner, and the door opened. The group had their weapons at the ready, waiting for the all clear. Scorcher gave the room a quick look, making sure nobody was hiding in an area they hadn't seen through the window.

Nothing.

After taking a deep breath, Scorcher relaxed his grip on his blades. Returning them to their sheaths, he placed one hand on Vincent's shoulder, patting it.

"After you, bud," whispered Scorcher. "Do the honors."

Vincent looked up to him, fear flooding his eyes as they widened. "You sure about that? I-I thought it was your job," he said, hesitating.

Scorcher shook his head. "Not anymore. You've earned it."

Vincent smiled wide, confidence replacing the fear in his eyes. Placing his gun into the holster, he walked forward, his posture the straightest Scorcher had ever seen, a slight bounce in his step. There was no sign of caution or fear in his body whatsoever, only excitement. Following Vincent inside the room, Scorcher looked out to the group. The faces of the younger kids as they watched Vincent stride over to the other box, doing such an important task, made it all worth it. He was just happy to do something he wished somebody had done for him when he was that age.

Scorcher looked to Ahna and smiled. She flashed a smile back, giving him a slight nod after her eyes darted toward Vincent. He chuckled, then looked back to see Vincent ready with the vial at the next door and knew it was time.

He raised his hand to form the balled fist, giving the all clear signal.

The door slammed shut, separating them and the group.

Scorcher looked toward Vincent, who had already placed the blood onto the box near the door. The door next to it didn't open, and the box glowed red, indicating a negative match. A red light blinked overhead, and a loud beep echoed around the metal room.

"What's going on?" asked Vincent. His face was flushed, his eyes darting side to side as he fumbled to hold on to his gun.

There was a bang at the door that had just shut on them, Ahna's face appearing in the window. She was yelling something to him, but he couldn't tell what she was saying. All sound was muffled through the door.

The nozzles on the walls to either side started to move, and Scorcher realized why they looked so strange.

No. No, no, no, no, no!

"Vincent, get d—"

Before he could finish, bullets flew from the nozzles on the wall into his body. Pain burned through his chest and arms before he went numb. Darkness seared the edges of his vision as he felt his body hit the ground, a heavy metallic taste coating his tongue. Light faded slowly, each breath becoming more difficult. The sounds around him became muffled, as though he were underwater. His eyelids felt heavy, his body weak and limp, and he realized he couldn't move. Tears welled in his eyes, clouding the already darkening vision before the rest of the room fell away into complete darkness. Ahna's scream was the last sound he heard.

Chapter Thirty-Five
Ahna

"Scorcher!"

She could hear her screams, feel her throat closing up, see the blood on the window from where she'd hit it over and over and over . . . but nothing felt real. Time seemed to slow, and she felt as though she'd been pulled out of her body and was watching everything from a bird's-eye view. Ahna continued to pound on the window of the door, hoping it would crack, wishing it would shatter, trying to make what she felt tangible—except she felt . . . nothing.

"Attention, Reject scum," said a voice through the speakers above the door.

You . . .

She froze. Her thoughts and senses returned, forcing her back into the moment. Pain coursed from her hand through the rest of her body, but she couldn't focus on that. The voice overhead couldn't be real. There was no way he was alive. Then again, when nobody could verify his death, she'd questioned it. Now she had the answer: Dean Tipper was the one responsible for Scorcher's death.

You're gonna pay for this.

"It appears you've found my trap. Well done." He clapped slowly, then continued. "Surrender now or face the same fate as your friends. Judging by the look of them, it won't be pretty!"

Your death won't be pretty. I can guarantee that.

His laughter felt like a dagger in her skin. He was laughing inside an office, while the only person she'd ever loved lay dead on the other side of the metal door.

I'll make sure you suffer, too . . .

She could feel her blood boiling, heat radiating from her face and body under the armor. Sweat joined the dried tears on her face as she tried to slow her breathing. Dean Tipper continued over the speakers.

"Should you give yourselves over, I can guarantee a swift end to your miserable existence. However, should you choose the other option, I can't make any promises. I would choose wisely . . . and hastily, as an army of Elite are descending upon your position as I speak. I am sure by now you've no doubt seen their upgraded armor. I would like to offer gratitude to Sticks for that. If you are here, my boy, know that we would gladly accept your return. Otherwise, enjoy the same fate as your friends. Until next time—well, there won't be a next time, but I do enjoy a good expression. Anyway, goodbye."

Ahna dug her nails into the rim of the window as her body was being pulled away. She fought as hard as she could, struggling to keep her grip despite it slipping.

"We have to go, Ahna!" said Felan. She was tugging at Ahna, trying to force her away from the door.

Ahna stole one last glance through the bloodstained window. Scorcher lay motionless in the middle of the floor, the once white-and-gray fur of his armor now saturated by scarlet. One of his arms lay outstretched, his fingers spread wide, reaching in the direction of Vincent's body. Ahna's heart dropped, and her grip loosened.

The door faded into the distance as she was guided toward the exit. She didn't care what was going on around her. All she wanted was to be in the room behind the crimson window.

It should've been me. It should've been me. It should've been me.

As they stepped into the snowy landscape, her thoughts flowed from her mouth and formed a cloud in front of her face, the words almost inaudible.

"It should've been me . . ."

AHNA STEPPED THROUGH the gate of Tent City and felt eyes staring at her, unblinking. With each step, City Hall seemed to move farther and farther away. Those who had been watching her moved in to surround her and began to point and laugh.

"Filthy Eksider!"

"Someone thinks they're better than us, don't they?"

"Drip, drip. Hope you slip!"

Ahna looked down at her feet to see a trail of blood behind her, a pool forming below her. Her heart began to race, and the red puddle grew until it was the size of a lake. The townspeople continued to laugh and jeer from the areas around her, safe on land while she began to tread. Her arms became tired as the lake grew even larger, now filling the entirety of Tent City. The walls broke down, tents floating away in the current. Ahna realized she was being carried off with the debris and struggled to swim against it.

Immediately ahead of her, she spotted a drop-off in the water level: a waterfall.

Red water splashed against her and the rocks that had formed on the side of the new river, Tent City now far in the distance, demolished. There was nothing around for her to grab on to, nobody to help save her from drowning or falling to her death in the waterfall ahead.

As if from thin air, a small raft sailed beside her, and a familiar voice called out her name.

"Ahna!" Scorcher yelled, reaching toward her. "Take my hand, Ahna!"

"Scorcher!" she cried back, swimming against the current to grab his hand.

The waterfall was much closer, and they had very little time to sail to safety. Once she gripped his hand, he pulled her onto the raft. Before she could get her bearings, the raft hit a large rock, sending her sideways. She slammed into Scorcher, who flew off the raft and into the water.

He yelled out to her, flailing about. Ahna reached out to him, yelling his name, but the raft sailed away. She hurried to the helm and gripped the wooden handle, but when she tried to steer back to him, the handle shattered into a million little splinters.

"Why did you push me in, Ahna? I thought you loved me!" Scorcher called out.

"I do love you! I didn't mean to do it, Scorch!" Ahna yelled back, but it was too late.

Scorcher sunk beneath the water, sending a rush of guilt through her body. The raft sailed downriver before heading right over the edge of the waterfall. Scorcher's body emerged from the water right in front of her. The raft followed his body over the edge and tipped downward, sending her toward the shallow water and rocks below. The air escaped her lungs as she tried to scream.

"Scorcher! Scorcher!"

AHNA JOLTED UPRIGHT in the bed, sweat dripping from her forehead. It felt as though she had just emerged from the depths of the ocean. She struggled to regain her breath, the light around her almost blinding. She sighed in relief as her surroundings came into focus. Sunlight streaked through a cloud of dust in the window, casting a silhouette at the foot of her bed.

"Guilty nightmare?" asked Sticks.

A glint reflected off his leg braces, shooting directly into her eye. She winced, blocking her eyes with her hand, and sat upright to face Sticks.

"How'd you know?" asked Ahna.

"You were screaming his name . . . but I could tell before that."

"How long have you been here?" she asked.

And why were you watching me sleep?

"Not long," said Sticks, shuffling on the edge of the bed. "Corrine wanted me to check in on you—make sure you were okay."

Ahna rubbed the back of her neck, resisting the urge to flinch when she felt the amount of sweat on her palm. She wiped her hand against the bedding as stealthily as she could, hoping Sticks wouldn't notice.

"I appreciate it, but I'm fine," said Ahna.

"No you're not," said Sticks. His tone was firm but soft. "There's no way you're fine right now. Honestly, it'd be weird if you were fine."

"What do you know? You have no clue how I feel," said Ahna.

Her body stiffened. Every single one of her muscles ached as she moved to get out of bed. Sticks held the cover down, keeping her from getting up.

"You're right," said Sticks. His tone was sharp, dry. "I have no idea what you feel, right? I forgot . . . I haven't had the only person I ever loved die."

"Sticks, I—"

"No, Ahna. It's fine. I mean, at least you got to tell him how you felt about him before it happened. With R—" Sticks hesitated before continuing. "I didn't even know she'd died until someone said it happened. I would have given anything to—"

Sticks turned away from her, but she saw the tears forming in his eyes. Ahna felt her eyes water, too. She started to wipe the tears away but instead reached out to Sticks, gripping his arm. When he turned to face her, his eyes were red and puffy. She assumed hers looked no different. It was surprising, but she felt like she could finally understand why he'd acted the way he had the day he found out Rollin died. She looked into his eyes, and it felt like she was staring at her own reflection. Ahna pulled Sticks into a hug, and they embraced each other tightly. Their quiet sobs ebbed and flowed for a few minutes, Ahna finally allowing herself the release she hadn't realized she needed.

When they'd both calmed down, Sticks backed away from her like a child meeting a stranger. He wiped his eyes and cleared his throat, taking a deep breath. For the first time in a while, he smiled at Ahna, and she felt like he meant it. As wrong as it felt given the recent events, she allowed herself to smile, too.

"Don't mention this to anyone," said Sticks.

"Don't worry, I won't."

Not that I have anyone I'd be excited to tell it to . . .

She felt the sadness creeping back in, but Sticks continued to talk, pulling her focus to him.

"Do you want to talk about it?" he asked. He must have seen her eyebrows meet because he continued before she could respond. "About Scor—his . . . passing, or anything?"

You're trying to be nice.

Ahna smiled slightly.

This is the Sticks I remember.

She shook her head. "I'm not really sure where to start."

Sticks nodded. The light reflected off the small metal piece still on the side of his head before he pushed the hair out of his face, covering it. It was almost like he knew.

"Death is . . . hard," said Sticks. She wasn't used to the soft, vulnerable tone he was using. She wasn't used to him being like this at all, actually. But it was . . . comforting. "In fact," he continued, "it's probably impossible to fully understand. But I try to . . . all the time."

He paused, swallowing. Wiping his eyes, he continued.

"I see her every day, you know. I hear her laugh in my head, hear her voice when I'm making decisions, egging me on when I lean toward the wrong one." He chuckled. "She'll always be there with me." He grabbed Ahna's hand. "Just like Scorcher will be there for you. It may take some time, but you'll realize . . . once you accept death, life becomes so much easier."

Ahna nodded, gripping his hand in her own. As weird as it felt to touch Sticks like this, she appreciated the gesture. She needed it.

As she thought of what to say, one thought kept returning to her. One face returned her mind. It was the same face she needed to rid her head and the world of: Dean Tipper. She'd had her hesitations before when planning their potential attack on the facility due to the risks involved. Now there was nothing left to risk for her. Everything she had to lose was lost. Dean Tipper may have taken everything from her, but he'd given her the only thing she hadn't had: a hunger for vengeance.

She pulled her hand away from Sticks, then stood up. She started putting on her armor, fumbling a bit as she did so. She was ready to move forward; she couldn't wait any longer.

"What are you doing?" asked Sticks.

Ahna slid into the breastplate, then pushed her feet into her boots, tying them as quickly as she could.

"Getting ready," she replied, grabbing her helmet and heading toward the door.

Sticks stood up, blocking her. "Hold on. Getting ready for what?"

She could see he was confused by her sudden change of emotion and overall state of being. She almost surprised herself.

"Revenge," said Ahna. "What you said made a lot of sense, Sticks."

"It did?"

She kept talking as though she hadn't heard him. "And I think we need to hit them harder than we ever thought possible. You still have the option to control those Wallers?"

Sticks nodded. "Well, yeah, but—"

"Good. Make sure those are good to go. I'll talk with Felan, Marie, Corrine, Baz and Taz, and everyone and make sure everything else is good, too. We need to gather the team, strike while the iron's hot."

"Are you sure about this?" asked Sticks.

Ahna nodded, a slight grin on her face. "More than ever. Like you said, Sticks, death is hard, but I need to learn to accept it. Once I do that, life will be easier."

Her tone shifted.

"Their death will be very easy to accept."

Chapter Thirty-Six
Sticks

Wallers were lined up like a battalion of soldiers standing shoulder to shoulder, all packed into a small area underground. Their eyes were open, but each one of them stared directly at the ground. A subtle breeze drifted near his ankles which Sticks realized was the collective breath of the Wallers. A twitch jolted his body.

Memories of his time within the facility, under the control of Dean Tipper and his walking mountain of a man servant flooded his mind. It had felt like forever when he was in there, as though he had been watching it all from afar and not actively doing everything himself. Even in his dreams he was forced to revisit the facility and all the death that followed.

He stared at the Waller directly in front of him for a moment.

Its shoulders moved up and down like buoys in the ocean, continuous and steady. If he looked past the grotesque, rotted skin he could almost see a normal person's face. Questions swam in his head. Thoughts of who the Waller might have been or become if it had been given the chance. Then, they disappeared in a flash when a hand gripped his shoulder.

Sticks leapt around, ready to strike when he paused.

"Easy," said Wick, pulling his hand back and holding them up in the air. "Easy, Sticks. I was just coming over to check on you. Everything okay?"

Sticks nodded.

"Yeah. Except you just scared me to death," he said. Sticks laughed after he realized he was no longer being attacked. "What made you think I wasn't okay?"

Wick shrugged.

"You were over here staring at that thing for a while. I called out your name a couple times. You didn't hear me?"

Really? Weird. I didn't think I'd been looking at it for that long.

Sticks shook his head. "Nope. Guess I was busy thinking."

"It's about time you started doing that," said Wick, laughing as he swatted Sticks on the arm. "Speaking of, what do you think? Is this amazing or what?"

Wick gestured to the army of Wallers behind him.

"It's definitely more than I could have imagined," said Sticks. "But do you ever think about . . ."

Wick's eyes narrowed. "About what"

Sticks scanned the crowd of Wallers, their biggest weapon against The Delivery Company.

"You ever wonder if Wallers are, like, real people?"

Wick started to laugh but stopped. He tilted his head.

"Oh. You're serious?"

Sticks nodded. Wick paused for a moment, taking another look at the army behind them. Then, he turned back to Sticks.

"I think, at one point, there was most certainly a time when they could have been."

"Like when?"

"During the beginning stages of their creation, however they are made. I'm not sure if they are all made the same way, but I would guess that if they are anything like us, then it wouldn't take much to alter their DNA one way or another."

"So, you're saying that they could have been just like us, had a more normal life like us?"

Sticks looked at the face of the Waller behind Wick again. He pictured its hair and face being clean, almost able to see a regular face if he looked hard enough.

"I guess so, yeah," said Wick. "But we don't exactly have a normal life either, right?"

Sticks nodded.

"I guess you're right. Beats having to live like an animal, though."

Wick chuckled.

"We are animals, Sticks. We just happened to work our way up the food chain a little bit quicker. Besides, there's always going to be predators and prey. We might as well be the predators, right?"

Sticks nodded.

"Good point." A slight pain shot through his knees, bringing him back to the task at hand. "We need to start checking on all the mechanisms. There's no way I'm gonna let all our hard work fail because of some stupid lock on the gate."

Wick chuckled. "That would be pretty lame, for sure."

"This needs to be perfect," said Sticks.

Wick shook his head as he was turning to leave. "Forget perfect," he said. "It just needs to work."

That's not a bad motto.

Sticks walked through the lines of Wallers, pushing all thoughts of their potential aside. They might have had the opportunity to become someone else at one point, but not anymore. Instead, he would make sure they would become something. That something would ensure that fewer Wallers would exist in the future. It had to.

At the gate, he checked the lock and took one last glance at the rows of Wallers. The way they stood next to each other reminded him of the Elite inside the facility on the day he gave the speech before attacking Tent City. So many stood ready to fight, awaiting his signal. Now, the Wallers awaited the very same. His signal would unleash their fury in a stampede toward The Delivery Company. As much as he hoped to never see another Waller again, he had a feeling their attack on the facility would be a sight he wouldn't want to miss.

Chapter Thirty-Seven
Felan

Where are they? I just need to get enough to last me through the next couple hours.

Felan crept through the maze of boxes and crates, searching for the pain killers. She knew from the time she'd taken an extra ration of meat that there had been enough of them in there before. Although, there'd been a few more kids go down with injuries since the last time. Of course, none of those kids were about to sneak into the facility alone and risk their life so she figured it would be okay to steal one or two. She definitely needed them.

She peeked into each crate as she walked by them. To her surprise, it took only a minute or so to find the syringes, thanks to Marie's organizational habits. Felan snatched two and pocketed them quickly before heading back toward the exit. As she turned the corner to leave, she doubled over.

Pain surged through her abdomen and Felan gripped onto the rough, wooden body of the nearest crate. Her knuckles whitened as she took quick, shallow breaths. It was becoming a usual occurrence and the pain wasn't getting any easier to deal with.

As it began to ease, Felan relaxed her grip on the crate and reached into her pocket for one of the syringes. She hadn't anticipated needing the pain killers so soon, but she hadn't anticipated many things as far as her illness was considered.

She removed the cap, but before she jabbed herself with the needle she heard her name.

"Felan?" asked Marie. She was adjusting her glasses, staring at Felan from the entrance.

Great. Of all the times this stupid illness decides to keep me from moving it had to be now. This can't look good.

"Marie! Hey. I, uh—"

Marie's eyes narrowed.

"Why do you have the pain killer without me giving it to you?" She paused. "Is it getting worse?"

Marie started toward her, her look of anger melding into one of worry. When she reached Felan, she held out her hand. Without saying a word, Felan knew to hand over the syringe. Once Marie had it in her hand, she held it up to the light and flicked the tube with her nail to get rid of any bubbles. Then, she pointed to Felan's waist.

"Shirt."

Felan lifted the bottom of her shirt, just enough so that Marie could pinch a bit of skin in her abdomen. Marie's fingers were ice cold, but she would gladly take that if it meant getting the shot. Felan looked away as Marie injected the medicine into her and once it was over, she let her shirt fall back down.

Marie stared at her for a moment, her eyes obscured slightly behind the foggy lenses of her glasses. Before saying another word, Marie took off her glasses and wiped them clean with her own shirt. While she was doing that, Felan felt the pain ease and her body start to relax a bit. Though, she wondered if it wasn't only the medicine that caused that sense of relief.

Felan took a few more deep breaths, trying to focus and figure out what to say. Before she could do that, Marie was already putting back on her glasses.

"It is getting worse, isn't it?" asked Marie.

Felan wanted to lie, tell her that everything was fine and that it was just a fluke, but she couldn't do that. Not to Marie. She deserved to know the truth.

"It's only been getting worse," said Felan. "It's like every day's a little death or something. Some days I feel like that might be easier, too."

"Don't say that." Marie's tone was sharp. "Don't you dare say that."

"Why not?" Felan shrugged. "It's the truth, Marie."

Marie shook her head.

"You're not dying on my watch."

Felan chuckled. "You can't save them all."

"I'm not trying to," said Marie. She looked behind her before returning her glance to Felan. "Don't tell me you were stealing the pain killer because you're still going out on that mission."

Felan shrugged. "There's nobody else who can, Marie. If I don't go, we risk losing all the data that can help so many people."

Marie adjusted her glasses again. The way she did that was always so precise, almost robotic. Most people would probably think it was a nervous habit or something, but Felan had seen it many times and knew Marie was not a nervous person. If anything, it was a move that signaled that whatever she was about to say was said with pure confidence. Her confidence was only one of many things she admired about Marie.

"You know there's a chance that you'll die out there, right?" asked Marie.

That was not what I was expecting you would say.

Felan shook her head. "I'll be fine. I always am."

"Just because something has always been, doesn't mean it always will be, Felan. You are getting worse and you might get hurt or worse. I can't have you dying, not before . . ."

"Before what?"

Marie started to answer but hesitated. She adjusted her glasses again, then locked eyes with Felan.

"Just promise me that you'll make it back in one piece."

Felan nodded. "I promise. As long as you tell me whatever it is you were trying to not tell me before. Deal?"

Marie walked over to the crate Felan had just rummaged through and pulled out a few more pain killers. When she returned, she placed them into Felan's hand.

"Deal."

Their hands touched as Marie handed her the syringes and Felan noticed Marie's cheeks glowing red. Before she could say anything about it, a noise from outside echoed around the building. Felan pocketed the pain killers and sucked in a deep breath.

"Sorry, gotta go," said Felan. Then, before she fully exited, she stopped. "In case anybody asks, you didn't see me, okay?"

Marie smiled, nodding.

"But I will, right?" she asked.

Felan nodded. "Yeah."

I sure hope so.

Chapter Thirty-Eight
Dune

"Ugh!" His fingers burned as the rope slid between them. Dune dug his feet into the snow trying to pull the wagon as much as he could but it wouldn't move.

Taz and Baz stood, their guns drawn, at the edge of the clearing, watching for any animal or Waller. Sarah was trying to push the wagon from behind, but to no avail. Finally, she quit trying to push and started up toward him. While he waited, Dune grabbed a handful of snow and cooled his burning fingers.

"Not moving at all, huh?" asked Sarah.

Dune shook his head.

"Nope. I have been pulling on it, but it keeps slipping through my hands. I don't know what else to do."

Sarah looked at the rope that he had dropped in the snow, then at him, then the wagon. Then, she smirked and snatched the rope.

"I have an idea."

Before he could ask, Sarah was already coming toward him with the rope. She held out her arms as though she were going to give him a hug and he felt very uncomfortable. Then, he realized she wasn't doing that at all. Instead, she was feeding the rope around his waist from one hand to the other, then tied it off at the front. As she tightened the knot, he grunted.

"Too tight?" she asked.

"No," said Dune, lying. "Not at all."

"Good." She gave one quick nod, then pointed to the wagon. "I'm gonna go back to the rear of the wagon and push, but you just walk as much as you can. Now that it's tied around you, you should have a bit more to pull with."

Dune waited until Sarah made it back to the wagon and gave the thumbs-up. He turned to face their facility at the top of the hill and started to walk.

His feet dug into the snow, slipping slightly at first. Then, once he figured out how to scrape away some of the snow with his steps he could dig more into the dirt. That gave him a much better grip and he could tell it was working.

Behind him, the wagon finally started to budge from its resting place. Thankfully, a lot of the supplies were still not inside it, but it wasn't empty. Unfortunately for him, the majority of what was in it was the weaponry and ammunition.

Each step he took seemed to get a little easier until eventually he was walking at a pace close to normal. He couldn't believe it. He felt strong, useful. Finally, he was proving to be helpful to the group, too. Of course, pulling a wagon up a hill wasn't the greatest thing in the world, but it was a start. He had to start somewhere.

As he neared the top of the hill, he spotted Ahna standing in the opening of the building. The look on her face made him laugh. It was only when he heard a yell from behind and felt the wagon pulling him backward that he had to quit laughing and focus on the wagon again.

Once they made it all the way back up to level ground, Sarah helped untie the knot from his waist. She then tied it around a large piece of metal jutting from the side of the building. That had to hold up much better than the tree that allowed it roll downhill in the first place.

"You drag that up here all by yourself?" asked Ahna.

Dune shook his head. "No. I had some help."

He pointed back at the wagon but realized that Baz and Taz were not walking next to it. Instead, one had their feet up in the air while the other stood on top of them inside the wagon.

"Looks like they were a lot of help," said Ahna, laughing. She turned to Sarah. "He came in handy, huh?"

Sarah nodded. "Couldn't have done it without him." She gestured to Taz and Baz. "Clearly."

They all laughed before another Gray Wolf ran out the gate, hardly able to catch their breath. A pair of binoculars hung from their neck and their eyes were wide.

"She's heading to the facility! All by herself!" he yelled, still catching his breath.

"Who is?" asked Ahna.

"Felan!" he yelled.

Baz and Taz suddenly stopped messing around in the wagon and hopped down to join them. Dune was impressed at their speed given how slow they tended to walk around the facility half the time.

"Did you say Felan went to the facility?" asked Taz.

"By herself?" added Baz.

The Gray Wolf with the binoculars only nodded, clearly still freaking out.

"She wasn't supposed to go down there yet," said Ahna. "She's going to mess up our plan!"

"What was she thinking?" asked Baz.

"We have to stop her!" added Taz.

The group argued back and forth about who or what to do as Dune listened. He pulled out the black stone from his pocket, running his thumb across his name. He thought of Vincent and all the others who had been killed by his old boss. He couldn't let that happen to Felan. She needed their help. She needed his help.

This is my chance.

"I'll go."

The group went silent after Dune spoke; all eyes were locked on him.

"You sure?" asked Sarah.

"Yeah, that's practically a suicide mission!" said Taz.

"She might die if he doesn't go though!" added Baz.

Taz stared at Baz with his mouth hung open and gasped.

"You're right!"

"I know!"

Dune pocketed his stone and put a hand on their shoulders, shutting them up.

"Don't worry. I'll make sure she makes it back and gets on the train."

Baz nodded. His eyes narrowed, his tone suddenly serious.

"You better," said Baz. "If she doesn't make it back to the train, you won't either."

The group started to argue, Ahna and Sarah trying to push back against what Baz had just said, but Taz starts defending Baz. Nobody seemed to be in full agreement.

While they were arguing, Dune was able to step away and head to his room. There, he gathered his stuff and put on the rest of his armor. There was a moment of hesitation before he finally let out a sigh and exited his room. He walked right past the group and out into the snow.

With the facility in sight, he took a moment to breathe. He never imagined returning. He had to remind himself that he was there for Felan, nothing more. Anybody who stood in his way would not be able to do so ever again. He was going to bring her back, no matter what.

Chapter Thirty-Nine
Scorcher

A metallic taste filled his mouth. His pants felt soggy, as though he had been lying in water for days. He struggled to open his eyes, his eyelids glued shut by the crust that had formed between them. Finally, after the water from his eyes soaked through the bulk of what he realized had been dried-up blood, he could take in his surroundings. As the room around him slowly came into focus, he could see he wasn't in his room. Instead, he was chained to a cold metal wall, shackled at the wrists. Not that it mattered since he couldn't move much of his body even if he were free to try.

Where's Vincent? Maybe he can help me.

Scorcher tried to call out to Vincent but quickly realized he couldn't speak. His throat was dry, and no sound escaped. Not that it mattered. Vincent wasn't in the room. Then he remembered everything.

He remembered going down into the cave. He remembered telling Ahna that he would be there for her the whole time. He remembered Vincent . . .

Pain surged through his body with each breath, and he shook while tears streamed down his face. It took a moment for him to calm down, but he was finally able to slow his breathing and focus on the situation.

Okay, Scorch, focus. What can you do in here? How can you get back to the group? Ah!

A small piece of the wall was rusty and pulling away from the screw where it was attached. As if a miracle, it was the same spot his right wrist was shackled to on the wall. He chuckled slightly, regretting it immediately. He winced, pain once again cutting his excitement short.

Emotion equals pain. Got it.

Scorcher yanked his arm forward, grunting with each thrust while he kept watch on the loose screw. Pausing in between each movement made it take twice as long as it should have, but he didn't care. As long as he could get one of his arms free, he could figure something out. He hoped. The screw moved millimeter by millimeter until, with one heavy pull, it popped out of the wall and landed in the blood next to his leg.

Gross.

His arm fell to his side like a heavy piece of rope. Light dotted his vision, pain surging through his arm and torso. He let out a howl of pain, the first sound he'd been able to make since waking up.

"Someone's finally awake, huh? About time!"

A voice outside the room called out behind the metal door. When Scorcher heard a jingle of metal, he knew he had mere seconds before someone entered his room. As the handle turned on the door, he snatched the large rusty screw from the puddle of blood beside him before flinging his arm back up to the wall. Pushing through the pain, he held his arm up against the wall as a guard entered the room.

If the guard was an Elite, he must have been in a bad batch because he looked a lot smaller than the ones they'd seen at the blockade. His size didn't matter when he carried a rifle, though. A smaller handgun rested on his waist, but it looked too clean to have been used regularly. When the guard looked at Scorcher, he placed his rifle back over his shoulder, smiling.

"Well, well, well," he said, moving closer to Scorcher. "The corpse lives, huh?"

Scorcher did his best to keep his arm from falling from its place, wanting to maintain the illusion he was still shackled to the wall. It took most of his focus to do so. The taunts from the guard didn't help.

"Not interested in talking? That's fine." The guard moved down to be eye level with Scorcher, crouching only inches from him. "I'm sure you have nothing good to say anyway. I don't know why the doctor wanted to keep you around. Once we don't need him anymore, we'll make sure you join him in the trash, where you and the rest of the Rejects belong."

He smiled, and Scorcher could barely contain his anger any longer. As he was about to attack, a siren wailed in the hallway. Lights flashed with each tone from the siren, and another guard appeared in the doorway.

"Leave the Reject; we're under attack! Let's go!" he shouted, then ran back out the door.

The guard in front of Scorcher squinted at him. "Looks like I'll have to deal with you later. Looking forward to it. Maybe I'll even let you free so you have a fighting chance," he said, laughing.

His eyes widened and his mouth gaped as Scorcher dug the screw into his neck. Scorcher twisted the screw as much as he could before having to let go. The guard fell to the floor, reaching toward his neck for the screw, which was now embedded inside it. While he struggled, Scorcher was able to grab the ring of keys from his belt. He forced each key into the hole of the other shackle until one went completely in and turned, releasing his other arm.

When it was free, his body slid toward the floor, finally free. It took a moment for his strength to come to a point that he could move his body fully. The guard across from him had stopped struggling, now lifeless in a mix of Scorcher's and his own blood. A shiver traveled down Scorcher's spine as he pushed the guard's lifeless body off and finally stood on his own two feet. He grabbed the handgun from the guard's waist and checked the magazine.

At least it's not empty.

One leg dragged as he limped toward the door, blood trailing behind him.

Lights and sounds battered his senses as he stepped into the hallway, where the loud noises echoed off the metal. Screams accompanied the sirens, gunfire in the distance. As Scorcher turned to head toward the tunnel, he spotted the Elite who had come to the room before. The Elite's eyes widened when he saw Scorcher, but he was too slow to pull out his gun.

Scorcher fired a round into him, sending the Elite to the ground. As the Elite struggled to stop his bleeding, Scorcher continued down the hall. When he passed a room near the end, he saw a handful of screens and buttons. On the middle screen, the largest of the group, he saw a camera feed of the front of the facility. In front of the gate were a handful of Elite and Dune.

You were coming to save me . . .

A tear welled up in Scorcher's eye, and he promptly wiped it away. He realized the Elite were causing a problem for Dune's plan, and the door still looked shut. Flashing buttons lay scattered beneath him like a starry mechanical sky.

One of these has to work, right?

Scorcher mashed buttons, watching the screen as he did. Once he saw the gate open, he destroyed the panel so nobody could shut it again. They didn't need more complications than they already had. Dune was destroying the guards at the front gate, but that wouldn't stop the problems they were about to face. Thankfully, he didn't have to do it alone. Scorcher smirked before heading out the door.

Now I can go through the main gate instead of those nasty Waller-infested tunnels. What the—

His smirk disappeared.

At the end of the hall was a set of metal bars barricading his way to the main gate. They hadn't been there before, but it appeared they had come from the ceiling as some sort of defensive mechanism.

Must've been one of those buttons. Dang!

He headed back toward the tunnels, no time for a new plan. There was no way he could fight the guards near the front gate like Dune—not that he'd have been able to find his way there very easily. Besides, he knew the tunnels were cleared from before.

Scorcher sucked in a deep breath, an image of Vincent filling his mind. He had heard the guards talking about him during captivity. The things they said were too terrible to dwell on. He couldn't bear the thought of Vincent being gone. He wanted to believe there was a possibility that he would see him again, maybe with the group. He just had to make it back to the group first. Then, his mom and Marie could patch him up on their way out of that dump.

He just needed to find the location of the tunnel entrance. Because he had been unconscious on the way up from there, it would be a guessing game—one he had very little time to play.

Scorcher paused for a moment against the wall, allowing his head to clear and vision to return to normal. Blood trickled sporadically from his body and pooled at his feet, his strength fleeting with every minute that passed. Once he'd gained a little energy, he powered forward.

If I remember right, there should be a stairwell leading down to the tunnel system. But where's the door?

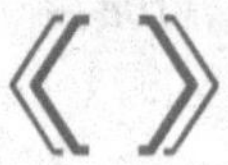

SCORCHER STOOD IN FRONT of a door marked "Employees Only." The door was from the prewar times, one that had a handle instead of opening automatically.

This must be it.

Scorcher opened the door, closing it quickly behind him so no one could see him enter. Once he was inside, he breathed a sigh of relief. He scanned the area, looking for any sign of the entrance.

It was a small room, probably ten feet by ten feet, cluttered with old desks and chairs on either side. The middle was left open, though, creating a pathway through the old furniture and supplies. At the other side of the room, a white coat twirled as a man moved quickly to see who had entered.

The man looked familiar, but Scorcher's mind was a bit foggy, making it difficult to place him. His hair was dark, though gray was scattered about the top and sides. A pair of glasses rested upon his pointy nose, obscuring his eyes but not his bushy eyebrows. His gasp indicated his surprise upon seeing Scorcher, who was equally surprised to see anyone inside. Scorcher raised his gun, pointing at the man in the lab coat.

"H-hold on, Scorcher," said the man. He raised his hands up in the air, cowering slightly as Scorcher hobbled toward him.

"How do you know my name?" asked Scorcher, trying to rack his memory. Nothing came to mind.

"I had to figure out who Ahna was with all the time," said the man. "I-I know I never got the chance to be there, but I'm trying to change that."

What craziness are you talking about?

"Who are you?" asked Scorcher. He moved closer again, stabbing the air with the barrel of the gun. The man stumbled back.

"Erik Sundry," he said. "Dr. Erik Sundry."

Scorcher's memory snapped back like a rubber band.

"If you're the doctor, then that means you're Ahna's—"

"Father," Dr. Sundry said. "Yes. Which is why I try to keep up with her life . . . and those in it." He gestured to Scorcher. "So, unless you want to tell her you killed her father, do you mind putting the gun down?"

Scorcher's mind raced. He had so many questions but no time. After a quick assessment of the doctor, he figured there was no risk lowering the gun. Besides, it was starting to get heavy, his arm almost shaking from exhaustion.

"Okay, there," said Scorcher, slipping the gun into his waistband.

"Thank you."

"What are you doing here?"

"Same as you, I'm assuming," said Dr. Sundry. "Trying to escape this wretched place before we all die. It would have been ironic for you to have shot me while doing it." He chuckled.

"So this is the way out?" asked Scorcher.

"Well, down, but yes," said Dr. Sundry. "It's not an easy way, though—especially not in your condition." He looked Scorcher up and down before he ripped a piece of his lab coat and started toward Scorcher.

Scorcher stepped back, reaching for his gun but not pulling it out yet.

"What are you doing?"

Dr. Sundry stopped, softening his tone. "I'm just going to patch you up the best I can so you have a better chance of getting back to Ahna in one piece. You know, without bleeding out on the way."

Scorcher glanced down at the small puddle of blood beneath him, realizing the doctor was probably right. If he was going to make it back to the group, he needed to stop the bleeding. Finally, he nodded.

"Fine, but hurry. She probably thinks I'm dead, so I'm hoping to get back before I really am," said Scorcher.

"Understood," said Dr. Sundry. "Just give me a moment, and you'll be good to go."

He started wrapping the bandage around Scorcher's leg, and the pressure was both relieving and painful. Scorcher winced, but he powered through, knowing it was only going to help. That didn't stop him from hating and loving the doctor for what he was doing at the same time. Once it was finished, Dr. Sundry pulled out a small flask and handed it to him.

"Drink this before you go."

"What is it?" asked Scorcher.

"Just water," said Dr. Sundry. "You're dehydrated. This should help, at least a little bit."

Scorcher took the flask, unscrewed the top, and lifted it up to his mouth for a sip.

"Thanks."

Dr. Sundry opened the hatch behind them, where Scorcher could see a ladder descending into darkness. It was going to be a difficult climb down and an even more difficult trek back through the tunnels, but he would do it. The water would definitely help, too. If nothing else, it would get rid of his dry mouth.

As he tipped the flask up to drink some more, the door at the other end of the room was flung open. Scorcher choked on the water, dropping the flask to the ground. Before he could do anything else, Dr. Sundry snatched the handgun from his waist and launched himself in front of Scorcher. A gunshot echoed in the small room, deafening him. The ringing in his ears continued as Dr. Sundry fell to the ground, bleeding. In the doorway, a large Elite was reloading their gun.

Scorcher started toward Dr. Sundry but was swatted away.

"Go! Just go before—"

A bullet whizzed past him, close enough he heard the air from it before the ringing intensified. Scorcher looked between the doctor and the hatch, then up to the Elite in the doorway, who was already reloading again and moving closer to them. Dr. Sundry raised the handgun and fired at the Elite until the magazine was empty, allowing Scorcher just enough time to get down into the hatch and close it behind him.

Chapter Forty
Felan

B *legh!* Vomit splattered in the grass, some getting on her boots. It had changed colors from the last time, too. Before it had been a light yellow. Now it was brown. She was worried not only by the color but by the frequency at which it happened. She'd thrown up three times in the last hour, each one robbing her of what little energy remained. She pushed herself back up from the ground, wiping the remnants from the corners of her mouth, her hands shaking.

Felan's field of vision darkened at the edges, like a burned picture, as she squinted through the immense pain that wouldn't fade. Each step was more difficult than the last, but she pushed forward, knowing the door to the facility was straight ahead. Her legs felt as though someone had attached chunks of steel to them. What felt like a mile couldn't have been more than ten feet.

Once she reached the door, her pain subsided just enough to see two Elite run past, heading down another hallway inside. After they were gone, she stepped inside, the bright light causing her to squint even more. Every few steps, Felan closed her eyes to take a break, focusing on the pain.

Stupid shot. It's never been this bad before.

It felt as though someone were inside her abdomen, wringing out her intestines—that, or she had swallowed a handful of razor blades. Either way, the pain was lower than usual, but that didn't make too much of a difference when it came to the severity. She'd thought she had experienced level-ten pain before, but she was very, very wrong. It was more than she'd ever felt and increased with each passing minute. She had to reach the main computer room, get the drives, and get out.

Even though it won't save me anymore . . .

Felan swallowed, wincing as another surge of pain sped through her abdomen, her fist clenching. She let out a small groan. It was a sound unlike anything she'd ever made. Sweat beaded down her forehead from her hairline. She wiped it away before moving forward once more, spotting a sign confirming the way to her destination. Nothing would stop her now.

BLEGH!

Felan wiped her mouth once more after depositing another batch of now-brownish vomit into a trash can. There was less than the previous time. She hadn't realized until now how much the amount had been decreasing. Her body felt weak; her armor seemed heavy upon her body as she stood still. She couldn't let that stop her from continuing. She wouldn't.

Now that she was in the control room, she felt a surge of adrenaline. Holding on to the side of the main desk, she shuffled past different monitors and switchboards. Buttons lit up in a myriad of colors, views of various parts of the facility playing on the large monitors above them. Yells from the halls outside alerted her to the situation at hand, reminding her of the time she didn't have to linger.

She began searching through the piles on the desks. She found a drive on one of them, but it couldn't be the only one, not in a facility this large. Lowering herself, she searched each of the towers below the desk. They were all hooked up to one machine, some sort of larger computer, but each tower had its own set of ports and inputs. She hoped that meant what she thought it did, but she didn't hold her breath. When she saw she was right, she couldn't believe it.

Jackpot.

Every single one of them had a drive. While some were smaller than others, only one of them was damaged. The others remained flawless. Their metal exteriors shone in the fluorescent lighting, reflecting her smile back to her. Even in pain, Felan couldn't help but smile. She'd searched for so long for individual drives and had now stumbled upon the mother lode. There was no doubt that they would find the cure for something on them.

Or everything…

Felan dropped a drive as another surge of pain snaked through her body. Her breath escaped as her eyes widened before tightening, closing and bringing her eyebrows together. She waited for it to pass, the noises in the halls growing louder.

Once it had passed, Felan picked up the drive she had dropped, hoping the crack in the casing wouldn't prevent Wick from retrieving the necessary information. She stuffed all the dri-

ves into the small sack hanging at her waist beneath her breastplate and started for the exit.

Chapter Forty-One
Ahna

"How're we looking?" asked Ahna.

Corinne and Marie buzzed around the hospital tent like bees, haphazardly tossing supplies into bins and carting them off to the assembly line of other kids. Those who could carry the supplies were heading off to the carts outside, where Ahna had set up the caravan.

The wagons were in position, one being loaded with all the supplies while the rest were being loaded with the kids who were unable to walk or run fast enough to get to the train themselves. The ramp that Scorcher had built for them was off to the side, one of the Gray Wolves rolling themselves up it in their wheelchair. The ramp had ended up being really helpful. Scorcher hadn't even been asked to do it; he'd just built it. He was always doing what was best for the group.

Now he never will . . .

Ahna's eyes clouded up, but she pushed the thoughts of him aside. She needed to focus on those who were actually there in front of her, those who would end up just like him if she didn't. Just because he was gone didn't mean she could let the others go with him. She wouldn't let him die in vain.

"Going as fast as we can," said Corrine. "There's not a whole lot left to grab. Granted, we don't have much room."

Marie sped past with an armful of bandages, a stream of white and tan trailing behind her. She spoke as she rushed by.

"I hope we can fit everyone on the train when we get there."

"We will. Don't worry."

Ahna answered before she'd even thought about whether she was telling the truth or not. She didn't know if there would be ample space, but she had to hope that they would create it if necessary. Everyone was used to sleeping practically on top of one another, so they would deal with it again. Besides, it was either sleep next to someone or sleep in the ground. She figured most people would choose the first option. Whether they actually made it onto the train was another question entirely. She knew it was risky—then again, so was living.

"This is the last batch of supplies," said Marie, a large box hugged to her body.

Ahna nodded. "Get it on the caravan and wait for my signal."

Marie nodded and hurried out the door, her glasses fogged up as she stepped back into the cold and headed down the hill toward the wagons.

Snow continued to fall outside, the temperature dropping in parallel with Ahna's hope. She felt like a turtle, her hard exterior helping to keep everyone else in high spirits while inside she felt soft, terrified. Nothing had gone the way she'd hoped since she'd joined the group. They'd lost so many supplies, so many people.

Rollin. Raider. Scout. Vincent. Scorcher . . .

Tears stayed frozen to her cheeks as she turned back inside. Everyone else was either at the caravan or carrying out their part of the plan. She had to make sure everything went smoothly, especially now that there was no other option.

The sound of her footsteps echoed across the front hall. What had once been full of kids chatting and playing, jokes and late-night stories around burning barrels, and the most comfortable beds they'd had in months now looked like any other scene across the wasteland they'd traveled through. Overturned chairs, leftover sleeping bags, and smoking barrels were all that remained of them inside. To whoever came after them, it wouldn't seem like much, but Ahna saw beyond the objects to the people, many of whom no longer remained. She held her breath as she passed by the old hospital room, trying to avoid breathing in the lingering odor of death and decay.

Once she reached the control room, she picked up the radio and let out a sigh. She pressed the button down, holding it in place as she spoke.

"This is Ahna. Sticks, you there?"

As Ahna waited for a response, her eyes were glued to the screen above. Felan was already nearing the front gate. Snow blurred the video, but even with that she could see that Felan was stumbling. Something had happened between her being in the facility and getting to the gate. She looked injured. Things were going downhill fast. They had to hurry.

"Sticks," Ahna said into the radio again. "You there? This is Ahna."

She waited again for a response, her fingers tapping the device as she watched Felan try to get inside the facility below. Wind must have picked up because the snow was flying past the camera providing the video, sticking to the lens. It had almost completely blocked her view. Felan disappeared behind the snow, only the top of the gate now visible. With Felan out of view and Sticks not answering, she was beginning to worry.

"Sticks!" Ahna yelled into the radio.

We don't have time for this, Sticks. Answer me . . .

Static was followed by a rustling noise from the radio.

"Hey, Ahna," Sticks said, his voice cutting in and out. "Sticks here."

"What took you so long? I've been trying you over and over."

"I know. We had a bit of an issue with one of the Wallers," said Sticks. Screeching echoed behind him from somewhere nearby. "But we should be good to go just as soon as—" A gunshot silenced the screeching in the background, and then Sticks continued. "You give the go."

"What just happened?"

"Inventory management," said Sticks.

Ahna looked at the screens above her, most of them entirely covered by snow or their video connection lost entirely. It was now or never.

"You're sure it's safe?"

Sticks forced a laugh. She could hear the fear in his voice.

"Nothing's safe anymore, Ahna. But I think it's the best shot we have at creating a diversion. We are almost back up to the facility now, too. Don't worry, once you give the signal, everything will be ready." He paused for a moment. "I just hope the plan works."

"It has to."

Chapter Forty-Two
Sticks

"You're 100 percent sure?" asked Sticks.

Wick nodded, a hum accompanying the nod. "Yeah . . . but let me see it again, just for a second. I-I want to make sure we didn't forget any of the most important pieces."

Sticks maneuvered the rusty wheelchair so that Wick could clearly see the scooter again.

A dim yellow light shone down on the scooter as if it were an exhibit in a dilapidated, forgotten museum. Sticks couldn't believe that Wick wanted to leave it behind, especially given the condition of his mobility. He hadn't said anything to Wick about it, but he noticed how much slower he was typing on the computer in the last few weeks. In addition to his deteriorating mobility, Wick wasn't doing as well as he let on. Sticks worried about that often, which was why it felt so wrong for them to be leaving the scooter behind. It was as though Wick and the scooter had been a part of each other. But Wick made a good point: they had little space, so unless Sticks wanted to leave him behind, they had to ditch the scooter. That was an easy choice.

Wick tapped Sticks on the hand and gestured toward the lift. "Okay, let's go."

Sticks nodded, turning the wheelchair back around and heading for the tram. His hands wrapped around the handles of the wheelchair brought back the memory of Rollin, her arms outstretched and flapping as she cackled. Her silly, vibrant imagination had been one of her best qualities. In all the dark times since that day, Sticks wouldn't complain about a little light.

Sticks looked back to the room before exiting, sucking in a deep breath. So much had happened in that room, in the building overall, and now they were leaving it behind. It wasn't the journey that he was worried about, though. What bothered Sticks most was the unknown destination. Of course, he would make wherever they went home for as long as it needed to be. After all, he'd done it before.

Sticks forced himself to focus on the task at hand and continued pushing Wick outside toward the tram, releasing a long sigh. He couldn't erase the image of the lone scooter destined to be forgotten in the abandoned facility.

Will anyone ever find this place after we leave? Will they know who was here, what we went through? Probably not . . . I wonder how many times we've come across a place of extreme significance to those who left it behind and thought nothing of it. I just hope I never end up like that scooter . . .

Chilly mountain air smacked Sticks in the face as they reached the platform of the rusty tram car that swayed in the breeze. All their belongings were already in the car, packed with only enough room for the two of them. Sticks pushed Wick over to the door of the cart before helping him into the metal contraption. Once Wick took a seat, Sticks compacted the wheelchair into its folded form and stuffed it into the tram with the rest of their belongings.

He walked to either end of the tram, quickly pulling on the straps that kept their stuff in place. After ensuring they were tight and secure, he knew they were ready. Before pulling the lever to the tram, though, he checked his pockets. Sticks felt the hard outline of the remote, relieved it hadn't fallen out earlier in the day during their hurried packing. He gripped the ribbed metal handle of the lever and called out to Wick.

"You ready?"

A thumbs-up shot into the air, followed by Wick's voice. "Ready!"

Sticks shoved the lever down, a grunt escaping him. Once it was down, the familiar hum of the machine whirred. The tramline started, yanking the tram forward, and Sticks sprinted toward it. Gripping the cold metal, he hopped while pulling himself inside. His body slid into the spot they'd reserved for him, snug against Wick and their collection of things. Wick laughed; their faces were not more than a foot apart.

"I almost thought you would miss the cart and be stranded up there," said Wick.

Sticks gulped, catching his breath. He shook his head. "Can't get rid of me that easily," he said, a laugh following.

Their laughter descended with the tram, and the lights of the facility fell away behind a blanket of snow. There was no turning back for them. Everyone else was already nearing the train, and the plan was in motion. All Sticks had to do was wait for the signal.

The signal!

Sticks reached for his pockets again, desperation quickly replaced by relief at the realization that the remote was still there. He didn't even want to entertain the thought of what might've happened if he had lost the remote. Ahna would most likely have killed him . . . if Elite or Wallers hadn't done it for her. Thankfully, he didn't have to worry about that. While important to the overall success of their mission, Sticks thought his part of the plan was not ideal. Playing puppet master to a horde of Wallers wasn't natural, and it certainly didn't feel that way. Sticks had lay staring up at the ceiling many nights attempting to think of alternate plans, anything to avoid the act of playing the Creator. There didn't seem to be another way.

A strange silence accompanied their initial descent from the facility. Trees danced in the mountain air, a dark outline of the cleared pathway on the mountainside below. The silence soothed Sticks's busy mind. Soon, however, silence would be replaced by chaos. Until then, Sticks planned on allowing himself to focus on anything but what was to come.

"When do you think she'll give the signal?" asked Wick. Clearly, he couldn't focus on anything but the plan.

So much for silence . . .

Sticks shrugged. "Could be any minute. As long as it happens, everything should be okay."

"If we never hear it?" asked Wick.

A lump formed in Sticks's throat and was quickly cleared by a gulp. "Then we just have to move a bit faster," he said. "We can't stay here, whether the plan goes well or not. Besides, everyone else should be on or nearing the train. We have to get them out of here before the train car becomes a mass grave."

Wick's eyes widened. Sticks could understand; he had surprised himself with that thought.

"Then I guess it has to work, huh?" asked Wick.

Sticks nodded. "I guess so."

Wick tilted his head, staring at Sticks for a moment. Sticks knew whatever he was going to say next would be something serious; it always was when he gave that look. He was consistent.

"Do you want me to push the button instead?" asked Wick.

Sticks was a little surprised at the question, considering he'd thought it was going to be about something totally different. He didn't rush to answer, though. Sticks had thought about the possibility of that, along with other methods of passing the blame or action onto someone else. But he was better than that. Besides, Seemore had always told him how much he admired that he was a man of his word.

I helped The Delivery Company get to the level they're at now with those suits. I helped innocent people get killed. This time, I'm going to make sure that I use what I created to keep that from happening.

Sticks shook his head, finally answering. "No, Wick. I need to do it."

I know what it's like to have your mind controlled like this, to be forced to kill people you didn't choose to kill. But this will be different, right? I mean, I'm only helping guide the Wallers toward them, right? Once they get there, whoever and whatever they kill is up to them. I'm not in full control of their minds.

"This doesn't make me as bad as Dean Tipper and them, right?"

"No," said Wick, shaking his head. "What they did was malicious, evil. You're doing this for good. You're making sure they die at the hands of Wallers while using their own tech against them. It's actually pretty poetic."

"So I made the right choice?" asked Sticks.

Wick shrugged. "It's your only choice."

Sticks nodded. Pushing the button was like pulling a trigger, only the bullet in his gun was a horde of Wallers. Sticks had killed people before, people who'd deserved it. Somehow, he felt worse about using the Wallers to do it. They were, after all, not so unlike him. They'd just happened to get the wrong strand of DNA. If he got the chance in the future, he would try to help them. First, though, they were going to be helping him.

Sticks wrapped his frozen fingers around the remote, waiting for Ahna to give the signal. Whenever she triggered the explosion, there would be no looking back.

Chapter Forty-Three
Scorcher

What little light remained in the tunnels below pulsed blue around him. Continuing deeper into the earth, he felt the temperature drop steadily, indicating the depth. His ears popped, but the feeling disappeared upon swallowing—a trick he'd learned from Seemore when they used to talk about diving.

I wonder if we'll ever see him again.

Scorcher continued through the tunnels, pushing himself to move as quick as he could. Thankfully, the bandaging held up well through the movements. He feared the doctor hadn't been so lucky. When he saw Ahna, he'd be sure to tell her that her father had died a hero; he'd saved his life for her.

Dirt particles rained on him from the ceiling after a trembling sent vibrations from the ground above. Whatever was happening up there had to be intense. He knew that it couldn't be good, whatever it was, so he tried to move quicker, knowing he had little time before the slight sprinkling of dirt became a cave-in.

Scorcher gasped, a smile spreading across his face.

She's helping me, even without being here. Man, I can't wait to see her.

Scratches marked his path along the wall; it was his trick, which Ahna had picked up after they'd gone to the beach the first time. He hadn't thought she'd been paying attention near as much as she had, but was happy he was incorrect. Those scratches would lead him out of the tunnels and back to her.

When this is all over, we can finally do everything we've always wanted. No more fighting, no more running, just us.

Memories of Ahna, his mom, and the rest of Tent City played like a movie in his mind. His energy grew with each memory as the faces of his friends and family flashed before him. When he got back, he was going to appreciate the everyday moments more with everyone. All the stupid jokes from Baz and Taz, all the moments with Ahna—good or bad—and even the fights with Sticks. Regardless of what was going to happen, he knew he would have their backs and that they would have his. They may not have all been of the same blood, but they were family. Once it was all over, he planned on starting one with Ahna, too.

A grin spread across his dirt-crusted face as he thought of the things he'd do with whatever kids they ended up having. He and Ahna could show them how to build their own raft, how to hunt, all the things they'd had to teach themselves. He knew, no matter what, that he would be better than his own father. He didn't plan on walking out on them or Ahna—ever.

I just hope you can forgive me for being so dumb half the time.

He started to laugh, which he quickly regretted due to the pain in his ribs.

His smile faded, energy draining from his body with each step. The memories weren't enough to keep him energized. His extremities felt heavier, as if blocks of wood had been tied to his body. Shuffling his feet, he headed toward what appeared to be a blinking red light illuminating the path directly ahead.

Scorcher thought he'd seen something like it before but thought he had been imagining it. As he got closer, he could see a large box-shaped object attached to the light. His eyes widened, his pace quickening. He didn't need to get any closer to know.

It was one of their bombs.

His breathing became shallow, his mouth as dry as a desert. Once it was blinking, it wouldn't be long before it blew. He had to move fast. Yelping with each step, he pushed through the pain and focused on finding his way back to the group, back to her.

I'm coming . . . Wait for me. I'm coming, Ahna.

Chapter Forty-Four
Ahna

Ahna stared past the trees as the caravan descended the mountainside toward the train. The group she was with was not the group she'd started with, and she had a bad feeling that it wouldn't be the group she ended with. Nothing ever stayed the same, and she was getting tired of the constant change. She hoped there'd be no more change once it was all over. That thought made her chuckle. Change was exactly what they were fighting for, after all.

Ahna's smile faded into a stern line. She pulled back the plastic cover, the red button staring back at her. Her body tensed up, her thumb shaking as it hovered over the button. She felt as though her breath had been knocked out of her body, her jaw tightening. Suddenly, she heard his voice in her head.

"BREATHE, AHNA. JUST breathe," said Scorcher.

Their raft got closer and closer to the edge, the water in front of them pouring downward to the sharp rocks below. Scorcher had been gathering what he could carry in his pockets before gripping her by the shoulders.

"How can I breathe when we're about to do a nosedive down a waterfall?" asked Ahna, her breath still shallow and choppy.

Scorcher shook his head. "Because we aren't. We're gonna jump."

"What?"

Ahna's heart raced even faster. Her eyes kept darting from the boat to the edge of the waterfall, which continued to move closer every time.

His warm hands gripped her face, and his emerald eyes stared right through her. Time seemed to slow as he spoke.

"Listen to me. We are going to jump when I say so, which is going to be very soon. Don't worry about the boat, don't worry about the supplies, and don't worry about me. Right now, focus on you. Understand?"

Ahna nodded.

Scorcher smiled. "You trust me, right?"

"For sure," said Ahna.

"Then listen closely. I want you to close your eyes and take three deep breaths."

Ahna fought her body's instinct to push back and forced herself to breathe deeply, just like he'd said. As she closed her eyes, she filled her lungs with the crisp, clean air of the mountains. Fear sailed out of her with each exhale, slowly allowing her body to relax and her mind to clear. Scorcher grabbed her hand, and she opened her eyes to see a large nest of trees quickly approaching their boat.

"When I say go, you're going to hold on tight and jump," said Scorcher.

"I don't think I can."

"But I do. You can do so much more than you give yourself cred-it for, Ahna. I know that, and I always have. It's time you know that, too. Trust yourself like you trust me. Think you can do that?"

Ahna wanted to say no, but something about the way he looked at her made it difficult. If nothing else, she would do it for him.

"Yeah. I can."

AHNA OPENED HER EYES, staring at the button. Less than a year ago, she had been part of the group she was about to destroy. She had wanted a family, had wanted to be the perfect Replacement. Instead, she'd been thrown out like trash, Rejected.

So many had died because of The Delivery Company, so many kids who should have had full, happy lives. Instead, those who survived fought to live only long enough to be killed by them at a later time. Ahna thought back to the cemetery where they'd buried Rollin, how she had seen so many other names scattered around it. Scorcher and Vincent would never get to be buried with their friends and family. For that, she would make them pay.

With the train in view, she knew it was time. Ahna took one last deep breath. Then she spoke aloud, as if he were sitting in the wagon with her.

"This is for you, Scorcher . . . and all the others they took too soon."

Chapter Forty-Five
Felan

Felan's mind began to clear as she stepped into the hallway. Now that she had the drives, she couldn't turn her focus away from the intense pain and discomfort tearing through her body. The light had become too bright, so she started to close her eyes more and more. She only opened them to see where the next turn was, which was more than she liked but necessary if she wanted to reach the group outside.

When Felan turned the corner, she slammed into something heavy. Her eyes shot open to see two Elite standing in front of her. Their eyes lit up, grins spreading across their faces as they chuckled.

"Look what we've got here," said one of them. "She doesn't look near as bad as the kid with the scars, huh?"

Scars? You're not talking about . . .

"No. In fact, she might have some uses," replied the other, a laugh following. "First thing's first, though," he continued, his tone darkening. "How'd you manage to get in, freak?"

Felan swallowed, her thoughts jumbled.

"The . . . door . . . idiot," she said. She winced, leaning against the wall as her body swayed. Her legs shook under her. There wasn't much time before they'd give out completely, making her unable to walk. She needed to get moving, get back to the group.

This can't be for nothing . . .

The Elite moved in front of her, now blocking the doorway entirely. They chuckled at her response, one of them tapping their weapon against their palm.

"Looks like someone needs to be taught their manners, huh?" said one of the Elite. Felan couldn't tell which one. Her eyes were clenched shut while another jolt of pain surged through her abdomen.

"Yeah, they do."

Felan opened her eyes enough to see the silhouette of her friend behind the Elite.

Dune?

A grin spread across her face. Dune wasted no time. Before the Elite could turn around to see who'd spoken, they found themselves in the air.

Dune launched them both into the wall across from Felan, their bodies denting the metal.

The Elite stumbled briefly as they stood up, brushing off the attack. Blades drawn, they crouched as Dune came toward them. Every time they swiped, Dune managed to dodge it. He was surprisingly fast for his size, but the moves weren't unknown to her. She'd seen him and Scorcher practicing those exact maneuvers before in the facility.

If only he were here to help now, too . . .

Dune tore the armor off one of the Elite before throwing him against the wall again. This time, he didn't get up. Before Felan could yell to watch out, the other Elite was on Dune's back. Dune fell to the ground, fighting to keep from going prone. They tussled for a moment before the Elite managed to force Dune fully into the ground after slashing his calf.

As the Elite pulled back his blade, Felan felt a surge of energy, and her eyes widened. She pulled out her knife and lunged toward the Elite. As her blade dug into their body, she felt as though she'd stabbed her own. A sharp pain spread through her abdomen again, this one the worst she'd felt so far. She squeezed her eyes closed and clenched her jaw. Her breathing became shallow.

Suddenly, an explosion rocked the room, the vibrations in the floor sending her tumbling. She tried to reach for the wall to catch herself but missed. Felan's body hit the floor. Debris tumbled toward her, pinning her body to the ground, adding to the pain.

More explosions reverberated through the facility, but they felt as though they were miles away. Fire was spreading from within the hallway, screams from every direction. However, Felan felt nothing but the pain that blanketed her body. She attempted to crawl out, to push the slab of concrete and metal off her torso, but every movement caused more pain. Even the thought of moving hurt. She couldn't think about moving any longer, though. Another surge of pain raced through her, a level higher than what she'd thought possible.

Sounds escaped her mouth, the worst sounds she had ever heard. Her only memory of anything similar was that made by the deer she'd killed with Elaine.

No one makes those sounds when they're gonna be okay . . .

She tried to fight, to keep herself from writhing around the cold metal floor, but she had already lost. Her body moved as though it were in control of itself. Tears rolled down Felan's cheeks as she realized her time was coming to an end.

I'm just like that deer . . . only my forest is of concrete, my own body the weapon that fired the final shot. I hope it's quick.

She choked on the smoke, more of it flowing across the ceiling like a black wave. Felan felt the familiar stabbing pain in her abdomen again and let out another moan. As the pain subsided, she could hear heavy breathing and what sounded like more debris falling nearby. Between heavy blinks, she saw Dune flinging rubble, racing toward her.

Her eyes closed again, energy draining. She was ready to fall asleep. Realizing she was still awake, Felan opened her eyes. Dune's dark eyes lit up, staring back at her.

"I've got you," said Dune.

A quick smile formed before he grabbed her. As he moved her, she winced, closing her eyes tight. Dune pulled her into a comforting embrace. It was almost like a tight hug. Then she felt air flow across her face.

Between surges of pain, she could open her eyes enough to see that he was carrying her through the hallway, its lights flickering. In the alternating glow of fluorescents and flames that now began to spread around the facility, she no longer saw a stranger, but a friend.

Felan opened her mouth, but no words escaped. Her thoughts remained solely her own. She wished, in that moment, that he could read her mind. Knowing that was impossible, she settled for the next best thing.

Felan used what strength she had remaining and tapped Dune on the arm. When he looked down at her, she mouthed the words she was thinking, hoping he would understand.

"Thank you."

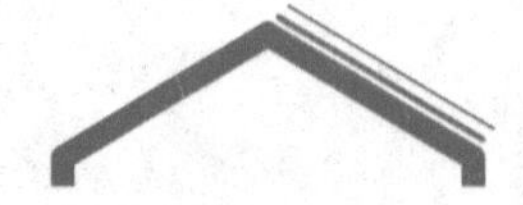

Chapter Forty-Six
Sticks

Sticks gripped the edge of the cart as it jolted sideways, the ground vibrating beneath them. Snow slid down the mountainside in response, a flock of birds shooting into the sky. It was time.

Sticks flipped the plastic cover up and stared at the button on the remote. His finger levitated above it as the memory of all those shocks surged through his mind. Now Dean Tipper and the entire facility were going to be shocked, especially when they were face-to-face with a horde of Wallers not under their control.

"What are you waiting for? That's the signal!" screamed Wick.

Sticks exhaled and pressed the button quickly. Then . . . nothing.

"What's happening?" asked Wick. "Where are they?"

"I don't know!" Sticks yelled. "Maybe the gate got stuck? Maybe we're too far away?"

Sticks pressed the button over and over, hoping that would help. Then, as all hope was fading, he heard a screech.

Sticks and Wick peered down below, the once clear path between the trees now dotted with bodies sprinting at full speed toward the facility. Sticks smiled.

"We did it. It worked!" yelled Sticks.

Wick laughed and cheered with him. Sticks closed the plastic cover to the remote and launched the remote into the air. With the remote gone, he felt a sense of relief return.

"What are you doing?" asked Wick, clearly confused.

"Allowing fate to take over," said Sticks.

They looked again at the horde stampeding down the mountain. It was a beautiful yet terrifying sight, a sea of color against a white canvas, almost like a painting. For a moment, everything felt right in the world. Their plan had gone off without a hitch, the Wallers were heading to take care of the enemy, and Sticks was able to help Wick get down the mountain with no trouble. Nothing had gone wrong.

A snap from above erased the smile from Sticks's face. The cart dipped, hanging lopsided in midair, still heading toward the bottom of the mountain. Their belongings started to fall out of the cart as it swayed side to side. Wick cried out in terror as everything around him shifted and he began to slip.

"Wick!"

Sticks reached out to grab him, barely catching Wick as he fell out of the cart. Sticks gripped tightly to Wick's hand, feeling the numbness of his own exponentially worsen in the cold. More vibrations from the ground sent the cart swaying again. If he didn't hold on, if Wick were to fall, he would never forgive himself. Thankfully, they were closing in on the drop site. Sticks had an idea.

"Hold on for a little longer!" yelled Sticks.

Wick looked down and back up at him, terrified.

"I don't know if I can!" Wick yelled back. "I don't want to die!"

Sticks shook his head. "You're not gonna die, buddy. I won't let that happen!"

Whether from the cold air battering his face or his level of fear, tears welled up in Wick's eyes. Sticks had to think, and fast. He felt his strength diminishing every time the cart moved. He wasn't sure he could hold on much longer.

"Do you trust me?" asked Sticks.

"Of course! Why?" Wick yelled back.

"When I count to three, I'm going to let go!"

Wick shook his head violently. "No! Don't let me go! Please!"

Sticks grunted with each movement Wick made, holding on to him becoming increasingly difficult.

"It'll be okay!" yelled Sticks. "The drop zone is close, so just pull your limbs into your body and trust that I'll help you up after! Can you do that?"

Wick nodded.

Sticks watched as they approached the drop zone, a pile of fresh snow waiting to cushion their fall.

As long as we land in the right spot, this should work. Oh man, I hope this works.

When the cart neared the spot, Sticks counted down while maintaining eye contact with Wick.

"Three, two, one . . . go!"

Sticks watched as Wick's body fell like a rock through the air. He held his breath until he saw a cloud of white erupt from the point of entry, Wick's body safe in the snow's embrace. Sticks inhaled deeply as he gripped the edge of the cart, watching the pile of snow come in and out of view.

Three, two, one . . .

Sticks leapt out of the cart.

For a moment, he felt weightless. It was as though he were a bird soaring through the sky. Thoughts of the birds within the forest surrounding Tent City flashed in his mind. He had always admired them, wishing to know what it felt like to be them, how it felt to fly. Now he had that chance. Unfortunately, it was time to land.

Sticks felt the cold, wet snow spray over his face as a dent in the shape of his body formed in the mountainside. A sudden crack echoed nearby, and Sticks looked up to see their cart fall through the air and crash on the rocky hillside down the mountain. Had they waited much longer, it would have been them. Sticks breathed a sigh of relief, happy that he hadn't waited much longer to jump after Wick.

Wick!

Sticks shot up and searched the surrounding snow for Wick, calling out his name. Laughter led him directly to Wick, where Sticks found himself joining in. Wick was moving his arms and legs side to side in the snow.

"Check it out!" said Wick. "A snow angel!"

Sticks watched as joy radiated from Wick's face. He thought about joining in the fun until a loud shriek echoed down the mountainside. The ominous reminder of their situation sent a shiver down Sticks's spine, Wick's laughter suddenly gone.

They stared at each other for a split second before Sticks extended his hand toward Wick.

"Come on," said Sticks. "We need to go."

A glance up the mountain confirmed his worries as a sea of bodies appeared at the crest of the hill. Sticks gulped.

"Now."

Chapter Forty-Seven
Dune

T*hud.*

Air escaped the body of the Elite as they finally came to a halt on the ground. Dune pushed forward, not wasting a glance in their direction. If another got in his way, he wouldn't hesitate to offer them the same fate as their fallen friend. Time was already wasting away, and Dune wouldn't let Felan do the same.

Her body felt more like a boulder, her weight pulling in toward her middle. Shaky breaths rattled her fragile torso, strained. Dune maneuvered her into what he believed to be the best position for her while still maintaining his strong, safe hold. Her positioning wouldn't matter if she fell from his arms.

If I can make it to the train, just get you out of here and back outside, everything will be okay. You will be okay. You have to be okay. I promised you would . . .

"Taking out the trash for us, D-72?"

T-3 was standing in the middle of the hallway as Dune rounded the corner, other Elite on either side of him. His blond hair bore streaks of dirt and blood, his stupid smirk still at home below. Scratch marks streaked across his suit of armor, except where entire plates of metal were now missing. Even though his voice was strong, his slightly hunched back and lean to one side said otherwise.

You always used to look so perfect. Not anymore.

Dune would have laughed, but he held it back given the situation. Instead, he put his energy into a comeback. Finally, he was able to speak to T-3 the way he deserved.

"No, but now that I see some that needs to go out, I can."

T-3's smirk melded into a grimace, his eyes narrowing. The Elite on either side of him started toward Dune, but T-3 put out a hand to stop them. Then, surprisingly, he laughed.

"I see you've somehow developed a sense of humor. Though, I guess it makes sense it took this long. From what I read in your files, you've always been a little . . . slow."

T-3 and the other two Elite laughed.

Heat radiated from Dune's face. A cough from Felan helped him realize he needed to loosen his grip on her. He did so quickly before turning his attention back to T-3.

"Get out of our way," said Dune.

T-3 shook his head. "You're not going anywhere, and certainly not with that Reject."

You don't control what I do anymore.

"Move," said Dune.

I won't ask again.

"Why are you helping those freaks?" asked T-3.

"None of your business."

Felan coughed again. Dune checked his grip, but it wasn't too tight. She was getting worse, fast. He needed to get her out to the train before they left.

"Everything you do is my business," said T-3. "In fact, Dean Tipper has been looking for you. He wanted to thank you personally. You wouldn't want to leave before he can do that, would you?"

"Thank me for what?" asked Dune.

I never did anything for him. I thought he hated me.

T-3 looked at the other Elite before smiling back at Dune, a chuckle escaping him.

"The tracking device. You don't remember?" T-3 clapped his hands. "Wow. You really are dumber than I thought."

"Shut up. Stop talking and get out of my way. *Now.*"

Dune narrowed his eyes, the speed of his chest rising and falling increasing with each breath. The drumming of his heart felt like a war drum, explosions in the distance adding to the symphony of chaos within the facility.

"That's no way to talk to your superior," said T-3. "But I'll let it slide if you come to your senses and give us the girl."

Dune nodded. "I understand."

Dune lowered Felan to the ground slowly, gently, as though she were made of glass. Her body remained coiled, the only movement coming from her chest when she sucked in a breath or coughed. Dune had never seen anyone in such a condition. He knew he had no other choice.

"I'm sorry," whispered Dune. "I can't risk you getting hurt in a fight."

He ran his hand over her hair, as though he were petting a cat. Heat returned to his face, but his heart rate had calmed. Finally, he felt in control.

Without warning, Dune charged toward the Elite, their eyes widening as they reached for their weapons. T-3 retreated a few steps as his blade extended. He may have been damaged, but that was only his body, not his technique. Dune would still have to be prepared to put up a good fight with him.

Dune's hand wrapped around the throat of the nearest Elite before their gun was even out of its holster. His grip tightened, and he heard a pop as he slung the Elite into the metal wall.

Wide-eyed, the other Elite stood rigid as a board, unable to pull their focus away from the motionless body of their fallen friend only feet away. Before Dune could react, the Elite extended their blade and swiped at him. A glint of light flashed as the blade skimmed the air mere inches from his face.

Momentum from the evasive maneuver carried Dune into the perfect position to retaliate. Pouncing like a lion hunting its prey, Dune tackled the Elite. The Elite tried to break free, but Dune's body weight pinned them to the floor. They weren't going anywhere.

Dune gripped the Elite's helmet and slammed their head into the ground. It took mere seconds for the movement beneath him to cease entirely. Rage boiled beneath is skin, heat radiating from his face. Once the Elite was no longer a problem, Dune smirked.

Now we play.

Terror painted T-3's face. Dune took advantage of that and sprinted toward him. It was only a matter of seconds before he was at T-3, his hands quickly gripped around T-3's shoulders. As he attempted to hoist T-3 from the ground, he realized right away that he'd made a mistake.

Pain jolted through his waist, and T-3 attempted to bring his knee up between Dune's legs for another strike. Dune let go of T-3's shoulders and instead grabbed his incoming leg. He was back in control and felt the adrenaline pumping through his veins.

Tightening his grip, Dune began to spin. T-3 stumbled as his balance dissolved. Once he had the right leverage, Dune used the momentum to lift T-3 into the air. He continued to twirl, the rate at which they spun increasing with each rotation. Finally, Dune launched him across the hallway into the wall.

A large dent had formed in the wall where T-3 had hit. Dune walked over to him, knelt on top of his chest, and extended his own blade. He stared down at T-3, his body broken and stained with blood, cowering beneath him. In any other circumstance, Dune would have laughed at the sight, but nothing was funny at the moment. Felan lay dying only feet away, and he needed to return her to the train, make sure she stayed alive. The last thing to take care of for that to happen was T-3.

"Please, D-72. Don't do this! Think of who you're about to kill right now. I took care of you, made sure you never got Rejected. This is how you repay me?"

T-3's voice sounded weak, shaky. Nothing about him seemed anything like the person who had been standing there only a minute ago.

"You deserve this for all the times you kept me from getting a family," said Dune.

"We are family, D-72. You and I come from the same place, share the same blood. That makes us family, right?" asked T-3. His eyes shifted between Dune's eyes and blade. His voice became strained, desperate. "Please, D-72."

Dune shook his head, an image of Vincent's face smiling at him in the light of his torch. "If you were my family, you'd know . . . my name is Dune!"

Dune thrust his blade into T-3, feeling the resistance fade as the flames in the background grew. A cough echoed in the hallway, pulling his focus away from the body beneath him and over to one now engulfed in smoke.

Felan!

Dune raced over and scooped her up from the floor, pulling her once again into a firm embrace. She felt heavier than before, as though all her energy had risen from her body to join the smoke filling the ceiling. Her breaths were weak, but she was still breathing. That gave him hope, but given how she looked in his arms, Dune was fully aware her survival would be entirely up to chance. Now that it was up to him, though, he planned to give her just that.

Just stay alive. That would be enough.

SMOKE BILLOWED FROM the train as it began to accelerate. Metal cried with each rotation of the wheels, shrieks from the horde of Wallers adding to the noise as it stampeded toward the facility. Dune looked down at Felan, then back up, then back down. His arms were wrapped around her like a boa constrictor, her groans muffled by the incoming train.

"This might get a bit bumpy."

As he held Felan to his chest, Dune pushed forward with his full weight. Dirt and snow kicked up from his feet as he sprinted toward the moving train, gaining on it, but only barely. If he didn't continue at this rate, it very well could leave them both behind.

I won't let that happen. I can't let you die here. Not without them, without her.

The world around him seemed to warp slightly as his focus streamlined. Nothing else existed in that moment besides him, Felan, and the train. He knew he could make it; he had to make it. If nothing else, he would make sure that Felan did. That was a promise he'd made to himself and intended to keep.

The closer he got, the louder the metal clunking and whistling of steam became. He'd been told about the train's history and how it had been old even for its own time. The fact that people used to use steam to power machines astounded him. Electricity was amazing, and he could understand how that energy moved from one thing to another; steam alluded him completely. One thing was for certain, though. It certainly didn't fail when it came to powering that train.

Dune pushed himself to run faster, harder than he'd ever gone. He pulled air in through his nose and allowed it to escape through his mouth, maintaining the cycle. There wasn't much he'd picked up on in the endurance trainings they'd had him attend, but that was useful, especially now.

Felan coughed, gagging while she bobbed up and down in his embrace. Dune's heart dropped.

"Hang in there. I've got you."

He sucked in another deep breath and pushed himself even harder. The muscles in his legs were starting to ache, and he felt every bone and joint move as he ran. That was something he had never felt before. He didn't care, though. It was worth it.

Almost there. Just . . . a little . . . more.

Dune sprinted forward, focusing only on the platform. Felan moaned as his grip tightened, but he had to do that to keep one arm free. He grunted as he thrust his free hand out in front of him. When his fingers wrapped around the cool metal handle on the outside of the train car, he hoisted himself up and in. A sigh of relief escaped him as he lay on the floor of the platform, Felan safely in his grasp.

When he stood up, he carried Felan in both arms, cradling her neck and legs. She had started to feel heavier, no longer struggling against him. He walked toward the group, and it didn't take long before Baz and Taz spotted him and Felan, announcing their arrival.

"Dune!" they shouted in unison. "He made it back with Felan! Just like we said he would!"

"Felan's back?"

Marie pushed her way through the others while Dune laid Felan down on the floor of the car. Marie fell to her knees, grabbing Felan's hand in her own. She was already crying. Dune wished he could help her more, but he didn't know the first thing to do when someone cried. He didn't really know what to do for himself when that happened.

A moment after he'd placed Felan on the ground, Corrine shouted his name.

"Dune! Are you all right?" asked Corrine, racing toward him. "You're bleeding. Did the Wallers reach you? What happened? How bad is it?"

Dune held up his hands, shaking his head. "She needs help. Not me."

Corrine tried to argue with him, but Felan let out another groan, helping to prove his point. Corrine hurried back to what little supplies she had available and then returned to Marie. A few of the others had grabbed pillows and other things for her, but it didn't look like she was going to even notice that they were there. It didn't seem like she knew what was going on or who was even there anymore.

I guess there aren't many people for her to see anyway.

A quick look around the train car told him everything he needed to know. The car was not near as full as he had expected. In the facility, there had to have been double the number. Somehow, between there and getting on the train, they'd lost all those people. Of course, that didn't include the people he knew weren't going to be there.

Poor Scorcher . . . and Vincent.

He suddenly remembered his promise and began to cry.

I miss you, little buddy. And now we'll never get to do all the things I told you we would.

Dune couldn't focus on that with everything going on, though. It was chaos inside the train car, with all the kids still dealing with their own problems and Felan now in the middle of the floor. It didn't compare to what was happening behind them, though.

Dune peered through the trees back toward the facility. Fire burned, black smoke filling the air above it. The facility was still falling, crumbling into the ground beneath it. He couldn't help but feel a slight sadness wash over him, but only for a moment. When the thought of losing his home tried to burrow into his brain, he dismissed it entirely. He hadn't lost anything, after all.

That's not my home anymore. You are.

He smiled as he looked around at the diverse group of people he used to know simply as Rejects.

Now he knew them for what they really were: his family.

Chapter Forty-Eight
Ahna

As the train barreled through the forest, the fire behind them grew distant, blending into the orange sunset on the horizon. Trees whipped by them, the winter air sending a chill through the car. Dune shut the door while Corrine tended to the kids on the cots at the other end. Almost everyone was injured, but no one as badly as Felan. She was throwing up into a bucket while Marie cradled her in her arms. Ahna moved to be close to them, joining Sticks, and they watched Marie stroke Felan's hair as she writhed in pain.

"How is she?" Ahna whispered to Sticks.

Felan's face was as white as the snow blowing around them. Felan gripped her stomach with one hand, holding Marie's hand in the other. Felan let out a long animalistic groan. A shiver traveled down Ahna's spine.

"Not good," said Sticks. "Seems like she's getting worse. Marie's been by her the entire time, but she said there's nothing they can do."

Ahna nodded, knowing there was nothing else she could possibly say. She'd never seen anyone struggle like Felan was. It was rough. Ahna and Sticks stood there, silently watching as

Marie brought the bucket to Felan's face for her to vomit again, but almost nothing escaped her mouth.

"It's going to be okay, Felan. Everything's going to be all right, I promise," said Marie. Her voice cracked between words as tears fogged up her glasses. She continued stroking Felan's hair after setting the bucket aside, her other hand still gripped within Felan's.

"Did . . . did you . . . get the drives?" asked Felan.

Her voice was weak, barely audible over the sound of the train and the other kids behind them.

Maire looked over to Wick, who nodded. Marie smiled faintly.

"Yeah, we did. We got them all, Felan."

"Will they—" started Felan. Her words were cut short by another surge of immense pain. Marie's hand lightened as Felan's wrapped tighter around it. Felan writhed again, another howl of pain escaping her.

"Just look at me," said Marie. "Focus on me and forget about the drives, Felan. Forget about everything but yourself for once, okay? I need you to hang on. Just hang on until we get to California, until we get to the others."

Tears fell from Marie's eyes onto Felan's forehead, and Marie sniffled. Felan shook her head, the motion minimal but obvious.

"You know I won't make it," said Felan. "We all—"

She stopped again, doubling over slightly as she gripped Marie's hand harder. Felan pulled herself into a fetal position as she experienced another wave of pain. Marie pulled her in close, holding on to her until she relaxed a bit, allowing her body to lie fully back on the ground again.

Ahna grabbed Sticks's hand, and they both cried as they watched. It felt good to just have someone there for it.

"Don't say that," said Marie. "You don't know that."

Felan forced a smile. "But you do. I sense it. I know you better than anyone."

"You always have," said Marie. "Please . . . don't leave me."

Felan blinked slowly. "I have to . . ." She paused again, groaning through another wave of pain. "Just don't let anyone else go like this. Use the drives, find their cures . . . please."

Ahna's heart dropped at the pain in her voice; she knew Felan was giving up.

Marie placed her hand on Felan's face and stared into her eyes, her own puffy and red from all the crying.

"I'll make sure you don't die in vain, Felan. I promise."

Felan smiled, though her eyes narrowed, showing her pain. "Marie, I . . . love you."

Tears flowed from Marie's eyes as she stared into Felan's. Marie moved in close to Felan, and Ahna couldn't help but lean in, barely able to hear her reply.

"I love you, too. So, so much."

Marie pulled Felan in close, hugging her tightly. Seconds later, Felan's fists relaxed and went limp. Felan's body melted into Marie, who gently lowered her onto the floor again. Sticks gripped Ahna's hand tightly as they watched Marie collapse onto Felan, sobbing.

After a moment, Ahna and Sticks moved in to comfort her, each placing a hand on Marie's shoulders. Ahna remained there for a minute before moving away from the group to retrieve a blanket so they could wrap Felan's body in it. Even though they didn't have all the required materials, they would do a send-off. It was only right.

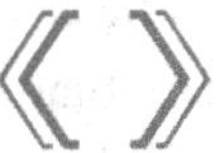

DUNE, WICK, MARIE, Sticks, and Ahna formed a circle, hands clasped. Felan's body lay at the center. Each of them said a few words before Dune opened the door of the car.

"It should be coming up soon," said Dune.

"Okay, thanks," replied Ahna. "Everyone, say your final words. We are coming up on the lake."

Everyone took turns individually approaching Felan's body to say goodbye. When Ahna walked up to her, she bent down on one knee and placed her hand on Felan. Tears no longer came, but her body shook as she spoke.

"I know we didn't always see eye to eye, but you were always there to help when I needed it. We won't be the same without you, and we won't let your death be in vain." She paused for a moment, swallowing. "And if what some of the others have said is true, you'll probably see Scorch up there, too. If you do, tell him I said hi, and . . ." Ahna inhaled deeply before continuing. "And that I love him. The two of you can spar or hang out until we can join you one day. We all miss you, both of you. It won't be the same without you all." She stood up and walked back to the others.

Marie was the last to say her goodbyes. As she was finishing up, Ahna spotted the lake coming into view as the train rounded the bend. She walked up to Marie and placed her hand on Marie's shoulder.

"It's time."

Marie nodded, wiping the tears from her face. Ahna nodded to Dune, who picked Felan up and held her gingerly in his arms. They all stood behind him as he stood on the edge of the doorway, the wind blowing Felan's blanket around. Once the train had reached the bridge over the lake, Dune bent down and bowed his head before lowering her, letting her go.

Marie dropped down to the floor, sobbing again. Dune moved to be with her, surprisingly comforting as he wrapped one arm around her. Ahna moved toward the edge and sat down, her feet dangling below the edge of the platform. She watched as the lake stretched out toward the mountains behind it, the sun almost entirely vanishing behind them. Cold wind battered her face, a welcoming change to the heat she'd felt from her own tears.

Sticks appeared next to her, allowing his feet to dangle like hers. They sat there for a few minutes, looking out at the wilderness as the lake view melted into a forest once again.

"What are we gonna do?" asked Sticks.

Ahna thought for a moment, trying to figure that out for herself. "What we've been planning all along, I guess. Take down The Delivery Company."

"Any idea how?" asked Sticks.

Ahna shrugged. "No idea . . . but I don't think they have any idea what they're going to do, either."

Sticks chuckled. "Let's hope so." After a moment, Sticks cleared his throat. "You think they're really out there? The rest of the Gray Wolves, I mean."

I sure hope so . . .

"They'd better be," said Ahna. "If they aren't, we're doomed."

They sat there listening to the repetitive, almost soothing sound of the train's wheels in the background.

"You know not everyone'll make it out alive, right?" said Sticks.

Ahna nodded. "Not everyone has."

They sat in silence on the edge of the platform, watching dusk transition to night. Stars filled the sky, the mountains becoming a blurry mass in the distance. Trees danced in the wind while more snow piled up on their branches. The frozen landscape seemed so serene, peaceful. Unfortunately, they had to leave it all behind.

Ahna sighed, realizing the fight that lay ahead of them. So many lives were at stake, so many already lost. The Delivery Company was falling; she just hoped they wouldn't go down with it. Ahna laid her head against the side of the doorway, watching the landscape soar by under a blanket of stars.

High above the mountains, a trail of light streaked across the sky. Laughter escaped her lips, briefly, before her laughter melded into a cry. Tears streamed down her face while the star streaked across the sky, but she didn't bother wiping them away.

Strength didn't come from holding things in, but from letting them go.

Ahna had let go of everything, everyone.

This moment, though, she would hold on to forever. It was her chance to witness one final moment of light before diving headfirst into darkness.

Thank You!

If you enjoyed this book, please leave a brief review on your retailer of choice. Reviews help authors in many ways. Thank you!

Acknowledgements

First, I would like to thank you, the reader. If you talk to any author, I think they will tell you that when it comes to trilogies, the sequel is the hardest. That most definitely rings true for me as well. However, something that made it a lot easier was all the wonderful reviews, critiques, messages, and questions I received from my readers. I want to thank you for sharing your honest opinions, ideas, and expectations and I hope to continue hearing from you after each book you read. From the beginning, this series has been about those who we surround ourselves with, our friends and family, whether we are born into it or find them along the way. I'm happy to have you included in my ever-expanding circle.

Secondly, this series would have never been what it has become without my family and friends, many of whom served as beta readers, proofreaders, and human walls off which to bounce my ideas. Without your constant support and critique, I would never have grown into the writer I am today. I will continue to share my ideas and new books with you and am grateful to have that opportunity. I appreciate each and every one of you.

Next, I would like to thank Natalia Leigh at Enchanted Ink Publishing. You have done so well in guiding me through the grammar, syntax, and style problems that seem to pop up more frequently than the Wallers. Thankfully, they aren't as dangerous, but I have no doubt you'd be able to handle them even if they were. Because of your wonderful comments and questions throughout the manuscript, I have certainly grown as a writer and for that I am immensely thankful. I'm glad to have you on-board so far and look forward to finishing the series together.

Even though we like to think that we never judge a book by its cover, that happens all the time. As usual, I need to recognize and share my appreciation for the amazingly talented, DePaul Vera. Your skill at graphic art and design and patience in dealing with last minute changes, some that never saw the light of day, will not be forgotten. You have been instrumental in helping me bring the world in my head to life with your beautiful and creative designs. Thank you for all you have done so far and for all you will continue to do as we finish the trilogy together.

I would like to give special thanks to those specific individuals who worked closely with me throughout this process as well. Without them and their thoughts and comments on many aspects of throughout, the book would not be what it has become either. These people include Eugene Harrell, Molly Nimmo, Adam Sowards, Trevin Hicks, and Hannah Buck.

Above all, nothing I do would be possible without the immense support of my wonderful wife, Shannon. You are constantly putting up with my random questions and ideas no matter when or where I have them. Your input, willingness to talk through stories and characters, and overall imaginative ideas have helped shaped this book and my writing overall. You are my ideal reader and ideal partner. Thank you for being in my life. Thank you for being you.

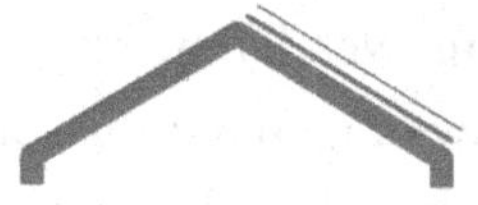

Discussion Guide

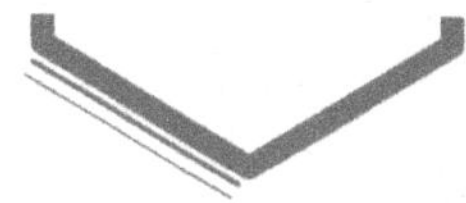

- Wallers have become a common occurrence, but it seems as though there is more to them than originally known. How do you feel about the Wallers overall? Do you think they are people? Was it right to use them as a weapon?

- *Rejected* added a couple new narrator main characters – How did their voice or viewpoint change your reading experience? Which one was your favorite addition?

- If you were to see the story unfold from the perspective of another character, which one would you choose? Why?

- Which event in the book was most like something you've experienced in real life? Do you think that you and the character going through it acted similarly?

- Which character is most like someone you know? How did that affect your perception of the character?

- What was your biggest takeaway from *Rejected*?

- Are there any quotes, passages, or scenes that you found particularly compelling or memorable? Share which one(s) and explain why you chose your selection.

- What was your overall impression of *Rejected*?
- Activity: Draw or map out the abandoned facility on the mountain based on the descriptions given. Then, redesign it however you'd like. Be creative!

About the Author

A Kentucky native, Lane currently resides in Brooklyn, NY with his wife and ideal reader, Shannon. *Rejected* is the sequel to his debut novel, *The Delivery Co.* and the second in the trilogy. When not writing, Lane is an actor, photographer, and enjoys bouldering at his local rock gym. In addition to The Delivery Company series, Lane is working on other books, screenplays, and more.